ONCE A
ROGUE

—

Allie Therin

carina
press

**carina
press®**

Recycling programs
for this product may
not exist in your area.

ISBN-13: 978-1-335-45264-1

Once a Rogue

Copyright © 2023 by Allie Therin

For questions and comments about the quality of this book,
please contact us at CustomerService@Harlequin.com.

Carina Press
22 Adelaide St. West, 41st Floor
Toronto, Ontario M5H 4E3, Canada
www.CarinaPress.com

Printed in U.S.A.

For friendships, old and new

Chapter One

October 1925
New York

Handsome men were a fucking menace.

Wesley stood under a tall arch, one of the many set into the row of passenger terminals and warehouses that separated the ocean liners at the Hudson's edge from the towers of Manhattan beyond. The October sky was a cloudless blue over the north river piers, the air crisp and tinged with salt and diesel. The cries of gulls mixed with the crowd's chattering as passengers disembarked down tall ramps.

By rights Wesley ought to be on his way to the hotel, not standing shoulder-to-shoulder on the pier with the other first-class passengers he'd had more than enough of. But the day before their ship had departed, he and Sebastian had received a cable from Jade Robbins.

MAY WE SEE YOU IN NEW YORK STOP
CLOCK NEEDS CURSE TO TICK CAN'T SAY
MORE HERE STOP

If anyone else had sent Wesley such an obfuscated message, he would have had his footman toss it in the fire. But it stood to reason that a telekinetic, bootlegging ex-spy might be speaking in code for a reason.

I think Jade could be referencing the siphon clock, Sebastian had said, when he'd read the telegram, referring to the astrological clock that had been used to create seven stupidly powerful magical relics during the Spanish Inquisition.

You never mentioned it requiring a curse to work, Wesley had said. *I didn't even realize you lot had curses—what are you, mummies?*

Curses are rare, Sebastian had admitted. *But the clock worked without a curse before and I don't see why it would need one now. They were supposed to use it to destroy the pomander relic; I hope they haven't run into any problems.*

Ah yes, just the pesky little pomander relic, the bit of fifteenth-century magic that could *enslave non-magic minds.* One would fucking hope that Jade and the others hadn't run into any *problems.*

That had been in Paris, more than a week ago. Today, they'd docked in Manhattan, and the moment Sebastian's foot had hit the pier, he'd said, *we should call Jade.* And as Wesley had opened his mouth to say *yes, we'll call her from the hotel like civilized men,* Sebastian had looked up with his big brown doe eyes and Wesley's traitorous mouth had instead said *of course, whatever you like,* and now Wesley was stuck waiting with the tourists while Sebastian was inside the passenger terminal, making his call.

With an irritable huff, Wesley pulled his cigarettes from his jacket pocket.

On his right, Sebastian's younger brother, Mateo de Leon, was leaning against the wall in the sun, reading a book in German—something about bees, perhaps.

"Don't you keep saying you're going to quit?" he asked, without looking up.

"I am," Wesley said unapologetically. "What a shame I don't have a fortune-teller to see my future and tell me if I ever actually succeed," which made Mateo crack a smile.

A few weeks ago, Wesley had fallen down a metaphorical rabbit hole into Wonderland, discovering magic existed along with paranormals like Sebastian, who had enervation magic, or Mateo, who could see the future of magic—well, *had* been able to, at least, and it had nearly killed him. Then Sebastian got himself a different relic, a fifteenth-century Spanish brooch, which bolstered his enervation magic enough that he'd managed to bind Mateo's magic. Now Mateo was almost as mundane as Wesley, and he seemed dead chuffed about it.

Mateo put out an expectant hand, gaze still glued to the book. Wesley held out the pack, and he helped himself. He was exactly the sort of social smoker Wesley envied, who seemed to be able to take them or leave them and didn't need to keep them on hand. Meanwhile Wesley fought all day long to keep his own addiction at bay, and still couldn't stop himself reaching for cigarettes anytime he got antsy.

He retrieved his matchbook from his pocket. "We could be in the club at the hotel right now."

"That would be nicer," Mateo agreed. "You could have bought me a Cuban cigar instead of the cheapest British smokes on the boat."

Wesley lit his own cigarette and breathed in vile, low-grade tobacco as he passed the matches to Mateo. Those few weeks ago, before he knew about magic, he had also been fully expecting to live the rest of his life alone, his own brother and parents years dead, he himself useless for anything except refusing invitations and growing ever more bitter. But then Sebastian had come into his life, and he'd come with magical quests and a family, including a refreshingly cynical younger brother, and now Wesley was still a cantankerous beast but he had purpose and acceptable company.

Eventually they'd all tire of Wesley, of course. But while it lasted, it was—not unwelcome. "I'll buy you a crate of Cuban cigars if you'll make your brother hurry up."

"Don't you have your own mail to read?"

"I read it," said Wesley, "and immediately realized my unforgivable error in telling my footman where I was going but not instructing him to withhold said information from society. I didn't cross the Atlantic for cards and parties; I have more pressing matters—or I *would*, if Sebastian would finish and we could crack on."

Mateo gestured inside the terminal with the cigarette. "He's off the phone, but a doll got him."

"For fuck's sake." Wesley looked through the window. A pretty flapper had joined Sebastian at the counter with the phone, pointedly displaying her cigarette in a long holder. "Ugh, he's like a polite lamb who naïvely believes the wolf actually forgot her own matches."

Mateo snorted and stuck his own cigarette between his teeth so he could turn a page. "You know Sebi doesn't flirt on purpose?"

"Yes, yes, I know."

"Not everyone does. A lot of people get mad at him, or think he's about to steal their girls. Or their boys, or their viscounts, apparently."

"You're a loyal brother, but you don't have to come to his defense with me. What kind of jealous fool do you take me for?"

Wesley had never been the possessive type. Jealousy was, after all, a feeling, and he was incapable of those. He'd come to America one time before in an effort to win a lover back, it was true, but that had been about sheer convenience. All those wretched romantic *emotions* were the provenance of posturing American hotheads and dramatic French poets, not stoic English viscounts.

Even if it was, perhaps, just a bit trying to watch others make a play for one's lover, who remained mind-bogglingly unaware of his own attractiveness.

Sebastian looked over then, to the arch Wesley was haunting, and even at a distance Wesley could see the slump of his shoulders, a sign of the fatigue that seemed to become more pronounced with each passing day on the ship. But when his gaze fell on Wesley, his handsome face visibly brightened, and what a good thing it was Wesley was incapable of feelings, because the thought of Sebastian being happy to see him came perilously close to causing one.

Sebastian said something else to the flapper—probably extricating himself from their conversion far more politely than necessary—and then he was heading toward Wesley and Mateo.

"Finalmente." Mateo dropped the cigarette to the pier, grinding it out beneath his foot as Sebastian came out from the terminal and joined them. "What did Miss Robbins say?"

Sebastian frowned. "Jade wasn't home."

"Wasn't home?" Wesley sputtered.

"Neither was Zhang." Sebastian was still frowning. "Maybe it was a bad time to call."

"It's late afternoon, shouldn't that be fine?" said Mateo. "Did you try their businesses?"

"It's not like I could ask the operator to put me through to Jade's illegal speakeasy," said Sebastian. "I talked to the Dragon House, but the waiter who answered said he hasn't seen Zhang in a few days." He held up his left wrist. A sliver of color peeked out from under his cuff, the top of his paranormal tattoo. "Maybe Zhang is here on the astral plane but I'm interfering with his magic."

"Then let's get to the hotel and maybe they can find us there," said Mateo. "Vamanos, I'll flag a cab."

They left the pier and terminal for the street, where the traffic was thick in front of the line of high-rises that formed the edge of Manhattan. As Mateo stepped ahead to the curb, Wesley hung back and gave Sebastian his best disapproving look. "So I had to wait with the tourists for nothing."

"They might have answered their phones—"

"But they didn't," Wesley said. "So now I get to be cross."

Sebastian made a contrite face. "How can I make it up to you?"

The corner of Wesley's lips curled up. "Come to my room tonight and find out."

He got to watch Sebastian shiver. Like usual, Sebastian looked stylishly casual, with a flat cap, loosened tie and attached collar. Unlike Wesley's homburg hat and double-breasted navy suit, his tie tight around his high starched collar—old-fashioned and out-of-style now, he was perfectly aware, but Wesley had never and would never give a damn about trends. Sebastian had no jacket under his unbuttoned overcoat, and Wesley could clearly see the chain of the brooch relic that Sebastian now kept in his waistcoat like a pocket watch.

That fucking brooch. Sebastian didn't complain, but

Wesley wasn't stupid; he could see for himself that no matter how long Sebastian slept on the ship, he couldn't seem to shake the fatigue. Up close, Wesley could see the dark circles under his eyes, the way he didn't stand quite as straight as he normally did. The brooch kept interfering with Sebastian's own magic, and every time he lost control of his enervation, it hit the auras of all the non-paranormals in the vicinity and they, in turn, hit the ground.

Must have been another large wave, Wesley had scrambled to tell the other passengers on the ship, after they'd all been knocked down yet again. He was willing to get down on his knees for the right man, but Sebastian did have a way of making everything just a little more interesting.

Wesley jerked his head toward the river. "Last chance to toss your new jewelry into the Hudson before we go."

"I can't just get rid of the relic where someone else could steal it," Sebastian said, like he'd said every time Wesley had suggested getting rid of it.

"They'd have to steal it during a murder to make it work for them," Wesley pointed out. "What are the chances of a murder occurring at the same time—" He paused. "I suppose we *are* in New York. Maybe it's not as improbable as it sounds. How close does the murder need to be?"

"Obviously we don't want to find out," Sebastian said.

"Except we do," Wesley said. "I'm not advocating a hands-on demonstration, but we want answers. Miss Robbins asked to speak with us—don't you think she and Mr. Zhang are going to want to help us figure out what to do with this brooch in return? Hell, you lot keep telling me that Arthur's surly little antiquarian can see history; let's ask him to take a peek at its past."

"But scrying relics is difficult," Sebastian protested. "I couldn't ask Rory to do that."

"I could," Wesley said unapologetically, as he took a slow drag from his cigarette.

Sebastian huffed, although he had a tiny smile. "I'm not asking you to take that one for me either."

"You didn't ask," Wesley pointed out. "Christ, let me do something for you once in a while. I'm clearly not accomplishing anything for myself; I can't even quit smoking."

"You go entire days without cigarettes now," Sebastian said. "Lots of people don't bother to try, but you do, and when you stumble, you pick yourself up and try again. Don't be so hard on yourself."

"Don't be so hard on myself." Wesley exhaled smoke. "Tell me, when you were on the phone just now, trying to get in touch with Miss Robbins, did you happen to call her dear friend Arthur?"

Sebastian winced. "Well—"

"Did you call her other good friend, Rory Brodigan, who might know where she is? No, don't bother to answer that, I'm certain you didn't call either of them."

"Neither of them should have to hear from me if there are others I can call," Sebastian protested. "I kidnapped Rory last winter. I held Arthur at gunpoint—"

"While you were under *blood magic*," said Wesley. "Do you really get to tell anyone not to be so hard on themselves?"

Sebastian folded his arms. "I get to tell *you*."

"Oh you do, do you?" Wesley said. "I was a captain; you were a corporal. I'm a viscount; you're basically the fae. You don't get to tell me what to do."

"Yes I do, because you're also my—because we're— well." Sebastian stuck his hands in his pockets. "You know."

A faint flush was blooming on his olive skin. And no wonder, because they'd yet to put a word to their relationship. A nice man would take pity on Sebastian and let it slide.

"Hmmm, no, I don't think I do," Wesley said, because he was a bastard and Sebastian's squirming was delicious. "I'm your what? Spell it out for me."

That earned him an even dirtier look. "My favorite person," Sebastian said, pointedly holding up his wrist again. "So I get to tell you not to be so hard on yourself."

Oh, that had to be cheating, didn't it? Because Wesley's eyes had, of course, gone to the partially visible tattoo under the coat sleeve, a tattoo that looked like swirls of colors to everyone else but let only Wesley see the lion hiding within. His ice-cold heart didn't know what to do with this damned tropical sunbeam, this kind-hearted darling who saw the world through the figurative rose-colored glasses, ignoring the ugliness of reality and choosing instead to see only beauty in mangy strays and beastly viscounts.

Wesley admired him for it, especially considering Sebastian's traumatic past under blood magic. But he wasn't deluded enough to think what Sebastian saw was real.

Or gullible enough to believe Sebastian would see him that way forever. Hope and faith were for the naïve; they led nowhere but disappointment. Wesley would enjoy Sebastian's warmth while it lasted, and not be foolish enough to trust that life would let him keep it.

Wesley's throat was a bit tight now, probably from

the smoke. "We should carry on," he said, purposefully changing the subject.

Sebastian held out a hand with a soft, questioning look. Not forcefully taking the cigarette, not shaming Wesley for the weakness of lighting it up in the first place. Just a quiet offer of help from someone who understood that Wesley's addiction sometimes rode him too hard to fight it off alone.

Wesley appreciated the support more than he knew how to put into words. He nodded once. "You owe me something else to put in my mouth now," he said, as he let Sebastian gently extract the half-smoked cigarette from his fingers and drop it to the pier.

Sebastian raised an eyebrow. "Oh yeah?" he said hopefully.

"Yes," said Wesley. "*Dinner.* I'm famished, let's go."

Chapter Two

From the pier, Sebastian found himself squashed into the middle of the back of the taxicab between Mateo, who was the same above-average height he was, and Wesley, who was three or four inches taller with long limbs and no practice sharing. The cab driver was ignoring them, shouting at pedestrians as the taxi crawled east and inward toward Manhattan's center.

"Are we sure it wouldn't have been faster to walk?" Wesley pointed out the window. "It wasn't a jest; that gentleman strolling on the sidewalk is covering more ground than we are."

Sebastian glanced out the window. A man with a long beard, holding the hand of a little girl of maybe three, was strolling past a storefront with a blue-and-white striped awning, the letters on the glass window spelling out *Abrams Deli*.

Sebastian had been in that deli, the last time he'd been in New York. On that trip he'd been with Shelley, a dream-reading paranormal, and Hyde, a paranormal with a monstrous second form. All of them had been on edge, the blood magic in their veins still following the most recent orders from the paranormal who controlled their bodies, the Puppeteer. They'd questioned the owner, and when that had been fruitless, an angry

Hyde had followed some hapless customer outside and into an alley. Then Sebastian had seen the flash of teeth, and had barely gotten between them in time—

He swallowed and looked away, taking a deep breath. It wasn't February. Shelley was dead, and Hyde was locked away with his mind trapped in another century. And Sebastian was here, with Wesley warm against his side and Mateo's elbow digging into his ribs every time he turned a page in his book. He wasn't under blood magic anymore. He was free now.

Sebastian felt the tug on his blood from the brooch, then, as if to remind him *freedom* was relative.

Did you call Rory Brodigan? Wesley had asked.

If only he could have. Was it normal for a relic to feel like lead chains, to pull on your blood like the moon on the tide? Rory had a ring relic that controlled the wind, but he'd always seemed fiery and bright, not exhausted by it. Sebastian's friend Gwen, who saw magic, had never complained about her relic that controlled the tide. Maybe it was their subordinate magic, so much more powerful than Sebastian's enervation, that made it easier for them to deal with having so much more magic flowing through them.

But then Ellis, with insubordinate invisibility, had never seemed bothered by his dagger relic either. More likely it was just something Sebastian had to get over.

Wesley turned his attention away from the street. "Maybe we'll have another message from Miss Robbins at the hotel."

"I hope so," Sebastian said. They were staying only one night before taking Mateo to Oberlin in Ohio. If they couldn't reach Jade tonight, it would have to wait for their return.

He was looking forward to seeing Jade and Zhang.

Arthur and Rory…that was a little more complicated, thanks to Sebastian's time under blood magic, and those were more memories like quicksand, ready to pull him under, back to terrible times. But he'd worked with Arthur and Rory once before; they could do it again.

The cab made a sharp left onto Madison Avenue, and Mateo closed his book with an air of reluctance. "Do we have our story for the hotel?" he said, gesturing to the three of them.

"I do," said Wesley. "If someone asks after my business, I tell them to fuck off. Works every time."

"That's not a story," Sebastian said.

"Once upon a time, there was a snooping gossip who fucked off, and I lived happily ever after," Wesley said. "Better?"

"How is that better?"

"You prefer the pulps? Picture the garish cover: me, with a large knife and far more muscle. You, clinging to my arm, your clothes strategically ripped. I'm fighting a crocodile, or perhaps an irate bear, and the headline reads *The Astounding Lord Fine: A Thrilling Tale of Everyone Fucking Off and Leaving Him Be.*"

Sebastian frowned. "Don't hurt the bear."

"It's not a *real* bear."

"I could have gone by myself to Ohio." Mateo pinched the bridge of his nose. "You're not going to tell anyone to fuck off, Sebi. How are you going to explain him?"

Sebastian frankly didn't know how to explain Wesley at all. They'd saved each other's lives; that had to make them more than casual, didn't it? But was he allowed to call a viscount something like *boyfriend*? Or did Wesley's world have rules about that, like how Wesley was addressed as Lord Fine even though his last name was

Collins? "What's to explain? I'm sharing a double room upstairs with my brother."

Sebastian was not looking forward to a night in a bed alone. For months in London, he'd been at the mercy of blood terrors, a holdover from the blood magic, waking from sleep to find himself a prisoner in his own body, unable to move until his blood remembered it was no longer under another's control.

Then Wesley had woken him out of a blood terror their first night together in the manor in Yorkshire— and he hadn't had once since.

But then, he'd spent all of his nights since Yorkshire with Wesley. They'd shared a room when they'd been in Paris, and then on the ship, he and Mateo had been next door to Wesley, making it easy for Sebastian to spend the voyage in Wesley's cabin.

You realize I've always slept alone, Wesley had said their first night on the ship, as they lay face-to-face on the bed in Wesley's cabin, panting and sweaty after Wesley had pinned him down and made him come twice. *And I've never indulged in anything as sentimental as cuddling.*

Your arm is around me, Sebastian had pointed out.

That hardly counts. This bed is the size of a matchbook. Where else am I supposed to put it?

Sebastian had hesitated. *Does that mean you want me to go?*

Wesley had skimmed his hand over Sebastian's shoulder and arm, the touch light and almost tentative. *Of course not. These are clearly conditions of this mad fae bargain I've apparently made.*

Sebastian had inched closer, running his thumb over Wesley's lips. *So what do you get in exchange?*

Sex. Obviously.

That doesn't sound like a fair bargain. It just sounds like you're giving me everything I want.

Yes, well. Wesley had brushed his fingers across the tattoo on Sebastian's wrist. *Perils of being a mortal in your world.*

Sebastian had kissed him, and then slept curled around Wesley every night, and he hadn't had a blood terror since Yorkshire.

Hard to imagine it was a coincidence that his blood remembered it was free when he had Wesley in his sleep. How mad was Wesley going to be if he ever found out Sebastian's suspicions when he was probably already sick of the clinginess?

But when they'd cabled from Paris to arrange their New York lodgings, the hotel had already been near-full, with no available rooms near their last empty suite. Sebastian wasn't going to ask a viscount to take a regular room when they were already staying in a travel hotel and not the Ritz or the Plaza, and he wasn't going to guilt Wesley into sharing a bed when he would welcome the chance to sleep alone in peace.

He needed to get used to giving Wesley more space in public anyway. They could hide away in a ship's cabin, but in public, people might speculate about what he was doing with Wesley. Sebastian knew all about that, and wasn't going to draw that kind of attention to Wesley.

So Sebastian would sleep in a bed alone tonight and survive; if he had a blood terror, he would open his eyes and see Mateo in the next bed, and that would hopefully end it.

But Wesley frowned. "As you say, what's to explain? It's fairly common in my circles to engage a traveling companion when venturing overseas—say, a worldly

Spanish patrician? The last time I came to America, I had a valet…although I suppose that didn't end very well for him, did it?"

To say the least. Wesley's valet had been smuggling the pomander relic into America, to sell to a textile mogul by the name of Luther Mansfield who traded in paranormal artifacts. Hyde had been the one to kill the valet with his claws and fangs; the police had written up the death as *mauled by a tiger.*

"No one expects me to travel alone, is what I'm saying," Wesley went on. "Then, of course, you can't walk into a bleeding ship terminal without catching a woman's eye—"

"What woman?" Sebastian furrowed his eyebrows. "Loretta?"

"Oh, she gave you her name, did she?"

"Yes, but I didn't *catch her eye.* She just wanted to talk about tattoos. She lives in Brooklyn and she said if I ever want an artist recommendation, I can call her party line and…" Sebastian trailed off in the face of Mateo's and Wesley's matching flat stares.

"My point—which you've just made for me—is that it's obvious you're popular with women, and that is what gossips will see," said Wesley. "It's also obvious what a demanding prick I am, and so no one will be surprised when I require my traveling companion to assist me in my quarters. Or when I require him to work *late.*"

Sebastian automatically glanced at the cabbie, who was leaning out the window and swearing inventively at a trolley.

Wesley leaned closer to Sebastian. "I've been watching him, you know," he said, in a sardonic whisper. "He's not listening to us. You seem to think I'm some sort of callow novice who requires your vigilance to protect my reputation, but I have done this before."

Of course he had. In fact, somewhere here in New York was Wesley's ex, the man Wesley had cared for so much he'd sailed across an ocean to try and win him back. Sebastian would have liked to find a reason to avoid ever thinking about it again, but back in Yorkshire, Wesley had spoken well of this man, whoever he was—might even want to visit him, while they were in the city.

And if that's what he wants, you'll support him, Sebastian told himself, as the taxi pulled up to the hotel.

They'd picked a hotel next to Grand Central Station, making it easy to catch the Ohio State Limited train the following afternoon. The Roosevelt was nineteen stories of brick in shades of gray and brown with rectangular windows across the higher floors. Near the ground, the second-level windows were arched and topped with carved faces, and black lanterns adorned the side along the street, their lights a warm glow in the gray October evening. There was a newsie on the sidewalk, just past the green-and-gold marquee.

"World championship!" the boy was shouting, as passersby slowed with interest. "Pirates versus Senators! Get the story in the *Evening Post*, just two cents!"

"Ooh, baseball." Mateo elbowed Sebastian. "Get a paper."

They got out and Sebastian gave the newsie a nickel, and then tucked the paper under his arm. He followed Wesley and Mateo through the wide doors into the white-and-gold lobby, a two-story space with pillars, two short staircases, and a crystal chandelier suspended from a gilt ceiling over an assortment of furniture arranged on the marble floors.

Sebastian resolutely did not think about how nice it would be to grab a rest in one of the leather chairs as Mateo stepped up to the suited man behind the check-in desk. Sebastian picked up a flyer on the counter and stepped back, next to Wesley. "The hotel has a rooftop patio."

"So we can join the million tourists to admire the *pretty view*?" Wesley scoffed. "Please."

"There are all kinds of things to see in the city," Sebastian pointed out. "Times Square, the Statue of Liberty, Central Park. Did you know New York has a menagerie and a zoo?"

"No."

"No, as in, you didn't know?"

"No, as in, I'm not going to a damned zoo."

At the counter, the suited man disappeared through a door into the back office.

"I've heard you can watch them feed the sea lions at the Bronx Zoo." Sebastian casually held out the flyer to Wesley, twisting his arm so the top of the tattoo would be visible to Wesley under his sleeve. "I thought you liked lions."

"You think you're so cute." Wesley's lips had curled in a grudging smile. He leaned in, taking the flyer, bringing his mouth closer to Sebastian's ear as he dropped his voice to an undertone. "You had best banish this notion that you can charm me into the zoo, or the park, or the roof. Because if you think I've gone that soft, then clearly I don't fuck you hard enough."

Sebastian nearly choked.

"Truly an unforgivable dereliction on my part," Wesley said, as he straightened up. "Rest assured I'll remedy that."

"We're in the *lobby*."

"Well, I wasn't planning to do it here."

There was a loud throat clearing. Sebastian looked over at the counter.

"I don't want to know what Fine just said to put that color on your face." Mateo jerked his head toward the elevator. "We have a double room on six and Fine's suite is on two. Our trunks are being taken up."

Sebastian appreciated Mateo keeping up the charade. Wesley might think he didn't need help protecting his reputation, but he wasn't the one who could flatten police and reporters with a thought. Sebastian would stay careful.

The clerk in the suit was returning, a small stack of mail in his hands. "We've been holding some correspondence for you and Lord Fine," he said to Mateo.

"I have *more* mail?" said Wesley. "Is half of London in New York right now? Why do they feel the need to get in touch?"

He accepted a sealed telegram from the clerk as Mateo took his own mail. "Do we have any other messages? Missed phone calls, perhaps?"

"No, sir," the clerk said.

Sebastian frowned.

The three of them stepped away from the desk to a quiet spot along the wall near the elevator. "Jade knows we're only here for the night," Sebastian said. "But no message."

"I really do want to hear what she and Mr. Zhang might think about the brooch." Wesley frowned. "I'd say let's pop 'round her business tonight, but I haven't a clue where it is. I was blindfolded last time, and Arthur is far too overprotective to give the location away through his driving."

"Maybe we go to the Dragon House for dinner?" Sebastian said. "I bet we can find that."

"The place you just called and the waiter said he hadn't seen Mr. Zhang for several days?" Wesley said. "I say we go to Arthur's."

Sebastian's eyes widened. "Arthur's?"

"I know the name of his building," said Wesley. "And there's probably somewhere near his flat where we can have dinner."

"You two can have dinner," Mateo said firmly. "I don't need to be there."

"Are you sure?" Sebastian asked.

"I don't know," Mateo said. "Am I sure that I don't want to share your table while the two of you fuck each other with your eyes?"

"Oh please," said Wesley. "You know who was fucking Sebastian with their eyes? Miss Loretta, that's who."

Sebastian rubbed his temple.

"I'm not coming." Mateo held up his bee book. "I want a sandwich and to read my books alone in my quiet room that's not moving. I've got weeks of work to catch up on. Sebi, come up, get what you need from your trunk, and then get out and don't come back until morning."

He headed toward the elevator. Sebastian lingered behind with Wesley. "You really want to go see Arthur? Are you sure?"

"He'll know where Miss Robbins is," said Wesley, "or at least he ought to know what's going on."

"But won't it be awkward?"

"Why would it?"

Sebastian sighed. His time under blood magic was heavier than the brooch in his pocket. "Because...you know."

Wesley gave him an assessing look. "Not because of him and me, surely?"

"Of course not." Why would Arthur and *Wesley* be awkward? They were friends. "No, you're right. It's a good idea, to go see him."

"Of course it is," said Wesley. "I'd hardly bother with bad ideas. Be back down in thirty minutes. Dress for dinner."

Sebastian stopped himself from making a face. Maybe it was the childhood on a tropical island, but he liked comfortable clothes and eating good food outside. Wesley, however, came from rules and structure, formal meals in formalwear. He despised the casual trend, so when he said *dress for dinner*, it probably meant he'd show up in white gloves and a top hat.

And it probably meant he'd pick somewhere full of people who would wonder why they were together. Sebastian had a brief interlude with a man he'd shared a tent with in the army, not serious enough to even call a fling, but Jasper had been adamant that he and Sebastian couldn't be seen together during the day. *You're pretty as a girl*, Jasper had snapped, the night after Sebastian had tried to sit at the same table at the mess. *And everyone knows Latin men love to fuck. If rumors start about us, it'll be your fault.*

Nine years later, Sebastian knew Jasper was a bigot and an asshole. But he'd probably been right about rumors, and people might be even more likely to gossip about a viscount like Wesley. But Sebastian was the one becoming embarrassingly attached to Wesley's company, and a suit was a much smaller ask than a boat across the Atlantic and a train ride to Ohio. Wesley had been willing to come with them, so Sebastian could do what Wesley wanted, including visiting Arthur and a formal dinner their night in New York.

The elevator let Wesley out on the second floor, and then Sebastian rode up to six to change and clean up. The hot water and needle shower were heavenly on his muscles, but he forced himself not to linger. *You have to get used to the brooch and the new magic,* he told himself. *You have to shake this malaise.*

He followed the shower with a quick shave, and then joined Mateo in the hotel room as he dressed in the clothes he'd grudgingly bought in Paris for first-class dinners on the ship: a black dinner jacket with a black bow tie and waistcoat.

Mateo was sprawled on the bed closest to the window with the newspaper open to the middle. "Who's winning the series?" Sebastian asked.

"Tied at three each." Mateo turned a page and sat up straighter. "What was the name of that asylum upstate? The one where your friend who sees the past was committed when he got stuck in his magic?"

Sebastian wracked his memory for a moment. "Hyde Gardens. Why?"

Mateo set the open newspaper on the mattress and pointed to a column. Sebastian stepped over to see it for himself.

"*Hyde Gardens reopens after September's mass escape,*" he read aloud. "I didn't hear about this."

Mateo was still scanning the article. "Not many details."

"You hear things though, about asylums," Sebastian said. "Inmates may have had good reasons to escape. Rory did."

"That could have been me," Mateo said, "except I had you."

Sebastian swallowed. This was exactly why he had to get used to the brooch, because subordinate paranormals like Rory and Mateo could end up trapped in their own magic, their minds lost. With the brooch, Sebastian might be able to help them. "The binding on your magic is still holding, yes?"

"Ugh, stop," Mateo said. "I can practically hear your thoughts."

"What thoughts?"

"You've been repressing my magic since I was eleven," Mateo said. "We're family. Just because you bound my magic doesn't mean you can do it with someone else. Do you really think you need to grind yourself into the ground with that brooch over a chance you can help subordinate paranormals?"

"But that's just it—why am I so tired?" Sebastian said. "No other paranormal I have known with a relic has had this problem. And it doesn't matter if I want to get rid of it; it has to be stolen during a murder and I hope it would be obvious that I don't want anyone *murdered*."

"Isn't Fine going to help you find a way to get rid of it?"

"Wesley was barely thrown into the paranormal world a few weeks ago," Sebastian said. "It's way too much, too soon, to ask him to help with a relic."

"Estás hablando como papí," Mateo said. "Dad is the one who always talks about the family legacy, like non-magical people are some helpless and completely separate species, but it's not really like that. Haven't you had any girlfriends without magic?"

"Por qué todo el mundo creen que he tenido tantas novias? I really haven't dated that many people," Sebastian said, so he wouldn't have to answer.

"You know what? It doesn't matter," Mateo said. "I dare you to suggest to Fine's face that he can't handle the paranormal world."

Sebastian could picture Wesley's reaction. He winced. "Don't tell Wesley I said any of this."

"Can I tell him you're being stupid?" said Mateo. "Let your boyfriend help you get rid of the brooch. Let Miss Robbins and Mr. Zhang and the others help you."

Mateo made it sound so easy. Wesley was straightforward and steady and he didn't rattle easily; there probably wasn't anything he couldn't handle. But Sebastian had gone into the army at eighteen and then into service for Baron Zeppler. He'd been on his own a long time; asking people for help meant remembering he had people to ask in the first place.

"I don't think Wesley is my boyfriend," Sebastian said, instead of voicing those thoughts. "I mean, we've never talked about it."

"But you're not going to call Loretta from the passenger terminal because you have Lord Fine," Mateo said shrewdly. "So what are the two of you, then?"

"Going to see a man I once held at gunpoint, apparently," Sebastian said. "I think I will always feel awkward around Arthur and Rory."

Judging by Mateo's expression, he knew Sebastian was dodging the question, but he let it go. "How do Lord Fine and Arthur Kenzie know each other, anyway?"

"They're friends," said Sebastian. "I don't know how they became friends, but Arthur's father is a congressman and Wesley is a viscount. They went to the same wedding here in New York in February, so their social circles overlap; maybe it was easy for them to meet in London."

"Arthur Kenzie is the one with magic in his aura?"

said Mateo. "The magic of the asylum escapee who sees history and has the ring relic, Rory Brodigan?"

Sebastian nodded. "Those two are also very good friends."

"They would have to be, for magic to work like that." Mateo tapped his lips. "So Lord Fine has a *very good friend* from his social circle, who's athletic and handsome, according to you, and that man is now *very good friends* with a different man?"

"Yes."

"And all of them are *just* friends?"

Sebastian paused. But no, of course they were all just friends, Wesley would have said if it was anything else. "Yes."

"If you say so." Mateo jerked his head toward the door. "Get out of here already; if Mr. Zhang is looking for us, he can't find me if your tattoo is screwing up his astral walking. Go try to call Miss Robbins again."

Sebastian couldn't argue with that.

Chapter Three

NEED TO MEET IN NEW YORK STOP CALL
ME AT THE WALDORF STOP

Wesley stood in the parlor of his suite, a corner room
furnished in a mix of practicality and luxury designed
to appeal to a wealthy traveler. His eyes skimmed the
telegram a second time.

The first message he'd received on the pier when
he'd disembarked from the ship had been easy enough
to dismiss. That had been an invitation for cards and
smokes with Sir Ellery Penfold, a baronet Wesley knew
well. Sir Ellery had been with Wesley on that godfor-
saken trip to New York in February, part of their group
that had come from London for Lady Blanche's wedding to the New York governor's son. Wesley had used
the wedding as a flimsy excuse to come chasing after
Arthur and had never intended to return to New York,
but apparently Sir Ellery hadn't had his fill and was
back in Manhattan, making friends who owned interesting establishments, according to him. Wesley still
didn't need to see him.

This telegram, however, waiting for him at the front
desk here at the Roosevelt, was from Major Charles
Langford.

A much harder man for Wesley to ignore.

He lowered the telegram. It had been some months since he'd last seen Major Langford, but Wesley didn't forget anyone, let alone a former commanding officer. Langford worked for the War Office now. Their post-war relationship was cordial enough, although on the occasions they still crossed paths, Langford would often imply that civilian life as a viscount was a waste of Wesley's talents and unsubtly mention they were recruiting. Wesley had never taken the bait; he might have felt useless and stagnant, but avoiding society was still preferable to returning to anything related to the war. He'd been a hard man most of his life, but never more so than under Major Langford.

Need to meet in New York.

Why? What was Langford doing in America, and how had he learned Wesley was here? What did he have to discuss that was so urgent it couldn't wait for London?

Wesley looked across his suite's parlor, to the candlestick telephone on the table next to the settee. He didn't have to see Arthur or take Sebastian to dinner. He could call the Waldorf, and spend his singular evening in New York with Langford instead.

But Jade had wanted to see them, and whatever Langford wanted to discuss, Wesley highly doubted it would be on the level of telekinetic bootleggers and fifteenth-century supernatural relics.

And the circles beneath Sebastian's eyes were only deepening as the days went on. And yes, Sebastian was the paranormal, not Wesley—a dangerous one, Jade had once pointed out. But, as Jade had likewise pointed out, Sebastian was also a marshmallow. One who needed help but was, frankly, shit at asking for it or accepting it. Wesley didn't have magic, but there was plenty else he could do, including finding answers to why the brooch was running a dangerous marshmallow into the ground, and their best lead right now was tracking down the other paranormals and Arthur.

He and Sebastian would only be in Ohio a few days before returning to New York; if Langford was still in the city, Wesley would get in touch with him then. He set the telegram aside, picked up his walking stick, and strode out the door without touching the phone.

He skipped the elevator, choosing instead to descend the wide, carpeted staircase that led to the lobby. He spotted Sebastian right away, once again on the phone, this time at the hotel desk. Wesley automatically slowed his steps to enjoy the view, because Sebastian took the damnable trend of dinner jackets instead of proper tail-coats and made it attractive.

Wesley had seen the suite's bedroom, which had a larger bed than a ship's cabin. It was going to be a good night, once they were done with said paranormals and Arthur.

But won't it be awkward? Sebastian had said.

Why should it? Yes, he and Arthur had fucked for six months, then Wesley had come to New York in February to try to win him back. And yes, that had been a humiliating mess, but Wesley had actually—ugh—learned something from it. And now he knew the difference between a partner he had no emotions for but made a convenient accessory, and—well. Sebastian.

Granted, it was perhaps admittedly a touch out of the ordinary to discover one's ex-lover was now shagging someone who could see history and control the wind, but Wesley had found a man who could destroy magic and pin him to the bed with his mind.

Lunacy all around. No cause to be awkward.

Sebastian hung up the phone just as Wesley reached him, a frown on his face.

"No Miss Robbins or Mr. Zhang?" Wesley guessed.

Sebastian's gaze darted toward him, and then Wesley was suddenly the recipient of a long look himself. And wasn't it ridiculous, for a man as effortlessly beautiful as Sebastian to find anything to appreciate in Wesley's crustiness.

"No." Sebastian sighed. "I don't suppose your telegram was from either of them?"

"Wouldn't that be refreshing, to get mail I actually wanted?" Wesley said. "Sadly no; it was from an army major who's apparently in town. Absolutely no reason for us to speak here instead of London; I'd prefer to finally have a meal on a table that's not moving. And speaking of tables." He tilted his head toward the concierge. "Can you recommend a place for dinner?"

"The Plaza, sir," the concierge said. "I can arrange for a reservation. How many?"

They'd have Arthur, which almost certainly meant Brodigan as well, and hopefully Jade and Zhang. "Could be six." Wesley tapped the counter. "I also need an extra blanket sent up to my room."

"You think you'll be cold in New York?" Sebastian sounded surprised as the two of them crossed the lobby toward the door. "Is it not colder in England?"

"Depends on the season," Wesley said. "But I was actually thinking a New York autumn is colder than *Puerto Rico.*"

Oh, Sebastian's lips formed. He looked a little lost. "That's considerate of you."

On someone else, the note of surprise might have been from disbelief that Wesley was capable of consideration. But this was Sebastian, who had spent three years under blood magic and then several months mostly alone. So more likely the surprise came because he was still recalibrating back to a life where he could rely on others, and Wesley really ought to have more patience while he adjusted—something that would have been easier if Sebastian didn't also have a galling tendency to forget that not having magic didn't make Wesley *useless*.

"I'm not being considerate, I'm being selfish," Wesley said. "I just spent a week on a ship with you. I'm well-aware now that if you aren't warm enough, you wake up constantly."

"How is that selfish?"

Because I don't know how to touch you when the fucking's over but I crave you more than I crave smokes so I want you comfortable in my bed so you'll keep coming back. Wesley cleared his throat. "Because I'm looking out for any light sleepers nearby. After all, if you're waking up, so are they."

Sebastian's gaze darted to Wesley. "You could have the extra blanket sent up to the sixth floor instead," he said tentatively.

Wesley could. He could sleep alone tonight in a big bed with only the blankets he needed. No crowded mattress. No overheating. No Sebastian wrapped around him, all quiet breaths and warm skin.

"Or you could appreciate that I have planned ahead so I can have my company yet not be woken through the night," Wesley pointed out. "Almost as if I have practice making battle plans. It's a tactical blanket, if you will," he added, which drew a quiet snort from Sebastian.

The doorman got them a cab, and soon Fifth Avenue was rolling past, the last of the soft glow of evening illuminating the tops of tall buildings as the city's famous night lights came to life along the darker streets.

"It really doesn't seem like Jade," said Sebastian, "to ask us to call and then not be reachable."

He was frowning, which would never do. Wesley poked his calf with his walking stick. "I said *dress for dinner.* Where's your tailcoat, brat?"

A small smile curled on Sebastian's lips. "I must have left it in Paris."

"If Paris was an imaginary place for the imaginary tailcoat you refuse to buy, then perhaps."

Sebastian's smile became a grin. "I think they look better on other people." He took another extremely unsubtle eyeful of Wesley, gaze lingering on the close fit of his overcoat, on his freshly shaved jaw above the white bow tie and wingtip collar. Sebastian opened his mouth, but then closed it, eyes darting to the cabbie.

Wesley kept his voice low. "I suspect I want to hear whatever it is you're hesitating over."

Sebastian's gaze lingered on the cabbie, and then, barely audible over the engine, he murmured, "Tan guapo como siempre."

Wesley went abruptly hot under the collar. Sebastian had translated that phrase one night on the ship. It was hard enough to resist flattening Sebastian against the nearest surface when he was sweetly clueless; a breathy *handsome as ever* had Wesley's gloved hands tightening on his walking stick, because none of the rigid formalities of his life had prepared him for honey-sweet Spanish compliments whispered like a secret in the backseat of a New York taxicab.

"How unsporting of you," Wesley muttered, also quiet, "to say something like that where I can't do anything about it."

Sebastian's small grin was back, the bastard. "It was your idea to go to dinner."

"Did you really just imply *I'm* the one with questionable judgment?" Wesley said. "You, the man who feeds strays, who decided Crumpet and Flan would make acceptable pets for my cook's daughter?"

Incongruously, Sebastian looked delighted. "You called the cats by their names."

Wesley pinched the bridge of his nose. "That isn't the point. That isn't even in the vicinity of the point."

"I knew you liked them."

Wesley sighed.

The cab dropped them off across the street from Arthur's building on Central Park West. The park's trees were bright with their October leaves, a riot of oranges, yellows, and reds woven like a tapestry into the last of the green.

They crossed the street, and Wesley spoke first to the doorman. "We're here to see Arthur Kenzie—is he in?"

Wesley could see the doorman assessing them, the cut and fabric of their suits, the ivory on Wesley's walking stick, the gold chain that led to the brooch in Sebastian's pocket.

"Viscount Fine," Wesley added dryly. "Or do we need to provide references?"

The doorman shook his head apologetically. "Sorry, sir," he said deferentially. "Mr. Kenzie isn't in. He left the city about a week ago."

Wesley and Sebastian exchanged a glance. "Do you know where he's gone?" Sebastian asked.

"I'm afraid I don't," the doorman said.

"Well, what about another man?" Wesley asked. "Curly blond hair, short and scruffy, wears specs?"

"Oh, Mr. Kenzie's nephew? No, he hasn't been around for a while either."

Nephew. Wesley's eyebrow went up.

With no Arthur to visit, they crossed back across the street to Central Park. Hardly pastoral when Fifth Avenue was within shouting distance, but Sebastian wanted to see the squirrels and Wesley could accept it was practical to take a shortcut to the Plaza through the park. They picked up one of the paths that wound through the trees. In the twilight, the autumn colors were soft, the city noises more muffled by the chirping of the birds and the fallen leaves crunching underfoot than Wesley had expected. He grudgingly amended his opinion of the park to *tolerable.*

"I didn't know Rory was Arthur's nephew," Sebastian said, as they passed an unnecessarily picturesque arched stone bridge curving over a little lake.

Wesley shuddered. "Christ, obviously he's not. It must be their cover story."

"Oh, good," Sebastian said. "I thought maybe I was missing something."

"I assure you, none of us would have missed *that.*"

"But why would they need a cover story?"

Wesley side-eyed him. "You thought *we* needed a cover story. Why not them?"

"They have less to hide, yes?"

"Well, *no,*" Wesley said, nonplussed. "Half of Arthur's family are in politics. He can't exactly parade his surly urchin around the city; it would raise questions."

"Oh," Sebastian said. "Arthur's family care about money, then? That is a shame."

It was more likely the *fucking other men* bit that was the problem, but perhaps the class difference was part of it. Wesley pursed his lips. "So Miss Robbins wasn't home, Mr. Zhang hasn't been around the Dragon House, and now Arthur isn't home and Brodigan hasn't been by either." He huffed. "Did they want to see us or not?"

"I've been thinking about Jade's cable," Sebastian said, his gaze darting to a cardinal in a tree. "What she might have meant by *the clock needs a curse to tick.*"

"That she's a rabbit in a waistcoat running late to an appointment, leading me into a particularly twisted version of your Wonderland?" Wesley said wryly.

That drew a quiet half-laugh from Sebastian. "Not exactly. Curses are rare, yes? But..."

"But what?"

"But Teo and I both carry a blood curse."

"Your blood. Is *cursed.*" Wesley came to a stop, and Sebastian mirrored him. "And you've never mentioned this *why*?"

"Because it just determined our magic—it doesn't do anything else," Sebastian said. "And it's from the de Leon who was a witch-hunter during the Spanish Inquisition; it's not like I want to brag about him. He cursed his own blood; that's why all his descendants have magic that works on other magic."

"Admittedly he makes even the worst Lord Fine seem like a lovely, reasonable ancestor," Wesley said. "Then you have *four* kinds of magic? The brooch, the tattoo, your enervation magic and a blood curse?"

Sebastian made a face. "It sounds like a lot when you say it like that."

"Christ," Wesley muttered. "So you think Miss Robbins's cable might refer to your blood? That this siphon clock needs not just paranormal blood, but *cursed* paranormal blood to work?"

"The pomander is evil magic," Sebastian said quietly. "Maybe it takes evil magic to destroy it."

"Stop it; you know you're forbidden to speak that way about my lion," Wesley said. "I don't care if your magic was the result of a blood curse; it's saved my life more than once. It isn't evil."

That put a small smile on Sebastian's face.

"Also," Wesley said, "not to reduce life to moral absolutes better suited for the preachiest of fables, but isn't evil generally vanquished by good?"

"In that case, you'd think the others could take care of it," Sebastian said. "They are very much the heroes."

"Take care of it without needing to send bafflingly cryptic cables to scoundrels like us, you mean?" Wesley said wryly.

Sebastian grinned, and they fell into step side by side again. "Hopefully Zhang will find Mateo at the hotel while we're at dinner. And in the meantime, the park is pretty." He glanced at Wesley. "We're walking through Central Park. Like tourists."

"Maybe *you* are. This is nothing but a shortcut to me."

"If you don't like Manhattan, we could visit the Bronx," Sebastian said, far too casually.

"And see the giant zoo, as you're transparently implying?" Wesley said. "You really do think I've gone soft for you, don't you?"

"There are the sea lions, and bears, and I think they have zebras," Sebastian went on, like Wesley hadn't even spoken. "And raccoons."

Wesley raised his eyes heavenward. "I did not sail an ocean to meet a fucking *raccoon*."

"There's also a fox den," Sebastian said. "But you're not allowed in there."

Wesley gave him a narrow-eyed stare.

"You can visit the sloth instead," said Sebastian. "As long as you don't hunt him."

Somewhere in a tree, a cardinal chirped, because even the damn birds were on Sebastian's side.

"I've never said I hunt—never mind, I'm not indulging a conversation about sloths and *foxes*," said Wesley. "We're supposed to have dinner. Let's go."

When they reached the hotel, they were shown to a spacious dining club upstairs with dark wood walls and crystal chandeliers.

"Would you prefer to wait for your other four companions?" the host asked, as he looked over their reservation.

Wesley and Sebastian exchanged a glance. "No," Wesley said. "Apparently it's only going to be us."

As the host took them to their table, Sebastian kept a little extra distance between him and Wesley than he would have with a friend, trying not to notice the lingering looks from the other patrons.

They were taken to a table along the far wall. The gentle light of the chandeliers played over Wesley's high cheekbones and keen eyes as they sat. "Did you just order coffee before dinner?" he said, as the host left with their drink requests. "Are you particularly tired, by chance? From, say, a bit of enchanted antique jewelry?"

Sebastian carefully didn't touch the brooch. "We just got off a transatlantic voyage."

"We did, but you're also trying to dodge the question," Wesley said. "Did they teach that tactic to you medics in the army? It won't get you very far with me."

Sebastian tried to smile. "I'm getting used to it."

"Hmm." Wesley didn't sound convinced by Sebastian's admittedly unconvincing lie. "Hopefully the others will have an idea for how to get rid of it, whenever they deign to let us find them."

"We're supposed to help them with *their* problem," Sebastian pointed out.

"Yes, duck," Wesley said, with exaggerated patience. "We can hopefully all help each other, imagine that."

Sebastian huffed as he picked up his menu. "You know, you've never explained why you call me that."

"Blatantly changing the subject, that's another tactic that doesn't work on me," Wesley said.

"I actually do want to know," Sebastian said, and meant.

Wesley picked up his own menu. "My old grounds-keeper, Fitz, was from Nottinghamshire. He used to call all the children that."

"Oh," Sebastian said knowingly. "So it's what you say when you're being patronizing." He paused. "Wait. You call me that all the time."

Wesley cleared his throat. "They have oysters."

"Now *you're* changing the subject."

"Not at all," Wesley said loftily. "I'm giving proper attention to this menu. I do realize this formal dinner, and the formalwear to go with it, is for my benefit."

Sebastian tugged the black bow tie. "I don't mind."

"A sweet lie, also for my benefit, and it's truly adorable you continue to think you can get that kind of thing past me," Wesley said. "It looks damn good on you, though. Which—yet again—is for my benefit, since I'm the one who gets to look at you in it. Well," he amended, "me and half the nosy Americans in this room. They're probably wondering what such a handsome Spanish playboy is doing with an unfashionable stick-in-the-mud like me."

Sebastian's smile wavered before he could stop it. Wesley's eyes narrowed suspiciously. "What did I just say that bothered you?"

The waiter was dropping off their drinks. "Nothing, Lord Fine," Sebastian said, with a muttered *thanks* to the waiter.

Wesley ordered first courses and soups. As the waiter left, he picked up his ginger ale. "Prohibition is a fucking travesty. And what happened to *Wes*?"

Sebastian gestured around the club. "Don't I need to use your title in places like this?"

"At our private table? Why?"

"Well, the waiter might think—"

"Why would I give a damn what the waiter thinks?"

"Because it's going to be how you say, isn't it? People will wonder why we are together?" Sebastian said. "It doesn't matter to me, but I'm not going to make trouble for you. I can be discreet."

"*Discreet*." Wesley took a sip, grimaced, and set the drink down. "And yet you've never asked me to call you Mr. de Leon in public."

"Of course not," Sebastian said. "You can call me whatever you want."

"I see," Wesley said, too lightly. "So I don't have to be discreet, but you do, so you don't make trouble for me? You can't publicly use the given name of the man you're sleeping with in case people talk, but I can use yours without a thought?"

"Yes, exactly," said Sebastian.

Wesley leaned forward. "That's bullshit."

"But—"

"What kind of contemptible lout would want that bargain? I'm not suggesting we give the restaurant a show, but I'm not about to fumble with your prick in private and then demand you act like a stranger in public," Wesley said, sharper than he'd been. "If the patrons here lack the manners not to stare and speculate about a handsome man from out of town, that is not your fault. You are not to blame for what gossips whisper about your lovers."

It was so completely different from what Sebastian had heard before that for a moment, he didn't have a response. Finally, he said, "But I have magic. I should be the careful one."

"You and you alone? Not a fucking chance," Wesley said. "That is not how this—this thing we're doing is ever going to work."

Aha. Apparently Sebastian wasn't the only one who didn't have a name for what they were to each other. "Why not?"

"*Why not?*" Wesley looked highly ruffled. "Because I will never require a nursemaid, not even in Wonderland, that's why not. There isn't even magic here; we're in a bloody hotel waiting for Oysters Rockefeller. Why would I insist we go out, choose the place, then make you solely responsible for protecting my maidenly virtue or whatever it is you imagine you're doing?"

Sebastian bit his lip. Wesley's wry smile had disappeared, and his shoulders had gone stiff. It brought back memories of their trip to Yorkshire, when Wesley had been bravely marching into a new world where others had magic and he didn't, refusing to show any nerves and instead being adamant that Sebastian *at least treat him like a competent man*.

It wasn't fair that life and war had forced Wesley to harden his skin into armor. But fair or not, he now resented anything he perceived as sheltering, and even if it seemed obvious that magic meant Sebastian would be the one to handle obstacles, Wesley clearly didn't agree.

"I just don't want to be the reason you get a reputation," Sebastian said.

"I *have* a reputation," said Wesley. "One that doesn't require protection. I'm well-known in my every circle for being a caustic prick and a discourteous bastard. Disagreeable, remorseless, unwelcome—"

"You're not any of those things," Sebastian interrupted. "Especially not unwelcome. You're always welcome. Everywhere—" He clamped his mouth shut before he kept going and spilled feelings all over Wesley.

But Wesley's lips curled up grudgingly. "You're truly an absolute nuisance, the way you insist on only seeing good in things. I could bring you a mange-covered dog and you'd call it cute."

"Why wouldn't he be?" Sebastian said. "It's not the poor dog's fault he's had a hard life. Suffering doesn't make someone ugly."

"I think you genuinely believe I could fall for this argument," Wesley said. "If you actually understood how cold-hearted I am, you'd know it's pointless to try to convince me to see the world in the rosy colors you paint everything in. But for all that softness, you're really fucking stubborn. You're not the only person who can handle things."

Sebastian winced.

Wesley sat back in his chair, gaze on Sebastian. "And how long has it been since you haven't dealt with everything alone?"

Sebastian dodged his eyes. "You and Jade and Zhang helped me get Mateo back."

"So you have a singular example over the past, what? Three years?"

"Um. Maybe," Sebastian admitted. He probably owed Wesley more of the truth. "And I'm not very good at guessing what non-magical people can handle, because I haven't ever—you know. With someone without magic."

Wesley blinked. "You haven't fucked someone without magic?"

"No, of course I have, I meant—I've never had a girlfriend without magic."

"You still don't have a girlfriend without magic," Wesley said wryly.

"Lord Fine," Sebastian said pointedly. "I'm trying to tell you why I'm so bad at this. You're not making it easy."

"Of course I'm not making it easy. You have met me, haven't you?" Wesley leaned forward. "Mr. de Leon," he said, just as pointedly, "I'm trying to tell you that you're not alone anymore. I'm actually frighteningly competent. Try relying on me."

Sebastian looked across the table, at Wesley's old-fashioned high collar and perfectly fitted tuxedo, because he wasn't swayed by trends or other people's opinions and wore what he liked. He was handsome, of course, but also steady and smart and refreshingly straightforward, and Sebastian had never felt as secure around someone as he did around Wesley.

He wanted to rely on him, to tell him everything. To say, *I haven't had a blood terror since I started sleeping with you. I think you're keeping them away. And they're more terrible than I ever admit and I don't want to go back to sleeping alone.*

But he hadn't forgotten Wesley's words from the ship. *You realize I've always slept alone. And I've never indulged in anything as sentimental as cuddling.*

Wesley didn't like sharing his bed. Was Sebastian going to take advantage of his tolerance and guilt him into it?

"You're really sweet," he said instead.

"How dare you," Wesley said, more amused than angry.

"I'm just saying things straight," Sebastian said innocently.

"No, you're being impertinent." Wesley still sounded amused. "I never hear you talk this way to anyone else."

Sebastian shrugged, smile still on his lips. "It's easier to talk to you than anyone else," he admitted. *Everything* was easier with Wesley.

Wesley tilted his head. "So I'm the only one who gets your cheek, then, is that what you're saying?"

Sebastian shrugged again. "Lucky you," he teased.

The corner of Wesley's mouth had turned up in one of his own rare smiles. "Lucky me."

Chapter Four

As they were finishing dinner, the host came by their table.

"Lord Fine?" he said. "I have a message from some friends of yours. They're in the gentlemen's smoking room and cordially request that you stop by."

Wesley and Sebastian exchanged a look. "Finally," said Wesley. "Although it won't be Miss Robbins, I suppose, and Arthur won't touch smokes of any kind."

"Maybe it's Zhang," said Sebastian.

Someone was fetched to take them to the smoking room. Wesley peered into the dim space, looking for the welcome sight of Mr. Zhang.

But as the waiter led them on, his eyes fell on someone he knew, and he nearly groaned out loud.

"Fine, old boy!" Sir Ellery Penfold was standing to give him a hearty wave. "There you are. Did you not get my message?"

Sir Ellery wasn't the worst person Wesley knew. He'd actually served in the war, and these days participated in many of the same shooting exhibitions as Wesley. Sir Ellery was second cousin to Sir Harold Kerrigan, the man who had stolen the pomander from the Earl of Blanshard in the first place, and had employed Chester the valet prior to Wesley—well, before Chester had murdered Sir Harold and smuggled the pomander into America with Wesley as his cover. Though of course, Sir Ellery wouldn't know that part, only that Wesley had hired Chester before the valet had been mauled by a tiger.

"How the fuck did you know I was in New York?" Wesley said, instead of hello.

"From Lady Tabitha." Sir Ellery said it like it was obvious, like it should have been expected that a pesky thing like the Atlantic Ocean wouldn't stop Wesley's relatives from interfering in his life. "She found out from your footman, and she's great friends with my aunt, who told her I was here too. Lady Tabitha says you'd turned down every girl in London and she's willing to resort to an American one."

Ugh. Wesley had found an American already, thank you very much, or, at least, a man with a complicated identity that included American. Next time Wesley would ensure his footman Ned knew not to tell anyone where he'd gone, particularly not distant family who were dead set on Wesley having an heir, or even better, finding his way to an early grave intestate.

"I had missed you when I called your hotel, but they said you had a reservation here," Sir Ellery went on. "Figured we could catch you and we did."

The other two men at the table had also stood, one of whom Wesley didn't know, and the other one he knew very well. "Major Langford," Wesley said to the white man on Sir Ellery's right. "How unexpected to see you in New York."

Where Sir Ellery was about Sebastian's height, with brown hair and pale skin red across the cheeks and nose, Major Langford was as tall as Wesley, his straw-colored hair still cropped military-short and his posture still ramrod straight. Not particularly surprising to find the two of them together, whether in London or Manhattan; Langford seemed to keep in touch with everyone he'd known since the war. Hell, perhaps the War Office was recruiting Sir Ellery now.

"Hello, Fine," Langford said neutrally. "I take it you didn't get *my* message either."

Wesley was spared having to answer by Sir Ellery, who was chattering again. "I don't think I've seen you since Lady Blanche's wedding—Mrs. Hartman now, of course."

"Since spring for me," Major Langford said, his gaze flicking between Wesley and Sebastian in a not particularly friendly way. "At a fundraiser in London. You had a different companion with you then, though. An American lieutenant."

Yes, Lieutenant Arthur Kenzie, and don't I wish it had been him here instead of the two of you. Wesley bit it back. Langford hadn't been his commanding officer for years, but old habits apparently truly did die hard, as he still couldn't quite bring himself to be rude to Major Langford's face.

Sebastian was being quietly polite, as he seemed to default to around most people. *A hard one to read*, that was another thing Jade had once said about him. But not with Wesley, not anymore, and he could suddenly appreciate the contrast; how much of himself Sebastian held back around others compared to how open and playful he was with Wesley. The world was different when it was just the two of them: Sebastian comfortable enough to slip into Spanish and badger him about animals; Wesley's jagged edges a little softer, his dark moods a little lighter.

He abruptly wanted that back. "I'm afraid I'm on a

schedule," he said brusquely, to Sir Ellery and Langford. "If you'll excuse us—"

"Hang the schedule," said Sir Ellery. "Come play the tables with me."

Doubtful that Sir Ellery could afford to lose to Wesley at cards. Rumor had it their family's finances were drying up, and Wesley might be a cad, but he wasn't going to empty Sir Ellery's pockets for him. "Can't."

"But you haven't met our friend." Sir Ellery gestured to the third man in their trio, who was pale and red-haired with freckles across his nose. "This is Mr. Findlay. Left Glasgow to make a name for himself in textiles here in New York."

"Please, call me Alasdair." The man, Alasdair, was probably around thirty, and still had quite a bit of Scotland in his accent. He was facing Wesley, for all intents and purposes paying full attention to their introduction. But his eyes hadn't once stopped darting to Sebastian. "And you're the Viscount Fine who hasn't told us who *your* friend is."

Major Langford snorted. "Fine isn't really the *friend* type."

Sebastian shifted. It was a tiny movement, but Wesley was attuned enough to him now to pick that sort of thing up, the reminder that a *dangerous marshmallow* might be soft and sweet, but was, in fact, still dangerous.

"He's got a companion, at least," Sir Ellery said. "Introduce us already, Fine."

Wesley met Sebastian's eyes for a brief second. If Sebastian was irritated at being the object of three strangers' stares and speculation, he was keeping it off his face. But then, he was keeping everything off his face right now. This Sebastian was closed off and unreadable, and would never shamelessly cajole anyone into the zoo.

Wesley bit back the less charitable things he wanted to say to the men who'd put Sebastian's walls back up. "Gentlemen, this is Mr. de Leon."

"De Leon?" Alasdair repeated. "Spanish, then? Quite a bit of history in the name."

"In some places, perhaps," Sebastian said, which was a tactful way to avoid saying *in the paranormal world, yes.*

"But that's fascinating, you must tell me everything about yourself." Alasdair had stopped pretending to look at Wesley or anyone else. "I can hear the accent— where in Spain are you from?"

"Puerto Rico, actually," Sebastian said.

"Is that right." Major Langford folded his arms over his chest. "And what sort of association do you have with Fine here?"

"Yes, are you two traveling together?" Sir Ellery added. "I don't believe you said one way or another."

"Since when does my business concern anyone but myself?" Wesley said.

"Everyone knows you rarely leave London," Sir Ellery said. "Of course we're curious why you've returned to New York."

"Tourism," Wesley said flatly. "Were you aware the Bronx Zoo has a fox den and a sloth?"

"Foxes, eh?" Sir Ellery said slyly. "And me without my dogs."

Sebastian's eyes almost imperceptibly narrowed.

Langford scoffed. "You're not here as a tourist."

Sir Ellery turned toward Alasdair. "I should have warned you, Fine is well-known in London for being, shall we say, abrupt?"

Sebastian's expression didn't change, but he went a little too still. Was he actually irritated to hear Sir Ellery say that? Wesley had warned Sebastian that he had a reputation. Not everyone saw Wesley through rose-colored glasses.

"It's quite all right," said Alasdair. "I could hardly be in my latest line of business if I minded sharp tongues, could I?" He leaned in, again toward Sebastian, like he had no interest in Wesley or anyone else. "If you get tired of all this ginger ale and juice, you'll let me know, won't you?"

Well, *that* wasn't subtle. Was *textiles* Sir Ellery's euphemism for bootlegging, then? Surprising that Langford hadn't objected, pedantic rule-follower that he was, considering Alasdair had practically just announced his bootlegging to the room.

"You look like a man who enjoys going out," Alasdair was saying to Sebastian. "With your very forward fashion sense. Do forgive the nosiness, I've been learning the textile business for a few years now; I always notice sartorial choices. But you have very modern sensibilities, unlike your viscount friend." He pointed to the gold chain that dangled from Sebastian's waistcoat pocket, the one that led to the brooch relic. "Although you've gone for a pocket watch instead of a wristwatch, that's surprising. It must be special, I take it. May I see it?"

Sebastian visibly stiffened.

Now they were absolutely done. Wesley didn't give a damn what people said about him, but he would not stand for Sebastian being made uncomfortable. "As I said: we can't linger."

Alasdair did look at Wesley then, with pale, watery eyes. Had the man come straight from some speakeasy somewhere? Too drunk to keep his line of business a secret or leave Sebastian alone?

"I asked to meet with you, Fine." Langford spoke like

a man accustomed to giving orders, a tone Wesley had heard too many times on the front. "You know I don't make idle requests."

Perhaps not. But they weren't in the army anymore; Wesley was the Viscount Fine now, and also accustomed to having his orders followed. "Forgive me, major," he said, "but it will have to wait."

Langford's gaze turned cooler, and went to Sebastian again.

"I'll see if I can get him on the list for Lady Blanche's party," Sir Ellery said to Major Langford. "Gives Fine a few days to wrap up whatever this business he's prattling about is, and she'll be delighted to have another peer at her Halloween masquerade."

Christ, absolutely not. Wesley would rather meet the sloth. "Good night, gentlemen." He set off for the door, Sebastian at his side, feeling eyes on their backs as they left.

Sebastian was glad to see a cab at the curb when they exited. It was close enough they could have walked, but between Wesley's dress shoes and Sebastian's exhaustion—and lack of a coat—they picked the ride, and in moments they were on their way downtown. It was fully dark, and colder now that no sun was left. The wind cut through the taxi's open windows as they crawled south through traffic. Sebastian tried not to look closely at Fifth Avenue; he'd been on the street too many times in that horrible February he'd spent here, and he didn't need more reminders of Hyde and Shelley, of the havoc they'd wreaked.

As if the brooch relic wanted to echo the terrors of his memories, a pulse of fatigue went through him, like his blood was mixed with lead.

Wesley's irritation was also palpable. He hadn't spoken since they got in the taxi, his jaw set, his arms folded, his long legs stretched out.

The cab driver was leaning out the window, trying to get through a traffic jam in front of St. Patrick's Cathedral, and didn't appear to be listening to the backseat. Sebastian bit his lip, and leaned in. "I have to confess something," he said quietly.

Wesley's gaze darted sideways, to him. "What?" he said warily, matching Sebastian's low volume.

"I am very glad you made us leave," Sebastian said, "because if your acquaintances ever imply you don't have any friends again, I might put them on the floor."

Wesley barked out a surprised laugh. "I assumed you were mortified by my rudeness," he said, a hint of the tension in his shoulders easing.

"You always frame things to make yourself the villain," said Sebastian. "But I was there. You made it clear you were busy and they did not respect that. They kept insisting to talk to you."

"Except for that Alasdair Findlay fellow," Wesley said. "He was only interested in *you*—your name, your accent, your clothes." He sounded particularly grumpy. "Frankly, I think *Mr. Call-Me-Alasdair* was drunk and trying to hide it. Sampling his own product, perhaps."

Sebastian had picked up on the bootlegging too. "Maybe they had come from a speakeasy."

"My thought as well," said Wesley. "Sir Ellery was with me on my singular trip here in February, when we were whisked off to Miss Robbins's speakeasy with the blindfolds and the cloak-and-dagger act. Maybe he found the Magnolia again. I should have asked, but as you might have noticed, I was rather preoccupied with leaving."

"Not like I wanted to linger," Sebastian admitted. "How do you know the major?"

Wesley grimaced. "He headed my company for a year."

"You reported to him?"

"On paper," Wesley said. "But my grandfather had a seat in the House of Lords. I might have been a captain under Langford, but he was shrewd enough not to treat me as a commoner. And in turn, I followed his orders—well." Wesley's gaze darted to the cabbie, then back to Sebastian. "Most of them. At any rate, he wasn't a friend, but we ran a tight company together. Maybe too tight."

Sebastian furrowed his brow. "What do you mean by that?"

"War doesn't exactly bring out the best in people," Wesley said. "And Langford had a talent for bringing out one's very worst."

His shoulders had gone tense again. New York was full of memories Sebastian didn't want, but Wesley seemed to have plenty of those from the war—had alluded to doing terrible things, to being the one called in when his troop had captured a spy who knew where Wesley's soldiers were held prisoner but wouldn't talk. Sebastian had seen Wesley with his staff, how he took responsibility for people in his care; it made his chest ache to think of Wesley's concern for his soldiers exploited in the worst possible way. Hopefully Langford had nothing to do with any of that. "He didn't say why he was in New York."

"He didn't, did he? Though could simply be wartime connections: Langford is well-acquainted with the new Mrs. Hartman's father, who was always a big military supporter. Langford has known Sir Ellery since the war as well, so perhaps he's here on one of their invitations. What a travesty that we ran into them instead of people I'd actually like to see."

And there it was again, the other thing about New York Sebastian was trying not to think about. But Sir Ellery had been with Wesley in February, and Sebastian couldn't forget why Wesley had come to America before, that there was some unknown man somewhere in the city that he'd sailed an ocean for.

He tried to keep his tone light. "You mean Jade and the others, yes? Or…well. Someone in particular?"

"Who would that be?"

"You know. The person you came here for in February."

Sebastian thought he got it out more-or-less steadily, but Wesley's eyes narrowed with suspicion. "We're not going to be awkward about this after all, are we? When I told you that story in York, you said it was a gallant gesture, hopping a ship in my doomed attempt to win back an ex-lover. Why be odd about it now?"

"Um." There was no good way to say it, but Sebastian obviously wasn't good at sounding smooth anyway. "Because when you told me the story in York, that was before we were—" *Boyfriends? Lovers? People who sleep together and save each other's lives but don't know what to call their relationship?* "—before we started…this."

So much for not broadcasting his own insecurity loud and clear.

But Wesley only shook his head. "It is not worth making it awkward," he said, more self-deprecating than mean. "That night with Sir Ellery at the Magnolia, I was pawned off on Miss Robbins. My ex couldn't lose me fast enough. I should have gotten the message then, but my head was so far up my own arse I couldn't see that I was chasing a convenience, not a passion. But I didn't know things could feel so—well."

He quickly cleared his throat. "Anyway. The entire fiasco was short and unenjoyable." He glanced at Sebastian. "Although, when it comes to terrible visits to this city, I think you win that dubious trophy."

Sebastian startled.

"You expected everyone else had forgotten what you went through on your last trip here?" Wesley said quietly. "I didn't forget. I likewise doubt your brother has. You do know you don't have to sugar-coat any of that either?"

Sebastian glanced outside the window as the cab pulled up to the curb in front of their hotel. Grand Central's traffic flowed around them, lights everywhere despite the night, honking cars and shouting people. The October air smelled like exhaust fumes and had a chill that hinted at the bitter cold of the February he'd spent here.

The past was stronger in New York, harder to ignore when his memories were constantly triggered by sounds and sights and scents. The brooch made it worse, not oily like blood magic but pulling at him like a magnet drawing energy out of his bones. It was better when they were moving, when he had distractions; in the stillness of the cab, his collar felt too close, cuff links too sharp where they touched his wrists, all of him raw to the touch like skin torn by claws—

Sebastian quickly looked away from the street, focusing on what he could see of Wesley's face in the dark interior of the taxi. "That's nice of you to say."

"None of that," Wesley said warningly. "This isn't about me being *nice*, which is a patently outrageous sen-

timent on its own." He dropped his voice even lower.
"You might have been a medic, but you were used as a
soldier, and now life expects you to play the tourist on
your former battlefield. That can't be easy."

The doorman was striding toward their taxi. Sebastian swallowed. "We're only here one night. I can just—
think of other things."

"Ah yes. Because of course the mind always cooperates when one instructs it to do that." Wesley eyed
him. "Perhaps someone needs to give you something
else to think about."

"Like what?" Sebastian asked, as the doorman
opened their door.

"I've got some ideas."

Chapter Five

They paused by the hotel desk, and Wesley waited while Sebastian gave their names. "Do we have any messages?"

"As a matter of fact, you do," said the clerk, reaching for a scrap of paper.

"Oh good," Sebastian said. "Is it—"

"It's from a Mateo de Leon, and it says *nobody called tonight, don't wake me up.*"

"Oh." Sebastian frowned. "Okay, then."

Wesley tapped the front desk. "If anyone telephones or sends a message, have it sent straight up to my room. Otherwise I am not to be disturbed for any reason."

"Yes, sir," the clerk said.

They skipped the elevator and walked up the stairs together. "We still have no word from the others?" Sebastian asked.

"Haven't the foggiest why not," said Wesley. "But our train isn't until three tomorrow. Maybe they'll be in touch in the morning."

They walked down the empty hall together as Wesley produced his key from his pocket. "The Plaza apparently has a butler on the suite floor," he said, as he unlocked the door. "But it also had Sir Ellery and the major in its smoking room, so I'm quite pleased that we're here." He held the door open and gestured for Sebastian to go in first.

The suite was on the corner and the drapes were wide-open, framing the streetlights and the traffic flowing to and from Grand Central Station. Wesley locked the door as Sebastian wandered into the parlor, toward the gold-trimmed settee and two wingback chairs set around a low table. The ashtrays were empty, but obviously Wesley wasn't anything as inane as proud of himself for managing hours without a smoke. It was the bare minimum, truly; he should have been able to quit long ago.

Sebastian's words from the pier echoed in his mind: *Don't be so hard on yourself.* Wesley pushed the memory away. Sebastian was far too kind when it came to him.

His skin was itching even now, hands twitching for his pocket, teeth clenched against the craving for a cigarette between his lips. He wanted something to touch and taste, to occupy his hands and mouth and sate the urges hounding him.

His gaze fell on Sebastian.

"So you served with Major Langford." Sebastian had stopped by the settee, already undoing his bow tie. "Do you know Sir Ellery quite well too? You said you traveled with him."

"He's a baronet I used to see at parties," Wesley said, "back when I was still willing to occasionally go."

Sebastian left the untied bow tie loose in his attached collar and slid the jacket off his shoulders. "Are they going to wonder why I was with you?"

Of *course* Sebastian was only thinking of Wesley's reputation. "Langford will, but not for the reasons you're worried about," said Wesley. "He's simply suspicious. As for Sir Ellery, he won't wonder that either, because we, ah." He cleared his throat. "We're also in a club together."

"You hesitated." Sebastian draped the jacket over the back of the settee. It left him in just the dress shirt and black waistcoat, which hugged the sleek lines of his body, no jacket blocking the view of trousers fitted to his hips and arse. "You never hesitate. What is the club?"

"One that makes society assume you couldn't possibly be the kind of man who wants to fuck other fellows."

"What club is *that*?" Sebastian asked, as he got his top two buttons undone.

"It doesn't matter."

"Is it a sex club?"

"No!"

"Are you sure?"

"How the devil would I *not* be sure of something like that?"

"Well, you have still never explained where your handcuffs came from." Sebastian bent his arm, efficiently removing first one cuff link, then the other. "And you seem to know an awful lot about things like floggers."

Wesley raised his eyebrow. "If you have a question, you can always ask," he said meaningfully.

"I did ask you a question," Sebastian said innocently, pocketing his cuff links and beginning to roll up his sleeves. "You still haven't answered."

Wesley gaze lingered as forearms were bared, the tattoo coming into view. "I am not in a sex club with Sir Ellery." He leaned his walking stick against the hat stand by the door. "If you must know, it's a hunting club."

Sebastian folded his arms.

"Yes, that's right, we shoot targets and occasionally

game together," Wesley said. "Sir Ellery did a tour of duty himself and is still an excellent shot."

Sebastian's eyes narrowed.

"I suspect you would have preferred to hear we used to fuck for an audience," Wesley said dryly.

"I wouldn't be judging you for that," Sebastian said. "Do you go on fox hunts together?"

"Surely that isn't relevant."

"It's always relevant, because you should leave the foxes alone."

"Would it soothe your marshmallow heart if I remind you that I don't own dogs and I despise most people?" Wesley said, placing his top hat on a hat stand hook. "I'd hardly join entire parties to track down a single fox. I'd sooner keep the damn thing in my garden."

"Oh." That looked like it had, actually, made Sebastian feel better. "You should get dogs," Sebastian said. "But not for hunting, to keep as pets. Like your neighbor's little Maltese, Powderpuff."

"Absolutely not—"

"And no shooting any of the animals when we go to the zoo."

"*When* we go to zoo." A hint of a smile played on Wesley's lips. "Listen to you, telling me what to do, confident I'll capitulate to your whims. Where did cautious, polite Sebastian go?"

Sebastian hesitated.

Wesley stepped closer, behind one of the chairs. "It's not an insult," he promised. "It's an observation. Or perhaps it's a brag."

"A brag?"

"You're so quiet and careful with everyone else." Wesley rested gloved hands along the high back of the chair. "But sometimes, when I get you alone, I get this other side of you, where you think you can order me around and give me a hard time."

Sebastian leaned forward, arms folded on the top of the settee. "I think you just called me a pain in the ass."

"I did, didn't I?" Wesley said, still with a hint of a smile. "And no one would believe me if I told them. They only know your reticent, unreadable side, but I get the impertinent, bossy side, and to be honest, it's maddening how attractive I find it."

"So you think I'm a *cute* pain in the ass?" Sebastian tilted his head, looking amused. "That's an odd thing to like."

"Not at all. At least, not for a man who keeps handcuffs in his bedroom."

Sebastian's amused look became a grin. "So you're finally going to admit what they're for?"

How could he rile Wesley up this much with nothing more than a little flirting? "And here you are again, talking to me like you never talk to anyone else," Wesley said. "I think you don't show this part of yourself easily, but I get it, just like I get you immediately stripping off every bit of your formalwear the instant you walk through my door. It's as if the real you comes out just for me, and so yes, that is a brag."

They were on the second floor, and with the wide-open curtains and glowing lamps, they were probably framed in the window like a play on a theater stage for anyone on the sidewalk. And what a sight Sebastian was, down to his waistcoat and rolled-up shirtsleeves, looking very much ready for Wesley to get the rest of those clothes off and get to the skin beneath.

Wesley's skin still itched for nicotine, and shadows still haunted Sebastian's eyes. Sebastian desperately needed a respite from his memories, and Wesley desperately needed something to occupy his hands and mouth.

How very lucky that they had each other.

There was a slight flush across Sebastian's cheeks that suggested he was also feeling the anticipation of touch. "I guess I do show you things I don't show anyone else."

Wesley's gaze automatically dipped to Sebastian's wrist, where his arm was turned just enough that he could see the edge of the tattoo. The edge of a lion that only showed himself to Wesley.

He stepped forward, from behind the chair.

"Curtains are still open," Sebastian said. "People in cars and on the sidewalk can see you."

"They can see you too."

Sebastian was already walking toward the drapes. "Yes, but really, no one cares about me," he said. "But we just ran into men you know who questioned why we were together."

"Yes, and I handled them," Wesley pointed out. "You still seem to be under the impression that you carry sole responsibility for shielding my delicate reputation. Do you not understand how terrifying I am to most of society? That I am always the meanest, most powerful person in any given room?"

"You're not *mean*," Sebastian said, because of course he did. "And you used to be."

"I used to be what?"

"You *used to be* the most powerful person in any room," Sebastian said, as he reached the windows. "Now…well, you know."

He wasn't teasing anymore, just speaking matter-of-factly, and was this magical brat actually about to *patronize* Wesley?

"I don't think I do," Wesley said lightly, with narrowed eyes. "I think you'd best explain exactly what you mean."

"I just mean that money and titles can't protect you from the things in my world." Sebastian had paused and turned to face Wesley. "So you're never going to be powerful the same way a paranormal is."

There was nothing the slightest bit belittling or condescending about his tone. If anything, he sounded bloody *earnest*.

"Oh, duck," Wesley said warningly. "Tell me you're not actually suggesting that having magic makes you more competent?"

"It's not about *competence*, it's just about magic." Sebastian leaned against the wall. "I don't need to be afraid of things like police; I've been able to flatten a room with my mind since I was nine."

"I have never needed magic to have you down flat on your back."

"Well, no," Sebastian said patiently. "But Wes, the only reason you're standing at all is because I let you."

"Because you *let* me?"

The shift in the air was tangible, like Sebastian had accidentally tripped an electrical wire and sent sparks into the air.

"Is that right." In two sharp tugs, Wesley pulled off one glove, then the other, and tossed them on the chair. "Close the fucking drapes, sweetheart."

Wesley crossed the room, giving Sebastian just enough time to yank the curtain closed. Then he put a hand on Sebastian's chest, flattening him against the window with a firm push.

"That's my ego you just came for." Wesley bent so their faces were an inch apart. "And I can't let you get away with that."

He brought their lips together. Sebastian's eyes flut-

tered shut as Wesley slid his arm around his waist, between the window and the small of his back, pulling
their bodies together. The window's glass was cool
through the curtain, a contrast to the heat of the kiss
and Sebastian's skin through his thin dress shirt.

He slipped his tongue along the seam of Sebastian's
lips, which parted for him. Wesley chased down the
taste of him, pressing him against the glass. Sebastian
made a noise in the back of his throat, and this was what
Wesley had been craving all day, the perfect fit of their
bodies, the arm around his neck and the hand in his
hair. The way Sebastian kissed like nothing mattered
but getting more of Wesley's lips, the way he clung like
a drowning man who'd found air, and Wesley wanted
to be that escape, to take Sebastian's mind somewhere
his demons couldn't reach.

Their cocks brushed, both already hard, and Sebastian groaned into Wesley's mouth. He jammed a hand
between their bodies, going for Wesley's zipper—

Wesley moved faster, catching his hands and pin-
ning them to the window next to his head. "What's the
rush?" he said lightly, and heard the hitch in Sebastian's
breath. He casually fit his leg between Sebastian's, forcing them farther apart. "We have all night."

Sebastian tilted his head up to meet his eyes. The
movement still sent shivers of want over Wesley, because
he was exactly the kind of bastard who enjoyed being
bigger and able to pin Sebastian like this. An illusion of
control, because Sebastian could always flatten him with
a thought, but that just made the yielding even sweeter.

"I need to touch you," Sebastian said, a bit breathless.

"Eventually." Wesley leaned in, but didn't kiss him
again. "Maybe. Or maybe I'll do all the touching, I
haven't decided yet."

Sebastian swallowed down another groan.

Wesley's gaze went to Sebastian's wrist where he held it to the wall, the inches of skin bared by the rolled-up sleeve. The sight made him feel like he'd touched lightning, electric from head to toe. "I don't think a single possessive thought had ever crossed my mind, before I met you. But every time I see this ink, I remember the lion is mine alone and I damn near lose my mind."

He ran his thumb over the tattoo, and Sebastian arched like Wesley had touched his cock, so that Wesley had to hold him down to keep him against the window, and both of their breaths were coming just a little faster now.

"A lion just for me." Wesley's voice had a rougher edge. "You'd best believe I'm not rushing this."

Wesley brought their lips together again, the kiss slow but deep. He kept Sebastian's hands pinned to the window as they kissed, their legs intertwined and their bodies tight together, the cacophony of Grand Central outside mixing with Wesley's heartbeat as it pounded in his ears.

Eventually Wesley moved to kiss his throat, exposed by the open buttons. Sebastian let his head fall back against the drape-covered window. "This is the best place, Wes," he whispered hoarsely. "No memories, no past. Nothing in my head but you."

Wesley's kiss stuttered, teeth grazing across skin, which drew a sharp inhale from Sebastian.

"I don't think I can let you talk." He pulled Sebastian off the wall and began steering him backward, toward the bedroom. "You say these things and I lose all reason, can think of nothing but sweeping the thoughts from your head so you only feel good."

Wesley pushed him through an open door and into

the darkened bedroom, the lamps off but the curtains partially open and letting in the lights of Midtown. The back of Sebastian's legs hit the mattress and he went down on the bed. Wesley was already climbing over him, sliding his leg between Sebastian's as he bent his head to bring their faces together.

"And I am going to make you feel so good," Wesley said, close enough Sebastian would have felt his breath on his lips. "But first, I've got a reprimand to get through."

Sweet, half-lidded eyes met his, Sebastian tilting his head against the mattress like he was reaching for Wesley's kiss. "Why?" he said, in a deliciously needy whine. "For what?"

Wesley let his thigh press down on the hard length of Sebastian's cock, drawing a lovely groan. "What was it you said? I don't have magic, so you're *letting* me stand?"

Sebastian winced. "Well—"

"I need to let you handle things?"

"I mean—"

"Go right ahead and take over," Wesley said. "Consider this my full consent for you to use your magic in any wicked way you can dream up." He moved his thigh again and heard the noise that caught in Sebastian's throat. "Unless, of course, you'd rather I keep going?" Wesley added lightly. "Find out what happens when I get your clothes off and my mouth and hands on you?"

Sebastian swore softly, his fingers twisting in Wesley's shirt, and that was an answer on its own, one that made Wesley's blood heat.

"I think I just called your bluff for what it is," he whispered. "It doesn't matter that you can use magic— you won't. Right now, you're as much mine as your lion is."

That got a full-body shiver from Sebastian under him. "Shameless," he said, his voice breaking on the word.

"*Competent*," Wesley corrected, his lips curling in a darkly teasing smile. "Or call it *in control*, if you like."

He lowered his weight on top of Sebastian, who responded by wrapping his arms around Wesley, as if their bodies could get any closer.

He brought his lips close to Sebastian's ear. "Where's your magic now, darling? I said you could topple me, why haven't you?"

Sebastian groaned. "Wes."

"I think you like being caught here under me." Wesley kissed the soft skin under his ear, making Sebastian's eyelashes flutter. "I think you like being mine and that doesn't have a damn thing to do with one of us having magic."

Sebastian's hands tightened on the back of his shirt.

Wesley shifted so their bodies rocked together, enjoying the shudder that ran through Sebastian. "Get comfortable," he said, like a half-whispered threat. "I could lecture you all night, but there are better ways to make my points, and I'm not going to rush this either."

Their clothes came off, and Wesley finally let his starved hands and body indulge in all the touch he constantly craved, drinking in the overwhelming pleasure of skin against skin. Sebastian could obviously have turned the tables anytime he liked, but he seemed to have chosen surrender, sweet enough to drive Wesley mad. He took his time, with slow kisses and slower touches that chased away tension until Sebastian was pliant and mostly incoherent beneath him, because he'd meant what he said—he wanted to sweep Sebastian's thoughts away, get them both to that state where nothing mattered but each other.

Finally, new tension began to tighten Sebastian's muscles, the kind of physical need that was purely body. Wesley fumbled around for the vial he'd left on the nightstand before he'd gone down for dinner.

Sebastian looked up at him with hazy eyes. "How do you have that so convenient? You already had it out of your trunk?"

"I might be insulted by how shocked you are." Wesley pressed two fingers inside him, drawing a hoarse, needy whine. "You don't have to think of everything. You don't have to handle everything. You can rely on me, and maybe if I tell you again while I'm inside you, you'll actually listen."

Sebastian groaned, and kissed him.

Wesley worked him open, his own need growing as he shamelessly watched Sebastian, the way his body responded to Wesley's hands and mouth, the way he was no longer forming real sentences. Fuck the cigarettes; they had nothing on the taste of Sebastian's lips and skin, weren't half as addicting as the sounds Wesley drew from him. Finally, Wesley slid into him, and then stilled again.

"Do you know how much I enjoy knowing that you could, at any moment, use your magic to take over?" He heard himself, half-drunk on pleasure too, as Sebastian tugged at his shoulders. "To fuck me senseless, or ride me to that release you're so desperate for?"

He kissed Sebastian again, his own lips throbbing from so many kisses. "But you won't. You're going to let me do whatever I want with you, let me take as long as I want with you, because you want to come, but you want to be good for me more."

Sebastian's entire body shivered, his fingers flexing tighter into Wesley's muscles.

"Maybe I'll do this to you again and again," Wesley whispered. "Torture you with pleasure every night until you learn you're not alone anymore."

"Wes," Sebastian said, his voice breaking.

Wesley let himself rock his hips, and pleasure jolted up his spine. Fuck, he was not going to last much longer. "But resist the lesson if you want, darling, because I'm a beast and I love this. The way you look, under me in this bed—I could spend weeks like this. So by all means give me more excuses to make you beg, squirming to come on my cock."

"Shit." Sebastian's fingers went so tight Wesley was absolutely going to have bruises on his shoulders. "Wes—come on, *please*—I can't hold on to my magic."

Wesley's hips jerked, and Sebastian swore again.

"Christ, you are not allowed to talk, you'll have me shooting off like a rifle." Wesley's voice was as wrecked as Sebastian's. "No more words from you. Just lie there and look pretty, it's already too much to resist."

Sebastian half-laughed, half-groaned. "I can't—"

And suddenly Wesley's limbs turned to water, as his aura gave way under the flood of Sebastian's magic. He made a startled grunt as he fell full onto Sebastian, but Sebastian was already pushing him over.

"*Christ*," Wesley said again, as his back hit the mattress.

"Need you," Sebastian said hoarsely, climbing on top, possibly the sexiest thing Wesley had ever seen or heard and he was going to ink this night onto his brain like his own tattoo. "Are you—okay?"

"Are you seriously asking? I am *so much better* than *okay*. Get the fuck back on me."

Sebastian straddled his hips, and Wesley made an inhuman noise as their bodies fit back together. Their

lips found each other's again, Wesley absolutely floating on the swirling mix of tingling limbs from Sebastian's magic mixed with the tight heat of his body—so
perfect that it only took a few movements before Wesley
was helplessly falling over the edge. Sebastian's head
dropped to Wesley's chest, his face against Wesley's
heart, and Wesley heard him falling too, soft sounds
muffled against Wesley's skin.

They stayed like that for a long moment, Sebastian's
forehead on Wesley's chest, Wesley drinking the close-
ness in as the loveliest of aftershocks coursed through
his limbs.

Finally, Sebastian raised his eyes, looking very
sheepish.

"Who's shameless now?" Wesley said, the words a
little slurred with effort.

Sebastian dropped his head back to Wesley's chest
with a self-conscious laugh. "You look like you were
mauled by an affectionate bear," he said, still sounding
very sheepish, and pressed a kiss over Wesley's heart
before he rolled off. Wesley was pushed over onto his
side as Sebastian spooned up behind him with an arm
slung around his ribs and *wait just one fucking moment.*

"Sebastian."

Sebastian rested his head against Wesley's shoulder
with a happy sigh.

"*Sebastian.*" Wesley forced his mouth to move.
"Have you forgotten something?"

Sebastian hid his face against Wesley's back. "Um—"

"I can't move my bloody limbs! Your magic is still
on strong enough the people in the next room might be
on the floor."

"I *know*," Sebastian said, into his back. "But I need
a minute."

Wesley barked out a laugh, a real one, with an almost rusty edge. "I fucked you to the point you can't rein your magic in?"

Sebastian groaned. "It's the brooch's fault. Don't be smug."

"I am going to be smug *forever*." Wesley still couldn't move, but it was fucking worth it. "What am I going to do with you?"

"Well, what I'd really like for you to do with me is cuddle. Er, when you can move again."

"*Sebastian.*"

"It's okay, I know you don't cuddle." The blankets were being pulled up over them. "But since you can't move, you can just lie there and let me hug you."

"You—"

"Shhh. My magic will ease fastest if I go to sleep."

"Oh it will, will it?" Wesley said. "How dashed convenient. And how do I know if you're serious or you're just fucking with me for vengeance?"

"I like to keep a little mystery alive between us," Sebastian murmured, which made Wesley laugh again. "Soy tan suertudo de tenerte, Wes, so lucky to have you. You make everything so good."

There was no way Wesley deserved those murmured words, but Sebastian was settling in closer against him, his voice soft and content and maybe even happy. Every inch of Wesley felt good, limbs tingling from the magic and the afterglow and the lovely sensation of skin pressed to skin, and he couldn't move anyway, so maybe for once Wesley could just—let himself enjoy the moment.

Chapter Six

Wesley woke as the first rays of the sun were peeking through the gap in the curtains. They'd shifted at some point during the night, Wesley onto his back, Sebastian now asleep with his head pillowed on Wesley's ribs. His arm was still across Wesley, curled to keep him close. Wesley had woken in positions like this since the night they'd started a physical relationship all the way back in York. If Sebastian was capable of keeping to his own space in a bed, Wesley had yet to see it.

It made no sense to share a bed after sex. Sebastian was probably half on top of him because there was simply not enough room for two tall men. Or because he'd spent his childhood on a Caribbean island and was cold in places like England and New York. He'd likely slept this close and clinging to every partner he'd ever had, because Wesley wasn't special, didn't bring any particular kind of comfort.

I know you don't cuddle.

Wesley most certainly did not. For fuck's sake, he didn't even know how. He'd be stiff and useless, nothing but awkward, misplaced limbs. He didn't cuddle and Sebastian should be grateful for that—he wouldn't want Wesley to.

Sebastian was admittedly very good at it, though.

The sun was falling across the bed, on the blanket around Sebastian's ribs. His shoulders were uncovered, moving ever so slightly with each breath Wesley took. He could probably hear Wesley's heartbeat in his sleep. The bare skin tempted Wesley's fingers, because he knew exactly how soft it was under his touch.

Stupid temptation. As if Wesley knew how to touch another person if they weren't fucking. But then, Sebastian was still fast asleep, wouldn't know if Wesley was getting it wrong.

Sebastian's arm was turned just enough that he could see the edge of the lion, and after a moment, he gave in to his own craving and ran his fingers over the ink. This he couldn't resist, a tattoo for his eyes alone, and surely that was understandable? A *magic* tattoo, when he'd driven that magic to escape Sebastian's control last night?

His lips softened into something like a smile. He'd spent so long wishing his memories weren't quite so sharp. Another change, to have things he wanted to remember.

He skated his fingers up Sebastian's arm where it was draped over his torso. Wesley loved sex, couldn't ever get enough of it. But the rare moments like this one, when Sebastian seemed content and Wesley's mind was at ease, when he let himself touch just for the sake of touch—these were moments it almost felt like his heart wasn't truly made of stone, just the hardest of earth, that maybe Wesley hadn't become bitter and cold beyond hope.

He'd never fall for the ruse, of course. Life delighted in finding ways to sabotage any spark of joy, and hope only made disappointment sting harder. Sebastian was brave to walk around with a soft heart; Wesley was far too much of a realist for that.

He ran his hand back down Sebastian's arm. Such an obvious soft heart that it became too easy to forget what Sebastian hid. How hard was it, for Sebastian to be back in New York? If Wesley didn't care for his memories of this city, how much worse were Sebastian's? Likely nightmare fuel beyond what even Wesley and his wartime actions could fathom.

And yet here, in bed with him, Sebastian's sleep was peaceful, as if he'd finally let go and trusted Wesley to keep them safe.

I'm so lucky to have you. You make everything so good.

Preposterous. The sort of thing only the kindest soul would say about a bastard like Wesley.

But damn if he didn't make the jaded, cynical stone of Wesley's useless heart want to bloom again.

The October dawn was cool, and the skin under Wesley's fingers was chilled to the touch. The ridiculous tropical flower would probably be shivering shortly. Wesley reached down and pulled the blankets up, tucking them around Sebastian's shoulders. A logical thing to do; they needed to rise soon, and if Sebastian got poor sleep because he was cold, Wesley might be dealing with a cranky lover all day. He was simply taking precautions. For selfish reasons, because he was a selfish bastard.

He wrapped an arm around Sebastian—not to *cuddle*, obviously, just to anchor the blanket in place so it wouldn't slip down again—and let himself drift back off.

The next time he woke, it was to a knock on his door.

Wesley groaned. "I told them not to disturb me for any reason."

He reluctantly sat up, dislodging Sebastian, who made

a displeased noise and buried himself completely under the covers as Wesley pulled on a full-length robe and went to the door. He opened it an inch.

There was no one there, but on the floor in front of his door was a rolled-up copy of the *New York Times*.

They'd disturbed his sleep for the fucking paper? He picked it up, slamming the door behind him.

He went back to the bedroom, where Sebastian was now sitting up in bed, looking as disgruntled as Wesley felt. The covers had pooled around his waist, and his wavy hair was sticking up at all angles. Nothing would get Wesley to admit there might be something to this sharing a bed thing, but what a pretty picture he made.

"You look tired," Wesley said slyly. "Rough night?"

Sebastian gave him a dirty look. "I thought you told them not to disturb you."

"Morning staff must not have gotten the message." Wesley unrolled the paper, and an envelope fell out.

He stilled.

"What's that?" Sebastian said, quite suddenly infinitely more awake.

"I don't know, but the last time someone stuck a letter in my paper, I was nearly immolated in an alley."

"Don't touch it." Sebastian was out of the bed, sheet wrapped around him like a toga.

"Modesty?" said Wesley. "Now? You think I didn't see every inch of you there is to see when my tongue was—"

"I don't want to be naked if it's *magic*," Sebastian said, which all right, yes, that was fair. "You should sit."

Which meant Sebastian was going to use *his* magic. Which put the memory of the night before into Wesley's mind, and he very quickly sat on his nearby trunk, because Christ, Wesley, *not the time*.

Sebastian knelt next to the envelope, his hand out.

Wesley felt the now-familiar wave of enervation sweep the room, rolling over his aura like the tide. His limbs went weak, but as soon as he'd registered he was slumping, the magic was gone.

"No traces of magic." Sebastian picked up the envelope. "But it has your name on it."

He held it out to Wesley.

Wesley frowned but took it. It was a plain, cream-colored envelope with no stamp. The words *The Viscount Fine* had been typed by a typewriter on the envelope's front, with Wesley's room number below, and it was gummed shut—no seal to give a clue. "Maybe we're finally hearing from Miss Robbins."

Sebastian sat on the edge of the bed, the sheet still wrapped around his waist. "I don't think so."

Wesley glanced at Sebastian.

"Jade is very kind," Sebastian said. "The last anonymous letter you got was not from a kind person, and she knows that. I do not think she would contact you the same way. She would not want to risk rekindling bad memories, no matter how small the chance."

That logic rang true. Wesley tore it open at the flap and pulled out a folded letter.

Lord Fine:

You once traveled with a man named Benedict Chester as your valet. Mr. Chester was a notorious international thief and you are known in certain circles to be his last employer before death.

You are not safe in New York. Beware the company you keep.

It was typed on a typewriter, same as the envelope, and signed with a typed—*a friend.*

Wesley raised an eyebrow. "Well, I think we can safely say this is, indeed, not from Miss Robbins."

He held it out to Sebastian, who took it. Sebastian's eyes tracked over the letter, and then widened. He looked up.

"No," Wesley said. "I can practically see the concern forming in that paranormal brain of yours, but we have discussed you not treating me like an infant. I will concede it's an unusual letter but there is no need for those big shocked eyes. We are not going to make a fuss."

"Yes, we *are*," Sebastian said, "because someone is threatening my boyfriend."

His boyfriend.

Sebastian didn't seem to realize what he'd said, rereading the letter with narrowed eyes. "Could this be from Major Langford or Sir Ellery?"

Wesley scoffed. "First of all, the letter styles itself as a warning, not a threat. And second, no. Langford is not a friend and Sir Ellery wouldn't know magic from a Mauser."

"Sir Ellery was on this same trip with you and your valet, Mr. Chester. He knew you employed him. How do you know they didn't collude?"

"How would a baronet get mixed up with magic and relics?"

"You're a viscount, and you're here."

Wesley opened his mouth, then closed it.

"I'm going to call Jade." Sebastian was on his feet, the sheet trailing after him as he strode into the parlor with the letter. "And Zhang. And I'm going to call Arthur and Rory and somebody is going to answer their phone and we are going to figure out what's going on."

"I'm sure it's—"

"No me digas que esta bien, it's *not* fine and I want to know who sent this to you."

"But—"

"And if there's a reason you're not safe in New York, I want to know that too."

"Sebastian—"

"Wesley, siéntate y ya no discutas conmigo."

Wesley didn't know what that meant, but he knew when an argument was over and he'd lost. He sat down on the edge of the bed with a huff. "Are you aware you slip into Spanish when you're emotional?" he called.

"Then now you know I'm worried about you."

Wesley watched through the bedroom doorframe as Sebastian picked up the phone, planning to call half of Manhattan while wrapped in a damn sheet because he was worried about his boyfriend.

What an utter bastard, making Wesley grapple with feelings before he'd even had his morning tea.

Except Sebastian's calls went nowhere. Wesley cleaned up for the day and repacked his trunk while Sebastian called the number they had for Jade, and then the Dragon House, then Arthur's flat, and then Rory's old boarding house. He tried the building where Rory's antiques shop used to be. He even called a pharmacy on the Lower East Side where Jade had mentioned her sister's paranormal girlfriend lived, but Mrs. Taussig, while very nice, said Sasha Ivanova and her brother Pavel were out of town.

Wesley joined Sebastian in the parlor as he hung up with Mrs. Taussig.

"Where *are* they?" Sebastian said.

Wesley gave a helpless shrug.

There was another knock on the door. "Sebi? Fine?"

Mateo. Wesley gestured at Sebastian's sheet. "I think you've got trousers in my trunk. I mean, don't get dressed on my account, but your brother might appreciate it."

Sebastian gave him a flat look. "Show him the letter, yes?" he said, and went into the bedroom.

Wesley let Mateo inside and filled him in.

Mateo was frowning as he finished. "We can't reach any of the New York paranormals and you're in danger."

"Someone *claims* I'm not safe here," said Wesley. "If they're such a friend, why an anonymous typed letter? Why not tell me in person?"

"And there is the other issue." Sebastian stepped into the bedroom doorframe, tying his tie. "They mentioned that Wesley's former valet was a thief. And you remember what he stole."

Wesley raised his eyebrows. "Is this also coming back to the pomander relic? The one Jade might have been telling us takes cursed blood to destroy?"

Mateo swallowed. "I think you need to take my enchantment off."

"No," Sebastian said flatly.

"I can try to see the future of Miss Robbins or the others—"

"No," Sebastian said again. "You already missed two months of school. The enchantment stays on and you're going back to Oberlin today."

"Sebi—"

"I agree with him," Wesley said to Mateo. "It was so difficult for him to bind your magic in the first place. I don't think he should take it off unless we have no other choice."

Mateo folded his arms. "And what's our other choice here? Yes, I had to pull every string our family has to get my program to let me come back, and if I don't show up, this might be it. But if there's danger—"

"Sebastian and I find it," Wesley said. "You take the train this afternoon back to your university. We'll stay here, in New York, and we'll seek out the others and the sender of this letter."

Mateo chewed on his lip. Wesley looked up at Sebastian, who was leaning on the doorframe. He still looked upset, but he nodded. "He's right, Teo," Sebastian said. "If we have no success, we can come to Ohio and get you."

"You won't," Mateo said flatly.

"He won't, but I will," said Wesley, "because you're a grown man who deserves to make your own choices. But you're also both compassionate and exceptionally intelligent, and I don't think you'll put your softhearted big brother through losing you to magic again when your logical mind can appreciate we haven't yet explored every other path."

There was a pause. "Well played," Mateo muttered.

Wesley looked up again, and found Sebastian's eyes on him, softer with gratitude.

Mateo stood. "I can at least help you question the staff here before I go. Maybe someone saw who slipped the letter into your paper."

Their questioning, however, was fruitless. They found the member of housekeeping who had left newspapers in front of all of the suites, a short man who'd been at work since midnight and kept yawning. But he swore he hadn't knocked.

"Your room had a note not to disturb you," the man said.

Wesley exchanged a look with Sebastian. "Did someone give you my mail to deliver with the paper?"

"No, and I wouldn't have taken it if they'd tried." The man sounded sincere. "I would have told them to leave it at the front desk."

"Did you see anyone when you set out the papers?" Mateo asked.

The man shook his head. "It was barely dawn and no one else was on the floor but me."

The knock on his door had come well past dawn, Wesley could attest to that. Not to mention the man had just blithely admitted he had no alibi and didn't seem to think there would be any reason to need one.

They renewed both rooms for another night, and Wesley arranged for a cable to be sent to his footman Ned back in London, so he'd know not to tell another damn soul where Wesley had gone. From the hotel, they went with Mateo to Grand Central Station to catch his three o'clock train.

"Write to Isa," Sebastian said, as the three of them stood on the platform next to the train cars of the Ohio State Limited.

"I do," Mateo said, sounding affronted. "I send lots of letters to everyone. You're the one who never writes and makes everyone worry."

Sebastian was suddenly very interested in his cuticles.

"Send me postcards from your travels with your viscount," said Mateo. "It's fucking cold in Ohio in the winter, I want you to send me something from San Juan and make me jealous. And take Fine to Spain."

"Aren't your parents there?" said Wesley, alarmed.

"It's not like you're going to say *cheerio, Mrs. D, I'm fucking your son*," Mateo said, and Wesley nearly choked. "They miss Sebi and want to see him. And they'll love you. Our mom will say *mijo, who is your handsome friend?* and Sebastian will say *mami, este viscount pobrecito has no parents* and she will gasp and kiss your cheeks and feed you."

Wesley glanced at Sebastian, who nodded. "But I'm a grown man," Wesley protested.

"She won't care," Mateo promised.

The porter's voice rang across the platform. "All aboard!"

The brothers hugged tightly, and Wesley carefully did not think about the last time he'd seen his own brother, at a train station in Sussex before Colin had met his death in France.

They hadn't embraced. They hadn't even bothered to say goodbye.

And then Mateo let go of Sebastian and turned to hug Wesley.

Wesley's eyes widened as Mateo wrapped his arms around him and clapped him on the back. "You write to me too."

"What?" Wesley said, in inelegant surprise.

"Escríbeme, I want your letters too," said Mateo. "And take care of Sebi. Make each other smile, you both need it."

And then Mateo was climbing aboard the train.

"I'm glad he's returning to the studies he enjoys," Wesley said, as they watched Mateo disappear. "But it wasn't terrible to have him around."

"I already miss him," Sebastian admitted.

"You're not going to go three years without seeing him this time," Wesley said. "See him for Christmas."

Wesley had spent the six Christmases since the war alone. His cook, Mrs. Harrick, was a war widow, and she'd leave Wesley meals that could be eaten cold before taking Elsie to see her doting grandmother in Lincoln. Ned, the footman, came from a large family in Nottingham, and he'd head up there to spend the time with his nieces and nephews, would probably meet a nice girl one of these days and get hitched himself. Wesley gave all the staff holidays and then would sit in his silent Kensington home, smoking too many cheap cigarettes and drinking too much expensive whiskey and resenting the hypocrites who would chirp *Peace on Earth* when they'd been happy enough to send other people to war.

There was no point being maudlin over any of it, because he had countless identical holidays to come. Wesley was, after all, beastly and intolerable company; unending solitude was simply reaping what he sowed.

Then Sebastian nudged him tentatively. "I've spent so many Christmases alone these last few years," he said quietly, like he was confessing. "The holiday is two weeks of happy chaos in my family. If I go, you have to come, but wherever we are, maybe we could be together, yes?"

Wesley stilled. He glanced at the beautiful man at his side, who had swept into his life and changed those endless identical days into adventures in new places. Who had filled the solitude with literal magic. Who had also had isolation and loneliness as his relentless companions, and if Sebastian was hoping they'd be together for the holidays, then Wesley would make damn sure he got what he wanted.

"As if you could possibly be rid of me by Christmas," Wesley said brusquely. "You owe me the Caribbean," which earned him a smile that made his knees a little weak, no magic needed.

As they walked through the Grand Central soaring terminal, however, two men he had no desire whatsoever to see were coming straight toward them.

"Fine, fancy catching you again!" Sir Ellery said, as Alasdair smiled politely next to him.

"Yes, fancy that," Wesley said. "It does feel a bit coincidental, doesn't it?"

"What are you talking about?" Sir Ellery asked.

"Did you send Lord Fine a letter this morning, by any chance?" Sebastian asked pointedly.

"No." Sir Ellery looked mystified. "I would have picked up the phone and called if I had anything more to say."

Hmph. He could be lying, of course. Wesley had played cards with the man; he had an excellent poker face. But would he really know anything about this business?

"Sebastian, it is so good to see you again," Alasdair said in his Scottish-tinged accent, breezily ignoring Wesley. "I love the fabric you've chosen for your waistcoat, light and flexible. I see you're still pairing casual clothes with the pocket watch chain; perhaps that's just your style."

"He's trying to get on my good side, appealing to my disdain for these blasted trends," Wesley cut in. "Transparent, really."

Alasdair turned his gaze on Wesley with lazy slow blinks, his light blue eyes as watery as they'd been the day before. Was the man day drunk? "Where are you two off to now?"

"Just playing the tourists again," Wesley said brusquely.

"Really?" Sir Ellery said skeptically. "*You*?"

"What about you?" Sebastian said, changing the subject.

"Tarrytown," said Sir Ellery. "Lady Blanche extended an invitation for her guest house. We're still a couple of days from the masquerade, but Alasdair here has some establishments up there."

"Does he." Wesley could well imagine what sorts of *establishments* a bootlegger like Alasdair might have.

"Her husband Walter is a very good customer," Alasdair added conspiratorially. "I've been to their new estate several times."

Of course the New York governor's son threw parties and invited bootleggers. Wesley had spent enough time around politicians not to be surprised.

Sir Ellery still had his friendly smile, but there was something slightly more calculated in his eyes. "Why not join us now? Lady Blanche was happy to add you to her guest list. It'd be no trouble at all to get you lodging in Tarrytown and have your things sent up. Your man here could come too," he finished, gesturing at Sebastian. "Alasdair's got plenty to entertain us all."

Wesley highly doubted Alasdair had anything half as entertaining as Sebastian panting under him. "Can't make it, itinerary to keep." After all, they were quite booked up finding where the devil the others had gotten to and then hopefully fucking straight up until their ship departed for San Juan.

"That's a shame," Sir Ellery said easily. "So you'll be staying at the Roosevelt for a few more days then? Are you liking it? The major was planning to stay in Manhattan until the masquerade and might need a new place."

Christ, no. What an absolute fucking disaster that would be, to have Langford in the same hotel as him and Sebastian. "You should tell Major Langford he's better off at the Waldorf," he said briskly. "More his style."

"If you say so." Sir Ellery glanced at the large clock in the center of the terminal and grimaced. "I'm afraid we've got to run."

"So good to see you, Sebastian," Alasdair said brightly.

Wesley narrowed his eyes, watching their backs disappear as Sir Ellery and Alasdair were swallowed up by the crowd.

Chapter Seven

From Grand Central, Wesley firmly vetoed the subway, so they took a cab to Mott Street on the Lower East Side. They wove through Chinatown, past shops and restaurants set into colorful, multistory buildings, following narrowing streets until they found the Dragon House at the ground level of a redbrick building. The English name was spelled out on the glass door under a red awning, and a white banner with red Chinese characters hung outside. It seemed to be just opening for dinner, and a few people could be seen already seated at tables inside.

Sebastian's tattoo was prickling as they stood on the sidewalk outside the restaurant's large windows. The buildings all around them rose four to five stories, with black iron fire escapes on the front. Next to the Dragon House's main entrance, a metal door was firmly shut.

Sebastian stepped to the side of the building and put a hand on the metal door. He closed his eyes, concentrating in effort, and sent out a tiny pulse of tightly contained magic, not enough to knock Wesley down.

The answering magic rose up like he'd thrown petrol on a fire.

Sebastian hastily scrambled back. His own enervation magic was instinctively simmering in response, like water ready to boil, and his blood was roiling like the brooch was rallying it to arms. He quickly and forcefully tamped all of it down.

"So do we have a plan for getting in?" Wesley was studying the building. "Do we, I don't know, sneak in the back? Is there some sort of faery veil to cross, or a rabbit hole to Wonderland?"

Sebastian made a quiet laugh. "Probably not, but the building is full of guardian magic. We're not sneaking in unless I tear it all down, and I don't want to do that. We're here as friends, not to try to destroy whatever magical defenses the Zhangs have in place. And it would be very poor manners to knock down everyone in his restaurant."

"Fair enough." Wesley eyed the fire escape. "How obvious would it be if we jumped up there and went in through someone's window? It's only a crowded street in broad daylight, after all."

That made Sebastian smile. "I say we just go in and have an early dinner. Maybe Zhang is inside, and I bet the food is good."

Wesley's gaze went back to the windows and the tables inside.

I've lived for years only a stone's throw from London's restaurants, yet I've tried almost nothing, Wesley had said to Sebastian once. *I don't change.*

Except a day after saying that, Wesley had saved Paris from magic with Sebastian, because Wesley believed a lot of things about himself that weren't true.

A paper menu had been affixed to the window. Wesley stepped forward to study it, closer to the building's guardian magic—and Sebastian's magic leapt up in response.

Sebastian slammed down on it, a hair too late. Wesley had already stumbled and grabbed for the redbrick wall. "*Sebastian.*"

"Sorry, sorry," Sebastian said, hands up in apology.

"What the hell was that for?" Wesley said, as he straightened up. "I thought we were staying away from the guardian magic so your magic would be fine. You didn't even move from your spot over there!"

Sebastian cringed, but he'd nearly sent Wesley to the sidewalk and owed him an explanation. "But *you* got close to the window and the guardian magic."

"So?"

"So I think that triggered my magic."

"But why would me approaching other magic trigger your magic?"

"To, um. To protect you."

Wesley blinked.

Sebastian pointed to his wrist, the one with the tattoo. "It obviously likes you more than anyone else."

Wesley's gaze went to the lion, and lingered.

Sebastian winced. "I'm sorry," he said again, awkwardly sticking his hands in his pockets. "Nothing is ever normal with me."

"Fuck normal," Wesley said, with feeling. "Buy me dinner."

Sebastian managed to squish his magic down enough to walk through the restaurant doors, and they were led to a table against the window.

Wesley picked up the dim sum menu from the table and scanned it. "Arthur mentioned something he liked here, back when he and Brodigan stayed with me in the spring. Pork buns, they were called."

"Oh, those are good," Sebastian said. "You know, I've never asked how you and Arthur became friends."

"I suppose it is surprising we pulled it off, given our

history," Wesley said. "We're far better suited as friends, though. But never mind, obviously you know all of that and we already decided we weren't going to make it awkward."

Sebastian furrowed his eyebrows. *I know all of what?* he was about to ask, when a waiter appeared at their table with a teapot and two cylindrical teacups. "Ready to order?"

Sebastian leaned forward. "We are friends of Jianwei," he said. "Is he here? Could we see him?"

The waiter shook his head. "No, sorry, he's not here. I haven't seen him in at least a week."

"Then where is he?" Wesley said.

"I don't know," said the waiter. "I think he left the city."

Sebastian and Wesley exchanged a look. "Do you know if he's with his girlfriend, Jade Robbins?" Sebastian asked.

"Maybe?" the waiter said unhelpfully. "We play her sister's record a lot, but Miss Robbins hasn't been here either."

Sebastian wracked his brain for details he'd heard about Zhang's family. "Is Jianwei's mother here? Or his cousin—Ling is her name, yes?"

But the waiter shook his head again. "Ling and Mrs. Wang are in San Francisco. They're staying a month, visiting family."

Then who is here? Sebastian wanted to ask. *Zhang said he has an entire paranormal library under this restaurant—who's looking after it?*

But what if the waiter knew nothing of magic? Who could Sebastian talk to and be sure he wasn't spilling all of the Zhangs' family secrets?

"Thank you," Sebastian finally said, and ordered the pork buns and several other things to share.

As the waiter left, Wesley was already drinking from his cup. "This is unequivocally the best thing I've had in America."

"I don't understand," Sebastian said.

"You don't understand why the tea is good? Have you truly no idea the millennia of tea history across Asia—"

"Not *that*," said Sebastian. "I don't understand why Zhang's not here. His mother and cousin are across the country. What would make him leave the family business if they're not here to watch it? And all his paranormal artifacts?"

Wesley glanced around. "There are paranormal artifacts here?"

"Zhang said his family has a whole collection, in a library in the basement." Sebastian leaned forward. "Apparently there is still a crack in the ceiling from Rory."

"Now I know you're telling tales," Wesley said dryly. "Brodigan can't reach any ceilings."

"Wesley, be nice," Sebastian said. "And he did it with magic. He lost control of his ring relic."

"Really." Wesley took another sip. "A paranormal losing control of their magic because they have a relic, where have I heard this story before."

Sebastian gave him a dirty look.

"When was this?" Wesley asked.

"February," Sebastian said, trying very hard not to think about what he'd been doing in New York that same week. "Jade said it wasn't her place to give me all the details, but apparently Rory had just discovered something that made him very jealous."

Wesley's hand jerked, spilling tea. "February, you said?"

"Yes." Sebastian tilted his head. "Why?"

"Ah." Wesley set the cup down. "Did Miss Robbins

happen to say if Rory's jealousy had anything to do with Arthur?"

"Why would it?" Sebastian said curiously.

Wesley stared at him. "For the obvious reason."

"What's that?"

"Do you not—do you actually not know? Do I know something your paranormal arse doesn't?"

"Probably lots of things," Sebastian said honestly. "You're very smart."

Wesley grimaced. "Actually, I have, at least on one occasion, done something that wasn't smart in the least."

Sebastian frowned. "Why do you look guilty all of a sudden?"

"Do I?" Wesley said weakly.

"You never look guilty," said Sebastian. "You have no shame."

Wesley rubbed his temples. "Truly, I assumed you had to know of all this."

"Know all what?"

Wesley gave the restaurant a quick glance, then leaned in and said quietly, "Did you really not know that Arthur and Rory are lovers?"

Sebastian stared. "Arthur…and Rory?"

"*Yes*," said Wesley. "They've been fucking since January. They're stupidly in love."

Sebastian sat back in his chair, eyes wide. "That explains so much."

"How did you not figure it out?" Wesley demanded. "They're not subtle in the least."

Sebastian made a face. "I don't notice that kind of stuff."

"Probably too busy feeding cats," Wesley said. "But no one thought to tell you?"

"Why would they? Arthur and Rory knew me as a villain; why would they trust me with that secret?"

"I thought Miss Robbins would have told you."

"Jade doesn't know I like men too," Sebastian said. "She would not give away her friends' secrets, even to other friends." He tilted his head. "Isn't Arthur much older than Rory?"

"Quite." After a moment, Wesley pursed his lips. "Although I suppose seven years isn't that much more than us."

"Wait." Sebastian furrowed his brow. "We're not the same age?"

Wesley pinched the bridge of his nose. "Are you serious right now?"

"Then how old are you?"

"How old am—you don't know how old I am?"

"Twenty-six?" Sebastian guessed.

Wesley's gaze flicked up, staring at Sebastian over his hand with an extremely unimpressed expression. "You cannot believe I'm younger than you. You *better not* believe that."

"Well—"

"I went to *war*. In *1914*."

Sebastian did some quick math. "So you're twenty... nine?"

Wesley's unimpressed expression didn't budge.

"Thirty-nine?"

Wesley's eyebrow went up.

Sebastian huffed. "You've never told me your age."

"I'm beginning to realize that I've assumed you know many things that you actually don't." Wesley fixed him with a pointed look. "But tell me that you do know why *I* came to New York in February?"

"To see your ex-lover." Sebastian was pleased he got it out without sounding as insecure as he still felt every time he thought about Wesley sailing an ocean after someone else.

Wesley blew out a breath. "Well, there's that, at least," he muttered, helping himself to Sebastian's tea.

Sebastian had a very strong sense he had just missed something.

But the waiter was approaching, with a tray of dim sum, so he put it to the back of his mind.

From the Dragon House, they walked up to Hester Street, and found the Taussig's pharmacy. The teenager behind the counter, Levi, confirmed that Sasha and Pavel were out of town on a tour with Jade's sister, Stella.

Sebastian got an ice cream soda from Levi, which Wesley firmly turned down in favor of a pack of cheap cigarettes. As they walked outside, Wesley began to count things off on his fingers.

"The paranormal siblings you've heard of, the Ivanovs, aren't in the city. Mr. Zhang isn't at the Dragon House. We don't know where Miss Robbins's speakeasy is. Arthur isn't at his flat. Brodigan no longer lives at his boarding house nor has an antiques shop to work at, and we don't have any other contact information for him."

"They are all gone, and someone is sending you cryptic letters." Sebastian didn't like any of it.

Wesley glanced down the street. "How far are we from City Hall?"

"Very close. We can walk."

"Then let's go there," said Wesley. "Because I know one more person in New York we can try."

They got to City Hall as smartly dressed workers were flowing out for the evening. Wesley strode right up to the guard. "Wesley Collins, the Viscount Fine," he said, and the guard immediately straightened. "I'm here for Alderman Kenzie. I don't have an appointment, but I need him to see me."

"I'll find out if he's still here, sir."

Minutes later, Sebastian was following Wesley as the guard led them through a rotunda and down a hall to an office.

"Lord Fine?"

Two white men had come out of the office. One was about Sebastian's height but stockier, with the same blue-gray eyes and light brown hair as Wesley. The other was a man even taller than Wesley, who looked shockingly like Arthur Kenzie, right down to the jet-black hair, blue eyes, and broad shoulders. He had a real smile on his face as he said, "Lord Fine, it is you. How good to see you again."

Wesley shook his hand. "John Kenzie, how are you?"

Sebastian nearly bit his tongue. This was Arthur's brother, the poor man who had suffered nightmares because the other paranormals Sebastian had been with in February had delighted in inflicting suffering, regardless of whether the blood magic in their veins made them do it.

"This is my friend, Mr. de Leon," Wesley was saying. "Sebastian, John here will be America's newest senator."

John modestly waved that away, although he looked very pleased. "Elections aren't for a while, but we're polling well." He gestured at the other man. "And you remember Walter."

"Of course," Wesley said, shaking the man's hand. "It seems married life agrees with you."

Sebastian placed him. This must have been Walter from the wedding Wesley had come for in February, the New York governor's son.

"Can't complain, can't complain," Walter said. "And how are you, Lord Fine?"

"Having a devil of a time, actually," Wesley said.

"Back in New York on business, and I thought I'd give Arthur a shout while I'm here. But I can't find the bloody man anywhere."

"That's because he's not in the city," John said. "Went up to Tarrytown, not far at all. He said he went to look at houses."

"You sound skeptical," Wesley observed.

"Because I am," John said. "He's still got the apartment on the Upper West Side, and what does an eternal bachelor want with a country house?"

Walter was nodding along. "I didn't buy mine until Blanche insisted. I offered my contacts, but Arthur didn't seem interested at all."

Now that Sebastian knew about Arthur and Rory, a private country house—without prying eyes—could be something Arthur might want. But then, there were plenty of reasons he might have gone, reasons connected to magic that Arthur's family and non-paranormal friends wouldn't have known about.

"So why do you think he went to Tarrytown?" Wesley asked.

John and Walter exchanged a glance. John's eyes then cut down the hall, toward the few other occupants several feet away, before he looked back at Sebastian, then Wesley. "You're both Arthur's friends?"

Would Arthur consider Sebastian a friend? That would be nice, but Sebastian wouldn't count on it.

"Both of us," Wesley said firmly. "You can tell us your suspicions, John."

John and Walter exchanged another glance, then John leaned in and lowered his voice. "I'm not supposed to know, you see, because I'm the law and all that. But I'm fairly certain Arthur's off chasing a bootlegging lead."

Sebastian stilled. "Really?"

"I'm also not supposed to know his pretty friend, Jade Robbins, runs a speakeasy," John said. "But look. Prohibition isn't popular, and you have to let a couple places slip through so the whole thing doesn't collapse, you understand?"

"You can't shut the Magnolia down," said Walter. "Do you know how few places get their gin from Canada, not a bathtub in the Bronx?"

"The secret is safe with us," Wesley promised. "So Arthur is in Tarrytown right now?"

"Yes, I spoke to him just a few days ago," said John. "I'm going up myself tomorrow, in fact, taking the boat out before the weather turns."

"Blanche and I are having a masquerade for Halloween, introducing ourselves to the neighborhood and all that," said Walter. "You'll come of course, won't you, Lord Fine? We've got a baronet on the guest list, and I know Blanche would love to have more of her peers."

"Parties. Hooray," Wesley said, without any of John's enthusiasm.

"Excellent, that's settled then," said John. "You can come up for the masquerade and see Arthur in one go. He's staying at the Horseman Inn—I'll get the information for you."

A few minutes later, they were walking down the steps of City Hall with the inn's address and exchange in Wesley's pocket.

"I come all the way to America and I still can't avoid parties." Wesley was frowning. "Frivolities aside, it seems Arthur could be chasing a bootlegging lead in Tarrytown—and here we just met a bootlegger on his way to Tarrytown."

Sebastian spread his hands. "Coincidence?"

Wesley looked doubtful. "Sir Ellery and Arthur have met through me."

In February, when Sebastian's companions had been tormenting John Kenzie and Sebastian himself had been driven by blood magic in his veins. He'd hurt so many people, the last time he'd been in New York; the blood terrors would have countless nightmarish memories to draw from, if they came back.

"It feels too close to be a coincidence," Wesley was continuing, "like it must be related, but fuck me if I could say how."

Sebastian pushed his thoughts aside best he could; there could be danger to Wesley and that was what mattered. "And none of it explains the letter you got. At least we have a place to call now."

They crossed the small park in the shadow of the skyscrapers on Park Avenue. The sun had set somewhere behind the Woolworth Building and the multicolored leaves on the trees nearly glowed, the reds and oranges like pinpoints of flame against the graying twilight.

"How do you know Arthur's brother?" Sebastian asked, as they walked.

"Met him during that whole mess around the wedding," Wesley said. "Talked to him at length after my valet was offed, and then spent some time making sure the New York governor understood that a viscount thought John ought to have his backing for senate."

Sebastian furrowed his brow. "You care about American politics?"

"Christ, no," said Wesley. "But helping Arthur's brother was really the least I could do, wasn't it?"

Sebastian once again had the sense that he was missing something very big. "Because Arthur is your friend?"

"Well, we're friends *now*, at least so far as anyone would consider me that. At the time, I also clearly owed him and Rory a very large apology."

"For what?"

Wesley stopped at the edge of the walkway, just before the park's end. He turned toward Sebastian, strikingly handsome framed against the autumn leaves in his long wool coat and old-fashioned high collar. Everywhere else Sebastian looked, he saw ghosts of his last trip to New York, but when his gaze fell on Wesley, it was enough to quiet the worst of his memories.

"What do you mean, *for what*?" said Wesley. "I put my lips where they didn't belong anymore and upset Rory enough he apparently cracked a ceiling. And I'm fairly certain that was *before* I showed up at his shop and tried to bribe him to leave Arthur. You know the story."

Sebastian blinked.

"Oh no." Wesley pinched the bridge of his nose with the hand not holding his walking stick. "You don't know this either."

"Know what?"

"If I have to talk about it, I need a cigarette." Wesley was already digging out his pack. "The day you kidnapped Rory Brodigan out of his antiques shop, you already know I was there, in the back room. Have you never wondered why a viscount from London was in a Hell's Kitchen antiques shop in the first place?"

Sebastian furrowed his brow. "No, I hadn't," he said slowly. "But why—"

His eyes widened.

Wesley had come to New York to win back an ex-lover and discovered they had found someone else.

"*Arthur* is your ex?"

Wesley winced so hard he almost dropped his cigarette.

"I held your ex-boyfriend at gunpoint and you didn't *tell* me?"

"I assumed you knew!" Wesley lit the match, blue-and-red fire against the deepening night. "Everything in your world has been new to me since the night you saved my life in London. It didn't occur to me there could be something you didn't know."

This was so much worse than some nameless, face-less man. "I tried to call Arthur today!" Sebastian said. "Was I going to see him again and not know you sailed across the entire ocean for him?"

Oh, Sebastian hadn't meant to blurt that out, to put his insecurity out there like a Times Square billboard.

But Wesley inhaled and quickly shook his head. "It wasn't like that." He blew the smoke back out in a hard stream. "I told you, I was chasing convenience, not passion. Arthur was handsome, and he fit conveniently into my life without me having to change. I'm a shallow prick who thought that was enough."

"You always find the worst way to see yourself," Sebastian said heatedly. "Arthur is very handsome, yes, but he is also brave and kind. He helped my family get our siphon back and forgave me for everything when he didn't have to."

"You truly don't have to extol the virtues of my ex-lover," Wesley muttered.

"But that's my point," Sebastian said. "Arthur is worth sailing an ocean for. Have you never stopped to think that maybe you're not shallow? That maybe you didn't just want him back because he's handsome, but because you knew what a good person he was?"

Wesley stared at him. And then, incongruously, he began to smile.

"What?" Sebastian said defensively.

"You, that's what." Wesley was shaking his head,

smile still in place. "I just told you a story where my every action was thoroughly reprehensible, and yet you're still trying to find a way to see it where I'm not a complete lout."

"Because you're *not*," Sebastian said. "You think I could stand being back in New York if I didn't have you?"

Wesley opened his mouth, then closed it.

"Is that something *you* don't know?" Sebastian swallowed. "You only see bad things when you look at yourself, but they aren't true, Wes. I know they're not true, better than anyone else."

Wesley had a funny, almost lost expression on his face. He put the cigarette back to his lips with an unsteady hand. "You should ask me sometime what I see when I look at you."

"You don't see a man as handsome as Arthur, that's for sure," Sebastian muttered, before he could stop himself.

Wesley raised an eyebrow. "You cannot possibly be jealous."

"Not really." Sebastian stuck his hands in his pockets. "It's more that I wouldn't blame anyone who wanted him back."

But Wesley only scoffed. "He is a lovely person, I'll freely admit that. A good friend. But we were terrible together."

"Really?"

"Wretched," said Wesley. "He drank like he could drown his demons and I couldn't see past my own miseries either. We quickly discovered we couldn't manage a conversation without fighting and ended up mostly ignoring each other. But it was the longest anyone had tolerated me and I assumed that was as good as relationships got. Until I saw him with Rory."

He shook his head. "It's night and day to how he was with me. Rory actually makes him happy, the way you—well." He cleared his throat. "Anyway. Point being, *you* are obviously also worth sailing an ocean for, as here I am."

Oh.

"You should see your face right now," Wesley said, sounding amused. "You didn't think of that, did you? Didn't stop and think, *Wesley wanted Arthur back in London the same way he wants his hats in a tidy row, but now Wesley is with me, sailing off wherever I want to go.* You do see the difference, don't you?"

He exhaled, smoke floating away into the yellow glow of the park's Victorian streetlamp. "And as for you not being as handsome as Arthur, well. I think you ought to know that Arthur came moping to me in London in May because he thought Rory was going to leave him for, and I quote, an obnoxiously handsome man."

"Really?" Sebastian said, surprised. "Who?"

"Yes, whoever could it have been," Wesley said dryly. "Who on earth is obnoxiously handsome and was spending time with Rory in London in May—no, don't guess someone else," he added, as Sebastian opened his mouth. "It was you, you impossibly attractive sod. So there will be no jealousy out of you. It's ridiculous and pointless, like all emotions."

It was Sebastian's turn to scoff, but he had a small smile. "You just spent ten minutes making me feel better."

"So?"

"If you really think emotions are ridiculous and pointless, why do you care about mine?"

Wesley narrowed his eyes. But he didn't seem to have a response to that.

Sebastian held out a hand. "You want me to take the cigarette away?"

"God, yes, please." Wesley held the cigarette toward him. "And for Christ's sake, don't let me make any more assumptions. If you ever want to know anything about me, just ask."

"I want to know everything about you," Sebastian admitted, as he took the cigarette and stubbed it out on the ground. "But I'm going to start with *how old are you?*"

"You truly don't know your lover's age?" Wesley said wryly.

Sebastian huffed. "I bet there's lots of things you don't know about me."

"You think so?" said Wesley. "Like what?"

"Um…" What would a man as smart as Wesley not know? "My full name."

"Juan Sebastián de León y Marin-Torres."

Sebastian stared. Wesley had even rolled the *rr*. "How—"

"I asked your brother, of course." Wesley's smile was amused. "Darling boy, you might be paranormal, but you're also Spanish. I am aware there are countries beyond England and that not every culture uses the same naming conventions. Thought the odds were fairly good that there was more to your name." The smile was still playing on his lips. "But I'm certain you don't know my full name. We've slept together how many times now? And you don't even know my age."

Sebastian winced. "This is so embarrassing."

Wesley only looked more amused. "You're twenty-seven. I'm thirty-two. So quite a bit older—and taller, while we're on the subject."

"How are we on the subject of height?" Sebastian said. "And you're barely older. Barely taller."

"Five years and five inches is not *barely.*"

"*Five* inches? You're one inch taller. Two at most." More like three or even four, but Sebastian didn't have to say that out loud. "Age and height don't matter between us anyway."

"I suppose you might be right," Wesley said delicately. "After all, none of that ended up mattering last night."

Sebastian's cheeks flushed. Hopefully it was dim enough Wesley wouldn't notice. "We're not going to talk about that."

"Why would I ever agree to not talk about it?" Wesley hadn't stopped looking amused; he'd almost certainly noticed the blush. "I'm not upset with you. I gave you full permission to use your magic on me however you like."

"The magic that knocked you over last night?" Sebastian said pointedly.

"The magic that flared up to protect me from a *restaurant*," Wesley countered, even more pointedly. "I'm also not afraid of you, even with that brooch. The offer stands."

Sebastian hesitated. He hadn't used magic on Wesley on purpose since their first night together.

He *wanted* to. Wesley was so good at sweeping every thought from his mind; he wanted Wesley pinned down and coming apart, so lost in the moment that addictions and harsh thoughts couldn't reach him. A mind like Wesley's didn't turn off easily, but Sebastian could make it happen.

Except, of course, for the brooch that made his magic too strong and unpredictable. If he could just get better control of it—

Sebastian sighed. Maybe he'd get there. Someday. "Let's go call the inn, yes?"

Chapter Eight

The cab pulled up at their hotel not soon enough for Wesley's tastes. They were going to call this damn Horseman Inn in Tarrytown, talk to Arthur and Jade, straighten the whole mess out. And then Wesley could get back to the only thing he actually wanted to do with his time, which was fuck Sebastian until he was bliss-drunk and loopy in Wesley's arms.

What would it take to get him to lose control of his magic again?

Wesley quickened his pace.

But as they crossed through the lobby, a voice called, "Fine!" Major Langford stepped into their path. "Glad I caught you."

For fuck's sake. Of course they'd been stopped by one of the only people Wesley couldn't bring himself to tell to fuck off. "Langford," he said, with a curt nod. "I didn't expect to see you again. What are you doing here?"

Christ, he hoped Langford hadn't actually moved to their hotel. Wesley was perfectly entitled to have anyone he liked in his room at any hour and not explain himself, but Langford was sharp and endlessly suspicious. He did not need to be turning those eyes and suspicions on Wesley's paranormal lover.

"Planning a tea party," Langford said sarcastically. "What do you think? I'm in New York on business, and in this lobby because I'm waiting for you." His eyes flicked past Wesley to Sebastian. "You and your friend, apparently."

Sebastian's shift in his posture was subtle, but once again loud and clear to someone as attuned to his body as Wesley now was. Langford might be suspicious of Sebastian, but Sebastian clearly didn't trust him right back.

Wesley folded his arms. "And why are you waiting for me?"

Langford gestured to the hall. "Concierge says the smoking lounge is down there. Join me, won't you?"

No, Wesley wanted to say, but Sebastian cleared his throat. "Lord Fine, the major did say he was waiting for you." His voice was soft but pointed, obviously thinking of the typewritten letter so clandestinely delivered to Wesley's door.

Not really Langford's style, but Wesley supposed it was worth asking. "Very well," he said shortly. "Indulge us, won't you, Sebastian?"

Major Langford's lips thinned. "Why would your companion join us?"

"Why wouldn't he?" Wesley said.

"I don't know," Major Langford said. "I don't know anything about him, because all you gave us was a name."

You don't need to know anything else was on the tip of Wesley's tongue, but again he held it back. "I'm considering some Caribbean investments, perhaps imports. Sebastian is advising."

Major Langford's eyes flicked over Sebastian's stylish clothes, then moved from the flat cap to linger on his face, the long-lashed eyes and soft lips. "Advising."

Sebastian didn't seem the least bit surprised to be the subject of a hostile stare, which implied a lot of things about how people treated him and Wesley didn't care for any of them. "I grew up in San Juan."

"How exotic," Major Langford said.

"He's an American in America; we're exotic foreigners from a distant island," Wesley said, a little sharply. "Let's have that smoke already."

A few minutes later, they were ensconced in the dimly lit lounge—mixed-gender, how very modern of the hotel—sitting in a trio of black leather chairs on the far side by the wood-paneled walls.

A man came by and offered a box of cigars. Wesley took one at random while Sebastian ordered sodas for them all, and what a fucking travesty it was that Wesley had to talk to Langford without a stiff drink.

Langford lit his cigar and leaned back in his chair. "So. Collins—Fine, sorry."

He wasn't sorry, Wesley knew, nor was the slip accidental. An unsubtle reminder to Wesley of his time as Captain Collins and the rank difference between them.

"You haven't told me why you're in New York," said Major Langford.

"Business," Wesley said coolly. "Same as you."

Sebastian looked between them. "Lord Fine said you served together, major?"

"That's right." Langford stuck the cigar between his teeth. "I assume you hid out the war in Spain?"

"He was a medic in the American army," Wesley cut in. "Healed up people like us."

"Or the unfortunates we got our hands on." Langford smiled at Sebastian around the cigar without an ounce of warmth. "And what has Fine told you about himself? Any stories?"

Sebastian's expression had gone unreadably blank. "Why do you ask?"

"You just don't seem like the type who'd want to hear the kind of stories men like Fine and I can tell," Langford said easily. "It's a shame; I've got some good ones."

It again would have been almost imperceptible to anyone who hadn't made a study of Sebastian's movements. But Wesley saw Sebastian's eyes narrow, the subtle shift in his body posture to lean forward. It made the hairs on the back of Wesley's neck rise, like an ocean breeze changing before a summer storm rolls in.

"I'm not disparaging medics, of course," Langford went on, unaware that he was pissing off a magical being with tenuous control on said magic. "Good place to be if you haven't got the stomach to be on the front lines with someone like Fine."

"There are people who would consider themselves lucky to be with Lord Fine." Sebastian's voice had gone quieter, which was actually quite a bit more alarming than if he'd yelled.

"Not anyone who's faced him in battle." Langford turned to Wesley and raised his cigar in a mock-toast. "It's a compliment. The world's gone too fucking soft. They don't make men as mean as Fine anymore."

Sebastian's eye twitched. Was it Wesley's imagination, or had his knees just felt a bit weak? "All danger, no marshmallow," he muttered.

"What?" said Langford.

"Nothing." Christ, was Wesley going to have to be the reasonable, subtle one this time?

"Why were you waiting for Lord Fine?" Sebastian said, still quiet.

"To talk. *Privately*." Langford sat back in his seat,

narrowed eyes on Sebastian. "You know, this hotel didn't have a room registered to a Sebastian de Leon."

"I travel under my second name," Sebastian said.

"Oh, do you?" Langford said. "You know, I actually couldn't find any information about you at all, not at the hotel, not in any records. Almost like you're a ghost."

Langford might have been trying to put Sebastian on the back foot but he was failing spectacularly. A man who'd been able to *flatten a room with his mind since he was nine* wasn't going to scare easy, and Sebastian's expression clearly said he didn't give a damn what the major dug up or how he spoke to him.

But Wesley cared. "Major, why the fuck are you digging into my personal affairs?" he said, as he tapped his cigar into the ashtray.

"I wasn't planning to talk about it for an audience."

Sebastian's mouth was opening, so Wesley cut in first. "Anything you have to say to me, you can say in front of Sebastian."

"Really." Langford picked up his drink. "Still have that soft spot for the Spaniards, then? You know, he seems to have such a rosy picture of you, maybe he does need to hear some stories. Should we start in the trenches? Or maybe with interroga—bloody hell," he swore, as his arm seemed to give out and the drink sloshed all over his lap.

But Wesley had felt it too, had nearly dropped his cigar.

Sebastian had shot to his feet. "I should—I think—the bar, I'll go get a new drink."

He didn't look at Wesley as he slipped away.

"Fucking clumsy of me," Langford said, now dabbing at his damp trousers with his handkerchief. "But damned odd of my elbow to give out like that."

"Maybe you should see a doctor," Wesley said, because it was better than saying *actually, we're lucky Sebastian scurried off to calm down before he had every mortal in this entire hotel on the floor in piles of useless goo.*

Langford set the handkerchief down and picked up his cigar. "Well, now that he's gone—"

"Did you send me a letter, by chance?" Wesley interrupted.

Langford's mouth thinned. "No," he said shortly. "But I know who did."

"Who?" Wesley said at once.

"A man you met last night." Langford stuck the cigar back between his teeth. "Alasdair Findlay."

"*Alasdair*? The textile fellow who's clearly wandering about day drunk?"

"That's the one."

Wesley frowned. "Major, what's going on?"

"If I'm perfectly honest with you? I don't know." Langford leaned forward. "I'm here on behalf of the War Office. We're investigating Sir Ellery."

Wesley's eyebrows flew up. "Ellery? Why?"

"The valet you hired in February, Benedict Chester, who met his death here in New York," said Langford. "The War Office was looking into him before he died. He was an internationally wanted criminal."

"Well, he hardly put that in his references, did he?"

Langford gave him a flat look. "Chester murdered his previous employer—Sir Ellery's second cousin, Sir Harold Kerrigan. Sir Harold and Chester worked together five years, ran quite a lucrative side business of collecting and selling rare artifacts."

Rare artifacts. Magic artifacts, perhaps? Wesley now knew Chester had been smuggling the pomander relic

with him, which had been among the Earl of Blanshard's collection. "So you think Sir Harold—what?
Passed the family business on to his cousin, Sir Ellery?"

"That's what we're trying to find out," Langford said.
"I asked for the case. I've known Sir Ellery since the
war, so easy enough for me to visit without raising his
suspicions. He's been in New York for a month, staying with his friend, Alasdair. Now you ought to know
that Alasdair's mad as a hatter, if you'll forgive the pun,
since the man is in textiles."

"He's a bootlegger," Wesley pointed out. "Are you
sure he's mad and not just constantly enjoying what he
purveys?"

"Quite sure. Alasdair's a teetotaler, doesn't drink
what he sells. Got strong beliefs and morals, that one."

They'd seen Sir Ellery and Alasdair today, heading
to Tarrytown—the same damn place Arthur's inn was.
"But if Sir Ellery is a friend of Alasdair's, why the devil
would he send *me* a warning letter?" Wesley said. "You
said it yourself, he and I met *last night*."

"I think Sir Ellery may be trying to bring Alasdair
into the business too," said Langford. "Alasdair is trying
to warn you away. From where I'm sitting, probably a
good idea; there's precedent for questionable decisions
when it comes to who you choose for company." His
gaze darted in the direction Sebastian had gone, then
back to Wesley. "Like your valet. A person you chose
to travel with."

Wesley wasn't going to rise to the bait. He sat back
in his chair. "You're telling me all of this for a reason.
What do you want?"

"You were a damn fine captain—again, pardon the
pun. Had a couple soft spots I'll never understand, but
the rest of you more than made up for it. War Office

could use more men like you." Langford took the cigar out of his mouth and leaned forward again. "There's more going on with Ellery than you could ever guess. I've got whiskey in my trunk. Come drink with me tonight and we can talk."

If Sir Ellery could possibly be mixed up with anything relating to Chester the valet and Sir Harold's theft of paranormal relics from the Earl of Blanshard, then Wesley wanted to talk to paranormals about it, not Langford. "I can't," said Wesley. "Sebastian and I are leaving for the Caribbean in a couple days. We have business to finish."

"Business and holidays are a damned waste of a ruthless man," Langford said. "Come up for a drink. Your advisor's already abandoned you. He's about to pull with that girl."

Fucking hell. Wesley turned, already knowing what he'd see. And sure enough, a pretty flapper in a sequined dress and matching headband over her black bob was leaning on the bar, talking to Sebastian.

"I can't take him anywhere." Wesley left most of his cigar in the ashtray and stood, ignoring Langford's irritable huff to cross over to Sebastian.

"—know a speakeasy called the Magnolia?" Sebastian was saying, as Wesley got within earshot.

"Heard of that one, it's supposed to be the best," the flapper said. "Don't know where it is, though." She flashed Sebastian a smile framed with perfect red lips. "We could go look for it."

Wesley cleared his throat. Loudly.

Sebastian glanced over, and relief crossed his face. "I'm sorry, not tonight," he said, sliding off his stool. "But it was nice to meet you, Matilda."

Wesley barely managed not to roll his eyes, both at

the flapper trying to move on his lover and at himself
for being a terrible hypocrite, because hadn't he just said
jealousy was *ridiculous and pointless* not an hour ago?

As they crossed the lounge, it was very obvious that
Sebastian was trying not to look back at Langford.

"What am I going to do with you?" Wesley muttered,
for Sebastian's ears alone. "You can't order a soda without someone trying to fuck you. You can't have a smoke
without nearly knocking the lounge to the ground."

Sebastian huffed as they passed through the lounge
doors and turned the corner to walk down the hall.
"Would have been worth it."

Wesley raised an eyebrow. "Am I to assume you
mean the bit about knocking Major Langford down
rather than the flirting with Miss Matilda?"

"I wasn't *flirting*," Sebastian burst out, with an edge
of genuine upset. "Wes, you were right there with that
asshole, I wouldn't—oh no."

The words rang simultaneously in Wesley's ears with
the clattering of dishes and someone's swearing, but
Wesley couldn't think about that because his knees had
collapsed and he was stumbling.

Sebastian grabbed him before his face had an un-
pleasant collision with the floor. "Dios mío, una y otra
vez." He pulled Wesley up to his feet. "I'm so sorry."

"Shush, I'm fine," Wesley said firmly—a bit of a
half-truth, as it was not his imagination that his knees
were still unsteady. "I had it coming. Thoughtless thing
to say when I know better."

"No, don't say that, you almost fell and it's my fault."

Wesley hated to hear him upset. Sebastian deserved
better than to be stuck with a cold prick like Wesley,
ought to have someone who could say the right things,

knew how to comfort him, to help him stop blaming himself for things he couldn't control.

Wesley's gaze lingered on Sebastian, who was looking miserably over at the hall's other occupant, a waiter who was being helped up by two others, an overturned tray and canapés scattered across the floor.

Oh, fuck it. Wesley only ever made things worse, but for Sebastian he would fucking try to make it better.

"Come on," he said, grabbing Sebastian by the sleeve and tugging him into a walk. "I have an idea."

Chapter Nine

Sebastian followed Wesley into the elevator. "Top floor," Wesley told the elevator operator.

Top floor? Sebastian didn't know what Wesley had in mind, but it wasn't as if he was making good decisions right then, so he held his tongue as the elevator rose.

They got out into a short hallway and Wesley led the way to a door. Were they going outside? "It's okay if you need to smoke in the room," Sebastian said.

Wesley got the door for him. "This is for you."

"Me? But you said you had a lot to tell me. And we need to call the Tarrytown inn."

"And we will, in a moment." Wesley jerked his head. "Go on. Out you get."

Sebastian furrowed his brow but walked out, and stilled. They were on the rooftop patio, which stretched the length of the hotel. There was a waist-high concrete railing at the edge, and beyond it rose even taller buildings. A soft rain was falling, chasing away the city scents and making the air smell fresh and bright, and the patio had gathered tiny puddles that glimmered with the reflection of the Manhattan city lights.

Sebastian went straight for the railing. "This is even prettier than I expected."

"If by *pretty* you mean *cold and soggy*, sure. You

talk about your rooftops in Puerto Rico and Spain and I'm sure they're warmer than this, but let's work with what we have, shall we?" said Wesley. "And the weather does mean we're alone, which is good. We don't need an audience."

Sebastian glanced over his shoulder and saw Wesley wedging his walking stick in the door. "An audience for what?"

"This next part. Though I am surprised you haven't complained about the cold yet."

Wesley was coming toward the rail. Sebastian leaned forward on it, ignoring the wet concrete against his clothes to get a better look at the cars several stories below. The rain was cold against the back of his neck, but he didn't care.

"I am freezing, yes," Sebastian admitted. "But it's worth it to be up here with you."

Wesley joined him at the rail. "You like the view that much?"

"I like the company."

"You think you're charming, don't you?" Wesley said wryly. "Save that talk for the Lorettas and Matildas of the world; it will never work on a prick like me."

"Oh yes, such a prick," Sebastian said. "Bringing me up on the rooftop you said you'd never come to."

"You can save your smug impudence for someone else too; we're up here for a reason."

"The pretty view?" Sebastian said, pointing to the glittering of the Manhattan skyline against the cloudy dark gray of the night.

"Of course not the *pretty view*, I will never be a fucking tourist," Wesley said, although his eyes stole to the skyscrapers around them. "We're up here so you can let go of your magic."

Once a Rogue

"*What*?"

Wesley gestured at the brick wall, which had a series of planters running its length. "I'm going to go have a seat over there—because yes, you've brought complete lunacy into my life but I'm not yet mad enough to stand at the edge of a roof while you use your magic—and then you can let go."

"But—"

"I don't have a speck of my own and I can see it's riding you into the ground," Wesley said. "You need a break. The others have all fucked off to Tarrytown, so we can't ask them for their advice, which means you're stuck with my ideas."

"I need to learn to control it—"

"And you will." Wesley took a step back, toward the wall. "You're the one who keeps telling me that I'm doing well with the smokes. This is me offering to take a cigarette from your hand. I brought you up here where it's just us and the skyscrapers. Let the wild horses you always talk about run free for a moment; maybe it will help them settle."

Sebastian bit his lip. "Then you go downstairs."

"No."

"Wes—"

"I didn't bring you up here to shove you outside and leave you alone," Wesley said pointedly.

"But the last time I let all of my magic go, I killed the Earl of Blanshard."

"And I got nothing more dangerous than a kip outside the Grand Palais." Wesley gestured at the night around them. "What do you think my life was like before I met you? Do you imagine I ever stood in the rain at the top of Manhattan with literal magic still in my aura? This is not a hardship for me, Sebastian. You're—it's—an adventure."

Oh.

Wesley looked a little wide-eyed, like he hadn't meant to say all of that. He added, quick and gruff, "I'm truly not afraid of your magic, you know. Your lion would never kill me. I'm his favorite."

Sebastian broke into a bigger smile. "Loco," he said, with exasperated affection, as he slid the coat off his shoulders and held it out to Wesley. "If you're staying, lie on my coat."

"I don't need it, I'm just going to sit against the wall—"

"Wesley," Sebastian said patiently, as rain fell on his flat cap and shoulders. "This time, you're going to need to lie down."

Oh, Wesley's mouth formed. He grudgingly accepted the coat. "Are you going to be insufferably smug if I admit that's a bit sexy?"

Sebastian bit back another smile. His stomach was fluttering with nerves, but Wesley always made him feel better.

Wesley found a spot farther away that was mostly dry and settled on top of Sebastian's coat along the wall. Sebastian could feel Wesley's gaze on him as he put his hands on the edge of the railing. He could feel his magic, like his blood was vibrating, like the brooch had the horses' reins in a tight grip and was yanking them the wrong way. He closed his eyes, and then he let the stampede go.

His magic swept the rooftop. He distantly heard Wesley hit the roof—he hadn't lain all the way down, because of course he hadn't—as his aura was swept under Sebastian's magic like a sunbather caught unaware by the incoming tide. He tried best he could to keep that sense of Wesley, to make sure it was only temporarily weakened, not hurt, as he let the horses spread out as far as they wanted.

It was like exhaling after holding your breath, a relief so intense that it left his limbs tingling. For that moment, he let it go, let it spread out over Manhattan's rooftops under the clouded night sky.

When the rush had left, and he was light-headed and dizzy, he finally pulled the magic back in. He gripped the railing as it settled into his body, like it was bonding itself to his bones, his blood.

He took two hard breaths, and then he hurried over to Wesley, who was still lying on Sebastian's coat on the rooftop. "Wes," he said, kneeling at Wesley's side. He was damp from the rain and a little shivery, but he ignored it to help Wesley sit up, propping him against the wall. "Wesley, are you all right?"

Wesley opened his eyes, which were only a little fuzzy. "Of course I am," he said. "I told you: I'm your lion's favorite."

Sebastian let out a quiet laugh of surprise and relief. Then he was kissing Wesley, needing the last inches between them to be gone. Their lips were also wet and cold, and they tasted like rain, and maybe like the magic that still crackled in the air. He threaded his arm around Wesley's neck, a barrier between his head and the hard bricks, trying to say *I'm so lucky to have you* through the kiss.

Sebastian finally pulled back, keeping his arm draped around Wesley's neck as he brought their foreheads together. He was soaked through his clothes to the skin, but his magic hadn't felt this stable since he'd taken control of the brooch relic. "That was such a good idea, Wes."

"Did it help?" Wesley whispered, his breath a puff of visible mist in the cold air.

"It did," Sebastian said, his own whisper into the private world made by their bodies. "I feel better."

"That's good." Wesley sounded a bit dazed, and his expression was soft in a way Sebastian had only seen in darkened bedrooms. "I wanted to make you feel better."

He wrapped his hand around Sebastian's wrist, over the tattoo, and Sebastian felt the touch ricochet through his blood.

He took an involuntary breath. "Let's go back to the room," he said, as his mind began to consider possibilities that involved more of Wesley's touch. "You can fill me in as we walk."

Chapter Ten

The last of the watery sensation had left Wesley's limbs by the time the elevator brought them back down to two. Wesley led the way to his suite, quietly recounting his conversation with Major Langford.

Sebastian was frowning again as Wesley opened the suite's door. "So Sir Ellery is related to the man who stole the pomander from the Earl of Blanshard? And Alasdair sent you the letter to—what? Warn you?"

"So it seems." Wesley held the door for Sebastian. "Major Langford did say the man isn't quite right in the head."

Sebastian slipped into the parlor. "Sir Ellery and Alasdair said they were going to Tarrytown today. That's where Arthur's inn is. I don't like the coincidence."

"Nor do I," Wesley said, stepping inside and closing the suite door.

"I don't like Major Langford either."

Wesley snorted. "You weren't particularly subtle about that."

"He's an asshole to you," Sebastian said, with feeling, as they stood in the tiny foyer and began peeling off wet coats and hats. Sebastian looked soaked all the way through. "I can't believe you talk to him."

Wesley hesitated, then admitted, "He did me a favor once. He's never let me forget it, but he did grudgingly do it."

Sebastian glanced at him. "Is this about the interrogation?"

"No," said Wesley, keeping his voice steady. "No, that was done on his orders."

Sebastian stiffened. "*Langford* made you do that?"

"It was war," Wesley said. "They had our soldiers; he hardly had much choice." He'd recommended Wesley for a medal afterward. Wesley had donated it, had never wanted to see it again.

"I don't care if he thought it was his only option." Sebastian's voice had gone very quiet again, and for a moment it was hard to reconcile the sweetheart who doted on animals with the paranormal taut with anger in front of him. "He shouldn't have given a command like that to someone under him."

"There's no point getting angry on my behalf," Wesley said. "I've told you I'm not a nice man. I did a lot of bad things during the war. And I was never under blood magic." He went on before Sebastian could argue. "The favor wasn't related. We had two soldiers in our platoon who were caught with each other."

Sebastian stilled.

"They were young and working class. Defenseless." Wesley's fingers twitched for a cigarette, as they always did when he didn't want to think about something. He curled his hand around the brim of his hat instead. "Major Langford was disgusted. Furious. Wanted every punishment in the book thrown at them, to have them flogged and sentenced to hard labor. And I—interfered."

Sebastian looked ill. "Did you succeed?"

Wesley gave a single, jerky nod. "I argued McGregor

and Reyes should only be transferred to another platoon under other pretext and the matter hushed up."

He took a breath through his nose. "Langford might have been my commanding officer, but he knew who my father was. We'd heard just the previous week of my older brother's death, so when I held my ground, Langford wasn't fighting his captain but the future Viscount Fine. He refused to transfer them to the same unit, there was no changing his mind there, but—he left them alone."

"That was good of you," Sebastian said.

"I have many faults, but I try not to be a fucking hypocrite," Wesley said. "I was keeping the same secret, wasn't I? And they were barely eighteen, so obviously enamored of each other. They should have been schoolboys in love, not suddenly armed in those hellish trenches and told to kill Germans."

"Did they make it?" Sebastian said quietly.

"I don't know," Wesley said honestly. "I've always assumed they did not; that would be far too kind of the war and the world. But I've never checked, so I'd never have to know. Cowardly of me, but there it is."

"Reyes," Sebastian repeated. "Was he from a Spanish family? Is that what Langford meant by the dig about *a soft spot for Spaniards*?"

"Without a doubt," said Wesley. "He'll never let it go. But then, in fairness, look at me now."

That put a tiny smile on Sebastian's lips.

"Speaking of soft spots, I've apparently gone soft enough to notice that your clothes are soaked," Wesley said. "I'm certain your tropical arse is freezing. Go put on something dry."

"Yeah, okay," Sebastian agreed, turning toward the bedroom with a shiver.

"You're not going to argue?" Wesley said dryly. "You're actually minding me? How refreshing."

"If that's what you want to tell yourself, Wes," Sebastian said sweetly, without a backward glance, in the easy tone of a man who can't be rattled because he knows he has nothing to prove.

The door to the bedroom closed behind him, which was probably good, because Wesley's fingers were still twitching for a smoke and he wanted to think about anything else besides the war years. Sebastian's self-assured attitude had sent a pulse of interest through him; his handcuffs weren't always for other people, after all.

But he needed to make the call first. He sat on the edge of the settee and picked up the phone. The operator put him through to the Horseman Inn. "I'm trying to get in touch with a friend of mine," Wesley said to the woman on the other end of the phone. "I've been informed by his brother that he's staying at your establishment. Arthur Kenzie is his name."

"I'll get the innkeeper," she said. "The name was Kenzie? With a *Y*?"

"No, with an *I-E*." Wesley heard steps from the bedroom, and looked up. "It's *K-E-N*—oh."

Sebastian had swapped his wet clothes for Wesley's deep green, monogrammed full-length robe. It was a little looser on Sebastian's shorter, sleeker frame, but could have passed for the right size to someone who didn't realize the bastard was now wearing Wesley's initials.

"It's *Z* next," Sebastian said, sincere and helpful.

"What?" Wesley said dumbly.

"Kenzie," Sebastian said, as he perched on the arm on the other side of the settee. He put his elbows on his knees, and the sleeve slid down to show the lion tattoo. "*K-E-N-Z-I-E.* How did you forget how to spell your ex-lover's name? You don't forget anything."

Wesley narrowed his eyes, lowering the phone. "You—"

"Sir?" The innkeeper's voice came, tinny and distant, from the earpiece.

Wesley pursed his lips. "We're going to talk about this," he said to Sebastian, and then put the phone back to his ear. "I'm looking for one of your guests, Arthur Kenzie. May I speak to him, please? It's urgent."

There was a sound in the innkeeper's background. "Just a moment, sir—can you hold?"

"Yes," he said grudgingly.

"Talk about what?" Sebastian said.

Wesley moved the receiver away from his mouth. "Are you wearing anything under that too-big robe?"

"It's not *big*—I told you, you're not that much taller than I am," Sebastian said, which was really not the important part of the question. He traced the embroidered, intertwined *WC* over his heart. "And it's *warm.* I'm going to get one for the times we go to England."

Wesley blinked. "You're planning to come to England again?"

"Of course," Sebastian said. "You came to Paris and America with me. You're coming to the Caribbean and maybe we will go to Spain. Why wouldn't I also come with you to England? Or wherever you needed or wanted to go?"

Wesley blinked helplessly.

"If we're in London, I can visit Crumpet and Flan," Sebastian went on. "I bet your cook's daughter is taking good care of her cats. We will work out the travel, yes? Figure out how to stay together?"

Wesley could suddenly *see* it—himself, in a shaded chair on the bright tile of a rooftop patio, drinking something cold under the warm sun with the endless blue ocean stretched out in front of him; Sebastian, in the green robe, curled up with a book in the chair closest to the fireplace as snow fell outside Wesley's study window.

Fuck. Life would never let one have anything so perfect.

He must have been staring, or quiet too long, because Sebastian bit his lip uncertainly. "Sorry, I assume too much sometimes. If that's not what you want—"

"I'm sure we're clever enough to work the travel out," Wesley said, because he'd never wanted anything more. "But it sounds like you're spending your next English holiday in the basement, because the cats are not allowed upstairs."

Sebastian broke into a grin. "You think they're staying in the basement while you're gone?"

"Of course they are. It's my home. I make the rules and I require obedience."

"You don't know cats very well, do you?"

Before Wesley could respond to that bit of impudence, the innkeeper was back on the phone. "I'm sorry, sir. But Mr. Kenzie isn't here anymore."

"He's left the inn?" Wesley said in surprise. Sebastian frowned. He moved from the arm to the settee next to Wesley, close enough he'd hear the innkeeper through the phone.

"Mr. Kenzie was a guest," the innkeeper was saying, "but he's no longer staying with us. He checked out yesterday."

Wesley and Sebastian exchanged a look.

"Is there a room registered to a Mr. Brodigan, or a Mr. Zhang, or a Miss Robbins?" Wesley asked.

"We're a small inn," said innkeeper. "Only nine rooms. There's no one here by those names."

Wesley frowned as he hung up the phone. "Arthur checked out of his inn in Tarrytown the day we arrived. Sir Ellery didn't leave until today, so perhaps there's no connection after all."

"But where did Arthur go, if not back to his apartment here?" Sebastian said. "Why did Jade not call?"

Wesley tapped his fingers on the arm of the settee as he frowned. "It is possible they simply changed their mind about seeing us."

"I don't think that's it," Sebastian said. "Jade would have said."

His hair was still damp from the rain, and he was chewing on his thumb. The damnable sleeve was falling down to show the tattoo again, and the robe was open enough to show his collarbone and a sliver of bare skin. He looked soft and inviting and infinitely touchable. Wesley hadn't taken off anything but his overcoat, still fully buttoned up in his waistcoat, jacket, and tie, and the difference in their states of dress was distracting.

"We do at least know where Arthur was yesterday." Wesley glanced at the clock. "I think we will have missed the last train tonight. But we should take an early train up to Tarrytown in the morning and search for ourselves."

"And even if we don't find the others, maybe I can have a word with Sir Ellery," Sebastian said, too lightly.

"Not so fast, de Leon," Wesley said, turning on the settee to face Sebastian. "You don't get to come to my defense like I'm an incompetent child when you don't even fill out my robe."

"It fits me," Sebastian insisted.

Wesley snorted. "It really doesn't."

"You're not as big as you think you are."

"*You're* not as big as *you* think you are."

Sebastian's lips curved in a smile that sent prickles of anticipation dancing through Wesley. He reached for Wesley's tie and casually pulled it free of his waistcoat, running the end of it through his hand. "Wesley?"

It was bleeding unfair, how Sebastian could make his name another kind of caress. "Yes?"

"I don't need to be bigger than you."

And he pushed Wesley in the center of the chest just as magic rose up, washing over Wesley and sending him sprawling backward onto the settee, his entire body heavy and tingling and *useless*.

Desire chased Sebastian's magic through his limbs, his breath caught in his lungs as Sebastian crawled over him. "This is a dirty trick," Wesley muttered, his cock hardening as Sebastian kissed his throat above the high, starched collar and he could do nothing but lie there and take it.

Sebastian's lips were moving across his jaw. "You're the one who said I could use magic any way I wanted."

"Yes, and now you're using it so you don't have to admit I'm right." Fuck, the robe was falling open as Sebastian balanced on hands and knees, baring more skin that Wesley couldn't fucking touch.

"I keep telling you I'm the worse scoundrel." Sebastian's lips found his ear. "You just keep forgetting."

"Rubbish. I never forget anything." It came out a lot more unsteady than Wesley had planned, as teeth gently grazed his hyper-sensitized skin. "Once a rogue, always a rogue, is that what you're trying to claim?

Please. The instant this magic is gone, I'll show you who the scoundrel is."

"Oh really?" Sebastian said, breath ghosting across Wesley's ear. "Then I guess I better not let you up."

And instead of easing, more magic flooded Wesley's aura, rendering him a boneless puddle on the settee. An embarrassingly breathy *fuck* tumbled from Wesley's lips.

Sebastian lowered himself flat on top of him, their bodies aligned, and Wesley's cock was so on board for this, the surreal sensation of being immobilized by a man not quite his own size. The magic wasn't the rush that had knocked him down on the roof; now it felt controlled, sweeping through him with precision. This magic wasn't reaching the next room; it was just for Wesley.

Sebastian dropped a light kiss to his lips, and Wesley groaned. "How is it that I can't move but my cock is hard as stone?"

"Because my magic is in your aura." Sebastian sounded fond and amused. "Your blood still works just fine."

Another kiss, this one lingering, Sebastian's tongue tracing his lips before slipping inside Wesley's mouth. Christ, he was good at this. After a round of drinks— well, a few rounds of drinks—Wesley might admit to a domineering streak in bed, and Sebastian's sweet nature stoked that side of him like petrol on flames. But this had an appeal all its own, and the way they fit together was dizzying, that Sebastian could dance between surrender or control and ensnare Wesley either way.

Sebastian pulled back, leaving Wesley's lips tingling and craving more. "Tell me again how you're just so much bigger than me."

Wesley attempted a glare under half-lidded eyes. "You tell me where my sweetheart Sebastian went. This Sebastian is a total bastard."

Sebastian grinned and brought their lips back together, intertwining his fingers with the ones Wesley couldn't move. "Do you remember when you hand-cuffed me to your bed?" he murmured against Wesley's lips.

A thrill sparked its way up Wesley's spine, memory and anticipation weaving together. "Not likely to ever forget."

Sebastian was leisurely maneuvering him alongside heady kisses, positioning Wesley's arms out of the way, over his head on the settee, like Wesley was a doll. "It was just like this, no? Except I don't need the hand-cuffs."

Wesley could only groan again. "And you call me shameless."

Sebastian's lips brushed his again as fingers worked to loosen his tie, open his waistcoat, untuck and unfasten his shirt and undershirt.

"What are you doing, fuck all of that," Wesley managed to say. "The *trousers*, get the trousers off."

Sebastian pushed his shirts up in between the braces, the cool air welcome against the heat of Wesley's trapped body. "What's the rush?" Sebastian said meaningfully.

"Oh, fuck you," Wesley said, his eyes rolling back as Sebastian's lips found his bare stomach, each kiss blazing like a firework. "You wouldn't dare."

"What is it you say? Turnabout is fair play?"

"There is nothing fair about this," Wesley slurred.

He felt Sebastian's lips curl in a smile against his skin. "I'm afraid life's not fair, duck."

If Wesley could have moved, he would have beaten his head against the couch at Sebastian's imitation of him, equal parts charmed and desperate. "Is this going to be vengeance? Are you going to draw this out, make me rue every time I've made you beg?"

Sebastian's fingers found his waistband.

"Fuck, *please* say no." Wesley's voice had gone gravelly and almost unrecognizable with want. "I'm a craven wretch who can't handle a dose of his own medicine."

A laugh rolled through Sebastian. "No. I don't have your patience, Wes." He opened the trousers with quick, deft movements. "I don't want to wait to make you come apart."

There was cool air and then a hot mouth, and it was a travesty that Wesley couldn't lift his head to watch, except being unable to move only wound him up further. Sebastian wasn't teasing at all now, wasn't holding back, his lips and tongue and hands all focused on Wesley—along with his magic, rushing him like a high tide, almost as tangible against Wesley's skin as Sebastian's touch.

Fuck, Sebastian was good at this too. Wesley couldn't think, couldn't second guess himself or force himself to wait, and he'd been too worked up since the roof to last. Pleasure swept him, and he arched into it as the magic in his aura let him go. His hands flew to Sebastian, needing to touch and finding his soft hair, the silky skin of his shoulder. He mumbled something, maybe Sebastian's name, as his head tipped back, the parlor ceiling above out of focus even for his sharp eyes.

Aftershocks danced through him as he raised his head enough to see Sebastian. He was sprawled out on top of Wesley, their legs tangled, his arms folded on

Wesley's chest and his head on his arms, so it rose and fell with Wesley's breaths.

"You are…" Wesley's brain was incapable of eloquence, so he simply said, "…enchanting," and really, it was the truth however one looked at it.

Sebastian smiled, and Wesley realized he was carding fingers through Sebastian's hair, almost *petting* him, for fuck's sake, what the hell did he think he was doing?

Except Sebastian had tilted his head into Wesley's hand, and his golden-brown eyes were warm and content, so maybe, just maybe, Wesley wasn't completely fucking up. Maybe he could just—enjoy the moment as the afterglow slowly faded. That's what people did, wasn't it? It was practical, when one needed to catch one's breath, and Sebastian had just left him out of breath and absolutely wrecked and was now sprawled contentedly on top of Wesley like there was nowhere he would rather be.

Wesley needed to say something and quickly, before he had a feeling about that. "Not an hour ago you couldn't hold your magic back in a crowded lounge, and now you've managed to perfectly wield it with a cock in your mouth. Quite the improvement."

"Because a very handsome and thoughtful viscount took me up to the top of Manhattan to let go," Sebastian said. "I couldn't have done it without being more in control of my magic, so it's actually the viscount's fault, if you really think about it."

Wesley had to smile. "So I did all of this to myself, is that what you're saying? I'm reaping what I sowed—"

Wesley cut himself off, but it was too late. Shit. He was most certainly having a feeling *now*.

"You had it coming," Sebastian said, blithely unaware

of Wesley's internal crisis. Then his gaze turned more serious. "If you ever don't want me to use magic—"

"Oh, Christ," Wesley muttered. "Are we seriously going to have this patently unnecessary conversation?"

"It's *important*—"

"If I ask you to stop, will you stop?"

"Always." Sebastian said it like a vow.

"Then that's settled," said Wesley. "Good talk."

Sebastian snorted. His waves were in disarray from Wesley's fingers. The deep green of the robe brought out the warmth in his olive skin. He was tracing patterns on Wesley's chest, a bit of ink peeking out from under the cuff of the robe. The top of the rampant lion, clear to Wesley's eyes and his alone.

And it was fine, all of it, Wesley could handle this, because afterglow wasn't *cuddling* and it wasn't *sentiment*. It was—it was a no man's land between sex and everything else, where touch and perhaps even a fleeting feeling was allowed. No need for these internal crises over it.

Wesley brushed his fingers over the stubble on Sebastian's jaw. "I would make any number of depraved faery bargains to have you inside me, preferably an hour ago, but I'd settle for now."

Sebastian's smile was fond and a tiny bit wicked, and then they were kissing again.

Chapter Eleven

"Sebastian, get up. Get *up*."

The urgency in Wesley's voice woke Sebastian with a start. He blinked for a moment, disoriented and lost. He could hear shouting out in the hall and pounding on their door.

And then, he smelled it.

Smoke.

"Come on." Wesley was pulling him from the bed to his feet, his grip tight.

The pounding on the door intensified. "Sir, you have to evacuate, everyone on the floor needs to get out."

Somewhere in the hall, a woman shrieked.

"Why is it always fire?" Wesley was scrambling into his silk striped pajamas, yanking the shirt over his head.

"Sir!" The voice came at the suite's door again, tinged with panic. "We're evacuating!"

"Clothes," Sebastian started, but Wesley was already throwing his robe Sebastian's way. Sebastian hastily pulled it on as Wesley strode to the hotel suite's door and opened it a couple inches.

"I'm up, I'm leaving," he barked at the man on the other side. "Go wake the next room."

The smell of smoke was worse with the door open. Sebastian grabbed his shoes in one hand. He waited a beat for Wesley to go first, and then followed out into the hall. The smoke hung thick in the air of the hall, and he couldn't tell where it was coming from. There was no heat he could make out, no crackling of flames indicating the source.

He frowned, his magic automatically rising up—

Wesley's hand closed on his sleeve. "Not the time."

"I just—"

"No excuses. I felt my knees weaken, I know what you almost did." Wesley tugged him down the hall, his voice a sharp whisper. "I'm aware your magic has a hair trigger these days, but I need to be able to move. Come on."

Sebastian wanted to protest, but Wesley's voice had a new edge. Their encounter with the fire paranormal Mercier had been only weeks ago; it was understandable Wesley didn't want to be rendered helpless near flames.

They both turned, not for the wide stairs to the lobby but for the narrow staff stairs that led up to the next floor. But a man in a housekeeping uniform blocked their path.

"Sirs, you need to go outside."

"But the people upstairs—" said Sebastian.

"We don't need a panic," the man said. "Fire's contained on this floor. NYFD is here to search for the source, then we'll let everyone back into their rooms." He pointed to the staff stairs. "That goes down to the sidewalk and outside. You two are the last on the floor, go."

Sebastian yanked the robe as tightly closed as he could. The stairs were cold against his bare feet as he followed behind Wesley in his slippers. The steps bottomed out in a concrete space with a heavy door. Wesley shouldered it open, and chilled wet air swirled in.

The displaced—and displeased—guests were crowded on the sidewalk, most of them in quality robes and pajamas. There was a white woman with her red hair in rollers, black silk peeking out from her robe; a circle of white men in dressing gowns gesturing with cigarettes. Staff in hotel uniforms were weaving in and out of clusters of guests, trying to soothe angry tempers. Everyone seemed to be snappish and arguing. Sebastian huddled deeper into the robe and gingerly stepped out to the sidewalk.

He followed Wesley to a spot just past the crowd. "What a fucking mess," a man behind Sebastian was saying. "A fire on our floor; damned lucky it didn't spread."

The rain was more of a cold mist than actual droplets, but the sidewalk was damp and chilled. Sebastian grimaced as he awkwardly balanced on the hotel's exterior wall so he could slide his wet feet into his shoes. He looked up at Wesley, who had his arms folded. He had to be freezing in nothing but the silk pajamas, but he simply looked irritated.

Sebastian's pockets felt unusually light, and a second later he realized why. "I forgot the brooch." He winced. "It's in the pocket of my waistcoat, in your closet."

Wesley took a breath through his nose. "I didn't think of it either."

Sebastian gritted his teeth. Perhaps the fire had thrown him too, but he shouldn't have left the brooch behind, should have kept his head. "I need to go back up."

"They're handling the fire. You'll just be thrown out again."

"But—"

"And your special abilities are right off the table. You can't knock down the firefighters, that's not going to do anyone any good, and if you're up there when they can't fight the fire, you'll be in danger too. So you're not running back upstairs for that relic."

"It could be stolen—"

"We should be so lucky," Wesley said flatly.

His shoulders were tighter than normal. Sebastian didn't argue about the brooch needing a murder too; he let it go, for the moment. The brooch was tucked away; someone would have to know about it and be searching their things to find it.

Wesley jerked his chin to the left. "There's your Miss Matilda."

Sebastian glanced down the sidewalk. Matilda from the bar was there, although she was still fully dressed, smoking cigarettes with the bartender from the lounge and two other flappers. She glanced back at Sebastian and gave him a wink.

"And now she's flirting with you, because this is exactly what I needed, for my night to somehow become more trying," Wesley said. "Think you can charm her into a smoke for me—"

Wesley cut himself off as his expression flickered with the closest thing to nerves Sebastian had ever seen on him.

"Fine!"

Fuck. Major Langford was making his way toward them from the crowd. The last person who could be trusted to see a man with Wesley, and Sebastian was at his side wearing nothing but a too-big robe embroidered with Wesley's initials.

Sebastian jammed his arms around himself and over the *WC* just as Langford strode up to them.

"Fine!" Langford said again. "Where's your dressing gown, man, there are ladies here."

"Being cleaned," Wesley lied easily. "Dashed nuisance, the timing. I thought you were staying at the Waldorf?"

"I was told to find somewhere cheaper. Figured this place must be all right if it meets your viscount standards." Langford's gaze went to Sebastian, sharp-eyed and fully awake. "Your advisor got caught out here too?" His gaze flicked to the bare skin Sebastian knew would be visible under the robe's collar. "Mr. de Leon. I thought *you* said you were staying upstairs. They only evacuated the second floor."

Sebastian tightened his arms over the monogram on his chest. "Um—"

"Christ, major, have a bit of subtlety," Wesley said, dry and unruffled. "Obviously he was in someone else's room. No need to be crass about it when, as you say, there are ladies present."

Langford's gaze flicked down the street to the group of flappers and landed on Matilda. "Oh. I see." Some of his suspicion cleared up, although the eyes on Sebastian were still unfriendly. He pulled a pack of cigarettes from his robe, jerking his head toward Wesley. "Couldn't wait to escape his company, eh? Not a bad job for you, is it, chasing skirts on his dime?"

Sebastian clenched his jaw. *I like his company*, he wanted to say. *And you're an asshole*, he wanted to say even more. But he was already risking revealing Wesley's secrets just by standing there, so he kept his mouth shut. Langford could think whatever he wanted about Sebastian if it kept him from wondering about Wesley.

Langford lit up and passed the pack and matches to Wesley in a reflexive way, like it was an old habit he'd fallen back into. "Fine, now. Never seen him meet a bird he likes."

"As if I would condemn a woman to my presence." Wesley had pulled out his own cigarette and handed the pack back to Langford.

"Not gentle enough for the gentler sex, Fine here," Langford said, gesturing with the cigarette.

Sebastian took a breath through his nose. Blew it out.

"But it'd be a shame to see you married," Langford went on. "So many *better uses* for a man with your talents."

"Yes, there are." Wesley lit his own smoke. "Imports, for example."

Langford smiled around his cigarette with no humor in it. "We really do need to have that chat, Fine. You have no idea how much we need a man as bad as you."

"He's not."

Sebastian hadn't realized he'd spoken aloud until Langford and Wesley had both turned his way. Shit.

"You don't think so?" Langford said lightly.

Sebastian's eyes darted up to Wesley, whose face was unreadable. "No." Sebastian swallowed. "No. I don't."

A new voice suddenly said, "Lord Fine?" A man in a hotel staff uniform was addressing Wesley. He had a clipboard and pencil in his hands. "If I could have just a moment to confirm any valuables in your rooms?"

Wesley blew out smoke in an irritated stream and turned to the man.

Langford took the cigarette out of his mouth, eying Sebastian. "American army, you said? Medical?"

Sebastian didn't answer, just kept his eyes on Langford and his arms tight over the monogram.

"All right, medic." Langford made the title an insult. "You think you know bad men better than me?"

Sebastian stayed still.

Langford tilted his head. "You ever see combat? Real violence?"

Sebastian took another breath through his nose. Even after the rooftop with Wesley, his magic was now simmering too close to the surface again, anger at Langford making it hard to keep the reins. He had too many bad memories from New York, had seen too much violence, been full of helpless anger then too.

"Not clean up the aftermath," said Langford, "but all that blood and gore happening right in front of your face—or at your own hands?"

Don't listen to him. You can't snap back and make him wonder about Wesley. You can't let him take you back to February.

"You ever had no choice but to do things civilians could never stomach?"

Sebastian bit down on his tongue, hard.

Langford leaned in. "I promise, nothing you can think of compares to Fine and I in the war," he said. "So you don't know shit. I know bad men, while a man like you will never know what men like us have been through or what we're capable of."

"Langford." Wesley had turned back to them, his tone knife-sharp.

But Sebastian was already backing up. He couldn't be here, couldn't risk losing his magic around all the guests, or losing his composure and revealing Wesley's secrets. He reached for a story that would help Wesley's cover. "I'm going to check on Matilda."

Wesley's expression flickered. "Sebastian—"

"All clear!" a man yelled, from down the sidewalk.

"Christ, finally," Langford said.

Wesley's eyes were on Sebastian. Sebastian cleared his throat. "I'll see you in the morning, Lord Fine."

And as the crowd pushed forward, he stepped backward, losing himself behind the bodies. Sebastian waited, arms shielding the monogram and holding the robe shut tight, as the crowd flowed around him. He waited for the last of the people to go in before he trailed in behind the other grouchy guests in their various night clothes.

Langford and Wesley were nowhere to be seen in the lobby, but at least a dozen snapping people were packed around the front desk. Sebastian stood off to the side, but when the desk clerk looked his way, he gave the room number on six. "Do you happen to have a spare key?"

The harried clerk shoved it at him and went back to the angrier guests.

Sebastian took the stairs up to six, avoiding the elevator, and let himself into the room he'd been in briefly with Mateo.

It was dark and silent, nothing but the trunk for show, since half his clothes were in Wesley's trunk now. Cold too, from the window Mateo had left cracked to try to chase out the smell of old smoke. The curtains were open, framing the lights of the building across the street. Six stories down on the street, cars were still puttering past, the city refusing to sleep, because he was back in Manhattan, like he'd been in February.

You ever see real violence?

Sebastian shook his head to get rid of the echo of Langford's voice. He sat on the edge of one of the single beds and pulled the chain on the light, flooding the room with yellowish glow. He caught sight of his reflection in the mirror, and winced. Between the rain on the roof and a night in Wesley's bed, his waves were a wild mess, paired with a stubbly jaw and deep shadows under his eyes that were ever-present these days from the brooch.

The brooch that was, of course, still in Wesley's closet, but was Major Langford staying on Wesley's floor? Would he see Sebastian, if he went back down? It was nearly two; too late for a suspicious man to believe business associates were at work and Sebastian had already put Wesley far too at risk because he couldn't keep his feelings to himself.

So he couldn't join Wesley now. He had to stay and sleep here, where there was no Mateo in the room anymore, no familiar paintings or anything else to anchor him or remind his blood it was free. Just a cold room with thin blankets, and the lights and sounds of New York, where he'd hurt countless others while under blood magic.

All that blood and gore happening right in front of your face—or at your own hands?

Sebastian's magic was still too close to the surface, like horses straining at their reins. If Wesley hadn't taken him up to the roof, he would have lost control completely down on the sidewalk. How welcome it would have been to see Wesley now; he was the only thing that made New York bearable.

Sebastian hadn't had a blood terror since York. But every night since then, he'd had Wesley, warm and solid, a constant reminder against his skin that the blood magic was gone.

But Wesley was probably asleep by now, probably sick of Sebastian's clinginess and enjoying having a bed to himself. Or maybe he was angry, because Sebastian had almost let his temper get away and revealed Wesley's secrets to Langford.

More reasons Sebastian didn't get to use Wesley as

an anchor, not tonight. He'd have to accept that tonight
there was a risk of blood terrors. He used to accept that
risk every night, back when he'd been resigned to it,
had known every night brought the potential for that
horror, that he might wake up trapped in his own body,
unable to move, with no idea how long it would last.

He just hadn't realized how desperately he didn't
want to go back to that place.

*You ever had no choice but to do things civilians
could never stomach?*

Sebastian shoved Langford's voice out of his head,
because if he thought about that any closer, his magic
would escape and he'd have the sixth floor on the
ground. Maybe he could sleep in Wesley's warm robe
tonight. Maybe all this extra magic would keep the
blood terrors away.

Unless having more magic made it worse. Or unless
it was like the relics themselves, and the longer they had
been buried, the stronger they'd gotten.

Maybe he was in for the worst blood terror he'd ever
had, the next time they came back.

He abruptly moved from the foot of the bed to the
nearby chair. He had letters to write, a book he could
read. He could keep the window open, take off the robe,
and he'd be cold enough to stay awake until he was
ready to try sleep.

Or he could just not sleep at all.

Chapter Twelve

Wesley's spine felt tight enough to snap as Langford walked beside him back to the suite. "Finally," Langford was saying. "The things I have to tell you—"

"He was a prisoner of war."

"What?"

Wesley stopped in front of his suite door, turning to face Langford. They were the same height, their eyes level. Langford's were the color of ice. Wesley suspected his own were even colder. "Sebastian," said Wesley, "was a prisoner of war."

Langford's lips thinned. "Did he claim that's his past? Because that's obviously bullshit. A soft ladies' man like that—"

"He's not lying."

"He's not a man you can trust. Use your head, Fine. Think how damned convenient it was of your last valet to show up right when you needed one—and how damned convenient it is that Mr. de Leon showed up right when you needed a Spanish speaker."

"Is *that* what this is actually about? You think he's a charlatan, like Chester was?" Wesley scoffed. "You're laughably off. We're not in the army anymore, and I'll say it to your face: your comments were out of line."

Langford's eyes narrowed. "Speaking of Mr. de

Leon," he said, too lightly. "He made me think of that other Spaniard you were so fond of. Reyes was his name. You remember him and Private McGregor, don't you?"

Wesley stilled. A rhetorical question; Langford, of course, knew he remembered.

"After I met Mr. de Leon, I thought, *whatever happened to those two*?" Langford said easily. "So I cabled home, asked the office to look into it."

Wesley's stomach didn't drop; it hardened like stone. Infatuated idiot children, he'd never wanted to hear they were dead—

"Turns out," Langford went on, still easy, "they're in Edinburgh."

Wait—what?

"Couple of injuries on the front, but they made it, the both of them," Langford said. "Doing all right for themselves, actually. Reyes writes for the paper and McGregor became a chemist." He smiled coldly. "They're flatmates—isn't that a coincidence."

They'd survived. But what was Langford doing? "Why would you have the War Office look them up?" Wesley said lowly.

"To remind you that when you insisted I listen to you, I did," Langford said. "So when I say now that you need to watch your back around your Spanish friend, you need to fucking listen to me."

Wesley kept his expression still. He put a hand on the doorknob. "I'm going to bed."

Langford's eyes narrowed. "Don't you want to hear why you shouldn't trust your friend?"

"No," Wesley said shortly. "I don't."

"You're changed, Fine." Langford's lip curled in a

way that made it clear he didn't think it was for the better. "You're not the Wesley Collins of the war anymore."

"Most people would consider that a blessing."

"Then they wouldn't know shit," Langford said. "Captain Collins was cold enough to handle a German spy. Saved a lot of lives. I don't think Lord Fine would be up to the task."

"Remind me, major," Wesley said, light and dangerous. "Who was it who gave that order?"

"You know why it had to be you," Langford said, without remorse. "You were the only one I could trust to be ruthless enough to do what had to be done."

Wesley tightened his jaw. "Good night," he said pointedly, and went into his suite, shutting the door firmly behind him.

It seemed very still inside. As still as Sebastian's face as Langford baited him with no idea the depth of the wounds Sebastian hid. Men like Wesley and Langford wore their scars on the outside, where everyone could see and know to keep their distance. Sebastian kept his inside, where they couldn't hurt anyone else.

I'll see you in the morning, Lord Fine.

Sebastian wasn't coming back tonight. Of course he wasn't; he wouldn't risk anything that might raise Langford's suspicions. Maybe he didn't even *want* to see Wesley tonight. Maybe he was finally realizing that Wesley was every bit as bad as Langford said and he should cut his losses now. Maybe he'd already gone to sleep, like a man with sense, because he didn't care what Langford said and he didn't need Wesley.

Wesley rubbed his temple. He was fooling no one; he had no idea how to have a relationship. He was inevitably going to ruin this one, and he'd be lucky if it hadn't happened tonight.

He did a quick search of the room, checking for the brooch as well as his own valuables, jeweled cuff links, his wallet, his watch. He lingered at the closet, eying his suit jacket and Sebastian's waistcoat with a small frown. Still, the brooch was in its place in the waistcoat pocket, and that was ultimately what mattered. Wasn't it?

He stepped back. The bedroom—the entire suite—felt silent and empty. Sebastian wasn't a loud person, but his presence transformed Wesley's spaces like having the fireplace lit on a winter's day. Except Sebastian wasn't coming back to warm Wesley's rooms, because Langford was on this floor, and he wouldn't do anything to put Wesley's reputation at risk. Langford would probably be delighted if he knew he'd succeeded in keeping Sebastian away.

With a jerky movement, Wesley grabbed his cigarettes and matches out of his jacket.

But as he turned, his gaze fell across the room, to where Sebastian's extra blanket was rumpled on his side of the mattress. He could almost see their ghosts in the bed, Sebastian curled up sound asleep against Wesley's side, Wesley pretending he didn't crave that touch more than he craved cigarettes.

Wesley abruptly shoved the cigarettes and matches back in his jacket pocket. He reached into Sebastian's jacket instead, fingers closing around the key to the room on six he'd pretended to share with Mateo. He then took Sebastian's waistcoat off its hanger, folding it around the brooch so he wouldn't make contact.

He turned to leave, and then he paused and looked back at the bed.

Three minutes later, he was walking out of the suite, still in his pajamas with a key in his shirt pocket, and the waistcoat and the extra blanket folded in his arms.

Langford didn't want Wesley to be with Sebastian. Sebastian didn't want Wesley to risk his reputation in front of Langford. Too bad for them that Wesley didn't listen to anyone except himself.

Up on six, he found the room, and unlocked the door. He eased it open as quietly as he could, because it was two in the morning and Sebastian was certainly asleep.

Except the light was on. And Sebastian was in the chair by the window, a book on the table that looked unread. He was dressed in only underclothes, a T-shirt and shorts, and as he looked toward the door, he blinked in confusion. "Wesley?"

Wesley came into his room, dropping his stack on the bed farther from Sebastian's chair. "You're still awake."

Sebastian dropped his gaze. "I wasn't really tired."

"And you didn't come back to the suite because of Langford?"

"I didn't know if the major was with you, or watching you."

"And that's the only reason?" Wesley pressed, because if Sebastian had finally realized Wesley wasn't the man he thought he was, better to hear it now, before his stone heart had any more cracks.

Sebastian definitely wasn't meeting Wesley's eyes now. "Well, you know."

"Maybe I do," Wesley said, as evenly as he could. "But spell it out."

Sebastian glanced at him, then away again. "I thought you'd be happy to finally get a bed to yourself again. And that you might be mad at me."

Oh.

There was nothing passive-aggressive in his tone. He seemed subdued and closed off, reminding Wesley of their early days together, only guarded politeness for everyone because Sebastian didn't know if someone's next words or actions were going to hurt. Gutting, really, to see those walls back up for him.

Sebastian drew his legs up onto the chair. "I'm sorry I couldn't keep my mouth shut around Langford."

"You think you owe me an apology?" Wesley was crossing over to him before he realized he'd started moving again.

"You said he works for the War Office now. He could make trouble for you. I could have ruined everything for you tonight."

Wesley stopped in front of the chair. Sebastian's arms were tight around his knees, the goose bumps on his arms visible in the lamplight. Wesley could see the green robe carefully folded on top of the dresser. Why the hell was he barely dressed and freezing in this chair?

"Langford should not have said those things to you," Wesley said.

"He's an asshole," Sebastian said. "And he shouldn't say the things he says about *you*."

Langford had hurt Sebastian because Sebastian had made himself a target, speaking up against him, and for what? To defend *Wesley*? "You really have to stop thinking you need to defend my honor. It's not only unnecessary but also pointless."

"It's not *pointless*," Sebastian said. "Langford doesn't know what he's talking about. He acts like you're heartless, like you want to be cruel, but that's not who you are. And now he keeps throwing the past in your face like the war doesn't haunt you."

And this was it, right here. This was why this magical thing he had with Sebastian was never going to last, because Sebastian turned everything around to find the kindest ways to see Wesley, and refused to listen to the truth about who Wesley really was.

"I know you don't want to hear this, but everything Langford says about me is true," Wesley said tightly. "But it's hardly surprising, since you refuse to see me through anything but those rose-colored glasses."

Sebastian's expression didn't change, but Wesley caught the flash of hurt in his eyes. "It must be the rose-colored glasses." His voice was barely louder than a whisper. "After all, how would I know anything about bad men?"

That brought Wesley up short. "Langford was out of line," he said. "I told him that."

Sebastian's voice was still quiet. "But you think he knows what he's talking about and I don't."

"No, that isn't—" Wesley uncharacteristically stumbled on his words. "That isn't how I mean it. You've been at the mercy of men that would make Langford and I piss ourselves with fright. I've never met anyone who knows evil like you."

Sebastian shook his head. "It can't go both ways."

"What does that mean?"

"You say I know evil better than Langford. But I'm saying that's he's wrong about you, and you won't listen to me."

Wesley's protest died on his lips. Because he *was* siding with Langford, dismissing Sebastian's past just like Langford had. Worse than Langford, because Wesley knew what Sebastian had survived and was still acting like it didn't count.

"But I know why you listen to him." Sebastian hugged his knees tighter to himself. "It's not because he's right. It's because Langford is the one who's as mean to you as the thoughts in your head."

Wesley winced. He was a man who prided himself on having no delusions, on facing any hard truth about himself.

But he had not been ready to hear that.

"But your thoughts aren't true either," Sebastian said. "And I can't change them tonight, but I also can't let you tell me Langford is right, not about this. Because I do know what I'm talking about. And I'm not the one who sees things the wrong way."

Wesley so rarely found himself at a loss for words. But for all he claimed to think with cold rationality, he'd forgotten that kind didn't mean gullible, that soft wasn't sheltered and sweet wasn't naïve.

"Sebastian," Wesley started, and then stopped. He ran a hand over his face. "I think I owe you an apology."

Sebastian shook his head, legs still tight to his chest. "You don't need to say sorry. You weren't trying to hurt me, you were trying to hurt yourself."

"It doesn't matter if you were the target or collateral damage," Wesley said.

"It's okay—"

"It isn't," Wesley said, sharp enough Sebastian furrowed his brow. "It's not *okay*, because I'm not *okay* with you getting hurt."

Sebastian swallowed. His gaze darted to the side and he blinked. "You brought a blanket?"

"Well." Wesley cleared his throat. "You were concerned about the brooch, so I was bringing that up. And obviously whatever blankets you had in here weren't going to be enough. Although then, of course, I find you like this." He gestured at Sebastian, still curled in a tight ball on the chair. "You're by an open window on a cold night in barely any clothes. You even took off the robe. It's almost like you're purposefully trying to be cold."

Sebastian made the tiniest flinch.

Wesley paused. "Come to think of it," he said suspiciously, "it's *exactly* as if your entire plan was to be cold."

Sebastian bit his lip. "Um."

"Why? And don't make something up, I know full well how much you hate the cold. Obviously you have a reason. How were you planning to sleep like this?"

Sebastian's shoulders hunched.

And Wesley recalled Sebastian's words from a few weeks back, the first night they'd spent together in York.

I'm not a good sleeper.

Wesley had woken to find Sebastian caught in a blood terror not long after that.

"Were you not planning to sleep?" said Wesley. "Why not? Do you actually think you might still have blood terrors?"

Sebastian hunched farther into the chair. "I don't know."

"You don't *know*? You haven't had one in weeks."

Sebastian looked away. "That's true."

"So aren't they gone?"

Sebastian still wasn't meeting his eyes. "I don't know," he said again, "because I also haven't slept alone in weeks."

"Wait." Wesley leaned forward. "You think you haven't had a blood terror because you've been sleeping with *me*?"

Sebastian shrugged jerkily. "I used to break the terrors with something familiar, to remind my blood that the magic is gone and I'm free now. And I—well. I think I always remember I'm free when I have you."

Wesley's heart did a funny twist in his chest as the way Sebastian stayed close in his sleep took on new meaning. "Why haven't you said anything?"

"What was I supposed to say? *I'm a mess who might still get magical nightmares, and you have to sleep with me because I think you're keeping them away?*"

Wesley could not let himself have a feeling about that, because then they would come and never stop. "Yes, say that exactly," he said brusquely. "And I'll say *all right, duck, I can do that.* Problem solved. Why are we having this conversation? Why would you ever risk putting yourself through one of those if I can keep it away?"

"What if Major Langford was watching your door?" Sebastian said heatedly. "I was supposed to risk him finding out all your secrets because I'm too broken to sleep alone? When you don't even like having me there, and only put up with it for me?"

Wesley drew a sharp breath. And then he said, "Get in the bed."

"What? Wes—"

"Now." Wesley grabbed his hand and pulled. Sebastian stumbled to his feet, but Wesley was already tugging him down on the bed. "Move up. Head on the pillow."

"Wesley—"

"Don't argue, I am shit at having feelings or knowing the right words to say so just—please. Get in the bed."

Sebastian furrowed his brow. But he shifted up the mattress as Wesley grabbed the blanket he'd brought, and the blankets off the other bed for good measure.

He turned off the light, and moments later, all of the blankets were piled on top of them as they lay on their sides, facing each other but not touching. The city lights still filtered through the window, just enough to see by. Wesley's heart was beating uncomfortably hard. This was a new door he was walking through and there was nowhere to hide right now. Sebastian was awake, could see for himself that Wesley was useless at this, didn't know how to touch a man if they weren't fucking.

"There's a difference between not liking something and being too cowardly to admit you like something." Wesley's voice was unsteady. "I came up because the bed looked empty without you."

Christ, he'd gotten everything wrong tonight. Every interaction was like a test he inevitably failed and he couldn't bear to fail with the person who mattered—

Sebastian moved into Wesley's arms.

Wesley stilled.

"I'm so glad you came." Sebastian pressed his face against Wesley's shoulder, the chill of his skin marked even through Wesley's silk pajamas. "You're right, I'm so cold and I hate it."

Wesley let out a breath. He should have known Sebastian would never make anything a test.

"I know you do." Wesley's voice was gruff, his hand finding the soft fabric of Sebastian's T-shirt, balling it up in clenched fingers and then letting go. "And you need to get it in your head that you don't need to handle everything alone anymore."

He was being too sharp again, but Sebastian pressed closer. "Okay," he said quietly, into Wesley's pajama shirt.

Wesley's hand slipped under Sebastian's T-shirt, over cold skin. "How do I warm you fastest?"

Sebastian rolled over, still under Wesley's arm, and squirmed backward so that his back was pressed against Wesley's chest, his hips and arse tight to Wesley's body as their legs tangled together. He pulled Wesley's arm more snugly around him, like it was another blanket, and their bodies suddenly aligned like two halves of a locket. "Like this."

They fit together like puzzle pieces, so perfectly there was no room for Wesley's doubt. Wesley's heartbeat was still too fast but it wasn't uncomfortable anymore. He also should have remembered that not all new doors lead somewhere miserable. New doors had led him here.

Wesley tentatively let his head relax against the pillow, which brought his nose closer to Sebastian's hair. "Your skin is like ice, I hope you know," he said, because his thoughts were too raw to voice.

"I know," said Sebastian, "but I'll warm up now that I'm with you."

He sounded so much better than he had, content, maybe even happy, and Wesley felt some of his tension bleeding away. He couldn't be irreparably fucking up if Sebastian was happy, could he?

Sebastian was tucking his legs under one of Wesley's. "I know you say you don't cuddle, but you're so good at it."

And maybe Wesley had his own things to get straight in his head. Like that perhaps he didn't get everything wrong with Sebastian—perhaps being with him wasn't about expectations and hidden rules with rights and wrongs at all. Maybe this thing they had was theirs alone, and they could build it together however they wanted.

Wesley let out a quiet breath. "How do you make everything so bloody easy?"

"Wes," Sebastian said, infinitely sweet. "You're not hard."

Wesley tightened his arm, and this was convenient,

wasn't it? Lying like this, where it was so easy to touch Sebastian, to pull him closer?

"I do owe you an apology," Wesley said softly. "I know you're not some naïve ingenue who only sees roses because you've never known thorns. It's just, well." He swallowed. "I might believe in magic now, but life letting me keep you—that's a fairytale I suppose I haven't yet believed in."

Sebastian ran his fingers along Wesley's arm in a reassuring manner. "It's because you're looking at the fairytale the wrong way."

"Oh, you think I'm looking at this wrong too?"

"Yes I do," Sebastian said. "Because you are the innocent mortal and I am the devious fae who steals people away to faery realms, yes? So you're not keeping me. *I'm* keeping *you*."

Wesley snorted, his lips turning up in the smallest of smiles. "Is that how this works?"

"Yes, and see, now you can be as cynical as you want. Like, *well, of course I was captured by the bloody fae and can't escape, isn't that just how life goes*?"

A huffed laugh escaped Wesley. "Christ, you cannot do an English accent to save your life. And I think I resent that you knew just how to turn this around on me."

"I really don't have my head in the sand about who you are," Sebastian said. "I'm not a—what is that bird? Emu? No, ostrich. I promise I'm not an ostrich in rose-colored glasses."

Wesley groaned. "Why did you mix those metaphors? It's all I can picture now."

A laugh rolled through Sebastian and Wesley felt the rumble under his arm, against his chest. He let himself reach for Sebastian's wrist, his palm and fingers loosely encircling the tattoo that let only him see it.

They were quiet for a long moment.

"Although actually, ostriches would be cute in—"

"Stop right there and go to sleep."

There was another long moment of silence, and then Sebastian spoke again, very quiet. "Wes?"

"Yes?"

His voice was tentative. "I'm a mess who might still get magical nightmares. And you have to sleep with me because I think you're keeping them away."

Wesley swallowed thickly. "All right, duck. I can do that."

He could feel it as Sebastian let out a breath, and settled in against him. Could feel the rise and fall of Sebastian's chest as he breathed, could run his thumb over the tattoo and feel the answering shiver that ran through Sebastian. His hair smelled like soap under Wesley's nose, his limbs finally warming where their legs tangled together, the sleek lines of his back and hips and arse tight to Wesley's body and everything about this was, in fact, absolutely brilliant.

Why the devil had he been letting Sebastian do all the holding? Why hadn't Wesley known this would satiate his endless craving to touch, that the ceaseless clamor of his addiction and demons would quiet when his arms were full? Why the hell hadn't Wesley fucked him like this yet, where he could position Sebastian how he wanted, had all the access he desired to see and taste and touch—

Wesley cut the thought off, filing it away for another night. He settled into the pillow, Sebastian tight against him, and let himself fall asleep.

Chapter Thirteen

It was later than they'd planned to rise when they finally stirred. Sebastian got dressed, but Wesley didn't keep clothes in his trunk—or fit into his clothes—so he disappeared to sneak down to his suite.

Sebastian lingered by the window after Wesley left, tying his tie as he watched Grand Central Station six stories below. The morning was chilly and the glass was cold, but the sky was very blue and the sun bright where it lit the umbrellas of the street carts. The sidewalk was full of people: three Black men in sharp suits walking into the train station; two young Italian boys selling newspapers; a Jewish couple with a young daughter, each holding one of her hands. The window was still cracked open, the city sounds drifting up, puttering engines and the shouts of the vendors. Someone was playing an accordion nearby.

For the first time since he'd stepped off the ship, the city in the present wasn't competing in his head with the New York of February. He wasn't seeing echoes of Hyde and Shelley; instead, out the window, Sebastian saw a street he'd crossed yesterday, lugging Mateo's trunk to the train while Mateo badgered Wesley to buy them pretzels from a man with a big wicker basket.

Sebastian tucked the tie into his waistcoat. The

brooch in his waistcoat pocket still tugged at him miserably, but something else had eased. Maybe because he wasn't bracing himself for the inevitable night when Wesley wasn't there; Wesley knew Sebastian's suspicions about the blood terrors and was going to sleep with him to keep them away.

You need to get it in your head that you don't need to handle everything alone anymore.

Maybe he needed to think about that.

Sebastian made his way down to the lobby and found a chair in a quiet corner to wait for Wesley. He'd picked his outfit entirely based on what would fit best under the overcoat he didn't plan to take off. Wesley, of course, came down the stairs in a perfectly fitted three-piece suit, crisp white shirt, and walking stick.

"You do know Tarrytown is not, in fact, the country?" Wesley said, gesturing at Sebastian. "Although I will admit that tweed suits you so well you can get away with it." He dropped his voice a little lower. "And everything is as it should be with the brooch?"

Sebastian blinked. "Of course. Why wouldn't it be? Was something odd when you brought it up last night?"

"Well, I rather would have led with *darling, something seems to be amiss with your deadly enchanted antique jewelry*," Wesley said dryly. "Only—" He hesitated.

"What?"

"A small detail, that's all," Wesley said. "You hung your clothes first last night, when we came in from the rain, and you hung them next to each other. I hung my jacket later, and I thought I stuck it in to the side of your things. But when I got back to the suite, my jacket was between your waistcoat and your jacket."

Sebastian frowned. He touched his waistcoat. "Everything seems normal," he said, which Wesley would know meant *I still hate it but have no choice about carrying it.*

Wesley held up his wrist. "My cuff links were exactly where I left them, in plain view, and these are real emeralds. If someone had gone into my suite rifling around, why not take them? Why on earth would someone only look in the closet and shift clothing?"

"Could it have been Major Langford?"

"I suppose," Wesley said. "If he'd moved very quickly to get down to us outside. But for what? Looking for the brooch? I have a hard time believing he's secretly paranormal."

"He's definitely not," Sebastian said. "I would have felt his magic, when I lost control for that second in the smoking lounge. And he wouldn't have dropped his drink—I weaken only a paranormal's magic, not an aura like I do in others."

"I suppose it could be Sir Ellery, looking for the pomander," Wesley said.

"We saw him in Grand Central yesterday," Sebastian pointed out.

"Yes, but he could have been lying about where he was going," Wesley said. "Or he could have gone and come back. But if he's looking for a fifteenth-century pomander, why not take the fifteenth-century brooch?" He pursed his lips. "Maybe I got it wrong."

Sebastian shook his head. Wesley's memory was near-flawless. "If you remember the clothes hung differently, then they were hung differently."

"Normally I would agree," said Wesley, "but in fairness, there's nothing normal about my life these days and I was highly distracted last night. I very well could be misremembering." He gestured at the hotel desk.

"What do you think? Keep the rooms, leave our trunks here?"

"I don't think we want to be managing them while we're looking for the others," Sebastian said. "We can always come back."

Wesley arranged for the rooms while Sebastian did a round of calls from the front desk, just in case the others had come home the night before. But it was the same: no answers and no news. Their best lead was still the name of an inn Arthur had been at two days ago.

"You've got a cable, sir," the man at the front desk said, as they were wrapping up. He held the paper out to Wesley. "From London."

Wesley took it and gave it a quick read. Then he glanced at Sebastian. "It's from my footman, Ned. He says he didn't tell anyone where I'd gone because he knows I hate that."

Sebastian frowned. "So Sir Ellery lied?"

"So Sir Ellery lied," Wesley agreed, with a frown that matched Sebastian's.

They crossed the street from the Roosevelt to Grand Central. In the station, Sebastian bought a newspaper for Wesley and coffee for himself, and then they found their platform. It was mostly empty, the morning commute over, the afternoon rush not yet begun.

Their train car had no first class or compartments for privacy, so they shared a gold-upholstered bench in an open car with three other people. As the train began its journey north through the subway tunnels, Wesley stretched his legs out under the seat in front of him.

"Miss Robbins says they want to see us when we arrive in New York." His profile was reflected in the window as they sped past the dark walls of the subway tunnel. "Arthur checks out of the Horseman Inn in Tarrytown the morning of the day we arrived."

"But Arthur doesn't come back to the city and none of them are anywhere to be found," Sebastian said. "Where did they go from Tarrytown?"

"I suppose we're hoping to find out."

The train came out from the tunnels, and sunlight filled the car. Wesley fit his monocle into place and spread out the newspaper as they rumbled toward Harlem. He looked very proper, but Sebastian missed the reading glasses Wesley only wore in private.

"Do you want the window?" Sebastian asked.

"Why would I?"

"The Hudson Line goes along the river. There are mountains and the fall colors are supposed to be very pretty."

Wesley didn't look away from his paper. "Tempting. Oh wait, no it isn't, because I can do something actually useful with my eyes and read my newspaper."

Sebastian elbowed him. "It's autumn in New York. It's famous."

The train slowed as it approached the elevated 125th Street station. "Please," Wesley said with a scoff, pitching his voice low enough it wouldn't travel to the train car's other occupants. "The leaves only turn those pretty colors because they're having one last screaming hurrah before they meet their maker. Probably a metaphor for how pointless life is."

"*Or,*" Sebastian said, "the tree survives the winter, and it grows, and the leaves come back in spring, and you get little bird nests and squirrels and chipmunks. Maybe that's the metaphor."

"Chipmunks." Wesley turned a page of his newspaper. "You're trying to convince me life isn't shit by using metaphorical rodents?"

"Oh no, life can be pretty shit," Sebastian agreed. "But sometimes the things *in* life can be pretty cute."

Wesley's gaze darted to Sebastian, and then back to the paper. "Maybe one thing."

The city gave way to countryside and the wide expanse of the Hudson River on their left, and soon enough, Wesley was disembarking in front of Sebastian onto the Tarrytown platform in front of the new station building. The entire scene was obnoxiously picturesque, the glint of sunlight on tiny waves, the fiery autumn leaves that covered the hills rising from the riverbank.

Sebastian, however, wasn't actually looking at the scenery, but was pointing off to the side, to a parked car. "*Mira la gatita,* Wes, look how sweet she is."

By now, Wesley understood *mira, Wes,* along with *gato* and *gatito* and *gatito chiquito*, and sure enough, there was a black-and-white kitten under the car. "We're not stopping to find food for that cat."

"What if she's hungry?"

"*I'm* hungry. Get in the taxi, you soft touch, let's go."

The train left behind them as they climbed into the taxi idling at the curb. "The Horseman Inn," Wesley said to the driver, who nodded with a grunt.

Tarrytown was bigger than Wesley had expected, a proper town and New York satellite, although with none of Manhattan's new skyscrapers. The main street was a row of three- and four-story buildings with small peaked roofs, a mix of Tudor-styled sidings and red-brick. Smushed in with the pharmacies and delis and boutiques was a church, with a small green yard and a tall, thin steeple that stretched up nearly as tall as the tallest buildings.

The inn was sandwiched between two buildings near the end of the street. It had an arched entrance on the ground floor, under a red awning, and there looked to be a small eatery to one side, its windows lined with tables and people.

The taxi left them on the sidewalk and puttered away. "I suppose we start here," Wesley said, eying the inn speculatively.

"It doesn't look like a town hiding bootlegging operations." Sebastian was looking around. "But it's got easy access to the river and the city."

"Well, I'd like to finally get some damn answers," said Wesley. "But I wouldn't mind a drink."

Through the inn's door was a small lobby with a modest staircase at the back. A wooden counter ran along one side, across from an archway on the other side that lead to the adjacent restaurant. A white woman, perhaps forty or so, was behind the counter, going through a stack of papers. Wesley hung back and let Sebastian approach first, because one of them was far more skilled at being pleasant and getting people to talk, and it sure as hell wasn't Wesley.

"Good morning," Sebastian said politely to the woman, as he and Wesley approached the counter and gave their names. "We were supposed to meet a friend of ours here at your inn, but we got our dates mixed up and he may have already left. A tall man, with black hair, his name is Arthur Kenzie?"

"Oh, *him*, yes, he's an easy one to remember," said the woman. "There were four in his party. But they've been gone a couple days now."

"Do you remember what time of day they checked out?" Sebastian asked.

"First thing in the morning." The woman hesitated. "They didn't check themselves out, though; Mr. Kenzie sent someone round to handle the bill and collect their things. That was day before yesterday."

Wesley and Sebastian exchanged a look. "So you haven't actually seen any of them yourself for three days?" Wesley asked.

"I suppose not." The woman pointed through the archway, into the restaurant. "They had dinner here that night. I assumed they went back to the city early and arranged for the delivery service to handle the bags."

Sebastian frowned. "What delivery service?"

"Didn't catch the name," the woman said apologetically. "Three men in a company truck."

Three men. It seemed like a long shot, but Sebastian must have also had the same question about the three men they kept running into, because he pointed at Wesley. "Did any of them sound like him?"

"Oh no," she said. "Locals, certainly. They settled the tab and the rooms were in tip-top shape when I checked."

"So they left nothing behind?" Wesley asked.

"Well, just the telegram from Miss Robbins," she said, like they should have known. "That's why you're here, isn't it? You said your names were Lord Fine and Sebastian de Leon." She held an envelope out to them, and Wesley could see their names on the front.

He and Sebastian exchanged another look. "Ah yes, the *telegram*," Wesley said, as Sebastian took it. "Why else could we possibly be here?"

"For the American history, of course." She smiled at

Wesley. "We get a lot of aficionados coming through to see the sights."

For fuck's sake. "We're not sight-seers," Wesley said flatly.

"Well, you could also be here for the pie." The woman pointed to the restaurant next door. "After all, it is apple season."

"Apple season." Were the river views and fiery leaf-covered mountains not sufficient? How quaint did one town need to be? "We're also not here for pie."

"I might be here for pie," Sebastian said.

Wesley fixed him with a stare.

"And to read our telegram from Jade, of course," Sebastian hurriedly added. He tilted his head toward the restaurant. "It's logical to read it over lunch, yes? You like logic."

Wesley sighed but followed him through the arch-way into the restaurant next door.

Chapter Fourteen

DEAR LORD FINE AND SEBASTIAN STOP
MUCH TO TELL YOU STOP
MEET ME TONIGHT MIDNIGHT STOP
TRY ON A BOWLER AT HUDSON HABER-
DASHERS STOP

"What the hell is going on?" Wesley said, across the table, as Sebastian read over Jade's telegram again. "Who the hell are the Hudson Haberdashers? How the hell did Miss Robbins know we would be here and why the hell is there a tiny pumpkin on my table?"

"Halloween," Sebastian said. "Sorry, that's the only *hell* I can answer."

The Horseman Inn's restaurant was charmingly decorated for the season, with wreaths of fall leaves, barrels of apples, and a scarecrow by the door. Wesley seemed annoyed by all of it. "So Halloween is made into a *thing*, in America? Big enough the governor's son is throwing a masquerade?" He sighed. "A pity Mr. Zhang can't find us on the astral plane. I can't believe you're magic yet we're resorting to telegrams."

The waiter came to the table with their lunches and two pieces of apple pie for Sebastian. "Excuse me," Sebastian said, before he could disappear. "Have you ever heard of Hudson Haberdashers?"

The waiter suddenly wasn't meeting Sebastian's eyes. "Men's clothes and accessories. The company used to have a hat factory on the river before they moved it up to Beacon, but there's a shifty little shop east of here that still sells the hats. That's all I know."

"Oh," Sebastian said. The waiter still wasn't looking directly at him. "Do you have an address?"

"I'm sure I've never been there," the waiter said.

Across the table, Wesley narrowed his eyes. "Then how do you know it's *shifty*?"

"Well—I mean—it's not the best neighborhood, so it's *probably* shifty, right?" the waiter said quickly. "Who goes to those kinds of neighborhoods? Not me, no sir. You ask anyone, they'll tell you Ernie only goes to work and church."

Sebastian opened his mouth, but Wesley had already leaned forward. "We don't have all day." He set a five-dollar bill on the table and slid it toward the waiter with one finger. "Does Ernie go anywhere besides church *now*?"

Ernie's eyes were on the bill. "Oh, *Hudson* Haberdashers, right right, actually I do know the shop that sells those." He flipped the paper menu over and began to sketch out streets on the back with his pencil. "It's east of here. Don't go north to the old church and cemetery."

"What church and cemetery?" Wesley said impatiently.

"From 'The Legend of Sleepy Hollow.'" Ernie glanced up from the paper. "Aren't you tourists?"

Wesley's eye twitched.

"Thank you," Sebastian said hastily. He took the map

from Ernie and moved Wesley's hand off the bill. Ernie snatched up the money and disappeared.

Wesley pinched the bridge of his nose. "It's a cover for a speakeasy, isn't it? Miss Robbins is sending us to a speakeasy at midnight."

"Seems likely," Sebastian admitted. He wasn't an expert on haberdashers or speakeasies, but Ernie's map had included the alley next door to the hat shop and marked it with an arrow.

"Is this a bootlegging thing or a paranormal thing? Are we going to have drinks or are you lot going to strip naked and howl at the moon? Because if you're planning to take off your clothes, I *will* clear my schedule."

Sebastian snorted. He set the map down on the table. "But what are we going to do until midnight?" he asked, because they still had some hours to wait. "Do you want to go back to the city?"

"No, we're here, and it seems the others are too, even if they're hiding still," Wesley said grumpily. "Might as well stay and see if we can learn anything." He eyed Sebastian's plates. "Two pieces of apple pie?"

"That's right." Adopting an innocent expression, Sebastian pointed to the second plate. "Unless you wanted this one?"

Wesley gave him an unimpressed look. "And why would I?"

"Because it's good," Sebastian said, "and you don't let yourself have enough good things."

Wesley pursed his lips. After a moment, he reached across the table and pulled the plate over to his side. "The things I do when I'm with you." He took a small bite, chewed for a moment, then paused.

Sebastian propped his chin on his hand. A pause like that from Wesley was practically a sonnet. "Good, yes?"

"Don't be smug, that's my job," Wesley said, going back in with the fork.

After lunch, they walked the few blocks of Tarrytown's main streets, stopping in at the stores. The bookstore clerk had sold a stack of recent issues of *Argosy All-Story Weekly* to a short, scowling man with glasses three days ago. The man behind the deli counter thought he remembered a tall man with black hair coming in to buy several sandwiches, also three days prior—and he was willing to give Sebastian some scraps of meat, which earned a suspicious look from Wesley.

They stopped in a pharmacy down the street from the inn and found a clerk stocking the shelves with headache powders. Sebastian stood by a display of liniments as Wesley asked him, "What are the chances one could hire a car around here?"

"You've come in the wrong season to hire anything," the clerk said. "Half the town closes up for the winter at the end of September. You'd be better off going back down to the city."

Sebastian sighed, gaze going to a row of vitamin tonics like it had any answers for why the others had come to Tarrytown but vanished three days ago. Did they have the pomander relic with them, and had it not been safe to bring it back to Manhattan? But why not get in touch with them sooner? Why make Sebastian and Wesley chase them up here before sending a message?

He waited as Wesley bought more matches and a pack of the cheapest cigarettes, and they went back out to the street.

"Could they really not have left anything more than another cryptic telegram?" Wesley said, lighting up. "I'd like to broaden our search, but I doubt we have time to get back to the city, hire or hell, purchase a car, motor back up here and investigate all before midnight." He inhaled from the cigarette and grimaced. "This tastes uncannily as if someone collected discarded butts along the subway tracks and rolled them back into another smoke."

Sebastian cringed. "That bad?"

"I guarantee licking an exhaust pipe would be an improvement." Wesley blew out the smoke. "Truly the one thing in New York that has gone according to my wishes. I wanted something vile, and this exceeds my wildest hopes. But we still don't have a plan."

Sebastian made a face. "We do have another option," he admitted. "But it's not great."

"What's that?" Wesley said.

"We steal a car."

"Sebastian de Leon."

"I *said* it wasn't great."

"Is this how it actually works, in the paranormal world?" Wesley said. "You pretend to play by our silly mortal rules, humoring those of us without magic, but the second those rules are an inconvenience it's straight to grand larceny?"

"I just want to find out what's going on," Sebastian said.

"Wait." Wesley inhaled with a raised eyebrow. "I thought I was speaking in hyperbole, but you're perfectly serious. You would help yourself to a car if you thought you needed it, mortal laws be damned." He blew the smoke back out. "Why do I find that so attractive?"

Sebastian huffed. "You make it sound like a crime."

"Yes, darling," Wesley said, slow and patronizing. "Because it *is*."

Sebastian folded his arms. "If the owner knew about magic, don't you think they would let me borrow their car?"

"*Borrow* their car? Is that how you'd explain it when the police showed up and you knocked them down like dominoes?" Wesley tsked. "As much as I unexpectedly find this side of you criminally sexy—you see what I did there—I say we taxi over to this shop that sells the Hudson Haberdashers hats and see if we find anything. No need for larceny and other larks."

"We should go back to the train station first," said Sebastian.

"Oh, we should, should we?" Wesley tilted his head. "And why is that?"

"You know, to investigate," said Sebastian. That sounded convincing, didn't it? "Maybe the station master saw Jade or some of the others."

"You're suggesting that maybe the fellow who sees hundreds, possibly thousands of people a day, will remember the four we're looking for?"

"Um." Sebastian tried not to squirm. "It can't hurt to ask, yes?"

"Sure, duck," Wesley said, as he dropped the cigarette to the ground and stamped it out.

It was a short walk through the town and down to the train station at the banks of the Hudson. But as Wesley had predicted, the ticket master was less than impressed with their questions.

"You think I remember who came through my station three days ago?" the ticket master said. "I don't know a one of these passengers from Adam. I don't remember who was here an hour ago. In three minutes I won't remember *you*."

Summarily dismissed, they stood on the platform, gazing across the tracks to the Hudson River beyond. "I think we should go to the river before we go to the hat shop," Sebastian said.

"Why?" Wesley said dryly. "Have Arthur and the others suddenly become mermaids?" He paused. "Is that possible?"

"My friend Gwen controls the tide," Sebastian said. "And some paranormals with water magic can breathe underwater—"

"You realize how casually you glossed over *my friend controls the tide*, don't you?" Wesley interrupted. "You've lived and breathed magic to the point that a sentence like that doesn't even give you pause, but I promise, I am very much still stuck on it."

Oh. Sebastian could hear Mateo echo in his mind, *haven't you had any girlfriends without magic?* "You're taking it very calmly," he said encouragingly.

Wesley narrowed his eyes. "You're not patronizing me, are you?"

"No." Of course Sebastian wasn't. Was he? He quickly went on. "I don't think Arthur suddenly grew fins," he said. "I just think we should look around the station. To, um. See if there are any clues about the others."

"Oh please," said Wesley. "What kind of hapless rube do you think you're fucking?"

Sebastian winced. "I just—"

"You're looking for that cat who was here when we arrived," said Wesley. "I know that's why you sweet-talked that deli into giving you some scraps."

"Maybe those are for me," Sebastian protested.

"Really," Wesley said flatly. "And for what purpose do you require a pocket full of ham?"

"...a snack?"

"A snack." Wesley tilted his head back. "Do you understand who you're talking to? What a terrifying and unapologetic bastard I am? There is not a soul in London who would talk to me like I'm a child bumbling through the adult world of magic, or who would undertake this transparent attempt to wheedle me into something as frivolous as traipsing after a stray."

Sebastian held up his hand. "Five minutes," he promised. "Then we can go."

Wesley pinched the bridge of his nose, muttering something indecipherable about *handsome men*. "Five minutes. Not one second more."

They crossed over railroad tracks to the green space at the river's edge. It was mostly empty, save for an older Black couple sitting on a park bench overlooking the water.

Wesley looked up and down the Hudson River. "Miss Robbins said Brodigan broke the ice on this river once. *Accidentally*, the way a normal person might accidentally break, oh, say, a china plate." He shook his head. "Not that I see any evidence of that, or signs of the others at all."

Sebastian squinted down the river. "There's a lighthouse."

"Is it hiding an ex-quarterback and three paranormals of varying heights and temperaments?"

"Probably not." Sebastian put his back to the river so he could scan the park around them. "Do you see the kitten?"

"Why would I see a mangy alley cat when I am in no way looking for said mangy alley cat?"

"Because you might see her first," Sebastian pointed out. "You have better eyesight than me and you're so observant."

"No, sorry, not going to participate in Sebastian's Sanctuary for Squalid Strays, no matter how you flatter my ego."

"But I don't see her anywhere."

Wesley raised his eyes skyward. "This is exactly why handsome men are trouble."

"Because they...feed cats?"

"Because I take one look at you and my cock goes *fuck, he's stunning. Give him whatever he wants.*" Wesley grudgingly pointed toward a clump of bushes, and Sebastian caught a flash of black-and-white fur hiding under it. "Your beast is over there. Feed her if you must, but mind you catch up with me; we are trying to get some answers today."

The cat would only watch warily from under the bush, so Sebastian left the food for her and followed after Wesley, who despite his words had only gone a few meters away and then waited.

They fell into step together. "You know what's bothering me about all this?" Wesley said, as they headed up the hill. "Well, *one* of the things bothering me, there's quite a lot to bother one, isn't there? But look. All this, sneaking around—it doesn't seem like any of their styles. Miss Robbins and Mr. Zhang are far too affable and congenial to treat us like this, Brodigan too surly to bother with it, and Arthur in particular would never employ this kind of secrecy."

"Well," Sebastian said, trying very hard to sound casual talking about Wesley's extremely handsome and dashing ex-lover, "Arthur does hide the paranormal world very well."

"Yes, because he's nothing but a giant, football-playing mother bear," Wesley said, as they passed an artist painting the mountains and a young woman pushing a baby carriage. "When it comes to protecting his surly antiquarian and the others, he keeps his mouth shut. But cryptic telegrams aren't Arthur's style at all."

"Mmm," Sebastian said.

Wesley waved a hand. "He ought to be charging into the inn with all the forethought of an impatient bull. Demanding whatever it is they all supposedly wanted to talk to us about."

Sebastian nodded. "I'm sure you would know."

"Because I know him biblically, you mean?"

Sebastian stumbled.

"A nice man would be sensitive and indulge you dancing around it," Wesley said dryly, "but as we've established, I'm an absolute bastard. I also thought I established unquestionably that there is no reason to make any fuss over the past. I understand we're a stone's throw from Sleepy Hollow; if you'd like a hands-on demonstration that I'm over Arthur, I will happily blow you on Ichabod's bridge."

"*Wesley.*"

"I'm just making my position on this clear."

Sebastian came to a stop, sighing as he turned to face Wesley. "I thought I was doing a good job pretending to be normal."

"It was a good act, yes," said Wesley, also coming to a stop. "But Sebastian, I don't want an *act* from you. Pretending is what you do around other people. Not me."

Sebastian stared at him for a moment. "You really are sweet sometimes."

"None of that," Wesley said. "I'm simply saying there's no cause for you to be insecure."

Sebastian stared a moment more. And then he started to smile. "I shouldn't be insecure about other people?"

"No," Wesley said, more slowly and suspiciously. "Why?"

"Well, see, I can't remember." Sebastian tapped his lips. "What do you call it when you're sleeping with someone and you're not supposed to be insecure about other people?"

Wesley opened his mouth, then snapped it shut. "You think you're clever, don't you?"

"No really, Wes, what's it called? I think you should *spell it out for me*."

"Are you sure that's what you want?" Wesley said pointedly. "Because I haven't forgotten what you called it at the hotel yesterday."

Oh. Shit. Sebastian had let the word *boyfriend* slip. He quickly waved for a cab. "Did you know Ichabod's bridge isn't actually there anymore? They built a new one, I saw it in a flyer at the pharmacy."

"Oh no," Wesley said, deadpan. "Will I need to arrange our liaison on a different American landmark, then?"

"We could find a car with a big backseat," Sebastian said innocently, as the taxi pulled to the curb. "And you could let me borrow it."

"See, these are the moments when I remember you are, in fact, from a completely different world, and I'm not talking about Puerto Rico."

Chapter Fifteen

The hat shop *was* in a less reputable area, where the sidewalks were littered with trash and the buildings had grime built up on the bricks. There was a closed apothecary next to the hat shop with boards hiding its windows, while a pair of big white men in black suits leaned against the wall just to the side of the hat shop's entrance, their eyes on the street.

There was a cigar store and newsstand across the street from the shop, and Wesley and Sebastian ducked inside. Wesley pretended to browse the selection of pulp magazines in the front window as he watched the shop. "Not really the kind of place one expects to go for a bespoke tuxedo, but looks normal enough from the outside," he said. "Then again, so did the abandoned tobacco shop that hid the Magnolia." He raised an eyebrow as a squarish truck with a wooden bed full of crates pulled up to the curb in front of the hat shop's windows. "That is, however, quite a large truck to be carrying hats for a store of that size."

Sebastian was a respectful distance away—which was a pity—watching from under his cap as the driver hopped down from the truck. "The woman at the inn said the others sent a delivery truck to pick up their stuff."

"And then they told us to meet them here," Wesley added.

Sebastian tilted his head. "Can you tell what's in the crates?"

"No, but hello." Wesley stilled. "Look who it is."

Alasdair Findlay had just stepped out from the front doors of the shop, wearing a close-cut suit with a fedora over his ginger hair. He met the driver on the sidewalk, listening with his head cocked and a polite, if vacant expression.

"I think we can safely assume exactly what type of business this really is," Wesley muttered.

"Langford said he's the one who sent you the warning letter." Sebastian was frowning. "You think he knows Jade?"

"I'd like to say no."

"Why?"

Because both times we met, he couldn't keep his bloody eyes off you. "He just doesn't seem like her type of fellow."

"No, I guess he doesn't." Sebastian watched out the window. "So he hides his bootlegging behind textiles and hats?"

"It's a clever cover," Wesley admitted. "He's always going to have an excuse to be transporting crates by road or river, and when it comes to imports, he could fabricate plenty of excuses to visit Canada, and I hope you appreciate that pun as well."

Alasdair was now directing the truck to the alley next to the shop. "Should we go talk to him?" Sebastian asked.

"Not here," Wesley said. "If Langford is even half right about Sir Ellery, I don't want to risk it getting back to him that we're in town. We know they'll be at that masquerade tomorrow night, if we do want a confrontation, but if Alasdair and Sir Ellery know the pomander exists, I'd rather find the others first."

A few minutes later, Alasdair had climbed into a car and driven away. Wesley and Sebastian walked past the haberdashery, peeking through the windows, but all Wesley saw was racks of men's clothes, hats on the walls, a tall cabinet with glass doors that looked like it held cuff links.

They found a perfumery Jade had visited with Zhang, and a restaurant that remembered serving Arthur and Rory. But no one had seen them for at least three days.

One street over from the hat shop, set into a row of narrow, three-story buildings, was an inn with none of the charm of the Horseman Inn they'd visited in Tarrytown. It had peeling paint on the trim and the shades drawn in every slim, rectangular window. A small sign with flaking letters jutted over the sidewalk.

"Tomcat Lodge," Sebastian read. "I'm not sure people come here to sleep."

"Not at all." Wesley eyed it. "In fact, if I were going to imagine an inn where drunks could stagger from an illicit speakeasy and hire company for the night, it would look just like that."

"I bet they do a lot of business, thanks to Alasdair," Sebastian agreed.

They had a late dinner about a mile away in a much more reputable-looking establishment that had three kinds of apple desserts. With nowhere else to go until their appointment, they lingered until ten-thirty, and then walked back to the haberdashery. From the outside, the shop looked convincingly closed, although Wesley caught the occasional silhouette of a body moving behind the curtains.

They went around the alley where they'd seen the truck turn. The two large men who'd been standing outside the hat shop earlier were now lounging against the alley wall on either side of a door. The bigger one straightened up as they approached. "You two lost?"

"Shopping for bowler hats, actually," Wesley said sardonically. "We understand they can be acquired here late."

The bouncer relaxed. "You can talk to Eddie, then," he said, as he opened the door.

Muted jazz and laughter floated up into the alley. Wesley and Sebastian exchanged a look, but stepped through the door.

A set of steep stairs took them down to another door, guarded by a smaller man in a pinstripe suit, the pseudonymous Eddie, presumably. He had a mean look about him, like he had more than one knife stashed on him and would be happy to use any of them.

Eddie appeared less than impressed to see them. "You're not from around here."

"Thank God," Wesley said, which made Eddie's eyes narrow.

"We're here to see friends," Sebastian said, unruffled.

Eddie sized up Sebastian, the stylish flat cap, loosened tie, and of course, the outrageously pretty face. "You can come in, the ladies'll love you," said Eddie. "But his majesty here doesn't seem like the friendly type."

Wesley opened his mouth again, tired of this posturing, but Sebastian got in between them. "He's *my* friend," Sebastian said, before Wesley could speak. "He can come in with me, yes?"

Wesley folded his arms. Sebastian was apparently going to get another reminder that Wesley didn't need a paranormal riding in to his rescue.

"Hmph." Eddie was grudgingly stepping aside. "Welcome to Hudson Haberdashers. Enjoy your evening, gentlemen."

They stepped through the doors and into a crowd. The speakeasy was dimly lit by a handful of flimsy drop lights, with dark walls ringed with booths and a low ceiling that made the cramped space seem even smaller. On stage, the band was performing "Big Bad Bill"—not up to the level Jade's sister had been, certainly, but Wesley suspected few were. In front of the stage and around the club, round tables dotted the floor, most of them full. A trio of men had whiskey shots lined up on the bar to Wesley's right, and to the left, a flapper with a cigarette in a long holder was getting a light from another flapper in a sequined headband, their eyes on each other, neither paying any attention to the men who kept looking their way.

"Sebastian," Wesley said warningly, as they headed toward one of the few empty booths along the far wall. "I don't need protecting from a bouncer with an axe to grind."

"But this time we're not here for Oysters Rockefeller, we're here to meet paranormals," Sebastian said, intolerably earnest. "Shouldn't I look out for you if there could be magic?"

"*No.*"

They reached the booth, sliding in across from each other as a waiter made his way over from the bar. Wesley pulled out his vile American cigarettes and lit one up as the man came to the edge of their table.

"What are you fine fellows drinking tonight?"

"Tonic water, please," Sebastian said.

The waiter raised an eyebrow. "Why come here for that?"

"He's perfectly entitled not to drink and doesn't need your commentary on it," Wesley snapped. "I want a glass of the finest stuff in the house. Granted, my expectations are rock bottom, so that very well may be piss in a cup, but supposedly hope springs eternal."

"You two seem like loads of fun," the waiter muttered, disappearing.

Wesley leaned forward, smoke drifting up from the cigarette between his fingers. "Stop treating me like I'm made of glass. I can handle the consequences of my own sharp tongue."

"But—"

"I like your magic in bed. Doesn't mean you get to lord it over me anywhere else."

"*You're* the lord," Sebastian said impatiently. "I'm just—"

"Magic isn't everything." Wesley brought the cigarette to his lips. "I've seen you drained of it, just as helpless as any other man."

"That was once—"

"Twice."

"Twice?"

"The time you had to bring your brother back from his visions, and the time Blanshard took it from you."

"That's still only twice—"

"Three times, really," said Wesley, "if you count the time you passed out in the London alley."

"En serio? Pero mira, Wes, I was saving your life that time."

"Yes, and you barely knew me. What if I'd run and left you unconscious by Fenchurch station? Left you vulnerable to Mercier or any number of London's crooks?" Wesley exhaled smoke, and then ground the cigarette in the ashtray. He might not be able to resist lighting them up, but he could put them out before they were done. *Progress*, someone might say, if that someone were an insufferably perky twit. "You saved my life with no care for yourself that night. I need to be able to hold my own in your world, for *both* of our sakes, and that's not going to happen if you feel like you have to coddle me like you're my nurse."

Sebastian gave him a suspicious look. "Are you in a mood?"

"A bit, yes," Wesley said testily. "I've been jerked around since we docked in Manhattan and I still don't know what's going on. Paranormals are not winning favor with me right now."

"*I'm* a paranormal."

"And you're cosseting me worse than Lady Pennington with her Maltese, Powderpuff." Did Wesley sound *sulky*? Christ, everything about this was unacceptable.

The waiter reappeared, carrying a tray of drinks. He set one in front of Sebastian and one in front of Wesley. "Tonic water and top-shelf gin. Try not to party too hard, gents." He disappeared again.

Wesley picked up the gin, sniffed it, and grimaced. Top-shelf his arse; this was likely distilled in a bathtub. He tossed it back anyway; Prohibition didn't exactly give him room to be choosy.

Sebastian took a sip of tonic water, cringed, and set his own glass down. "This tastes off. I don't want to think about the state of the kitchen here," he said. "And I don't think you're Powderpuff."

"I should hope not, or you've been wildly reticent about your previous sex life."

"Wes."

"Might explain the affinity for animals, though."

"*Wesley.*" Sebastian leaned forward. "You are the smartest, most competent man I've ever met. You know you don't have to prove anything to me, yes?"

"I don't know anything of the sort," said Wesley. "You come from a completely different world, where you grew up with magic and a family legacy to protect those without it. And you don't know what to do with me."

He gestured to himself. "I can admit to my own shortcomings here. As I've told you, I've spent several years knowing I was the meanest, most powerful person in almost any room. Now the paranormal shoe is on the other foot, so to speak, and it's fantastical and thrilling and also humbling, and I am shit at being humbled."

"But you're doing great," Sebastian protested.

"And that, right there, is exactly it," said Wesley. "In my world, no one would dare say something to me as patronizing as *you're doing great*. In your world, you don't give a solitary fuck if I hold you at gunpoint. And I can admit I am not handling that with aplomb, but *you* are not making it easier by insisting on shielding me like *I'm* the delicate tropical flower."

Sebastian huffed. "I just didn't think you liked Eddie the bouncer—"

"Do I have to like someone to speak to them?" Wesley said testily. "If that were the case, I'd never utter a word to a single person on the planet besides you."

Sebastian propped his chin on his hand. "So you still

like me even though you think I treat you like Powder-puff?" he said ruefully.

Wesley snorted. "Do you still like me even though I just took you to task for ten minutes over it?"

Sebastian smiled, just a tiny bit sly. "You should have given the lecture in the bed again. I learn better that way."

"No you don't," Wesley said wryly, like Sebastian's words hadn't just made heat bloom in his core. "If you did, we'd hardly be having this conversation, would we?"

"I guess next time you'll have to lecture me harder," Sebastian said, with a straight-faced innocence that sent that heat stealing through Wesley's blood. Everyone else got quiet, polite Sebastian; only Wesley got this flirtier side, and it was headier than the gin.

"I know you don't try this shameless impertinence on anyone but me." Wesley leaned forward. "And before you get cocky, remember that the last time I *lectured* you, it was hard enough you lost control of your magic."

Sebastian gave him a dirty look. "We agreed we weren't going to talk about that again."

"No, *you* don't want to talk about it again," said Wesley. "*I* plan to bring it up in perpetuity. We'll be eighty years old and I'll still be teasing you—"

He hastily cut himself off. It was one thing to jest with Sebastian over what to call their relationship, quite another to assume they would spend decades together.

But Sebastian grinned. "*You'll* be eighty. *I'll* be seventy-five."

He said it with no hesitation, his eyes and smile warm enough to melt even Wesley's cold heart. "You're so proud of yourself for finally knowing how old I am," Wesley said, to cover his moment of fluster.

"What if we pretend I always knew?" Sebastian said hopefully.

Wesley's lips quirked. "You mean you don't want to tell the others you've been helping yourself to my body for weeks without bothering to ask me the most basic of questions about myself?"

Sebastian winced.

"I mean, really," Wesley said, picking up his empty glass. "A man could almost get the impression you only want him for his *lectures*."

"They're such good lectures," Sebastian mumbled, which put a bigger smile on Wesley's face.

"Speaking of the others," Wesley said, as he waved the glass pointedly at a passing waiter. "It's nearly midnight now. Let's hope they show soon."

Chapter Sixteen

By one a.m., Wesley and Sebastian were still in their booth, Wesley on his third gin, Sebastian's tonic water half drunk. The band was on break, and the club patrons had grown louder and rowdier.

And the others had not arrived.

"Where the hell are they?" said Wesley. "Miss Robbins says to meet her here, and she doesn't show?"

Sebastian didn't like anything about this. "This doesn't feel right at all, Wesley. I wish I could see Zhang."

"Well, I don't see Mr. Zhang, but look who's behind the bar."

Sebastian glanced over. Alasdair Findlay was behind the counter, chatting with the bartender. "The major said Alasdair sent you that letter."

Wesley pursed his lips. "I still find it odd that he sent me a letter when he's so clearly interested in *you*."

"Is he?" Sebastian said in surprise. Wesley leveled a flat stare at him until Sebastian squirmed. "I mean. If you say so. You're probably right, you always are."

"Thank you," Wesley said pointedly. "As I was saying, it's odd."

Sebastian chewed on his lip. "I think we should talk

to him. He might be able to tell us more about Sir Ellery, and he's a bootlegger, so maybe he's met Jade."

Wesley considered Alasdair for a moment, then sat
back in the booth with a huff. "You should probably
talk to him alone," he said grudgingly. "I think he's
more likely to talk to you and we need some fucking
answers."

Sebastian frowned but got to his feet. He wove
around tables until he'd reached the bar. Every stool was
full, but he found a tiny space where he could squeeze
in and lean on the counter. "Alasdair," he called.

But Alasdair was already heading his way. "Mr. de
Leon!" he said brightly. "Or Sebastian, wasn't it? I can
call you that, can't I?"

"Of course," Sebastian said. Alasdair was partially
shadowed in the dimly lit speakeasy, making it hard
to see his face, but his friendly greeting seemed genuine enough.

"I didn't expect to see you here." Alasdair leaned
on the bar across from him, in a mirror of Sebastian's
pose. "This is one of my haunts, you know. I keep these
shelves full. What are you drinking tonight? Let me
get you another."

Sebastian shook his head. "Just the sodas for me."

"Oh really." Alasdair raised an eyebrow. "Not many
people come to a speakeasy *not* to drink."

"I don't handle a drink well," Sebastian admitted,
because *alcohol makes me lose control of my magic and
I'll send this whole place crashing to the floor* was a bit
more explanation than Alasdair needed.

"Is that right?" Alasdair smiled. "Me either," he said,
as if confessing a secret.

"But you're a bootlegger?" Sebastian said in surprise.

"I don't sample my wares." Alasdair's tone was still

friendly, almost teasing as he said, "But why did you come to my speakeasy not to drink?"

Why did you send Wesley a letter? Sebastian wanted to ask. *What do you know about what's going on?*

"I was supposed to meet a friend," he said carefully, "but she isn't here. She's in, um, your line of work, and I was hoping maybe you knew of her? Jade Robbins is her name."

"I've heard of Stella Robbins," said Alasdair. "One of the finest singers on the Eastern seaboard. I'd love to get her in one of my bars. But I don't know a Jade Robbins, I'm afraid."

Another dead end. Sebastian hesitated, then said, "Where are *your* other friends tonight? The major and Sir Ellery?"

"Indulging in the other vice I support," Alasdair said cheerfully. "Gambling. I've got a place with tables not too far from here, above a fabric and sewing store called Ace Up Your Sleeve, isn't that fun? Do you play cards?"

"Yes, but I'm not very good," Sebastian admitted. "Lord Fine is an excellent player, though. He knows your friends; maybe they would like him to join. Unless you think he shouldn't?"

He waited, but Alasdair's gaze didn't go to Wesley. It didn't leave Sebastian at all, just flicked from his flat cap down to the chain of the brooch in his waistcoat before returning to Sebastian's eyes. "If Lord Fine would like to, he's welcome," Alasdair said warmly.

Sebastian kept the frown off his face, but nothing in Alasdair's tone or expression gave any indication that he was worried about Wesley's safety in the company of Sir Ellery.

"I hope you'll stay a bit, even without your friend Miss Robbins," Alasdair said sincerely. "I'm afraid I have another place to check on and can't linger, but I'm putting your tab on the house. I insist," he said, as Sebastian started to protest. "My treat."

"Alasdair!" someone down the bar called.

Alasdair smiled. "No rest for the wicked," he said brightly. "Maybe I'll see you at the tables soon. I have a feeling our paths will keep crossing."

Sebastian watched as Alasdair headed down the bar to talk to a pair of men in suits and fedoras. With a sigh, he picked his way around the crowd until he was back to the booth.

Wesley had a half-smoked cigarette in his hand and a cranky expression. "Any luck?"

Sebastian shook his head. "He doesn't know Jade." He relayed the conversation to Wesley. "Are we certain we believe Major Langford that Alasdair sent the letter?" he said, as he finished. "He didn't seem to think you'd be in any danger playing tables with Sir Ellery."

Wesley was frowning. "Maybe not. But for fuck's sake, if that's the case then we're even more lost than we were this morning. I think we should talk to the bouncers. Maybe they saw Jade or the others tonight, and they just didn't make it inside."

Sebastian nodded. He picked up the tonic water and tossed back the last of it in one sip, and then followed Wesley out of the speakeasy.

Eddie was gone as they climbed the stairs, replaced by a tall and fit woman standing guard at the door. Sebastian and Wesley took the stairs back up together, emerging into the alley. It was unexpectedly empty— no cars waiting, no tipsy loiterers propped against the wall, no couples making out in the darker corners.

"Did the bouncers cut out early?" Wesley asked,

scanning up and down the narrow space. "Where did everyone go?"

"I got rid of them."

Sebastian and Wesley turned as one.

Sir Ellery had emerged at the mouth of the alley. He wore a three-piece suit as crisp as anything in Wesley's closet, but now he had a gun in one hand, held at his side.

And at his other side was Alasdair, with his bright smile. "Sebastian," he said, in a friendly manner, like no one was armed. "I told you we'd cross paths again."

"Hello again, Fine," said Sir Ellery.

Wesley's eyes had widened just slightly, and they were fixed on Sir Ellery. "What the hell are you doing here, Ellery?"

Sebastian kept his eye on the gun in Sir Ellery's hand. He wasn't aiming at Wesley, but the instant Sebastian saw it move, he was ready. "What do you want, Alasdair?"

Wesley shot him a glance. "Alasdair?"

Sir Ellery cut in. "I want the pomander that valet of yours stole from my cousin."

Wesley's attention was back on Sir Ellery. "Sir Harold stole it from the Earl of Blanshard, who stole it from someone else, probably another relative of Sebastian," he said testily. "It's not yours."

"I've got more claim to it than *you*," Sir Ellery said. "Someone out there has offered a price for it and I want to sell."

Sebastian stayed tense, magic simmering just under the surface. Alasdair was looking between Sir Ellery and Wesley with an interested expression.

"Probably in debt, I'd wager. Christ, can none of the aristocracy manage the money they had the good fortune to inherit?" Wesley said. "You want nothing to do with this business, Ellery."

"I want to sell that pomander," said Sir Ellery. "So you're going to return it to me."

And at his side, the hand with the gun twitched.

Sebastian let his magic loose.

Twin yelps of shock filled the alley as both Wesley and Sir Ellery went stumbling.

Except Alasdair—didn't.

"And that must be your enervation magic," Alasdair said, sounding delighted. "I wish I could hear it. Packs a punch, doesn't it? Or at least, I'm sure it does when you haven't been poisoned."

So many thoughts rushed Sebastian's mind at once he could barely sort through them: Alasdair was a paranormal; Alasdair knew Sebastian was a paranormal; Alasdair didn't care that Sir Ellery was armed.

And Alasdair had just said *poisoned*.

"What are you—" Sebastian froze.

A searing burn was creeping through his veins, spreading from his core through his limbs.

"Sebastian de Leon," came Wesley's irritated voice, not nearly as weak as it should have been. "I had everything under control."

Sebastian couldn't answer. His magic had reversed itself, pulling back into him like the tide rushing back into the ocean. The alley had gone blurry, the bricks blending together. Sebastian's breaths were starting to come too hard, sweat drops beading on his skin.

"I'm afraid your magic has a new target now," said Alasdair. "Good thing, too, otherwise your enervation would have spoiled my illusion, and then Lord Fine would see me and my jig would be up."

Sebastian tried to take a step, but his knees buckled. He stumbled as fever rushed him, chills and burning heat together, far too fast to be natural.

"Sebastian." Wesley's voice was strong, not touched by magic at all, not slurred. "Sebastian, what's going on?"

Sebastian opened his mouth, but no words would come out. He shook his head helplessly, and then his knees gave out completely, and he was the one tumbling down to the pavement.

"Sebastian!"

"What the fuck was that?" Oh no. Sir Ellery was getting to his feet. He was still armed—and Wesley—

There was a thud, and a man's grunt of pain.

"Watch where you're aiming that thing," Wesley snapped, and then there was another smacking sound, another yelp.

Sebastian tried to push up, to see what was going on. Down the alley, Wesley was shoving Sir Ellery up against the wall. Sebastian's arms were trembling as he tried to start an army crawl toward the fight. "Wes—"

A boot wedged itself under his ribs. "Let's let the Englishmen work it out, shall we?" Alasdair's boot shoved up, flipping Sebastian over and onto his back. "Winner takes all."

Shit. Sebastian tried to sit up. Alasdair planted his boot on Sebastian's chest. "There's nothing you can do to help now," he chided. "Just enjoy it."

Sebastian turned his head. He could barely make out Wesley and Sir Ellery, a blurred scene like a movie projector out of focus. Their voices seemed very far away.

"I know damn well how good you are with that

weapon." Sebastian had never heard Wesley so furious. "Don't you dare point it at Sebastian."

"Fuck off, Fine," Sir Ellery spit out. "You stole from me."

"I don't have the bloody pomander," Wesley snapped. "I don't even know where it is. Give me that."

Wesley grabbed for the gun. Sir Ellery took a swing at him, and the men began to fight in earnest. Alasdair watched them with an expression of delight, like he was at a sporting match. "I poison all my non-alcoholic drinks."

What, Sebastian wanted to say at the non sequitur, but he could only loll his head to the side.

"It's harmless to anyone without magic," Alasdair went on, eyes on Wesley and Sir Ellery. "But when a paranormal swallows it, it goes into your bloodstream. Then you've got a little booby trap in your own veins, ready to be sprung as soon as you use your magic."

But why, Sebastian tried to ask, but his voice didn't seem to be working, just like his eyes.

"Really quite an amazing poison," said Alasdair. "Turns magic on the magic user, makes it attack your own blood."

The burn in Sebastian's limbs was worsening, and he was shivering under Alasdair's boot even though he could have sworn his skin was flaming to the touch.

Down in the alley, Wesley seemed to be gaining the upper hand. His fist connected with Sir Ellery's face, sending him reeling. Alasdair gestured to the fight. "Now this is better than magic. No tricks and slippery gimmicks. Just fists and brawn, as it should be."

Wesley was on Sir Ellery, the two of them struggling for a moment before Wesley shoved Sir Ellery to the ground. He stepped back, the gun now in his hand, pointed at Sir Ellery. "What the fuck is going on, Ellery?"

"You tell me," Sir Ellery snarled.

"You pulled a gun on us, I wouldn't tell you shit," Wesley said. "Hands on your head. No sudden moves; you know I won't hesitate to shoot."

"All right, all *right*," Sebastian heard Sir Ellery snap, the voice coming as if through molasses. "Lower the goddamn gun, Fine, let's talk."

"And it sounds like Sir Ellery has thrown up the white flag." To Sebastian's horror, Alasdair was now raising a gun of his own. "The match goes to Lord Fine."

Sebastian tried to move, to shout, anything—

But a sudden crack split the alley, muffled as if the gun was under a pillow. *Silencer*, Sebastian's army brain supplied.

"Ellery!" Wesley's shocked voice echoed off the bricks. "Ellery, *fuck*, who the fuck fired that?"

"I better hurry now," Alasdair said pleasantly. "Lord Fine seems like a sharp one, he'll figure it out."

Through the fog of his blurred vision, Sebastian saw a glint in the streetlight. A knife in Alasdair's hand.

Then the knife was coming straight for Sebastian.

Except there was no fresh pain. Instead, Sebastian heard a soft clink. Then Alasdair was straightening up, a cut chain dangling uselessly from the brooch relic in his hand.

Stolen during a murder.

"Mine now," Alasdair said, bright as ever.

And then he sprinted away, just as the wild horses of Sebastian's magic cut loose, and Sebastian's world went dark.

Chapter Seventeen

Sir Ellery was dead. Shot. By someone else in the alley, someone Wesley hadn't seen. He registered the sound of an engine turning over, tires screeching as it pulled away, but his eyes were on the crumpled figure near the mouth of the alley.

"Sebastian—"

But then Wesley hit the pavement.

"*Fuck.*"

Sebastian's magic was rushing the alley, but not in the steady tide Wesley had come to expect. Instead, it was jerky, an uneven pulse of varying strengths that made Wesley's joints protest and his eyes water.

Wesley tried to lift his head. He could just make out Sebastian up ahead, an unmoving ball in the alley. The hairs on his neck rose as dread crept into his stomach.

"Sebastian, *stop*," he said, more a plea than an order. "I can't get to you if you don't stop your magic."

Sebastian still didn't move. Wesley got his palms flat on the alley, tried to raise himself. "Sebastian," he said again. "You *promised* your magic would always let me up if I asked. I am *fucking asking*."

Wesley held himself in a half-press for a moment, limbs shaking, magic rushing over him in stuttering peaks and valleys.

And then, it was gone.

Wesley blinked. Then he jumped to his feet and stumbled down the alley. "Sebastian." He fell to his knees at Sebastian's side. "Sebastian, are you all right?"

No response.

Panic climbed up Wesley's throat. He shoved it down, compartmentalized it for later. Some bits of the war he would never lose, and his brain remembered how to instantly calm itself; no feelings, just cold, rational observations and action.

He did a rapid assessment of the scene. Sebastian was alive. Unconscious, yes, but his chest was rising and falling. There was blood on his face but not much, and no strange smells. His face was pinched, however, and faint sounds of pain occasionally escaped him.

Wesley felt for the pulse in Sebastian's neck and found it, more sluggish than it should have been but steady, at least. Sebastian's skin, though—burning up, far hotter than he should have been. Fever, then. A high one.

Wesley scanned his body, gaze zeroing in on the waistcoat pocket. A cut chain dangled out of it, and there was no longer a bulge for the brooch. He touched the pocket to confirm his growing suspicion, but he was right. The brooch was gone.

Wesley sat back on his heels.

Someone had murdered Sir Ellery and stolen the brooch—the two-part key to transferring its magic to a new paranormal. It seemed highly unlikely the two events occurring together could be an accident.

He closed his eyes, and called up the events of the past few minutes, starting with Sir Ellery emerging at the alley's mouth.

"Hello again, Fine," Sir Ellery had said.

Wesley had answered. "What the hell are you doing here, Ellery?"

Then Sebastian, whose eyes hadn't been on Sir El-
lery. *"What do you want, Alasdair?"*

Wesley's eyes opened. "Like Mr. Zhang," he said
under his breath.

Alasdair was likely a paranormal. Whether it was
his innate magic, like Mr. Zhang's astral walking, or
some other magic, Sebastian would have been able to
see him, but Alasdair had been hidden from Wesley.

Maybe the car Wesley had heard had been Alasdair
fleeing. Or he could still be around, watching them,
armed with the gun that had shot Sir Ellery and now
with the magic of Sebastian's brooch relic.

There would be no way for Wesley to know.

Wesley tensed, a sickening shiver going through him.

But then his eyes fell on Sebastian's wrist, where the
top of the lion tattoo was visible.

Sebastian's magic had reared up when Wesley had
gotten close to the guardian magic at Mr. Zhang's restaurant in Chinatown. And Wesley realized that he now
believed, with bone-deep certainty, that if Alasdair was
still around—if there was a threat to Wesley—Sebastian's
magic would still be filling the alley.

Wesley shoved the thought into the compartment
with his panic. He might have feelings about that later;
he couldn't afford them now.

Wesley got his feet under him and got behind Sebastian, levering him up into a sitting position with his
arms wrapped around his chest. "How many times are
you going to make me carry your unconscious body
out of an alley?" Wesley said with a grunt, resolutely
pretending Sebastian could hear him. "I know I teased
you about not filling out my clothes, but you're not exactly *small.*"

Sebastian's eyelashes fluttered. "Wes," he said, thick
and quiet.

The sound was like music to Wesley. "I'm here, of course I'm here," he said into Sebastian's ear. "Can you walk at all? It will be easier to explain this as too much drink."

Sebastian gave something that resembled a nod, his eyes barely open. Wesley would take it. He got Sebastian to his feet, then wrapped his arm tightly around his waist.

"Lead," Sebastian slurred.

"What?"

"Lead. Somewhere."

Wesley did not have time to worry about *lead*. Sebastian needed a bed. Shelter and safety to recover. Medicine for the fever. Wesley needed somewhere close to go, and only one place was coming to mind—a place he could bring a supposedly drunk friend and it was unlikely anyone would alert the police.

Wesley grimaced. "Apparently we're going to the inn of ill repute after all."

He got Sebastian over to the next block and into the Tomcat Lodge's lobby—a generous term for the filthy room with an ancient settee and a wooden counter. The woman behind the counter gave them a bored look, like two men staggering in, one nearly unconscious and the other sweating and swearing, was the least interesting thing that had happened to her night so far.

"A room, if you please," Wesley said, holding Sebastian upright. God, he was alarmingly hot, even through clothes. "My friend here could use a quick kip."

Above their heads, the room over the lobby must have had at least five occupants throwing a bash of their own, judging by the stomping of feet mixed with bawdy laughter and catcalls. The woman behind the counter didn't seem to even notice the noise as she sized them up, the way Sebastian's head was resting against Wesley's chest, the tightness of Wesley's arm around his waist.

"*Friend*, huh," she said, her tone as unbothered as her expression. "Isn't he pretty. For a friend."

Wesley narrowed his eyes. "How would you prefer I describe him? May I please have a bed for the man I sexually service on a regular basis?"

She actually cracked a smile. "Now *that* will get you a room here," she said, pulling out a set of keys. She pointed to the stairs in the corner. "Second floor, third door on the left."

Wesley accepted the keys. "Have you got any first aid supplies? Water and extra blankets?"

"For your pretty friend? Why not." She bent down, rummaging behind the counter and gathering things.

A first aid kit was probably close to useless, as Wesley was fairly certain tonics and powders were going to do fuck all against magic. But there was still blood on Sebastian's face, and they might need the bandages.

The woman straightened back up. "There's a bathroom on the floor; you can fill the canteen in the sink." She handed the canteen over along with a large tin and two stacked blankets. "What did he drink, anyway? Tell me it wasn't the gin at the Haberdashers; ain't no one oughta be drinking that swill. They make that in an old factory. Still got pieces of hats in the tubs."

Ugh.

It took some wrangling, especially since they had to maneuver around a pair of tipsy women giggling at the top of the stairs and a couple sharing cigarettes in the hall, but Wesley finally got Sebastian up the stairs and into the room. The carpet was every bit as filthy as Wesley had expected, and the room held only a bed and a nightstand. But the sheets were clean and the radiator seemed to be somewhat working, taking the worst of the chill off the night air.

Wesley sat Sebastian down on the edge of the mattress. There was a small lamp on the nightstand, and when he pulled the chain, it lit the room enough to see Sebastian's flushed skin, how his hair was damp with sweat despite his shivering. The blood on his temple was clearer now, and Wesley quickly wiped it away with his sleeve so he could see the cut below. Small mercies here, at least; just a shallow scrape at the hairline, maybe from hitting the pavement.

Sebastian's eyes were closed again and he was probably not going to be able to sit upright for more than another minute or two. Wesley reached for Sebastian's hands, to check for scrapes where he hit the pavement, and his heart stopped.

The lion was gone.

Wesley scanned the tattoo frantically, seeing only swirls of colors on Sebastian's skin, even the scars now lost to the blend of abstract, vivid hues. Wesley took a breath, and this might be it, the moment when his panic would refuse to be contained—

The lion appeared within the colors.

But before Wesley could feel relief, it faded again, like it was slipping underwater beneath the colors of the tattoo.

He wrapped his hand around Sebastian's wrist. "We need you to stay," he whispered urgently, brushing his thumb over the ink that hid the lion. "We need you to hide us from the man who did this to Sebastian."

The lion did appear to Wesley's eyes then, as if it had bobbed to the surface—but only to fade away again, lost within the ink. Coming and going in stuttering pulses like the uneven waves of Sebastian's magic that had rolled over Wesley as they filled the alley.

Wesley took a breath through his nose. Panicking would not help Sebastian; he needed to keep his head.

There was muted laughter, maybe the pair of women from the stairs, passing by the outside of their door as Wesley ran through the night's events in his mind, detached and observant. In the alley, he'd felt Sebastian's familiar magic start to weaken his knees, but then it was gone and Sebastian was down on the stones of the alley. Sebastian had fallen *before* the shot that killed Sir Ellery—before the brooch had been stolen.

Was it more than just losing the brooch that was making his magic unsteady?

Wesley clenched his jaw. He knew nothing right now, had no idea what he was dealing with. But he would focus on what he could do: bandage cuts, make sure Sebastian was warm. Keep his eyes on the lion.

And most of all, he could stay, in case Sebastian fell asleep, to keep blood terrors away and make sure his blood damn well remembered he was free now.

In the hall, there were new voices, a man bragging, a woman flirting; the couple who had been sharing cigarettes, perhaps. A moment later, the door to the room next door slammed shut.

Sebastian's eyelashes fluttered again. "Wes?"

Wesley let out the breath he hadn't realized he was holding. "I'm here. Do you know what happened to you?"

"Poison."

"*Poison?*"

"For paranormals." Sebastian's eyes were hazy, his face very flushed. "Alasdair."

"You were poisoned by Alasdair? Because you're paranormal? Even though he clearly is too?"

Sebastian managed a nod. "My drink."

"Your drink." Wesley some quick calculations. Sebastian had sipped from a single glass of tonic water over their time in the speakeasy. But he'd had about half of that tonic water remaining when they got ready to leave, and he'd tipped all of it back in one go right before they left. That was half of the poison dose, and he'd imbibed it not that long ago. They had to try.

But this was not going to be pleasant.

"You might be magic," said Wesley, "but I'm afraid all we've got are mortal remedies. And in the first aid kit is a vial of ipecac."

Sebastian winced.

It was not easy to get a half-conscious man down the hall to the bathroom, and then Wesley had to hold him upright enough to vomit. A middle-aged white drunk staggered in for the loo while Wesley held Sebastian over the sink.

"Oy, Fancy Man, what'd your friend drink?" the man slurred. "Not the Haberdasher's gin, was it? Got a piece of fedora stuck in my teeth from that rotgut once." He paused. "Didn't stop me from another round, though."

Wesley was never drinking in America again.

Sebastian was possibly even less enthusiastic about being corralled into a cold shower.

"Don't give me that look, you were a medic, you know this is to bring your temperature down," Wesley told him, as the first reprobate got into a loud argument with a new drunk who'd stumbled in, and Sebastian somehow found the energy to glower at him while shivering under the spray. "I know it's a magic fever, but you still have a human body, and I'm trying everything I can think of."

All in all, it was not going to make anyone's list of *most romantic nights*.

But Sebastian looked the tiniest bit more alert, as

Wesley wrapped him in three towels and got him back to the room. He propped Sebastian on the edge of the mattress again, sitting next to him to keep him up, and then handed him the canteen and two aspirin. "Drink."

The man and woman from earlier seemed to be getting on quite well, if the noises now coming from the neighboring room were any indication. Wesley tried to ignore the squeaking of cheap springs as he helped Sebastian take several sips of water and then lie down on the mattress.

Wesley shook out the blankets, then stripped off his own suit. He crouched at the edge of the bed so their faces were level. "The next time you try to treat me like lacking magic makes me incompetent, I'm going to remind you of this night," he said, reaching for the blankets. "Which means you have to make it through, because I won't have you denying me a chance to gloat."

That got a tiny smile. It would have been nice to get the smile without the grunts of the man next door, but Wesley would take what he could get.

"Also," Wesley said, pulling the blankets over Sebastian, "I think I've been egregiously underestimating myself. I just held your head while you *vomited*; whatever this thing we're doing is called, I'm fucking excellent at it. You're a very lucky man."

Sebastian's eyes were half-lidded, his skin still flushed, but his tiny smile stayed. "Told you."

Wesley put a hand on Sebastian's forehead. Still too hot, but at least a bit cooler than he had been. "You were the medic. Am I doing this nurse thing right?"

"Need the uniform," Sebastian murmured, closing his eyes.

Wesley's lips twitched. He let his hand linger against

Sebastian's face, just for a moment. Then he said, "Scoot over. Come on."

He helped Sebastian shift backward, and then Wesley got in the bed too. Sebastian immediately curled into him, and Wesley had to do some awkward maneuvering so he could look at the tattoo. The lion was still coming into focus like the rotations of a lighthouse beam, there one moment, gone the next.

Wesley frowned, and Sebastian must have felt it, because he tensed. "Stay?" he said, eyelids cracking open as he glanced up at Wesley.

"Obviously."

Sebastian relaxed, eyes trustingly closing again, and it made Wesley's chest ache. He would not be looking closer at that. There would be no feelings right now; they had to get through the night first.

The couple on the other side of the wall sounded particularly loud now that he and Sebastian were in bed and quiet. "Think you can sleep?" Wesley asked softly.

"Depends on if our neighbors finish," Sebastian said, without opening his eyes.

Wesley snorted. "Miss Neighbor sounds like she's having a good time at least."

"She's faking," Sebastian muttered.

"Really?" Wesley tilted his head, and yes, Sebastian was right, her moans did sound staged. "Is she putting on a show for his benefit? Doesn't say much for Mr. Neighbor's performance, does it?"

"Tell him to use his tongue."

"Ugh, *no*, that is not the kind of thing a polite boy like you says; you're learning terrible habits from me." Wesley reached for the light on the nightstand and pulled the chain, sending the room into semi-darkness lit only by the streetlamp outside. "You know, it's four times now. Four times I've seen you where you haven't had magic. You're really terribly lucky to have me."

"So lucky," Sebastian murmured. "Talk?"

Because he wanted to hear Wesley's voice. Because when he was ill, he wanted Wesley.

Wesley quickly cleared his throat. "Right. So you already know I only have one thing I can talk about, and that's myself. I could once again attempt to relay the history of the Viscounts Fine, but..." He wet his lips. The words on his tongue were affectionate, even hopeful—not the kind of thing a cold, cynical bastard like himself said, and he was clearly also learning terrible habits from Sebastian. "Instead of the past, I'm going to tell you about the future. A story about an Englishman on a Caribbean beach, and a Caribbean boy in an English snowfall."

"Love that."

Sebastian's words were thick and slurred with sleepiness now. But he'd definitely said *that*. Certainly not *you*. There was no way he could have said *you;* what a flight of fancy that would have been, to imagine that was what Wesley had just heard.

Though it had sounded—no. No, of course it wasn't.

Wesley let himself settle in as well, let himself drape an arm over Sebastian's ribs, so he could feel his breaths rise and fall. Reassure himself those breaths were still coming. Then he took a breath of his own. "So first, obviously, you're going to feel much better, and all of this American nonsense is going to be wrapped up. Then we'll pick our ship—I know I haven't sailed frequently, but I have strong opinions about my ships nonetheless..."

Chapter Eighteen

Sebastian woke with a headache, a parched throat, and sweat on his brow. But he was mostly alert and his mind mostly clear, both a significant step up from his night. And even through the physical weakness, there was a lightness to his body that he hadn't felt in weeks.

Wesley was already awake and dressed, standing by the window with his gaze on the street. The early morning light was gray again, illuminating his profile, the stubble on his sharp jaw, the eyes that matched his suit and the sky.

Wesley's words from Manhattan came back to him. *I might believe in magic now, but life letting me keep you—that's a fairytale I suppose I haven't yet believed in.*

His fingers curled around the edge of the blanket. Wesley was the one who talked about suddenly stumbling into a world of magic, and it was true in the literal sense. But there was a kind of magic in a person who carried you when you couldn't walk, who stayed by your side during a dark night and saw you through to the dawn. And maybe Sebastian had been just as much of a skeptic, unable to quite believe life would let him keep someone like that. Keep someone like Wesley.

Sebastian watched him watch the street. He wanted to say something charming about how handsome Wesley was, the kind of compliment that would have him falling right back into bed.

What he actually managed to say was "Hi."

"Hi indeed." Wesley turned away from the window and toward Sebastian as he sat up against the pillows, wincing as bruised, stiff muscles protested. "How is the patient this morning?"

Sebastian made a face. "Humbled."

"Are you now?" Wesley's lips curved up, like that had surprised a smile out of him. "Don't tell me you're about to acknowledge that magic isn't everything?"

"You were amazing," Sebastian said, rueful and soft.

The small smile was still on Wesley's lips. "Generally the kind of thing I like to hear after a fellow has enjoyed himself in my bed, not vomited in a loo."

Sebastian wet his lips. "I don't know if I would have made it without—"

"No, stop, it's too early for sentiment." Wesley had stepped away from the window, toward the bed. "You're just very bad at relying on other people."

He sat on the edge of the bed. "But I hope you now unequivocally understand that the next time you think you might have a blood terror, or any other kind of trouble, and you're wondering *should I go to Wesley for help*, the answer is always yes. Actually, let's just make the question *should I go to Wesley*, because the answer to that is also always yes."

This close, Sebastian could appreciate the light brown stubble on Wesley's jaw, the high cheekbones and the hint of a smile lingering on his lips. The night was a blur, but Wesley was in every memory, helping Sebastian when he couldn't help himself. Wesley said he didn't want sentiment, but Sebastian had a lot of it right then.

He leaned forward and kissed Wesley, who made a

small noise of surprise, his lips softening under Sebastian's. The kiss was brief, almost chaste, and then Sebastian was pulling back.

"You wouldn't let me say it with words," he said wryly.

"You're incorrigible," Wesley told him, but he had a grudging smile. He reached for Sebastian's hand, rotating it so the inside of his wrist faced him. "The lion is still stuttering."

A statement, not a question. Wesley had already known, must have already checked on the tattoo that morning. Sebastian looked down at his wrist, and sure enough, the lion in the ink was hidden, visible only for a moment before slipping away again.

Wesley ran his thumb over the tattoo, and Sebastian shivered. "Well, you still feel that at least, that's promising," said Wesley.

"Wait, you know the skin is sensitive there?"

"Like I haven't memorized every touch that gets a response from you." Wesley fully encircled his wrist, his thumb still over the pulse point and tattoo, his hand warm against Sebastian's skin. "Do you know what's happening to you? Why the lion is doing this?"

"Not exactly," Sebastian admitted. "But Alasdair said the poison was activated by magic, that it turns the magic on the magic user and makes it attack our blood. Perhaps the poison is still active in me."

"So the pulses could be a sign that your magic isn't recovered—that using it might trigger the symptoms again?"

Sebastian nodded.

"Well, welcome to the mortal plane for an unknown amount of time, then," Wesley said. "How do you feel otherwise?"

"Like I was run over by a stampede," Sebastian said

ruefully. He hesitated. "But I also feel…better, somehow? Like I've taken off chains now that I've lost the brooch."

Wesley raised an eyebrow. "So is Alasdair going to regret stealing it?"

"I don't know," Sebastian admitted. "I don't know what it's going to do to him, because I don't know what Alasdair's magic is. The brooch makes magic work on other magic. Maybe it's only too much for a paranormal whose magic already works on other magic."

Wesley's thumb skimmed over his wrist again in a distracting way. He was looking at the tattoo thoughtfully. "Which magic was it?"

"What do you mean?"

"You said in Central Park that you had four kinds of magic. If you've lost the brooch, I assume you're back down to three, but which one was interacting with the brooch before?"

Wesley was tracing the tattoo now and Sebastian was having a hard time concentrating. "The enervation magic. Well. I think."

"You *think*."

"I assumed it would be interacting with the most innate magic. I suppose I could be wrong, but it doesn't really matter now." Sebastian tried to find something else to look at besides the hypnotizing motions of Wesley's thumb on his skin. His eyes fell on some rust-colored spots on Wesley's white cuffs. "You have blood on your sleeve. Did you get hurt?"

Wesley shook his head. "It's yours." He tapped his own temple. "From the cut on your head. It's not as if I have another shirt to change into, and at any rate I'm hardly concerned about a stain right now." He let go of Sebastian's wrist. "What's our plan, then? I think we assume that telegram wasn't actually from Miss Robbins."

"Alasdair, or perhaps Sir Ellery, or maybe both," Sebastian said.

"But then where are the others?" Wesley said. "This is the same damn problem we've had since we set foot in this country and they're farther away than ever."

"How did Alasdair know about the brooch?" Sebastian said slowly. "Jade and the others would never have told him."

"Never have told him willingly," Wesley said grimly. "What if he knows where they are? What if he's the fucking reason we can't find them?"

"Alasdair said he also runs a gambling den," Sebastian said. "He said it's not far from the speakeasy, in a fabric store called Ace Up Your Sleeve."

"I bet he thinks that's clever," Wesley muttered.

"He could be lying," Sebastian said. "Obviously he was lying about Sir Ellery being at the tables, but it's still a lead. Maybe we should try to find it."

"Maybe." Wesley's expression was pensive. "But last night, in the alley, as we were leaving, you said there was lead somewhere."

Sebastian frowned. He tried to think back to the night before, which was a fuzzy, blurry mess.

"We'll walk through it," Wesley said, like he understood. "From my perspective, it appeared that Sir Ellery showed up alone. You started to use your magic, then fell. Sir Ellery aimed at you then, I disarmed him, and then a shot rang out and he dropped dead in front of my eyes. Alasdair, I presume?"

Sebastian nodded.

"But I don't understand," said Wesley. "I was defenseless. Why shoot his friend instead of me?"

Sebastian winced. "He wanted to let you two fight it out. Winner take all."

"Christ." Wesley's jaw tightened. "So Langford was right, Alasdair is mad as a hatter, and he can turn invisible?"

"Not necessarily," Sebastian said slowly. "The invisibility could be his magic, but there are potions and totems that can cause that effect as well. I'm starting to think his magic is something else."

"Why?"

"Do you remember how Mateo was, in Yorkshire and Paris, lost to visions of the future? Or how Isabel painted her home in Spain to keep her mind from getting lost in colors?"

Wesley's eyebrows went up. "You think he has some kind of subordinate magic? And that's what's affecting his mind?"

"It's possible."

"Mad magic men, why not," Wesley muttered. "So he murders Sir Ellery and steals the brooch. Then what?"

"He ran," said Sebastian, "and my magic went wild."

"Yes, it did," Wesley said bluntly. "I could barely think."

"I heard you, though," Sebastian said, eyes closed as he tried to bring the memory up. "It was like—like there was a stampede in my head, loud as thunder. Magic everywhere. Then I heard you, and that let me call the horses back."

Sebastian kept his eyes closed, trying to remember what he'd felt. "Alasdair was gone. I think he knew my magic would go haywire and didn't want to be affected." He suddenly opened his eyes. "But there *was* lead. I felt it when my magic was loose, like a boulder at the edge of the water. Something big."

"Lead in the alley?"

"No, a little farther," Sebastian said. "I think we need to search the area."

Chapter Nineteen

They walked back down the sidewalk, which had few people at that time of the morning. As they passed back by the alley, however, there was no evidence to be seen of the night before: no police officers, no blood stains on the bricks.

"No police," Wesley observed, "despite there being a murdered baronet right in that alley. But then, it probably wouldn't have taken more than a phone call for Alasdair to have a body outside his speakeasy cleaned up. In fact, the bouncers may have been expecting it."

They ducked back into the cigar shop and newsstand, where they could survey the shop from across the street. The hat shop had a large *Closed* sign on its door, although Sebastian could see someone moving around inside, tidying and setting up.

He frowned. "How are we going to do this? Normally I'd just do a sweep with my magic, but—"

"But you're not allowed to use your magic right now," said Wesley. "You will answer to me personally if you so much as try."

"But how do we search without magic?"

"With our eyes," Wesley said dryly. "And our brains."

Sebastian scrunched his nose.

"I'm choosing to interpret that face to mean that you

can't wait to show me how humbled you are now that you've realized magic isn't everything."

Sebastian sighed. "It was a lot of lead. We're looking for something big."

"What, like the paint on the shop's walls?"

Sebastian shook his head. "That would have felt like—well, a wall. This felt like a boulder in the river of magic."

"Large and leaden." Wesley pulled out his cigarette pack, then stuffed it back in his pocket without taking a cigarette out. "A safe, perhaps? That seems like something Alasdair might have in the back of his hat shop or speakeasy."

"And it would be a convenient place to hide anything magic," Sebastian said.

They exchanged a glance. "I say we search." Wesley's face was set. "As I said last night, I'm tired of being jerked around. Alasdair decided to pick this fight; I don't intend to run away."

"I didn't plan to show up at the fight unarmed," Sebastian muttered.

"We'll just have to get creative," Wesley said, eying the shop across the street. "Come on. I have an idea."

Sebastian trailed at Wesley's feet as he confidently strode up to the haberdashery and banged on the window. "Excuse me. Sir! I need to speak with you."

The man inside gave him a narrow-eyed look. "We open at ten," he said, his voice muffled and just audible through the glass.

Wesley meaningfully pressed a twenty-dollar bill to the glass.

The shopkeeper's eyes widened, and then he was hurrying over to the door. "Come on in, come on in," the shopkeeper said, holding it open for Wesley and Sebastian. "We do sometimes open early, for special guests."

The store was one small room, well-stocked with hats and ties and coats of all kinds. There was a counter at the back wall, and behind it, a door that was firmly shut.

"We're quite special, I assure you," Wesley said, as the bill changed hands. "I'm in a frightful bind. Masquerade tonight, haven't got a tailcoat or top hat with me in America."

"Happy to help you, sir," the shopkeeper promised.

"Well, that's a relief," Wesley said. "And is there anyone else here who could attend to my companion?"

"It's just me right now, I'm afraid," the shopkeeper said apologetically. "Steve won't be in for another hour at least."

"So you're here alone? And will be for another hour?" said Wesley. "Well, I suppose we'll make do, then. Where do you keep your formalwear selection? Is it over here?"

Wesley strode off toward the far back corner of the shop. Sebastian walked up to the counter instead, eyes on the door behind it. If there was a safe, he'd bet it was in the back.

Sebastian leaned on the counter, frowning. If only he could use his magic now—keep the shopkeeper down while he broke the back door—

There was a thud, a muffled yelp and then another thump. Sebastian looked over his shoulder in surprise.

"I've got him down and I'm tying him up," came Wesley's voice, from the back corner. "Do hurry, won't you? Steve might show up early, after all."

"Be careful, they might hear him in the street—"

"I'm not an *amateur*, duck, he's already gagged."

Sebastian hurried behind the register. The door was unlocked, and he slowly opened it, revealing a set of stairs trailing down out of sight.

Down, where the speakeasy was.

Another muffled, indignant yelp came from the back corner of the store, then Wesley was walking his way.

"Our new friend is tied to the radiator. I've no idea how skilled he might be at escape, so let's assume we have only a couple minutes, shall we?" He glanced past Sebastian. "Back door into the speakeasy?"

They took the stairs down together in quiet, cautious steps. The final step opened into a short hallway. The kitchens were up ahead while a door stood along the wall. They stopped for a moment and listened, but the speakeasy was silent.

Sebastian opened the one door to a small room that held a messy desk, a filing cabinet—and a free-standing black safe on the back wall, a sizable one with a keyhole.

"Got the safe, now we need the key," said Wesley.

Sebastian went straight to the desk and began opening the drawers, scanning each one and pulling it out to check underneath, as Wesley slipped out the door and back into the hall.

Sebastian had just reached the final drawer when Wesley strode back in, holding up a metal key.

"How'd you find that?" Sebastian said, delighted.

Wesley coughed. "I might have been watching Alasdair very closely when the two of you were talking."

"Really? Why?" Sebastian said curiously. "We didn't know he was a paranormal then."

"No, but he was so bloody interested in you, and I was—well, I'm sure it doesn't matter," Wesley said quickly. "Point being, I saw him put something in the drawer beneath the cash register at the bar. And now we have the key."

A moment later, Wesley was swinging the safe door open. "Let's see." He crouched in front of the safe.

"We've got the usual suspects: cash, papers, cash, jewelry, yet more cash. Apparently bootlegging is quite lucrative."

Sebastian's gaze had gone straight to the tiny box on top of a bundle of bills. "Wes."

Wesley followed his gaze. "Is that box for cuff links? Or a ring, perhaps?"

"Rory kept his ring relic in a box like that when I saw it in London," Sebastian said.

"You think that could be *Brodigan's*?" Wesley said, eyebrows flying up. "But if Alasdair already had a relic, why not use it?"

"It's bound to Rory," Sebastian said. "It's not going to work for anyone else until he's dead."

They exchanged a glance.

Sebastian swallowed. "What if—"

"No," Wesley said brusquely. "Brodigan's not dead. No one who vexes me that much would ever die. We're proceeding on the assumption the lot of them are alive."

Sebastian let out a breath. "Okay," he said, reaching into the cabinet. He touched the ring box, and painful pinpricks shot up his fingers.

"This is lead too." He ignored the needle-like sting against his skin as he encircled the box in his hand. "So we should take this—*Wesley*," he said, as Wesley took him firmly by the wrist and pulled his hand away.

"Why are you touching something that hurts you?"

"Because—"

"Why are you touching anything magic, period?"

"Well—"

"We're not taking chances with things that might send you back into that fever daze," Wesley said. "Hands to yourself."

"But—"

Wesley had already reached into the safe and picked up the ring box. "You have a perfectly serviceable mortal right here. I'll do it."

"I don't want you touching magic either!"

"What kind of posturing fool do you take me for? Of course I'm not touching magic. But I can hold this lead box and open it for your eyes with neither of us taking the risk or experiencing pain." Wesley cracked the top of the ring box.

Sebastian stilled at the sight of the familiar jewels, a ring he'd seen in a pub in London in the spring, when he and Rory had talked about relics. "Yes," Sebastian said quietly, "it's Rory's."

"I see." Wesley snapped the box shut. "Well. We're taking this with us, then. Or *I'm* taking it with us, to be precise. You're not touching it until we're certain your magic is healed." He tucked it away in his jacket. "Come on. Let's get out of here."

They scrambled back up the main stairs. "But why does Alasdair have Rory's ring?" Sebastian said, as they stepped into the alley. "And where are the others?"

"Maybe we find this gambling den next?" Wesley said. "Alasdair told you it was close. We should search—shit."

Sebastian followed Wesley's gaze down the alley. "Oh no."

Major Langford was across the street, looking in the cigar store with a grim expression.

"Hell and damnation." Wesley pursed his lips. "How could it possibly be coincidence that he's this close to where Sir Ellery was shot?"

"It can't be," Sebastian said. "We have to get him out of here."

Major Langford stepped farther down the street,

disappearing from sight. "Come on," Wesley muttered. They quickly darted out from the alley. Sebastian scanned the street: two pedestrians. A car parked at the curb. No Alasdair.

Wesley started crossing the street. "Major," he called brusquely.

Langford turned, his gaze going to Wesley, then Sebastian. His expression went stonily unreadable. "Fine, what are you doing here?"

"I could ask you the same thing," Wesley pointed out, as Sebastian joined them in front of the pharmacy.

"I'm looking for Sir Ellery," Major Langford said testily. "We went out last night, played cards at another place Alasdair runs. I turned in after, but Sir Ellery said he was popping 'round here to see Alasdair and get a last drink. We were to meet for breakfast this morning, but he didn't show."

Sebastian just managed not to wince.

"He told us he was staying with the Hartmans, in their guest house," Wesley said, expression blank and not at all like he'd seen Sir Ellery shot the night before. "Did you try there?"

"Of course I did. He's not there either. Lady Blanche also mentioned her husband is weathering a flu." Major Langford's eyes darted to Sebastian and narrowed. "That's all I can say. For the moment," he finished meaningfully.

A flu—or an illness like Sebastian had gone through the night before? Could Sir Ellery or Alasdair have slipped something to Walter Hartman too? Alasdair had said it only worked on paranormals, but what was to say he'd draw the line against poisoning someone without magic?

Wesley's jaw tightened, but Sebastian spoke first.

"Lord Fine, maybe you and the major should have a conversation."

Wesley's irritated expression didn't budge. "I've told the major he can speak freely in front of both of us."

Langford smiled without humor. "Remind me: when were you put in charge of who I decide to speak freely with?" He turned back to his car. "I'm going over to the Hartmans' home now, see if I can get some goddamn answers."

Wesley again looked like he was about to speak. "Maybe you should go with him," Sebastian said first.

Wesley's gaze snapped to Sebastian. "*Just* me?"

"Someone should stay and finish our business here." They'd found Rory's ring; they needed to follow that lead, but if someone in the Hartman home had been poisoned, they needed to know that too. "We can meet back at the inn—the horse one, not the cat one."

Major Langford gave Sebastian another long, suspicious look. Then he turned away. "Are you coming, Fine?"

Wesley turned to Sebastian.

"We need to know what he knows; we need to know why Walter Hartman is sick," Sebastian said quietly. "And he's not going to talk with me there. I'll check Alasdair's other place."

Wesley's lips pinched. "Fine. I'll go with him to Walter's home and see what's going on, and then I'm borrowing his car and meeting you back in Tarrytown."

"So it's borrowing when *you* do it?" Sebastian said wryly.

Wesley's lips twitched in a grudging smile before he strode off toward Langford. "Major! I'm coming with you, hold up."

Chapter Twenty

Wesley sat in the passenger seat as Major Langford began to drive them north. He briefly touched his inner jacket pocket, where the heavy lead box with Rory's ring was concealed. "How far are we going?"

"About ten miles. They've got a manor on the mountain, overlooking the river." Major Langford's gaze darted to Wesley, then back to the road. "You haven't explained why you and your man were in that shop. Getting outfitted for tonight? Going to the masquerade after all? Didn't think you had it in you."

Wesley frankly wouldn't go to a masquerade under threat of torture, but he couldn't exactly say *Sebastian and I thought we'd pop 'round to Alasdair's speakeasy cover and look for magic*. Instead, he made a noncommittal sound, which Major Langford seemed to take as agreement.

"Are you going to tell me what you were refusing to say in front of my business associate?" Wesley said.

"You've lost your touch if you can't figure it out," Langford said shortly. "You and Sir Ellery were here together in February—why? To attend Walter Hartman and Lady Blanche's wedding. And now Mr. Hartman is ill."

"You said flu," Wesley said slowly.

"I have reasons to suspect it's more than that." Major Langford had turned onto a main road and was heading down it quite fast. "And now Sir Ellery's missing. I don't know what the fuck is going on, Fine, but I don't like it."

Wesley touched the pocket with the heavy ring box again, and didn't respond.

They were soon beyond the town, but the shops had given way not to the manicured estates and sprawling homes Wesley had expected, but to industrial buildings and grimier streets.

Wesley frowned. "Major," he said warningly. "This is not the way to Walter Hartman's home."

"You're right," Major Langford said. "I have to show you something."

"But why the fuck—"

"I'll give you all the answers in a few moments. Christ, Fine, there was a time you trusted me."

Wesley glanced ahead. A multistory brick building that had seen better days loomed at the end of the road, at the river's edge. Langford headed up the gravel drive into some kind of industrial complex, with smaller buildings surrounding the main brick building and a few trucks parked in front—unmarked trucks, just like the one that had pulled up in front of the hat shop the previous day.

"Langford—"

"You remember what I said, in Manhattan?" Langford brought the car to a stop just outside the main building, a factory of some kind, perhaps. "That I listened to you when you asked me to, and you need to start fucking listening to me?"

This again. Once upon a time, Langford might have listened to him about two soldiers in their company, but in the present he'd gone and had the War Office snoop on them. Wesley perfectly remembered how Langford's strategies worked; it was obvious where this conversation was going to go. "Is this the part where you're about to try some kind of threat against a pair of men who served our country?"

"Do I need to?" Langford said coolly. "I know you had a soft spot for them. You know exactly what kind of threats I can make, and that they're not empty. We understand each other." He pointed at the building. "I need to show you something in there. This is not negotiable. People are in danger."

Shit. What had Langford stumbled into? Alasdair was a paranormal, supposedly in textiles. He supplied the gin at the Hudson Haberdashers—rumored to be made in a hat factory. Was this factory his? Had Langford found magic?

Wesley reluctantly stepped from the car, slamming the door. "Are you armed, at least?"

"Of course I am." Langford had drawn a revolver already, and gestured with it. "In there. Let me show you what I found."

They walked through the doors of the factory. It felt asleep, like a museum after hours, the skeletons of frozen machines only weakly lit by the gray light that filtered in through dirty windows. Dozens of empty crates were stacked at the base of the machines, all of them labeled *Mansfield Textile Wholesalers*.

Wesley tensed. "Why are we here, Langford?"

"So we can talk," a new voice said brightly.

Wesley whirled around to see Alasdair smiling at him. The two bouncers from the speakeasy the night before stood just behind Alasdair. They weren't smiling.

"My little charm from last night wore off. So you

can see me now, can't you, Wesley?" Alasdair went on. "I can call you Wesley, can't I?"

"No you may not," Wesley snapped. "Langford, the gun." He shot a glance in Langford's direction, and stilled.

Langford's gun was out, all right. And it was aimed at Wesley.

"Langford, what are you doing?" Wesley said warningly, gaze darting between Langford and Alasdair. "This man is dangerous."

"Nowhere near as dangerous as your friend, Mr. de Leon," Langford said.

"How is dear Sebastian doing, by the way?" Alasdair said, still friendly. "I hope he hasn't tried anything rash. That tonic water—strong stuff, you know. Packs a kick, sticks around in the system quite a while."

Wesley tightened his jaw. His gaze darted around the open room in emotionless assessment: Alasdair, a paranormal. Two bouncers, possibly armed. His former commanding officer—definitely armed.

"What do you want?" he said, addressing Langford.

"What Alasdair said." Langford smiled his humorless smile. "To talk."

Sebastian was on his third cup of coffee in the eatery adjacent to the Horseman Inn in Tarrytown, and Wesley still hadn't arrived.

"You all right there?" the waitress asked, as she stopped by to check on him.

"I am, thank you," Sebastian said politely, trying not to let his worry show.

He drummed his fingers on the table, eying one of the tiny, decorative pumpkins that Wesley had found so irritating.

He'd found the fabric store and gone in, found a young woman who sold sewing machines during the day and delivered drinks at night. She let him upstairs under pretext that he'd left his hat behind and let him look around. He'd left with her exchange in his pocket and no further clues to where the others had gone.

Now, he was back at the Horseman Inn in Tarrytown, still waiting for Wesley. How far away was Walter Hartman's home, exactly?

"Excuse me?" The woman from the inn's front desk was approaching his table, a small piece of paper in hand. "Mr. de Leon, wasn't it? Someone called just a few minutes ago and left a message for you."

"A message?" Sebastian said in surprise.

"Yes," said the innkeeper. "It's from your friend, Lord Fine."

Sebastian let out a breath of relief. "What did he say?"

"He said he's afraid he's going to be detained longer than expected, and to meet him at the masquerade tonight."

Sebastian blinked. "Lord Fine said *masquerade*?"

"Yes."

"And you're sure?"

"Absolutely," the woman said, with certainty. "I said *oh, you mean the one for the governor's son—he lives around here and it's been in the papers*—and he said *that's the one. Tell Mr. de Leon I'll make sure he's been added to the guest list.*"

"Oh." Sebastian sat back in his chair. "Okay. Thank you."

She handed him the piece of paper and then went back out through the restaurant into the lobby.

Sebastian looked at the paper, but it didn't say anything more than the woman had said. He set the note down on the table.

Had Wesley found evidence of poisoning? Evidence of Alasdair at the Hartman home, or maybe a connection to the others, and he needed a reason for Sebastian to join him?

Whatever the reason, Wesley wouldn't be at a masquerade unless it was important. Apparently Sebastian was going to need a tuxedo.

Wesley glanced around the factory, from Langford with the gun to Alasdair with his bouncer bodyguards. "Just to be clear, you do know Alasdair is a murderer?" he said to Langford.

"Oh come now, I've heard Langford's stories about the two of you in the war," Alasdair said pleasantly. "We're all murderers here."

"If you think a transparent attempt to throw the past in my face will solicit some sort of emotional response, you're sorely mistaken," Wesley said coldly. "Langford, I demand an explanation."

Langford gestured with the gun. "Do you have any idea what you've gotten mixed up in?"

"Do *you*?" Wesley said incredulously.

"Your friend." Langford spat the word. "Sebastian de Leon. And Alasdair here. They have magic."

"*Magic*?" Wesley forced every ounce of derision he could muster into the word. "Did you just hear yourself? Has Alasdair been plying you with his wares?"

"Do I seem drunk or drugged?" Langford said.

No. He didn't. Neither did the large men standing behind Alasdair, who were staring at Wesley with unfriendly expressions.

Wesley took a breath. "Magic isn't real, major."

"I suppose you think Sebastian carried a bit of antique Spanish jewelry on him for sentimental reasons, then?" Alasdair said.

Wesley shrugged. "He said he inherited it from his grandfather."

"Shut up, Fine," said Langford. "It's pointless to lie to me, I remember your tells. And I know why you're nothing like the old Captain Collins. You're under de Leon's enchantment; that much has been obvious since Manhattan."

"I have no idea what you're talking about," Wesley said, ignoring how his pulse had picked up speed. He turned to the men behind Alasdair. "You two are just going to stand there and listen to this lunacy?"

"We've seen it," the bigger one said. "It's a lot scarier than the whining of a fancy lord."

"Don't underestimate Fine," Langford said warningly. "He might be under a spell, but he's quick. Inventive. Ruthless. And if things go south, he's got an iron stomach for other people's pain."

The men exchanged a glance.

"Oooh, you really should let me call you Wesley," said Alasdair. "It sounds like we could be great friends."

Wesley drew a breath through his nose. "Langford, if you believe Alasdair here has magic, why are you aiming that gun at me?"

"Because Alasdair is on my side," Langford said. "He understands exactly how dangerous magic is, and he understands that magic, and all who use it, must be destroyed."

Wesley went very still.

"It's true," Alasdair said easily, like Langford hadn't just called for the man's own destruction. "Magic does nobody any good, you know."

"But you just said *you* have magic," said Wesley.

"So who would know better than me?" Alasdair tapped his ear. "I hear magic. Turns out, that's the sort of skill that makes one quite attractive to those looking to trade magical artifacts." He leaned forward. "And I was very good at it, but as you might imagine, hearing magic does make it rather difficult to hear one's own rational thoughts. I'm afraid I've been quite mad for some time. Was committed last year, actually—well. Until Sir Ellery got me out."

Christ. Had Sir Ellery had some cocked-up delusions about using Alasdair to find the pomander, or other things he could sell? "Why would he have done something like that?"

"Because Ellery was a fool," Langford said. "A man who thought magic could be controlled. Some things are meant to be eliminated."

"I'm working my way through my former partner's collection," Alasdair said brightly. "He had all sorts of powders and trinkets and I'm using them all up. Convenient to be invisible sometimes, isn't it?"

"That doesn't sound like *destroying* to me," Wesley said pointedly.

"I suppose you're right," Alasdair said. "But magic is so terribly difficult to destroy—well. Unless you're Sebastian, I suppose. He's the only exception I've heard of, and it still takes his innate magics enhanced by a relic to do it. The rest of us can only hope to transfer magic—or steal it."

Wesley's gaze darted to Langford, but he hadn't lowered the gun.

"Speaking of stealing." Alasdair pulled his jacket lapel to the side, revealing the brooch relic pinned to his shirt. "Now *this* is far more exciting than powders and trinkets, isn't it? I quite like its song. Granted, I couldn't hear it when Sebastian was *wearing* it." Alasdair shook his head. "That tattoo he's got might as well be ear-muffs. I had to set that fire to get him out of the way so I could search your room, and *then* the brooch told me its secrets, told me all about Sebastian's magic. But I could hardly steal it at that moment. No, the brooch told me that if I wanted it to be mine, it would take a murder too."

"So you shot Sir Ellery?" Wesley said. "The man who freed you from the asylum?"

"It's not as if Sir Ellery's actions were out of the goodness of his heart. I'm very useful," Alasdair said earnestly. "And I had to kill somebody. I imagined Sir Ellery was very surprised, though."

Wesley turned to Langford. "You know all this and you're *partnering* with him?"

"It's war, Fine," Langford said crisply. "I shouldn't have to tell you there are costs. Sir Ellery thought he could find that pomander and sell it, and he paid the price."

"But we don't want to kill Sebastian," Alasdair said, as if that would reassure Wesley. "The de Leon family is really quite famous in the paranormal world, you know. They're descended from a notorious witch-hunter. Se-bastian's ancestor had the right idea, same as Major Langford here, getting rid of paranormals. We're noth-ing but a threat to ourselves and the world. I say we get rid of magic, and I think Sebastian could be very use-ful in that mission."

Alasdair clapped his hands. "But look, you haven't even heard our proposition."

"You're threatening me at gunpoint. What on earth

do you imagine I would agree to?" Wesley said incredulously.

"To help us destroy magic," said Langford. "Use your head, Fine. There are people like Alasdair loose in the world."

"Yes, I'm terribly dangerous," Alasdair agreed, completely sincere. "Mad as a hatter—ha. I never tire of that pun. But truly, I know what magic has done to me. Let's rid the world of it and everyone who has it."

The cold, rational part of Wesley's mind could appreciate that a world without Alasdairs might be a good thing.

But a world without Mateo, or Isabel, or Miss Robbins or Mr. Zhang or even Rory Brodigan would be a very boring place indeed.

And Wesley didn't want to return to a world without Sebastian.

"I'm not you," Wesley said to Alasdair.

"Well, no," Alasdair agreed. "You're English, for one."

"I meant that I don't kill my friends," Wesley snapped. "I'm not going to join you in a mission to kill Sebastian."

"I already said we're not killing him," Alasdair said patiently. "We're *using* him. That's why I sent him a message."

Oh no. "What message?" Wesley said grimly.

"Well, I said it was from you, actually," said Alasdair. "That you were detained and to join you at the masquerade tonight. I had to get a bit creative, you see, we weren't expecting Sebastian to recover so quickly and we're going to need him and his blood."

"What do you want with his *blood*?"

"You can worry about that when you decide to join

us," Langford said curtly. "What do you think? Are you in?"

Wesley's hands had balled into fists. "I think this is the part where I tell you both to go to hell."

"I told you he was enchanted too," Langford said to Alasdair. "It's been clear since we met him in New York that Fine isn't himself."

"I do hear a tiny bit of magic on him, it's true," said Alasdair. "I can't quite tell what it is, though, it's very muffled."

Wesley very carefully did not clap a hand to the ring box in his pocket. Surely Alasdair couldn't hear the ring through lead? Sebastian had said no magic got through.

"We'll lock him up with the other one," said Langford. "They're soldiers, they'll come around."

The other one?

But at that moment, Alasdair moved, quick as a cobra, and clapped a cloth over Wesley's mouth.

He breathed in a sickly sweet scent.

Fucking villains with chloroform.

"I love the elegance of solutions without magic," was the last thing he heard Alasdair say, and then the world was dark.

Chapter Twenty-One

Sebastian sat in a car he'd borrowed—yes, *borrowed*, he told the Wesley in his head, he'd leave it where it could be found and returned—on a hillside just outside of Tarrytown, under the cover of tall trees with bright autumn leaves.

After the message, he'd bought a tuxedo from a store—not the haberdashery over Alasdair's speakeasy, obviously—and asked around town until he'd found someone who could tell him where the governor's son's mansion was. Now he was parked up the road from the open gate, watching the cars turn in. The grounds covered several acres of the hillside and probably had lovely views of the river and Catskills in the daylight. In the darkening evening, the stone pillars on either side of the gate were topped with giant carved pumpkins that glowed like lanterns. The house could be seen in the distance, four stories high and illuminated with pale white lights against the night.

Tell Mr. de Leon I'll make sure he's been added to the guest list.

Part of him wanted to sneak in. Always easier when you didn't draw attention to yourself, and Sebastian wanted to find out what was going on. Alasdair had mentioned that he was going to be supplying this party with alcohol; there was a chance he was delivering it personally.

Of course, sneaking in was a lot easier when you could knock guards down and keep them there.

He glanced down at his wrist. The lion was there, but still fainter than usual, occasionally slipping away completely before coming back. Using magic would be risky, and something he wanted to avoid if at all possible. If he slipped back into the fever daze, he'd be no good to anyone.

Which left the front door. Sebastian started the engine, and drove forward, turning in through the gate toward the lit mansion beyond.

"Wesley. *Wesley.*"

Wesley's head was pounding, but he heard the familiar voice calling his name as if from a distance.

"Come on, Wesley, you've been out for ages. Wake up."

Wesley forced his eyes open. He took in his new location: a small room, with concrete walls, a sink in the corner, no windows and a bare light bulb high above. Across from him was a bunk bed stacked three high, like the sailors' quarters on a navy ship. He himself was on a coarse mattress on what seemed to be another bunk, the bottom of the one above quite close. At the wall beyond his feet was an open doorway where the air seemed almost glittery, and beyond that he could see through another open doorway into the room across the hall.

And standing in the other room, calling his name, was Arthur. He had three days' worth of black beard on his face, dark circles under his blue eyes, and his suit looked like he'd been sleeping in it, but it was Arthur.

"Christ, Arthur." Wesley forced himself up, having to hunch to avoid the bunk above. He reflexively touched his jacket, relieved to find the heavy lead ring box still tucked away in his interior pocket. "We've been looking for you, where the fuck have you been?"

"Really?" Arthur said incredulously. He gestured around them. "Take a look around, Wes. I've been *here.*"

"Where's *here*?"

"A barracks of some kind. Used to house factory workers, I'd guess." Arthur reached toward the open doorway, and then his hand stopped, like he was a mime. "No doors, but my room's got a magic barrier of some kind. Might as well be another concrete wall."

Wesley stood on shaky legs, trying to shake the last of the chloroform. He approached the doorway, but he could see the glittery air in front of him. He reached for it himself, and just past the doorframe, his fingers hit something invisible yet solid. He tapped around, but Arthur was right: there was a barrier, impassable as concrete.

He looked across the hall at Arthur, barely three feet away and completely unreachable. "Are you hurt?"

"No," Arthur said, with a shake of his head. "I've had a bed and blankets, plenty of food and water, books to read. Been treated well, all things considered. There's an English army major here—"

"Major Langford, yes. He headed my company."

"Oh good," said Arthur, "so you already know he's an asshole."

"Quite familiar with that, yes," Wesley said. "Although now he's apparently mad as a March hare, with some lunatic plan to destroy magic."

"It might take me a second to adjust to you knowing

about all this paranormal business," Arthur said. "Jade said they'd told you."

"*You* could have told me," Wesley snapped. "We fucked for six months. Just slipped your mind to mention magic is real?"

"Would *you* have told you? Would you even have listened? Jade said the only reason you finally believed in magic was because you were literally *on fire* and Sebastian had to put you out."

Wesley pursed his lips. "Yes. Well. Anyway. Apparently I'm lucky your urchin didn't use the fucking wind to blow me straight through a window."

"That's fair enough," Arthur said weakly. "But Wes—I don't know where Rory is." He looked wrecked as he said it.

"Shit," Wesley muttered. "We've been looking for you lot since we docked in New York. What happened?"

"We have the de Leons' siphon clock that created and can destroy relics. Except it won't work on the pomander."

"Won't work?"

"The pomander is made from what Zhang calls violation magic. With the other relics, we were able to make the clock work with paranormal blood, but that didn't seem to be enough. So Rory did more scrying, and our best guess is that we need *cursed* blood, which of course is even harder to find."

"Except you knew Sebastian and Mateo de Leon were on their way to New York and they both carry their ancestor's curse."

Arthur nodded. "We were waiting for you all to arrive when Jade got a cryptic message from another bootlegger, based in Tarrytown, implying he knew she was paranormal."

"And you came racing up here to find the threat," Wesley guessed, "instead of waiting a handful of days for two de Leons and an ex-British army captain to join your team."

Arthur winced. "We did arrange for Jade's family to get out of town with the Ivanovs before we left, and we were going to come back to meet you in Manhattan. But of course it was all a trap and we were ambushed at the Hudson Haberdashers speakeasy."

"It was Major Langford?"

"Along with your baronet friend, Sir Ellery, and a paranormal, Alasdair, did you meet—never mind, I can see from the look on your face that you've had the delight of meeting the Mad Hatter. I drank something at the speakeasy that knocked me out, and when I woke up, I was here, separated from the others."

"But why?"

"Alasdair heard Rory's magic in my aura and Langford thinks I'm enchanted," Arthur said grimly. "The major knows my name, my father and my war record, and he's convinced I'll shake the enchantment and come around to his plan to destroy magic. Says he need more soldiers."

"Langford's lost his fucking mind," said Wesley. "He's still working with Alasdair after he murdered Sir Ellery." He quickly filled Arthur in on everything that had happened with Alasdair, Langford, Sir Ellery and the brooch relic.

Arthur looked paler when he finished. "So the brooch is Alasdair's now?"

"But what good is it going to do him?" Wesley said. "He said he hears magic—doesn't that mean his magic already works on other magic?"

"You said Sebastian was bound to the brooch the past few weeks," Arthur said. "What did it do to him?"

"He was able to bind his brother's magic, and destroy the Earl of Blanshard's magic," Wesley said. "Otherwise it mostly seemed to run him ragged. And speaking of relics." He pulled the ring box out of his pocket and held it up.

Arthur's eyes widened. "Is that—"

"Sebastian said it was." Wesley carefully opened the top so Arthur could see inside.

"Oh God." The look in Arthur's eyes was heartbreaking. "How do you have Rory's ring?"

"We found it in the safe at Alasdair's speakeasy. And I have it instead of Sebastian because we didn't know how he might react. Alasdair slipped him something last night that makes him sick when he uses his magic."

"Did he do that to Rory too?" Arthur said worriedly. "To Jade and Zhang? Is Sebastian still at least free?"

"I don't know," Wesley admitted, closing the box. "We weren't together when I was captured, but Alasdair said he sent a message to Sebastian pretending to be me."

"Well, shit," said Arthur. "So you and Sebastian are friends now, then? Jade said you were, but I confess I wasn't going to believe it unless I heard it from your lips."

"Friends." Should he explain Sebastian was his— lover? Boyfriend? Were they telling the others anything at all? Maybe not yet. Wesley cleared his throat. "You have Rory's magic in your aura. I have Rory's ring. If I can somehow get this ring to you, can you use it?"

Arthur shook his head. "Rory's magic holds my aura together; it doesn't give me the power to use magic."

"But surely we can do something with this ring? It's

bloody powerful, isn't it?" said Wesley. "Alasdair was able to feel it through the lead box."

"What?" Arthur scrunched his nose. "He couldn't have. No magic gets through lead, a paranormal who sees magic told me that."

"He must have," said Wesley. "Alasdair said he heard magic on me—muffled so he couldn't tell what it was, but he did hear it. It had to be the ring. Sebastian didn't actually enchant me—well. In any literal sense. What other magic could it possibly be but the ring?"

Arthur made a helpless gesture. "The longer I'm around magic, the less I know."

"So we need Rory to work this ring, but we don't know where he is." Wesley frowned. "It's a big property. Lots of other buildings. And at least some of the non-magical people around here are willing to work for Alasdair. Perhaps we're not the only ones being kept here, but the message Alasdair sent to Sebastian—he told him to meet me at the governor's son's masquerade tonight."

"Walter's masquerade?" Arthur said. "Why?"

"I don't know. I think we can assume it's not for a good reason." Wesley hesitated, but if it had been him, he'd want to know. "Your brother John was planning to be there."

Arthur flinched.

"I'm sorry," Wesley said, and meant it. "I finally find you and I can do nothing but make it worse."

"Not your fault." Arthur ran a hand over his face. "But Wes, what are we going to do? How are we getting out?"

Wesley helplessly shook his head.

For once in his life, he didn't have a smart response.

Chapter Twenty-Two

There was a man in a uniform with a list in hand, checking with each driver as they pulled through the mansion's gate. As the car in front of him disappeared down the long drive, Sebastian eased the borrowed car up to the man. "Sebastian de Leon. I was added to the list today."

The man in the uniform scanned his list. "Yes, sir. Here you are." He gestured down the drive. "They'll help you park at the house."

A few minutes later, Sebastian was parked and climbing the mansion's wide white steps. Jazz drifted from the wooden double doors at the top of the stair, each propped open with another giant jack-o'-lantern. Beyond the foyer, he could see the mansion's crowded downstairs, men in black suits interspersed with women in bright dresses. Several of the guests were wearing pieces of costumes— odd hats, wigs, boas and feathered half masks—and most hands held a cocktail glass or cigarette.

Sebastian stepped into the first room, a circular space under a giant chandelier. Two wide staircases carpeted in red curved up to the second floor. Sebastian stayed to the edge, gaze darting around the room. John Kenzie was there, like an older but equally dashing version of Arthur in a tuxedo and top hat. His arm was around an elegantly beautiful woman with strings of beads and a dress that shone in the light, and they were laughing, their attention on a boisterous man dressed as Uncle Sam.

Sebastian approached quietly. John saw him first and smiled. "Mr. de Leon, wasn't it?" He held out his free hand to shake Sebastian's, introducing the woman at his side as his wife, Emma, and the man dressed as Uncle Sam as another New York City alderman. "Pleased to see you again. If you're here, does that mean Arthur and Lord Fine are hiding somewhere?"

Sebastian's heart fell. "I was hoping you could tell me."

"Haven't seen either of them," John said regretfully.

"Perhaps they're with Walter." Emma held a glass of what might have been champagne.

"Is he feeling better?" Sebastian asked.

"Who, Walter?" Emma seemed genuinely confused. "Was he ill? He seems in great health tonight."

Langford had said Walter had the flu. "Maybe I misheard," Sebastian said, unease threading through him. "I'll keep looking for them."

"You'll come back when you've got them, won't you, and I'll find Blanche?" said Emma. "I know she would love a chance to talk to someone from home, and if you're one of Arthur's friends, I already know I want to hear all about you."

"Arthur has the most interesting friends," John said.

That was one way to describe that everyone Arthur spent time with was paranormal. Sebastian tried to smile. "Of course," he promised, and slipped away in the opposite direction. Whatever was going on tonight, he'd make sure Arthur's family wasn't hurt by magic ever again.

He accepted a glass off a waiter's tray, more as a prop than with any intention of drinking anything that might be in it. The music became louder as he skirted the edge of the crowd into a large ballroom, where a jazz band in costumes played in the corner. The ballroom had been decorated for Halloween, with paper skeletons and bats on display. Glass windows lined the long back wall, overlooking a stone patio with several more pumpkins, their glowing faces visible as dots between partygoers' legs.

Sebastian scanned the room, but Wesley's tall form was nowhere to be seen. He turned back to consider the first room, with the prominent curved staircases.

Had Langford lied about Walter's flu? But why? And where were Langford and Wesley?

He hadn't searched upstairs yet. Guests didn't seem to be climbing the stairs, but a waiter was disappearing down a narrow hall with a tray of empty glasses. Heading for a dumbwaiter to return the dishes to the kitchen, perhaps, and there might be staff stairs nearby.

Sebastian set the glass on one of the bar-height tables that lined the edges of the room, not far from a man playing an upright bass, and followed the waiter down the hall.

Sure enough, a set of narrow staff stairs disappeared both up and down from the main floor. Sebastian had just stepped through the doorway when he heard a voice behind him.

"Sir? Are you looking for something?" Another waiter was peering at him politely.

"Um." Sebastian's mind raced. He couldn't knock the waiter down. What would Wesley say in this situation? "I'm looking for the…smoking room? I just need a quick break from people?"

"Oh!" The waiter smiled. "Yes, that's upstairs, second floor. Should be empty," he said sympathetically.

Sebastian offered him a smile and turned back to the

stairs. They weren't carpeted like the main staircase, so Sebastian moved as quietly as he could as he climbed.

It was an uncomfortable feeling, not being able to use his magic, as if he'd shown up to the fancy party naked. He braced himself with a quick breath and stepped into the hallway of the second floor.

The hall had no wall on one side, just the railing overlooking the hanging chandelier and central room downstairs. The noise of the guests drifted up, conversation and laughter, already quite loud as people hurried to drink while they had the chance.

There were several doors off the hall. Hopefully he wouldn't disturb anyone by checking; the couple was newly married, no children, so he shouldn't be risking waking any young ones.

The first door was an empty office, loudly masculine with a giant mahogany desk and three stuffed stag heads mounted on the wall. Sebastian narrowed his eyes but shut the door.

The next room held a billiards table and smelled like cigars. He stepped inside, holding the door mostly closed behind him, but the room didn't appear to have been used recently: no ash in the ashtrays, none of the billiards equipment out of place. He turned to leave.

But as he opened the door, he came face-to-face with a revolver, held by Major Langford.

"I know what you are."

Sebastian's eyes widened.

"Hands up. Now."

Sebastian raised his hands. "Where's Lord Fine?"

"Here's the situation," Langford said, ignoring his question. "We're surrounded by tipsy idiots who have no idea my gun is currently aligned with your brain. The poison Alasdair gave you is going to take at least another day to work its way out of your system, so if you use your magic, nothing will happen to me, but you'll make yourself useless. If you cry for help, I have an entire party of hostages to shoot. And I will."

Sebastian swallowed. He could take a swing at Langford, try to grab the gun, but he was only passably useful in a fight; his magic had meant he'd never needed to learn more than that. Langford had years of combat under his belt; Sebastian had been a medic.

"Hands on your head. Take two steps backward. Any more than that, I start shooting guests."

Sebastian gritted his teeth but complied. "Where's Wesley?"

"Somewhere safe from you," Langford said. "Once we finish with you, your enchantment will break and he'll come to his senses."

Langford thought Sebastian had bespelled Wesley. But he was safe and that was all that mattered.

Sebastian didn't have time to feel relieved when Langford stepped forward, gun never wavering. "Get walking. We're going up."

Wesley had gone over every inch of his small barracks room and come up with nothing. No cracks in the walls, no weakness in the sink, no way to break apart the metal bunks with his bare hands.

But then, he hadn't expected to find anything. Logical to still check, but if there had been a weakness to find in the rooms, Arthur would have already found it.

Arthur was sitting on the floor of his barracks room, in front of the barrier. He'd been watching Wesley and occasionally calling out ideas, but mostly looking unbearably despondent. Wesley couldn't blame him; Arthur had been here three days with no news of the others.

And now Wesley was here so they could both be fucking useless.

He sat down across from Arthur. "This is a terrible kind of torture, being safe oneself but not knowing how the others are faring."

"Langford truly believes we're enchanted. I suppose he can't imagine someone could have discovered magic is real and been delighted." Arthur huffed. "Why is it always *control* or *destroy* when people find something new? What's wrong with *befriend*?"

Wesley blew out a breath. "Find the answer to that and maybe no one else will ever have to go to war."

"What, really?" Arthur looked up. "The Viscount Fine isn't going mock me for my sentimentality? Are you, in fact, actually enchanted after all?"

Wesley couldn't be insulted, because that was fair. A month ago, he certainly would have mocked Arthur. "Sebastian's a terrible influence."

Arthur snorted. "Jade said you let your cook's daughter adopt two cats because of him. I didn't believe her."

"They're called Crumpet and Flan and they live in my *house* and it's entirely Sebastian's fault. He's as incorrigible as he is handsome."

The corner of Arthur's mouth quirked up. "You noticed that part, did you?"

"Hard to miss." Wesley ran a hand over his face. "Sebastian's going to go to that masquerade, even though he can't use his magic. Going to end up walking right into their trap." He clenched his jaw. "Langford and Alasdair said they want to use him, somehow use his magic in their plan to destroy magic. Or his *blood*."

"A paranormal once told me there's very little stronger than magic made with blood," said Arthur. "Pavel Ivanov was once able to use *my* blood to work his alchemy just because Rory's magic is in my aura."

"And that still doesn't let you use Rory's ring?"

Arthur shook his head. He was frowning again. "I

really don't believe Alasdair could have heard the ring through the lead box. I'm telling you, Gwen said no magic gets through lead and she knows what she's talking about. She wouldn't be wrong about this. Alasdair must have heard something else."

"There's nothing else magic on me to hear," Wesley said.

"Are you certain?"

"I think I would know—" Wesley cut himself off. His eyes had fallen on the cuff of his sleeve, on the rust-colored stain where he'd wiped blood away from Sebastian's face so he could check the cut below.

Arthur was watching him. "What is it?"

Could it—no. Wesley shook his head. "Flight of fancy. It can't be what Alasdair heard, it can't possibly."

"What, Wes?"

Was Wesley actually considering this possibility? He'd well and truly lost his mind. He held up his wrist, showing Arthur his stained sleeve. "This is Sebastian's blood."

"Sebastian's?" Their eyes met, and Arthur's eyes had the most life in them he'd seen yet. "As in, the Sebastian de Leon with the enervation magic that weakens other magic?"

"I was trapped by a barrier somewhat like this once, and Sebastian obliterated it." Wesley's heart was pounding. "But Arthur, really, what are the chances it works?"

Arthur was already on his feet, pressed against the barrier. "It's magic, isn't it? Come on, fucking try it already."

Wesley stood as well. This was absolute madness. It was a small patch of blood. But he reached out with his hand again, putting his fingers against the invisible wall just beyond the door.

Maybe my magic just likes you, Sebastian had once said.

Heart still too fast, Wesley turned his arm to press his sleeve to the wall. Hope, faith—truly these were the worst of all emotions, and damn Sebastian for creating them in him.

For a moment, nothing happened, and Wesley's heart plummeted. This was exactly why one should never have hope—

And then his arm went through like the invisible wall had turned to tissue, the glittering magic in that space dissipating into the air like dust blown off a shelf.

"*Yes*," Arthur said, tightening his fists in excitement. "Bless his stupid magic that knocks us to the floor. Think you can make openings big enough for us to climb through?"

Wesley nodded, throat momentarily gone too tight to speak. Sebastian wasn't even here and his magic was still going to free them, and fuck, Wesley was having emotions again.

A few moments later, Wesley was out of his room and working on Arthur's barrier. Then Arthur squeezed his way out and grabbed Wesley in a giant hug.

"God, thank you, Wes," he said.

And it was a funny thing to be struck by in that moment, but it was almost exactly like being hugged by Mateo—a hug that felt nothing like an old lover and everything like a brother. Like no matter how winding the path, he and Arthur had found their way to the friendship they were meant to have.

"Move your legs, Ace," Wesley finally said, "or I *will* mock your sentiment."

Arthur clapped him on the back, and then they took off down the hall.

Chapter Twenty-Three

Arthur and Wesley crept down the hall on quiet feet, eyes and ears alert. At the end of the hall was a window, and just to its left, a flight of stairs. Wesley paused at the window and very carefully glanced outside, then quickly flattened himself to the wall. "One guard."

"Just one?"

"It's not like Langford and Alasdair would expect us to escape magically sealed cells," said Wesley. "I saw this one earlier. He knows about magic and also bounces at Alasdair's club. He's big and loyal."

"Is he." Arthur smiled with narrowed eyes. "We're big. And angry. I like our odds, let's go."

And he was slipping down the stairs, fast and graceful enough to remind Wesley he'd been an athlete before the war and still boxed for fitness. It wasn't an actual plan so much as it was Arthur charging into danger like an idiot, but Wesley seemed to have caught the disease as well because he followed.

At the bottom of the stairs, they stood on either side of the door. Hinges on the outside. No lock.

They met each other's eyes, and Wesley nodded once.

Arthur turned, and in one smooth, powerful motion, kicked down the door.

The man outside turned, already reaching for a holster under his jacket, but Wesley and Arthur had the advantage of numbers and surprise. Before their guard could aim, Arthur landed a lead hook that sent the man staggering and the gun clattering to the gravel. He tried to steady himself and swing back, but Arthur dodged, then followed up with a jab-cross combo he'd probably learned in the ring.

The man went down. Arthur planted a foot on his chest. "Where are the others?"

The man turned his head to the side, spit out blood. "I'm not saying shit. Throw all the punches you want. I've seen magic; I'll take my chances with you two."

Arthur's jaw tightened.

Wesley picked the revolver up off the gravel. "My turn."

He strode back over to the pair, where Arthur's oxford was still pressed to the man's chest to keep him pinned.

The man's gaze was on Wesley. "You shoot me, you still lose," he said, but this time, it lacked conviction.

Wesley crouched down next to the man's head. With any luck, his words and reputation alone would be enough; he refused to think about the possibility they wouldn't. "We met earlier."

The man's expression flickered.

"What was it Langford said about me?" Wesley said, in a conversational tone better suited for chatting about the weather. "Inventive? Ruthless? Oh, that's right: iron stomach for other people's pain. Does magic have that?"

The man shrank back.

"I need to know what happened to everyone who was with my friend here," Wesley said, nodding toward Arthur. "Are we going to have a civilized conversation about it, or will I have to start digging in your pockets for other weapons that might be put to interesting uses?"

"I don't know who else is here," the man blurted. "But there's a warehouse, all the way down by the river on the other side of the tracks. Used to store hats and other shit before they were shipped out. It's in worse shape than the factory, but Alasdair made himself an office in there."

"Keep going," Wesley said lightly.

"We weren't allowed inside until last week, when he paid Mick and me to carry in crates of army rations. Just like the ones you two got." The man swallowed. "It's on the second floor, at the back."

"Thank you," Wesley said, and cracked him over the head with the pistol.

They stuck the unconscious guard in the barracks and hurried down the gravel drive, the gun still in Wesley's hand, not raised but ready. It was fully dark outside, which meant Wesley had been unconscious for some hours.

The masquerade had probably started.

They headed toward the river as quickly as they dared, sticking to the trees and listening for others. "I forgot how well you bluff," Arthur murmured, as they paused to scan for a patrol. "No wonder I've never beaten you at poker. I think he actually believed you're capable of that."

"Bluffing." Wesley let out a quiet breath. God, he missed Sebastian. "Of course."

They moved forward, paused again.

"You said you rode here with Major Langford," said Arthur. "How far are we from town?"

"Not too far," Wesley said. "If we can get our hands on a car, I can find the way back."

"And if you can get us to Tarrytown, I know where Walter lives." Arthur gestured in front of them, where the skeleton of the run-down main building rose above the trees. "Is that the factory?"

Wesley nodded. "Hat factory, according to Langford. It's still full of crates that say *Mansfield Textile Wholesalers*."

"Mansfield?" Arthur repeated.

Wesley glanced at him. "You know the name?"

"Textile moguls, make my parents look like paupers," Arthur said. "One of them, Luther Mansfield, used to trade in magical artifacts—well, until he was killed by one."

"Magical artifacts." That would be one hell of a coincidence, and Wesley hadn't believed in coincidence even before he'd known about magic. "Alasdair mentioned a business partner, said they used to work together to find magical artifacts."

"Was that Luther, then?" Arthur said. "I'd almost feel sorry for Alasdair if it was. Luther was a nasty piece of work; if he'd found a paranormal who could hear magic so loudly he was struggling to think, he would have taken full advantage, probably made Alasdair's condition even worse."

"Alasdair seems aware of how dangerous he's become. He's fully committed to whatever scheme they think they have to supposedly destroy magic," Wesley said. "Back in Manhattan, he said he'd be supplying the masquerade with liquor, and that he was familiar with Walter's property." He shook his head. "I've no idea what he's planning."

"I'm not exactly going to stand by idly and watch him come after Rory and the others," Arthur said, dark and angry.

"Nor I," Wesley said, in a matching tone.

Arthur glanced at him. "You know, you used to mock

me for being a mother bear, not get growly and over-protective right along with me."

"Ah." Wesley quickly pointed forward. "I think I hear something, up there."

They'd reached the end of the drive, the run-down factory up ahead. Wesley could hear others now, shouts and grunts. There were lights in some of the ground-floor windows.

"Bootleggers?" Arthur guessed.

Wesley pointed to the drive, where two rough-look-ing white men were carrying boxes out from the fac-tory to stack them in the back of a truck. "Bootleggers driving a delivery truck."

They watched for a moment as the men bickered with each other and loaded the boxes. Finally, a bigger man came out of the factory, and Wesley recognized him as the second bouncer—Mick, apparently. He snapped at the pair of bootleggers, and then they all turned and went back into the factory.

"Come on," said Arthur. "To the river."

They stuck to the shadows, staying out of the boot-leggers' sight as they crossed behind the main building. The warehouse could be seen up ahead, a windowless structure with a squat appearance from being wider than it was tall.

They approached on quiet feet, the area dark com-pared to the lights spilling from the factory.

Arthur glanced at Wesley. "Alasdair's office?"

Wesley kept the gun at the ready. "Alasdair's office."

The warehouse door was locked with a chain and padlock. Arthur examined the lock. "Fairly simple one. Any chance you're wearing a stickpin? I've only got a clip."

Wesley extracted the gold and emerald pin from his

tie and handed it over to Arthur. "You pick locks?" he said incredulously, as Arthur bent over the padlock.

"I figured since I don't have magic, I'd pick up other skills." Arthur slipped the stickpin into the keyhole. "You're going to fit right in with your sharpshooting."

You're going to fit right in. That was a phrase Wesley hadn't heard often. Maybe ever. He cleared his throat before any untoward emotions bubbled up. "Hurry the fuck up, come on."

A couple minutes later, Arthur had the door open and they were stepping into an expansive space scattered with crates. The electricity was still on, although many of the bulbs had burnt out, leaving the cavernous area dimly lit.

The second floor looked to be little more than the equivalent of a walled-in hayloft along the back of the warehouse, with only one set of narrow stairs leading up to it.

"Go first, I'll cover you," Arthur whispered.

"I'm the one who's armed," Wesley said testily. "I'll cover *you*."

Arthur rolled his eyes but mercifully went first up the stairs. Wesley's skin began to prickle as they climbed— faint enough he could have dismissed it, if he weren't on alert.

"I think there's magic in the air, do you feel it?" Arthur said under his breath.

Wesley nodded. "But Langford thinks paranormals are the enemies. If he still strategizes like he did during the war, he'll have put a lot of thought into keeping paranormals in—and not enough into keeping the non-magical out."

The stairs opened onto a platform. There was a hall that ran the length of the back of the warehouse, windows overlooking the floor on one side and a row of doors on the other. Warehouse offices, Wesley would gamble.

The first door was ajar, nothing inside but a desk that had been pushed into the corner and a few odds and ends: an assortment of hats on the desk, a filing cabinet, a few rolls of fabric against the wall. Wesley's gaze fell on the hats, and he stilled.

"Come on," Arthur started.

But Wesley shook his head. "Look at the *hats*."

The hats were *moving*. There was no pattern to the movements, no finesse, just small motions as the hats bumped into each other along the desk.

"What's doing that?" Wesley whispered.

"A spell." Arthur took a breath. "Or a telekinetic."

They scrambled to try the second door, and found it locked. Arthur swore as he checked the door. "Old door, but it's bolted and not much room to maneuver. I'm not kicking this one down." He put his ear against the crack between the door and the frame. "I don't hear anything." He knocked on the door with some force. "Jade? Are they keeping you all in there?"

Wesley gestured with the revolver. "Back up."

"Are you screwy? Those bullets are going to ricochet—"

"I'm not shooting the door, I'm bashing the pins out of the hinges." Wesley side-eyed him. *"Are you screwy*—you picked that up from Brodigan."

"And I'd give anything to hear him say it in person," Arthur said impatiently. "Give me that."

Wesley let Arthur take the gun from him and stepped aside. Arthur brought the butt of the revolver down on the higher of the two hinges, and old wood splintered under the strength of an angry ex-quarterback's throwing arm.

Moments later, Arthur was pulling the door off its

hinges, revealing an office space with three cots and two figures curled together on the cot at the far end of the room.

"Miss Robbins." Wesley hurried forward. "Mr. Zhang."

He dropped to a crouch next to the cot where the couple was pressed close to each other, Arthur at his side. Wesley reached for Zhang's wrist. "Steady pulse," he said, letting out a breath. "They're alive."

"But unconscious." Arthur was scanning the room. There were opened army rations on the floor, a couple blankets, a radiator and a single light bulb on the ceiling. "What happened to them?"

"Ace?" Jade's eyelashes were fluttering.

"Christ, Jade." Arthur leaned forward, touched her face. "Are you all right?"

"Not hurt," she mumbled. "Just…hot."

Zhang's wrist under Wesley's fingers was likewise too warm. "Alasdair poisoned Sebastian, slipped something in his drink. Told Sebastian it turns magic on the magic user, causes the magic to attack the blood. He was just like this, feverish and weak, after he used his magic."

"Ace," Jade said again. "They took Rory."

Arthur went very still.

"He was in here too," she said, "but they took him, today, not that long ago."

"Shit," Wesley muttered, while Arthur's words seemed to have stuck in his throat. "They sent Sebastian on a false trail to the masquerade; maybe that's where they took Brodigan."

Arthur blew out a breath. "How long have you been in here?"

"I don't know." Jade sounded just like Sebastian had, fuzzy and distant. "Since the speakeasy? Magic makes the fever worse but it's hard to stop using it."

Wesley looked more closely around the room. There were a few canteens next to the army rations. "Alasdair could have slipped more of the poison into your water, and then not given you lot anything else to drink."

Jade touched Arthur's arm. "Jianwei keeps getting trapped on the astral plane," she said thickly. "The fever makes it hard for him to come back."

Arthur swore. "Come on. We have to get them out."

Langford's gun stayed pressed against Sebastian's back as he was forced back to the servants' staircase. He didn't dare shout; Langford's demeanor was cold as ice, and Sebastian didn't doubt he meant it when he said he'd shoot someone else.

"Up," Langford said, as they reached the stairs. "Hands stay on your head. How did you shake your symptoms so fast? You shouldn't be walking."

Sebastian ignored the question. "Is Wesley upstairs?"

"Of course not," Langford snapped. "I told you, he's somewhere safe from you. Move."

Sebastian set his jaw and began to climb. They went two flights up, bypassing the third floor and coming to the top of the staircase on the fourth. The ceiling was low and steeply pitched, and there was a single, short door on the landing, short enough Sebastian would have to duck to pass through.

As they crested the last stair, the door swung open. "There you are," Alasdair said brightly. "Come in, come in. It's a veritable symphony of magic in here."

Sebastian's eyebrows went up. "You hear magic?"

"Most magic. Not you, of course." Alasdair held the door open expectantly. "I'm glad you're here, though. We can't start without you."

That didn't sound good. "Start what?"

That got him jabbed in the spine by Langford's gun. "We didn't bring you here for questions."

"It's all right, major," said Alasdair. "Of course Sebastian has questions. I certainly would in his shoes."

What could be seen of the room beyond Alasdair was dimly lit and seemed to be all wood: wood floors, paneled walls, wood beams. The attic, perhaps. "Are you planning to kill me?" Sebastian asked warily.

"*Planning* to? No," said Alasdair. "*Willing* to? Absolutely. But that's how I feel about everyone." He clasped his hands together. "Now, before we go in: Major Langford and I would very much like you to use your magic again and reactivate the poison."

Sebastian tried to keep his surprise off his face.

"I know what you're thinking," Alasdair said anyway. "You're thinking *why would Alasdair announce that to me?* You see, we can't force you to use your magic. But I do think we can convince you another way."

Using magic again would make him useless; it wasn't an option. Sebastian shook his head.

"So stubborn." Alasdair opened the door a little wider. "Such a shame; you might be his only hope."

Sebastian's eyes widened, but Langford was already prodding him with the gun, forcing him forward to duck under the door. The rest of the room came into view, and Sebastian went rigid.

It was an attic space, maybe the size of a modest bedroom but with a lower ceiling that just cleared Sebastian's head and would have made Wesley hunch. There was a window in the gable at the far end, tightly shut. A pair of kerosene lamps lit the space from either side of the room.

And in the center of the floor was Rory. His eyes

were closed, glasses askew on his unhealthily flushed face. He was still as a corpse except for his lips, which were moving slightly, as if he was mumbling.

You might be his only hope.

Sebastian's magic understood before his mind did. It leapt from his control, sweeping over the room and everything in it.

Behind him, there was a crash, and Langford swore, but Sebastian couldn't take advantage of weakening him; he was already staggering as fever rushed him so fast his knees gave out. He hit the floor, a small grunt escaping him.

"Heroic," Alasdair said sincerely. "Useless, but heroic."

Sebastian winced as heat spread through his limbs, skin breaking out into sweat. He'd done exactly what they wanted, and Alasdair was right, it had been useless, just like he now was—

Across the floor, Rory's eyes opened. "Sebastian?" he rasped.

Langford swore. "You said de Leon couldn't actually wake him!" he snapped, somewhere above Sebastian's head.

"Sebastian." Rory was blinking. He sounded as sick as Sebastian now felt, but there was awareness in the eyes behind the glasses.

"Major, I can't hear Sebastian's magic," Alasdair said reasonably. "Mr. Brodigan's magic is very strong and the poison sent him spiraling into it as designed. But obviously Sebastian's magic is stronger than I expected. Simple mistake—"

"Shut up." Langford was moving away, deeper into the attic.

Rory's hazy eyes met his. "What's going on? Where's Ace?"

Sebastian weakly shook his head. "You okay?"

"*No*," Rory said. "I've been stuck across five centuries. How long've I been out?"

"Let's focus on tonight." Alasdair crouched down between them. "We've got very big plans," he said conspiratorially. "We're going to get rid of magic, and both of you are going to help."

Wesley got Zhang over his shoulders in a soldier carry while Arthur picked up Jade bridal-style.

"I should walk," Wesley heard Jade say blearily, to Arthur, as they made their way out of the room.

"In this state, down these stairs, in those heels?" Arthur said.

"Fair," she said reluctantly.

"But rest assured you are the only person I know who can spend three days locked in an office and still look like you stepped out from the pages of one of your French fashion magazines."

She gave a soft laugh. "Thanks for coming."

"Always," Arthur promised.

They got down the stairs and across the warehouse floor. As they reached the front door, Zhang said, "Fine."

Wesley nearly dropped him in surprise.

"*Thank you*," Zhang said, slurred but heartfelt. "Help me walk?" Wesley got him down to his feet as Arthur set Jade down and they stumbled into each other's arms.

"You're out." Jade's arms were very tight around his neck.

They looked a little precarious. Wesley tried to stay in catching distance. "Sebastian went through the same thing. Took a night of no magic to clear. Can you two hold off on the magic for a bit?"

Zhang pulled back slightly from Jade, but not far

enough to separate. "But I can check the path forward from the plane—"

"Not this time," Arthur said firmly.

"But you said Sebastian has been lured into a trap," said Jade.

"And we need to find Rory," Zhang started.

"Rory of all people would not want you to lock yourself back on the astral plane," Arthur said. "We're going to rely on Wesley's eyes."

"And Arthur's fists," Wesley added.

Jade's brows drew together as she seemed to consider that. "You're certain Sebastian cleared it by not using his magic?" she said to Wesley. "You stayed with him all night?"

Arthur glanced at Wesley curiously. "You didn't mention that part before. In fact, you also didn't explain how you got Sebastian's blood on your sleeve."

"Ah." Wesley coughed. "Can we focus on the situation at hand? We passed bootleggers at the main factory. They were loading trucks."

Zhang tilted his head. "I think I just heard you say we're stealing a truck."

Sebastian was going to be insufferable when he found out. Wesley cleared his throat. "Come on, then."

Arthur supported Jade while Wesley helped Zhang, and the four of them got out of the warehouse. The perimeter around the windowless warehouse was dark, especially compared to the lights of the main factory. They quietly made their way down the side of the warehouse until they reached the corner, and then Wesley peered around it.

Up ahead, there were two trucks parked outside the factory. The lights illuminated the two bootleggers hefting more crates toward them.

Wesley scanned the area. "Not much cover on a gravel drive."

"Do we need cover?" Arthur said tightly. "Can I not just go in swinging?"

"That is a ludicrous but admittedly tempting thought," Wesley said. "Except our guard was armed so these blokes probably are too." He glanced at the trucks, their transportation to find Rory, to get to Sebastian before Langford and Alasdair sprang their trap. "Then again, I'm armed too."

"Look, they've put the crates in one of the trucks." Jade still sounded a little fuzzy as she pointed. "They're going back in the warehouse."

"This is our window, let's go," said Arthur.

They crossed the dark gravel drive as quietly as they could. "Quickly now," Wesley said, as they reached the closer truck. Out of habit, Wesley went for the right side of the vehicle and accidentally ended up on the passenger's side, but it was too late to correct.

The truck had a single bench seat. Wesley helped Zhang in first. "This truck is full of hooch," Zhang pointed out.

"No time to unload," Arthur said, helping Jade in through the other side.

"I'm the one who knows how to get back to town, you don't even know where we are," Wesley hissed across the seat, as Jade made space by sitting on Zhang's lap and Arthur got up into the driver's seat behind her. "Let me drive."

"American car, American roads, American driver. Hurry up and get in; this is going to be loud." He turned the engine over, which came to life with a roar.

"Shit," Wesley said, scrambling up into the truck as

he heard the shouts in the warehouse behind him. "If you're driving, then fucking drive."

Arthur hit the gas. The truck screeched as it shot down the gravel drive. "Tell me where to go."

Wesley glanced behind them. Three people were already sprinting out of the warehouse. "Straight ahead, then a left." He heard the roar of another engine. "They've got the other truck."

Arthur took the left so sharply that the back of the truck fishtailed and two crates of moonshine went tumbling out.

Wesley tightened his grip on the revolver and leaned out the window. The other truck had just taken the same left, just as fast, and they'd have the advantage of knowing these streets and these vehicles. "Why are your cars like this? I'd have to be a contortionist to use my right arm." Wesley swapped the revolver to his left hand as Mick the bouncer stuck his head out the passenger window. "*Drive*, Ace."

"I'm *trying*."

Wesley's eyes widened as Mick the bouncer leaned out farther and his firearm came into view. "Christ, that's a fucking *tommy gun*."

Nothing for it; Wesley had to aim left-handed. He sighted down the barrel, and took the shot.

The tire burst. There was a terrible screech as the wheel's rim hit gravel, and Mick was thrown back into the truck as the vehicle went careening off the side of the road.

"Oh, well done, Wesley," Arthur said, just as Zhang said, "What a shot" and a "Bravo" came from Jade.

And Wesley was absolutely not going to have an emotion about a truckload of people praising him, or about the pounding of his heart, or how a few weeks with Sebastian had transformed his life from avoiding parties to rescuing paranormals and shootouts with bootleggers.

"Absolute lunacy," he said instead, twisting back into his seat. "And credit to Arthur; I wouldn't even have a gun if he hadn't taken down our guard."

They got out on the open road, the cold night air whipping through the truck.

"I do have a brutal right hook, and that's not hubris," said Arthur. "Ask Sebastian sometime."

"Absolutely not," Wesley said shortly, holding on to the side of the truck as Arthur pushed it to its limits. "We're not reminding him of what he did under blood magic, he self-flagellates too much over it already. Take this right here."

"Did you just tell me to spare someone's feelings?" Arthur took the turn with his eyebrows raised. "*Are* you enchanted? I'm asking seriously this time."

Wesley huffed. "You know, for a man who was dead set on driving, you're doing a lot of talking."

"Am I?" Arthur glanced at Jade and Zhang. "Did I tell you two that Wesley here cabled me asking about Sebastian?"

"Oh, that was my suggestion," said Jade.

"He was convinced Sebastian was a terrible scoundrel," Zhang added.

Wesley managed not to wince, but it was a near thing. "Was I?"

"Like you ever forget anything," said Arthur. "What was it you wrote in your cable? Something along the lines of *Arthur: you won't be duped by good looks. Confirm: Sebastian de Leon is a criminal.* Yet you're terribly concerned for him now?"

Wesley cleared his throat. "We're taking another right, just up here."

"And now you're dodging a question?" said Arthur. "What has gotten into you?" The tires screeched as he made the turn. He glanced across Jade and Zhang, to Wesley. "You don't—you don't fancy him, do you?"

Wesley just managed not to groan. Arthur's voice had been filled with *pity*. "Christ, Ace. Really? *Now*?"

"Oh boy," Jade murmured.

"Why not?" Arthur said. "Jade and Zhang know you're my ex."

"I think that actually makes the conversation *more* awkward," Zhang muttered.

Wesley pinched the bridge of his nose. "Arthur. Will you just fucking drive?"

"Wes, you're my friend," said Arthur. "I know you haven't dated since me, but I would hate to see you pining after someone you can't have. You have to have noticed that Sebastian adores women," and really, this entire line of conversation was intolerable. "I understand that he's very handsome but—"

"Yes, he is," Wesley snapped. "So handsome you came crying to me in London that Rory was going to leave you for him. You also remember that bit, don't you?"

Jade and Zhang turned to look at Arthur.

Arthur opened his mouth, then snapped it shut.

"Take the second left," said Wesley. "Without commentary, this time."

Arthur rolled his eyes and drove on.

Sebastian stared at Alasdair. "You want to get rid of magic?"

"Oh swell," Rory said hoarsely. "Woke up to a fella screwier than me."

"Not about this," Alasdair said pleasantly. "This is Major Langford's plan. He's very tactical."

Sebastian tried to focus. He was so hot, then so cold, in alternating bursts. "Alasdair," he tried. "What are you doing? Where are Wesley and the others?"

"*Wesley*?" Rory groaned. "You gotta be kidding me. Fine's in New York?"

Alasdair tsked. "He doesn't let *me* call him Wesley."

"Enough." Langford stepped into view. The gun was still in his right hand; something Sebastian couldn't quite place in his left—metal and glass and cloth, perhaps? "We weren't supposed to have two of you awake." He looked between them consideringly, then pointed the gun directly at Sebastian.

Sebastian met Langford's eyes and refused to flinch.

"*Don't*." Rory was trying to push up.

But Alasdair had straightened. "I know you'd like to shoot him, and probably all of us," he said to Langford, "but we do need Sebastian alive."

Langford narrowed his eyes, gun still aimed at Sebastian. "I know you enchanted Fine," he said harshly. "As soon as you've served your purpose, you're dead."

"Yes, yes, we're all very dangerous men here," Alasdair said. "Major, a moment."

They stepped toward the wall and began to talk in low voices.

Rory narrowed his eyes at Langford and Alasdair. "No chance you've got my ring, is there?" he said to Sebastian, in an undertone.

Did Wesley still have the ring? Where was he, and was he okay? "Sorry," Sebastian said, shaking his head.

"S'okay," Rory slurred. "You got me outta my magic. Appreciate it. Can't burn off whatever's making us sick, can you?"

Sebastian shook his head regretfully.

"You all drank the poison. It's in your bloodstreams, Sebastian can't do anything about that." Alasdair had walked back toward them. He reached into his coat and withdrew a box that Sebastian recognized all too well. His stomach dropped.

"You bastard." Rory's glare had intensified. "You stole the pomander."

"No, I stole the *brooch*," Alasdair said patiently. "The pomander has been up for grabs, waiting for someone who could listen to it and be up to the task of unlocking it."

Rory went very pale.

"Now see, Mr. Brodigan here already knows what it takes to unlock the pomander," Alasdair said to Sebastian. "Unlike the brooch, this one takes quite a bit more than a single murder to bind it to someone. There's a lot of pain involved. But luckily I've got plenty of people downstairs."

Sebastian's gaze went to Langford. "You're going to let him enslave non-magic minds?"

"Of course I'm not," Langford snapped, from over by the wall. He was moving around, dressing perhaps. "That's why he needed to steal that brooch of yours first."

"Oh no," Rory whispered.

"Yes, see, now you're getting it," Alasdair said proudly. "The brooch makes magic work on other magic. It's going to let me make the pomander relic work on other paranormals, and then I'll have plenty of options for how to get rid of all of you."

"You can't control two relics," said Rory.

"That brooch alone—" Sebastian started.

"Yes, it told me. It was far too much for you," Alasdair interrupted. "But *only* you, because when you wield the brooch, it draws on your most innate magic."

"Yes, the enervation—"

"No. Your blood curse."

Sebastian stared.

"I'm sure you felt quite terrible, having a relic literally yanking on your blood," said Alasdair. "It would have eventually killed you, and sooner rather than later. You're very lucky I stole it."

Sebastian swallowed. "But you murdered a man to steal it."

"Unfortunately these days, I'd kill anyone."

"These days?"

"Once upon a time, I had more of my mind," Alasdair said. "It was even better after I found a lodestone that helped. But when Luther and I had a falling-out last year, he stole the lodestone away and had me committed. I haven't heard many of my own thoughts since."

"I've seen the lodestone," Rory said in a scratchy voice. "Was your partner Luther Mansfield?"

"Oh, did you know him?" Alasdair said. "I was poor as dirt when he and I first met, and I thought he had done me such a favor when he pulled me off the street in Glasgow. Got me into both of his businesses, textile and paranormal, in exchange for me using my magic. I would have done anything he asked, but turned out, he was kind of a bastard."

"You think?" Rory said sarcastically.

"How did you fall out with him?" Sebastian asked.

"You might not believe it, but I was upset he had someone killed." Alasdair put a hand on the top of the pomander box. "Bit ironic, isn't it, considering how many people *I'm* about to kill."

Sebastian tried to move. "No, Alasdair—"

The attic door opened. "Major Langford? Alasdair?" Eddie, the mean-looking man who'd been standing guard at the entrance to the speakeasy, stuck his head around the door. "It's top of the hour." He stepped inside, closing the door. "You wanted me to come up?"

"Don't come in," Sebastian managed to say, as Rory slurred, "Get outta here."

Eddie gave them an unimpressed look. "Like I'd listen to either of you. The major said you're evil magic users." He squinted across the room. "Major? Why're you wearing that?"

"Eddie, I appreciate your reliability," said Alasdair. "Good help is so very hard to find."

"*Run*," Sebastian rasped.

Alasdair opened the pomander.

Sebastian gagged as the vile scent filled the attic, a stomach-turning blend of decaying flowers and rotting flesh. Rory likewise gagged.

But Eddie began to choke.

"*Alasdair*," Sebastian said. "Alasdair, stop."

"You both know the pomander has this effect on the non-magical," Alasdair said pleasantly, like Eddie hadn't hit the attic floor on his hands and knees. His face was turning purple. "It's not pleasant for those of us with magic, but for someone without magic, it shreds their aura. In a tiny space like this, it's going to happen quite fast."

"*Don't*," Rory said.

Eddie made a retching noise, and Sebastian couldn't let this happen. He forced himself up onto his arms. Rory was trying to do the same.

"You're both trying to be heroes, I know, but we *need* a first death to get started," said Alasdair. "It's our champagne bottle against the ship's prow."

Sebastian pulled himself forward. He was going to

get to Eddie, cover his nose, get him out of the room, something—

A shot rang out.

Eddie dropped to the floor.

Sebastian froze as Rory cried out.

Major Langford stepped forward, gun in his hand, and Sebastian now recognized what had been in his hand earlier: a gas mask, the kind they'd had on the front. Langford was wearing it now.

"You tried to save him and forced the major's hand." Alasdair shook his head slowly. "We can't let you interfere, you know."

Rory was staring at Eddie's unmoving body. Sebastian's jaw tightened as he looked up at Langford in the gas mask. "You planned this with Alasdair. You're killing innocents."

"The major understands it's a war on magic," said Alasdair. "There are going to be casualties."

Eddie's eyes were open and staring lifelessly forward, blood beginning to pool under his head. Langford was moving around the room again, gas mask in place. The stench of the pomander in this small space was nauseating.

"Alasdair, I know part of you understands this is wrong," Sebastian said. "Part of you cares about people. You sent that letter to Wesley, didn't you? You tried to warn him about Sir Ellery."

"Yes, because Lord Fine was in danger. *Everyone* is in danger, when magic is involved," Alasdair said. "Look what it's done to me. I'm killing people now, Sebastian. Magic has to go. I'm trying to save everyone, paranormals drowning in it, people like Lord Fine without it."

"But this is not the way," Sebastian pleaded. "I can take the brooch back. I can bind your magic."

Alasdair raised an eyebrow. "I just told you the brooch will eventually kill you."

"Not important now," Sebastian said.

Alasdair appeared to be thinking it over. "No, I'm afraid that won't work," he finally said, with what seemed like genuine regret. "I don't think we should let all the other paranormals keep their magic; most of them are dangerous too. Better to just destroy it all."

Sebastian winced. "Alasdair—"

"You of all people should understand," Alasdair said. "You're descended from an actual witch-hunter. He would have approved of all of this." He glanced at Langford. "The major is very smart to keep that gas mask on; this pomander is truly deadly for anyone without magic. Well, I suppose not Arthur Kenzie—I heard your magic in his aura, you know," he said to Rory. "But you better hope no one else without magic comes up here and tries to be a hero, or, well." He gestured at Eddie. "You see what happens."

Shit. Well, that was the only thing Major Langford had done Sebastian would be grateful for. Thank goodness Wesley was nowhere nearby.

Chapter Twenty-Four

Arthur had known where to go from town, and soon enough, their stolen truck was climbing up a hillside road.

"I'm certain we're both on the guest list to this party," Wesley said, as Arthur slowed the truck in approach to an open gate topped with jack-o'-lanterns. "Do we just tell the gate guard who we are and that we brought plus ones?"

"Absolutely not," said Arthur. "You said John was here. I'm not going to make him explain why his vagabond brother crashed the masquerade with a stolen truck full of bootlegged liquor."

Wesley considered the house. "Well, Alasdair said he was supplying this party. Convenient we're driving one of his trucks."

"*I* could have supplied this party," Jade muttered.

"You don't poison the customers," Zhang agreed.

"Or sell gin with pieces of hat in it," said Wesley.

Arthur cringed. "I drank that gin."

They turned through the gate, and Arthur stopped the car next to a man with a list. The man eyed Arthur's stubbly beard and the dirt on Wesley's face. "And who are you?"

"We're making a delivery," Arthur said winningly.

"From Mansfield Textile Wholesalers," Jade added meaningfully.

"Oh." The man stepped away. "Drive around to the back, they'll direct you to the kitchens."

Arthur followed the drive around the side of the house and to the back. A pair of men in black-and-white suits were patiently waiting.

Arthur hopped out of the truck and turned to help Jade down. "All yours," he said to the men, as Wesley and Zhang stepped out of the other side of the truck.

"Where now?" Arthur said, under his breath, as the men in the black-and-white suits began to unload crates. "These grounds cover a large part of the hillside, and they could be anywhere."

"I'm going to use magic." Zhang had steeled himself. "We have to find them—"

"You won't be able to find Sebastian with magic, because of the tattoo," Wesley pointed out. "We have other options to try first." He pulled Rory's ring box out of his jacket.

Jade blinked. "You have Rory's ring?"

"Yes," said Wesley. "And Arthur has Brodigan's magic in his aura. Ace, can you not tell if he's here somewhere?"

"No, Wesley, it's not a leash," Arthur said testily. "Look, give me the ring and I'll show you I'm useless with it."

Wesley handed over the box.

Arthur opened it. Emotion flickered on his face as he lifted the jeweled ring out.

Nothing was happening. "At least put it on," Wesley said.

"It truly doesn't work for me, Wes." Arthur tucked

the lead box away in his pocket and slid the ring onto his right pinkie. "There. See? Nothing—"

The ring went flying off Arthur's finger.

It shot up into the sky, a tiny flash of gold that caught the house lights.

And then it was gone.

The four of them stared up at the sky, at the stars beyond.

"What the fuck just happened?" said Wesley.

Jade's gaze was still on the sky. "The ring is full of the magic of the wind. And it's always responded to Rory's stronger emotions."

"He once set it rattling around in our library, despite being across Manhattan at Arthur's place," said Zhang.

"So that means Brodigan *is* here?" Wesley said.

In the distance, glass shattered.

Arthur's eyes had gone wide. "I think it means," he said, in a voice that was equal parts hope and trepidation, "that we better evacuate the house."

Alasdair was humming to himself as he carefully set the pomander on the makeshift pedestal made of stacked boxes, as if there wasn't a body crumpled in an unmoving ball a couple feet away. Langford was leaning against the wall, gun in hand, a discomforting presence with the gas mask still in place. The smell in the claustrophobic, enclosed attic was getting worse.

"You know, we have a murder right here," said Alasdair, "and neither of you two can even stand." He opened his jacket to show off the brooch pinned to his lapel. "If you could just find your feet, you could steal this from me in the next couple of minutes, and then my plan would be foiled. I'd have to settle for enslaving all the non-magic minds instead of binding all the paranormals to me."

Across the room, Langford cocked his gun.

"I don't think he likes that idea," Alasdair said to Sebastian and Rory.

"Listen, buddy," Rory said, hoarse and tense. "You can't be king of two relics, understand? That's too much magic. I would know."

Alasdair tutted. "You really ought to be a little more ambitious. We picked you out of your merry little band of misfits to sacrifice tonight because you have the most magic, the most powerful blood. Think of what you could do with it—well. If you were going to live through the night," he finished apologetically. "I'm afraid neither of you will."

"You said you weren't planning to kill us," Sebastian said.

"No, I said *I* wasn't planning to kill you," Alasdair said patiently. "I do plan to take control of you, though. That might kill you, and if it doesn't, Major Langford will. He's dying to shoot all of us."

He looked back at Rory. "I wonder if the magic you put in Arthur Kenzie's aura will live on in him after your death. Do you think I'll be able to control him too?"

"If you've hurt Arthur," Rory said lowly, "I'm gonna make you regret it."

"We haven't hurt Arthur," Alasdair said impatiently. "It's the paranormals we want to hurt. And speaking of pain."

He crouched down again, and Sebastian saw the glint of metal in his hand. "We've got a nice fresh murder, and now I'm just going to help myself to a bit of your cursed blood," he said brightly. "Can't unlock the pomander without it. Then, of course, it's going to take many painful deaths, but one step at a time."

"You can't—" Rory stopped mid-sentence, his eyes going very wide.

"And he calls me *screwy*," Alasdair said, as he reached for Sebastian's arm. "I can at least finish my sentences."

"The pomander is evil," Sebastian said. "You need to stop listening."

"Oh, but I can't stop," said Alasdair. "I love its song."

Sebastian squinted up at him, seeing red where he shouldn't. "The pomander is lying to you. It's killing you."

Alasdair scoffed. "Killing me?"

"Your ears are bleeding."

Alasdair touched his ear. "Fancy that," he said, looking at his now red-tipped fingers.

"Alasdair—" Sebastian started.

But then Alasdair stilled. His gaze went straight to the window. "Oh. We didn't plan for this."

Sebastian furrowed his brow. "What—"

The attic window shattered like it had been hit by a bullet. Something tiny and gold zipped across the room.

Straight onto Rory's finger.

"Langford," Alasdair called, but Langford was already pushing off the wall, raising his gun.

Sebastian's heart went to his throat. With a burst of adrenaline, he shoved himself forward, landing over Rory's chest. Rory was so small, even younger than Mateo. He'd cover Rory from the shot—

A blast of wind swirled around the room, blowing the gun straight from Langford's hand and sending it clattering to the floor. A muffled shout could be heard inside the gas mask as Langford stumbled uselessly after it.

Then, in the distance, Sebastian heard a high-pitched whistle.

And suddenly scrawny little Rory was the one covering *him*.

"Stay down," he hissed.

And then the storm hit.

They left Jade and Zhang to evacuate the kitchens, and then Wesley was sprinting up the manor's stairs, Arthur at his side. As they crested the stairs, he heard it: a high-pitched whistle.

Wesley startled. "What the devil—"

"Oh shit, he's called it from the southeast," Arthur said. "That's the ocean."

They burst through the door into a large foyer with a massive chandelier and two curved staircases winding up to the second floor. Heads jerked in their direction.

"Everyone!" Arthur shouted, rather needlessly. "If I could have your attention—"

He was cut off by the crash of glass—a *lot* of glass, like the windows along an entire wall had just blown out. A series of screams came from somewhere in the back.

"Oh hell," said Wesley.

They scrambled toward the crash. Guests in tuxedos and sparkling dresses, wearing odds and ends of costumes, came pouring past them, out the front doors and down the steps. As Wesley and Arthur reached the source and what seemed to be the ballroom, the wind roared, whipping through the house in a mighty gust.

A *wet* gust.

Wesley was slapped in the face by wind and rain, his suit almost instantly drenched. "Ugh."

Arthur wiped at his face with his jacket sleeve. "There is going to be hell to pay if they've upset Rory enough to call in a hurricane."

"A *hurricane*—" But Wesley caught sight of one of the guests. "Arthur, your brother!"

John was still in the ballroom. A cabinet bigger than a man had toppled onto the grand piano, trapping frightened people in the corner, and John was frantically trying to get to them.

"John," Arthur said, voice strangled. "Emma."

"Help him." Wesley was already turning. "I'm going to find Rory and Sebastian."

He didn't wait for Arthur to respond, instead sprinting back into the foyer. The ring had flown off Arthur's hand and up into the sky; wherever Rory was being held, there was a chance it was up, and the only place that could be was the upper floors of the house.

He could only hope Sebastian was with him, and that he'd make it on time.

The attic window and part of the roof were torn straight off, spiraling out into the sky and disappearing. Rory held Sebastian down on the ground as Alasdair and Langford smashed into one of the attic walls. The pomander went careening into the corner closest to them, spinning like the world's most repulsive top.

"Rory? Sebastian?" Zhang's astral projection had just materialized in the middle of the attic. Relief poured through Sebastian.

"Zhang." Rory rolled off Sebastian onto his back. "Damn it, he can't see us with your tattoo, can he?"

Zhang was facing in the opposite direction. "I think you have to be here," he said, "because I can't see anyone and that has to be Sebastian's fault. I'm using magic so my body is sick as hell again, but the others are looking for you."

The others. Sebastian's heart leapt to his throat.

"Not Wesley," he said, even though it was useless and Zhang couldn't hear him. "Don't let Wesley near the pomander—"

But there were footfalls, feet running up the stairs to the attic, and the next moment came Wesley's voice. "Sebastian! Where are you?"

"Wesley!" Jesus, his voice was useless, Wesley would never hear him. Rain poured in through the window and missing roof, soaking him as he began to crawl toward the door, closer to Alasdair and Langford. "Wesley, *no*—"

Someone shouldered open the attic door with force. "Sebastian—"

His name became a choked off retch as Wesley stumbled forward, a revolver falling from his hand and skittering away on the floor.

Against the wall, Alasdair began to laugh. It shook his shoulders, the light catching the brooch pinned just within his jacket. "Too late, Sebastian," he said, as Wesley hit the attic floor on hands and knees. "The pomander has been free, growing stronger, saturating the air with its magic. Fine's aura will never make it—"

Sebastian was already moving. With the bouncer's corpse just feet away, Sebastian staggered onto hands and knees, swiped the brooch off Alasdair's jacket, and fell on top of the pomander just as the brooch's magic rushed him.

He could feel the pomander, its magic slick and oily like the Puppeteer's magic had been. As the brooch's magic charged painfully through him, like it was drawing from his bones, Sebastian reached for every bit of magic he had, let the brooch's magic strip the curse in his veins, and let it go.

Beneath him, the pomander burst open, dust and bits of flowers spilling out.

"Rory," he tried to say.

But a zephyr was already swirling around him, sweeping the pomander's ancient remains into the tiniest of tornados, which lifted up into the sky and disappeared.

Sebastian flopped over onto his back. Everything hurt, his chest, his heart, his lungs. He looked at the brooch in his hand, feeling the pain all the way down to his veins.

"Goodness, that was deafening," Alasdair said, drawing Sebastian's attention. Blood was still trickling from his ears. "Very selfless. Suicidal, in fact. You drew too deep: you destroyed a relic, but your magic is gone."

Sebastian took a heaving breath, Alasdair's words ringing true. He felt like scorched earth, like he'd been stripped of color and left a husk of gray.

"And without magic the brooch will pull on your life force instead," Alasdair said. "You saved Lord Fine just to die in his place."

Sebastian's eyes met Wesley's, who was also breathing too hard, his expression unreadable.

There were shouts in the hall, echoing footsteps on the stairs, but Sebastian's eyes went to Langford. He had scrambled up onto his feet, ripping off the gas mask. "You've ruined it all," he snarled at Alasdair, as his hair and clothes flapped in the wet wind. "You murdered Sir Ellery for nothing."

"It does seem that way, doesn't it?" said Alasdair. "What a shame Sebastian destroyed that pomander."

Langford's nostrils flared. He swooped down onto the floor, snatching up his gun.

"Langford!" Wesley's shout came as if from a distance, because Sebastian was now staring right into the barrel of Langford's revolver.

"If we can't control the paranormals, I can still kill all of them. Starting with you."

Langford's finger was moving on the trigger. Rory was raising his hand, but even the wind wasn't going to be fast enough this time—

A shot rang out through the room. Langford hit the floor.

Sebastian drew a breath of surprise—

A hand swiped the brooch straight out of his.

An involuntary gasp left Sebastian as he felt the brooch's hold on him disappear like ashes on the wind. He tipped over onto his back as a thud shook the attic, voices blending into a blur. For a moment, all Sebastian could process was the glimpse of the night sky peeking through a gap in the clouds, stars twinkling at him through the torn roof.

Finally, with a deep breath, he turned his head to the right.

And stared.

Langford was crumpled on the ground, while Alasdair was off the ground—slumped and apparently unconscious, but still pinned in place against the wall.

He jerked his head left, and there was Jade, kneeling on the ground next to him, the brooch relic sparkling in her hand.

"That really does pack a punch, doesn't it?" she said with a wince. "I feel like I could move a truck. I was only trying to lift Alasdair and accidentally knocked his head against the wall a bit harder than I meant." The curtains were rising up from the floor to wind around Alasdair like ropes. "He's alive, but it may take him a few minutes to wake back up, as well as a few minutes for me to regain enough control to get everything else down."

Sebastian glanced around to see all of the attic's boxes now floating in the air. "Jade?" he said, voice breaking.

Jade glanced at him out of the corner of her eye. "I stole your brooch," she said, with a wry smile. "Should be safe enough for me, and I don't think any of us wanted to say goodbye to you."

"Jade, bless you." Sebastian took another deep breath, and let his head fall back, catching sight of Langford's unmoving body. "So who—"

"Sebastian." Wesley stepped over him, holding a revolver.

Emotion welled in Sebastian's chest. "Wes," he whispered.

Wesley reached down with his hand. Sebastian took it and let Wesley pull him to his feet.

"Are you all right?" Wesley said, looking into Sebastian's eyes. "Sebastian, your magic—"

Sebastian stumbled forward, into Wesley's arms, and planted his lips right on Wesley's.

Wesley made a surprised noise.

"Estás ileso, I'm so glad you're okay." Words were tumbling out of Sebastian against Wesley's mouth as he wrapped trembling arms around Wesley's neck and kissed him with exhaustion and relief. "You saved my life—"

Someone cleared their throat.

Sebastian froze.

The attic had gone very quiet. Slowly, he turned his head. Arthur was frozen in the doorway, supporting Zhang. Jade and Rory seemed to have stopped midway through helping each other stand. All of them were staring at him and Wesley.

Wesley coughed. "I hadn't actually told any of them yet."

"Oh," Sebastian said weakly.

The attic burst into a flurry of voices and movement.

"I refuse to deal with anything else right now. Teddy, are you hurt—"

"Ace, if you've got so much as a bruise I'm blowing this Alasdair fella all the way to the Hudson and will you tell your ex to *stop kissing people*—"

"One surprise at a time is enough—Jade, love, are you okay with that relic—"

"Yes, but I can't believe I missed this and is Rory ever going to turn off the wind—"

"Sorry," Sebastian said sheepishly, to Wesley, under the voices of the others as they scrambled around the attic.

"I'm not," Wesley said firmly. He dropped his eyes, and then he stilled.

Sebastian furrowed his eyebrows. "What?"

Wesley reached for Sebastian's wrist, encircling it with his hand and pulling it down from his neck, turned so the pulse point was facing up.

All of the color of the tattoo was gone. All that remained was a black ink outline of the lion, almost like he'd been branded into Sebastian's skin.

"Is that—a lion?" Arthur said.

Wesley slowly ran his thumb over the lion. Sebastian looked up and found Wesley's gaze on him.

"Was Alasdair telling the truth?" Wesley said quietly. "Do you have any magic left, or did you give it all to save my life?"

"I don't know," Sebastian admitted. "But if I did, it was worth it."

This time, Wesley was the one to kiss him in front of everyone.

Chapter Twenty-Five

The storm had finally stopped—exactly the moment that Arthur had pulled Rory into his arms, obviously not a coincidence. But the guests would be returning, and they had the unconscious Alasdair to deal with and two bodies to explain.

Somehow Wesley ended up talking to Rory, of all people, about the plan for Alasdair and the bodies of Langford and Eddie the speakeasy bouncer.

"They locked Arthur up for three days," Rory said flatly, before Wesley could even finish asking for his opinion. "The bulls can have them."

Wesley raised his eyebrows. He glanced around the attic. Alasdair was still passed out and tied in curtains. Jade and Zhang were stuck together like glue on the attic floor, Arthur only a foot away from the couple as he checked Sebastian for a concussion.

Wesley took a pointed step toward the wall, and Rory followed until they'd gotten just a little more distance between them and the others.

"Major Langford worked for the War Office," Wesley said. "The local police can address the bouncer's death, but they are not handling Langford. I'm cabling home."

"If Langford didn't want the American police in-volved, he probably shouldn't've sailed over and kidnapped a bunch of Americans," said Rory, which was an obnoxiously sound point. "He locked all of us up. He was going to *murder* all of us, starting with Sebastian."

That was true. Wesley nevertheless leaned down so they were closer to level. "Langford was my commanding officer for a time during the war. I will handle his death."

Rory pursed his lips, studying Wesley. "You know blame's on him, yeah? He forced your hand?"

"I know," Wesley said tightly.

Rory considered him for another moment. "Ace said his brother is here," he said. "And we're in the governor's son's house. You can handle it how you want, but work with them and Ace; they'll keep any heat off you."

That was surprisingly clever advice. Had Wesley been underestimating Rory's mind as well as his magic all this time? Ugh, what a humiliating thought. "And Alasdair?"

Rory's gaze went to Alasdair's unconscious body. "I felt Sebastian's magic sweep the attic. Strong enough to destroy a relic."

"And?"

"I had my ring on, and I've got Ace's aura in my magic," Rory said. "I'm fine. But I don't know how much of Alasdair's magic will have survived under Sebastian's."

Wesley raised an eyebrow. "What does that mean?"

"It means that maybe he'll hear the world now, not just magic. Maybe he'll be a different person when he wakes up." Rory looked back at Wesley. "Can you and Ace get him put somewhere to heal up? *Not* Hyde Gardens again. Find somewhere he'll be safe."

Wesley opened his mouth, then closed it. Rory had been lost in magic before. Maybe Wesley should lis-

ten to him. Just this once. "Very well," Wesley said,
straightening up.

"That was easier than expected." Rory tilted his
head. "Sebastian's that much of an influence on you?
How'd you even get together?"

"Why would I tell you that story?" Wesley said
shortly.

"'Cause I *asked*," Rory said.

Wesley fixed him with a stare down his nose. "Remind me: when did my relationships become any of
your business?"

"When you forgot where your lips are supposed to
go."

Wesley raised his eye skyward. "Are you ever going
to let that go?"

"Nope," Rory said, popping the *p*.

Wesley took a breath through his nose. If he were a
humble man, he'd take this moment to thank Rory. To
say *you opened my eyes to new paths when I saw you
with Arthur. I didn't know a damn thing about real feelings before then. You showed me what making someone happy looks like and gave my cold heart a fighting
chance when someone incredibly special came along.*

And maybe someday, Wesley would be a bigger man
and tell Rory all of it.

Today was not that day.

"Sebastian and I met in London and our association
grew from there," said Wesley. "I'm sure that's all you
need to know."

"And just to be clear, *association* is your fancy way to
say you decided you oughta put your lips on him too?"

Wesley narrowed his eyes.

Arthur's voice drifted over. "Everything all right,
you two? You're not fighting, are you?"

Rory's gaze went to Langford's body. "Nah, Ace," he said, a little softer. "We're good."

Wesley rolled his eyes but didn't argue.

Rory looked back at Wesley. "Thanks for saving Arthur and the rest of us," he said, with complete sincerity. "You're real brave. Loyal too. We're lucky you were here."

Christ, really? *Rory* was going to be the bigger man? "Stop it," Wesley said, because he absolutely, positively was not having feelings tonight. "Stick to yelling at me."

The corner of Rory's mouth turned up in a grudging smile. "Come on. I want outta here."

Zhang had seen a second-floor library from the astral plane, one with plenty of seating and windows still intact from the storm. Wesley and Arthur moved Alasdair into an empty bedroom on the third floor and locked him in, in case he woke. They came back up, and Wesley covered Langford's body with his jacket before walking over to Sebastian.

Sebastian's fever was gone—disappeared with his magic, it seemed—but he'd had an alarming amount of magic run through him and looked ready to sleep on his feet. Wesley got him standing, his eyes catching the outline of the lion again, and no, he couldn't think about Sebastian's sacrifice right now, because it made his throat tight and overwhelming sentiment want to spill from his tongue.

He supported Sebastian with an arm around his waist, and the six of them began making their way downstairs. It was slow going, with Sebastian leaning heavily into him, Zhang and Jade both unsteady, and Arthur and Rory stalling everything to kiss on the landing.

Having to dodge the occasional decorative vase zipping through the air didn't make the progress easier, but Jade's quick thinking had saved Sebastian from the brooch. As far as Wesley was concerned, her telekinesis was entitled to every knickknack in New York.

"Arthur, we're going to need a car to get back to the city," Wesley pointed out, "or a place nearby for the others to sleep. Miss Robbins, Mr. Zhang, and Mr. Brodigan are probably in need of food as well."

"Alasdair left us water and rations in the office," said Rory. "We were sick, but we got each other to eat. Now I just want Ace."

Arthur tsked. "As much as I return the sentiment, when was the last time you slept in a real bed?"

"What about *you*? You said those dicks had you locked up this whole time—"

"No, sorry, I have a monopoly on being overprotective, you don't get to do it too—"

"I don't know how I missed it before," Sebastian muttered, listing into Wesley's shoulder. "They really are obvious."

"My point," Wesley stressed, to the group, "is that you are all going to wait in the library. Arthur and I are going to handle the rest."

"'Cause it's gonna be real easy to explain," Rory muttered.

"We'll tell the story without magic," Wesley said. "Arthur came up to Tarrytown because he heard there were dangerous bootleggers, and he didn't call the police like a sensible fellow because he was too busy charging into danger trying to protect others."

Arthur winced. "John will believe that, yes."

"But then Arthur was kidnapped by these villainous bootleggers," Wesley went on, "and so were his friends. What luck it was that Sebastian and I followed

John's lead on Arthur's whereabouts and we all foiled the bootleggers' plot. We don't have to tell them what that plot was."

"What about the bouncer?" Zhang asked.

"Langford killed him," said Wesley. "That's perfectly true."

"And the storm?" Jade said.

"I hear the weather in New York is very unpredictable in the fall," Wesley said.

"And Alasdair?" said Arthur.

"Needs a hospital," said Wesley. "I think it's pretty obvious Langford was the true mastermind," he said, a little tensely.

"I'm sorry," Sebastian whispered.

Wesley tightened his arm around him. "None of that. It's not on you; this was all Langford's plan."

"Was it, though?"

Wesley glanced over at Jade, who looked deep in thought.

"Was Langford truly the mastermind behind this?" Jade said. "Or could there have been someone else pulling his strings as well?"

That was not a reassuring idea. "Something to think about," Wesley said, meeting her eyes.

Chapter Twenty-Six

As they emerged on the second floor, the police were coming up the main stairs, John and Walter with them. Sebastian found himself propped in a large leather chair in a well-appointed library with a thick rug and built-in bookshelves that stretched to the ceiling. Jade and Zhang smooshed themselves into a single chair across from him, murmuring softly to each other.

"How're you feeling?"

Sebastian glanced to his left, where Rory had taken a seat in the chair next to him. "Tired, but alive," he said, a little cautiously. He and Rory had gotten on well in London, and Sebastian liked him a lot, but it was hard not to feel guilty every time he looked at Arthur or Rory.

Rory sat back in the chair, eying Sebastian. "So. You and Fine."

"Um." Sebastian couldn't exactly deny it; he'd kissed Arthur's ex-boyfriend in front of all of them. "Yes."

"Guess when we asked you to keep an eye on him, you took us real serious, huh."

That started a smile out of Sebastian. "I guess I did. Is that—does that make everything even more complicated?"

"Nah," Rory said. "I'd say you're screwy for wanting

him, but he said Langford was his commanding officer. Fine must be for real, when it comes to you."

Sebastian winced. "Wesley never should have been put in that position."

"You're not the one who gave him no choice," Rory said. "Don't go blaming yourself. I get the feeling you might be good at that."

Several books pulled themselves free from the bookshelf to hover in the air nearby. Jade grimaced. "I'll get the hang of the brooch," she promised. "Probably not until I've had some sleep, though."

"I always enjoy having a book to read," Zhang said supportively.

Rory's eyes flicked down to Sebastian's wrist. "So is your magic really gone?"

"Feels like it," Sebastian admitted. "The fever has cleared up. The lion has changed. And I can't sense anything left."

Rory nodded slowly. "You must like Fine a lot right back."

It was strange to see the lion now, without his colors. Sebastian's emotions were a jumbled mess of uncertainty and loss, but there was no regret mixed in, because he would have given so much more for Wesley. "Yes," he said quietly. "I do."

"Can I see the tattoo?" said Zhang.

Jade and Rory were looking too, so Sebastian held his wrist up. Zhang tilted his head. "So it was always a lion?"

Sebastian nodded. He hesitated, but it felt relevant to all that had happened that night, so he said, "Wesley—er, Lord Fine—he could see the lion. Even before."

Zhang and Jade exchanged a look. Zhang leaned

forward. "Obviously I can't promise it," he said, "but I think your magic will come back."

"It's okay if it doesn't," Sebastian said, and meant it. "I don't regret it. I'd do it again."

"I know," Zhang said, as his hand intertwined with Jade's. "But your magic went up against a relic's magic, and won."

"Your magic could have survived," Jade said, resting her head on Zhang's shoulder. "And it could come back."

Sebastian swallowed.

They were quiet for a moment, and Sebastian very carefully did not close his eyes, because if he did he was liable not to open them again for at least twenty-four hours.

"You're not on the plane anymore," Rory said to Zhang. "You're resting?"

Zhang nodded. "But that means I have no idea what Arthur and Fine might be saying."

"Or where they're gonna stick us," Rory grumbled. "How'd you get here? Did you drive? Let's just take that car back to the city."

"I'm afraid the truck didn't survive," Jade said. "Most of the cars on the grounds didn't."

"Survive what?" said Rory.

"The storm," Zhang said pointedly.

"Oh." Rory rubbed the back of his neck. "Guess I was pretty mad," he said sheepishly.

Sebastian took a deep breath, letting their voices wash over him. It was so nice to hear all of them, even if it gave him an achy feeling of being an outsider, trespassing where he didn't belong.

"Hey." He glanced over to find Rory looking at him again. Rory's voice was quiet as he said, "You were ready to take Langford's bullet for me, before the storm. You're a good friend."

Sebastian glanced away again. "I don't think *good friends* kidnap each other."

"But you know no one's still mad at you over the blood magic, right?" said Rory. "That we all understand?"

"Maybe *I'm* still mad at me over the blood magic," Sebastian muttered.

"Then that's something you gotta work out with yourself," Rory said wisely. "'Cause the rest of us— we're all square. No one blames you but you."

Sebastian opened his mouth, then closed it. That was going to stick with him awhile. "Grazie," he finally said, some of the scant Italian he remembered from the war.

Rory smiled, one of his rare, real smiles. "Di niente."

"And once again I find myself agreeing with Brodigan; this truly must stop." Wesley had come up behind Sebastian's chair. "Are you all aware there are books floating in the air?"

Sebastian glanced up at him.

"I'm working on it," Jade said, as Arthur appeared next to Wesley behind Sebastian's chair. "But you know, once I get control of this brooch, I'm going to be so dangerous. I'm going to cable Gwen. Maybe we'll start that ladies' society after all."

"Gwen is our friend who sees magic," Arthur said to Wesley. "And auras. Can touch auras, actually, have a man on his knees in agony."

"Sebastian mentioned her." Wesley frowned. "Doesn't she also control the tide?"

"That too," Arthur agreed.

Wesley's gaze darted to Jade. "That's one hell of a ladies' society."

"Yes, we're very lucky they're on the side of the angels." Arthur paused. "Well. Except for that time Gwen tried to drown Brooklyn."

Wesley opened his mouth.

"Where are we *sleeping*?" Rory interrupted. "And *eating*."

Wesley gave him a flat look. "John has offered us his yacht for the night."

"A boat?" Rory groaned. "Tell me you at least brought food, not just bad news?"

"What am I, your hall boy?" Wesley said.

"You won't get seasick on the river," Arthur cut in. "Well. I hope you won't get seasick."

Rory gave him a dirty look.

"John's arranging for cars as well," said Wesley. "They can take us to the marina."

"Did the police believe the story?" Zhang asked.

Arthur nodded. "Walter is pretending he had no idea anyone was bringing liquor into the party. Swears he thought the trucks were delivering crates of soda. But he was quick to back us up that bootleggers were the villains. Alasdair is being transported to a hospital."

"And Langford?" Sebastian said quietly.

"I wrote a message for the War Office," Wesley said. "They'll see that it gets cabled home." He held out a hand to Sebastian, as he had earlier in the attic. "It's taken care of. Come on."

Two drivers had been called to take them down to the waterfront. Arthur and Rory took the first car, so Arthur could check the accommodations, and Wesley and Sebastian rode with Jade and Zhang to the pier. Sebastian wanted to lean into Wesley the way Jade was with Zhang, but he settled for stretching his leg out to rest his foot alongside Wesley's. To his surprise, Wesley found his hand in the dark of the backseat, loosely entwining their fingers so that his thumb rested on the lion on the inside of Sebastian's wrist. The skin was sensitive, as delicate skin always was, but it didn't send sparks through him the way it had before.

Zhang might believe Sebastian's magic wasn't gone forever, but Sebastian wasn't so sure. He'd meant what he said, though. He had no regrets.

Their car pulled into the marina, and Sebastian made it down the ramp with the others, unsteady legs not helped by the swaying of the dock under his weight. John's boat was at the far end of the pier, a modest, well-kept cabin cruiser. Aboard, Arthur directed Jade and Zhang to the aft stateroom, insisting he and Rory were sleeping on the deck, where the fresh air would help keep Rory's seasickness away. Sebastian and Wesley ended up on the port side of the bow, in a room that was more of a cubby and obviously designed with children in mind—a low ceiling, round portholes and a bed that filled almost the entire space, which meant poor Wesley would spend the night kicking the wall with his long legs.

Sebastian, on the other hand, was tired enough he'd have happily slept on the pier. Wesley had lingered in the cruiser's galley, speaking in quiet tones with Jade, but Sebastian gratefully sat down on the edge of the mattress, more than ready to call it a day.

"Sebastian."

Sebastian looked up to see Arthur just a couple of feet away in the hall, hunching under the short ceiling. "Arthur." He swallowed, trying to look nonchalant and not at all like he'd once held Arthur at gunpoint and was now sleeping with his ex-boyfriend. "Hi."

Arthur took a hesitant step forward. Then he held out a hand. Confused, Sebastian took it.

Arthur pulled him to his feet and into a hug, and Sebastian had to smother a noise of surprise.

"I was under blood magic for only hours," Arthur said quietly, hugging him hard, "and I still have nightmares. He made me hurt *Rory*. I am so sorry for what was done to you and if you need to talk about it, I'm here."

Sebastian's throat went very tight. And then he was hugging Arthur back, also hard, not quite able to form words for what that meant to hear but maybe Arthur understood that too.

After a minute, they pulled apart. "Is there anything I can do for you?" Arthur said, very seriously, his hand still on Sebastian's shoulder.

Sebastian swallowed and shook his head. "You already did," he said quietly. "You helped me find the path to Wesley. And he is—the best thing, he makes everything so much better."

Arthur smiled softly. "Okay," he said, squeezing Sebastian's shoulder. "I really am here if you need anything. And I'm happy for you two."

"Thank you," Sebastian said, and he realized he was smiling too.

He heard a throat clear. "May I have Sebastian back now, Arthur?" Wesley said, sardonically, arms folded. "Only if you're finished with him, of course, by all means don't let me interrupt."

Arthur rolled his eyes. He let Sebastian go and turned toward Wesley. "I'm sure John has cigars on board somewhere if you need one."

Wesley shook his head. "Sebastian's half asleep already. I don't leave when he's asleep."

Arthur's eyebrows went up. "Wow," he said slowly, smile coming back. "All right, then. I don't think I know who you are, but I'll leave you two, shall I?" He squeezed past Wesley in the narrow hall that was definitely not designed to accommodate a man of Arthur's size. "Let me know if you need anything."

"I most certainly will not," said Wesley. "If I need something, I'll get it myself. No force on earth could get me to interrupt you and Brodigan tonight. I like my sight unviolated, thank you very much."

"And there's the Wesley I remember." Arthur clapped him on the bicep. "It's good to have you here. Both of you," he said, and disappeared down the hall.

Sebastian crawled up the bed, and Wesley joined him, stretching out next to him so they faced each other on their sides. "And now you've landed yourself on Arthur's mother bear list," said Wesley. "You poor sap."

"He's nice," Sebastian protested.

"Oh, he is. But when you're awakened at two a.m. because Arthur ironically needs to be sure you're sleeping well, you can't say I didn't warn you."

Sebastian reached out, needing to touch him, and ran his fingers over Wesley's jaw. "I'm so sorry about Langford."

Wesley raised an eyebrow. "You didn't put a gun in his hand and bespell him to point it at you. He was going to kill you and as many other paranormals as he could."

"I know," Sebastian said softly. "But I also know it was complicated, and he wasn't all bad to you."

Wesley acknowledged that with a tilt of his head. "You know, he kept telling me I'd changed, that he wanted the stone-cold bastard of wartime back, heartless and willing to kill. Perhaps ironic that he got what he wanted in the end."

Sebastian shook his head. "You weren't *willing to kill*. You pulled that trigger to save my life. To save the lives of your friends. You're anything but heartless, Wes."

"You're trying to turn the tables on me again," Wesley said, voice a bit gruffer. "Trying to make me see things another way—"

Sebastian gently pressed his fingers over his lips to stop the argument. "You're not heartless," he said again. "Or cold, or made of stone. I know you better than that. It was a terrible choice to have to make."

"And what about your choice?" Wesley said. "You might have given up your magic. Forever. For *me*—"

"I'd do it again," Sebastian said.

"But—"

"I almost *lost* you," Sebastian said. "I meant what I said. If it's forever, it's worth it."

"You say that now, because you're exhausted and possibly in shock," Wesley said. "Come tomorrow—"

"It might be hard. I might miss it," Sebastian admitted. "But I'll never, ever regret it. If I have a choice between *Wesley* or *magic*, I will choose *Wesley*. Every time."

"Stop that at once; you're going to make me have an emotion."

Wesley reached for Sebastian's left arm, turning it so the inside of his wrist faced up. He tilted his head, gaze on the tattoo. "There's the lion. Not all mine anymore, I suppose, if everyone can see him now."

Sebastian swallowed. "I'm sorry," he said. "I know you liked the way the lion was before—"

"How can you imagine for one moment that I don't adore him all the more like this?" Wesley said, a little more hoarse than normal. "I mean, yes, it's unforgivable, because every time I see your tattoo now I will remember what you sacrificed and be in danger of experiencing feelings. But the lion, and the man who carries him, are enchanting. With or without magic."

Sebastian's throat was tight again. "You're not looking at my tattoo through rose-colored glasses, are you?"

"How dare you." Wesley's thumb skimmed over the tattoo in a light caress that still lit Sebastian's skin, even if it was different without the magic. "It's not rose-colored glasses, it's cold facts. Most people want things from me. Sometimes they want money or status; sometimes it's war and violence and cruelty. But you—you've only ever given, from the night we met. That kind of enchantment has nothing to do with magic."

Sebastian bit his lip against the feelings welling up. "Definitely rose-colored glasses," he said lightly, "because I know I've wanted things from you in bed."

The corner of Wesley's lips curled up. "Yes, but you begging is still you giving me exactly what I want, isn't it?"

Sebastian shivered. He was exhausted, but he was craving Wesley, to feel him solid and real and alive against him. "I could beg now."

"That is a transparent attempt to make me forget how exhausted you are and I'm ashamed to admit it's working."

Wesley shifted, rolling Sebastian onto his back as he moved to lie half on top of him. He ran his fingers down Sebastian's side, skating over his ribs, lighting Sebastian's nerves in their path.

"What was it you said? That I was looking at the fairytale from the wrong angle—that I was actually an innocent human held captive by a devious fae?" His fingers slipped over Sebastian's hip, inching their way closer to his belt buckle. "The tables have quite turned, haven't they? Now you're the one who's caught in my world. And *I'll* be keeping *you.*"

Sebastian stretched up, needing to kiss him, closing the distance between their lips. His hand found the back of Wesley's head and pulled him closer to deepen the kiss.

When his head was starting to spin, he tried to push up, wanting to roll Wesley over—and got nowhere. "Wes."

"I'm sorry, are you trying to move me?" Wesley shifted his kisses to Sebastian's neck, and he automatically tilted his head so Wesley could reach more of his skin. "I weigh a good bit more than you. Without your little paranormal tricks, you're the one who's not moving unless I let you."

Oh.

Wesley must have felt him flinch, because he pulled back. "Which is very new to you," he said, more slowly, sharp eyes tracking over Sebastian's face, "and so I'm not going to make light of it."

"What? No, it's fine, why wouldn't it be fine?" Sebastian said, although his heart was beating a little faster. "I've been around you without magic lots of times—you're the one who keeps pointing that out."

"But you always knew it was temporary," Wesley said, "and right now we don't know anything."

Sebastian looked away, to the porthole window.

"You know," Wesley said wryly, "there's a difference between someone who likes being helpless, and someone who likes *playing* at helpless while always keeping the power to knock the other person on their arse."

Sebastian became aware he was twisting the fabric of Wesley's shirt in his fingers. But he didn't stop. The tumult of feelings was hard to parse through. Wesley was warm and solid on top of him, and he wasn't sure he liked being pinned but he wasn't sure he didn't. "It *shouldn't* matter. I trust you."

"And remind me, when did I say *since you trust me, you have to let me do whatever I like with you?*" Wesley said lightly. "Because I trust *you*, yet I seem to recall you insisting on a so-called *important conversation* about how your magic would always let me up if I asked."

"Yes, and you told me it was *patently unnecessary* to talk about it."

"I did," Wesley said. "But perhaps this isn't just new for you. Perhaps you have significantly more reasons than most to dislike the idea of a true loss of control."

Sebastian bit his lip. He experimentally flexed up against Wesley's weight. "I don't dislike it," he said, before Wesley could move, trying to put his feelings into words. "It might be complicated; that doesn't mean bad."

"I'm afraid my ego isn't going to settle for *not bad* or *don't dislike*. Whatever we're doing, I want you to *need* it. *Crave* it." Wesley kissed beneath his ear, and Sebastian felt the rasp of stubble, a nip of teeth. "You sweet, lost faery. You don't have to adjust to an entire new world in one night. You should know by now I'm never in a rush when it comes to you."

The last of the tension left Sebastian. He pushed up and Wesley went over, rolling onto his back with Sebastian on top. He crawled forward, fitting himself between Wesley's legs, eager for more of him. He lowered himself down, their bodies fully aligned, and swallowed Wesley's groan with a kiss. He was warm and hard and alive under Sebastian, his heartbeat strong in his chest.

When they broke for air, Wesley ran his hands up Sebastian's spine. "Now see, I *am* a man who thoroughly enjoys being pinned down and ravaged," he said slyly. "Maybe we should get you handcuffs."

Sebastian grinned. "I'll just borrow yours."

"I did tell you they come in useful."

Wesley's hand reached Sebastian's head, tangling in his hair and bringing him back into another kiss. Sebastian closed his eyes and let the world fall away, welcoming the place where nothing mattered but the fingers against his scalp and the planes of Wesley's body under his hands, solid and real.

"I heard what you said to Arthur," Wesley murmured as they kissed. "That I make everything better. How dare you say something so soft about me, something I'll never forget."

"It's true," Sebastian whispered. "Look at us now. Look how good things are with you."

"And now you're making it worse." Wesley sounded ragged and raw. "I have been on the verge of feelings all night and I expect you to make that up to me."

Things blurred after that, a heady blend of desire and pleasure and exhaustion that was almost like being drunk. Most of their clothes were shoved to the foot of the bed, and then Wesley got his hand between their bodies, encircling both of their cocks in his palm.

Sebastian swore in Spanish, burying his face in the juncture of Wesley's neck and shoulder.

"Christ, you feel good." Wesley sounded as overcome as he felt.

"Wes." Sebastian rolled off Wesley and tugged him over too, so they were on their sides again, facing each other, so Wesley had more room to work their cocks and Sebastian could kiss him without crushing him.

"Tonight was unacceptable," Wesley whispered, against Sebastian's lips, as his hand drove all the thoughts from Sebastian's head. "We had this discussion weeks ago. You were already forbidden from coming so close to death ever again."

Sebastian wanted to drink him in, weld them together so they could never be lost to each other. "You were the one who almost died."

"Was I?" Wesley's breath tickled his lips as his hand glided over them and Sebastian was losing his mind. "Oh wait, no, that was *you,* because you nearly traded your life to save mine. And that's unacceptable, because regardless of whether you can knock me on my arse, there's no magic in my life without you."

Sebastian pushed him onto his back again, knocking Wesley's hand away to take over stroking them. He kissed him again, because he couldn't stop, because they felt so good together, because Wesley had gone pliant the way he only did when he was close to the edge and Sebastian wanted to drive him over it. The gentle motions of the boat on the river gave every movement just a little more sway, a little more depth that added a weightless, almost floating sensation.

It didn't take very long before Sebastian was close too, for sweat to bead on his skin from the effort of holding back, the sweetest kind of torture. He tried to keep his eyes open enough to see Wesley. "You really are the best thing that's ever happened to me. You know that, yes?"

Wesley groaned. "Haven't I also told you that you're not allowed to talk? It's too much." He always looked good, of course, but right now, unraveled and sweaty, breathing hard, his hair in disarray, his cheeks flushed and his eyes bright—Sebastian wanted to drink in the sight.

"I want to talk," he said. "So I can tell you that you make everything better. That you make my demons disappear. That my life was so bad, but now I have you, and it's so good, Wes, you're so good."

Wesley's hips stuttered against him and Sebastian caught his breath. "You arsehole." Wesley's voice was unsteady. "I told you to make up for almost giving me a feeling, not give me more of them."

"You have to get used to it," Sebastian whispered. "Because we both made it tonight. And someday we *will* be eighty, and who knows where in the world we will be together—"

Wesley's sharp inhale filled his ears, and then they were kissing again, the angle awkward and messy and perfect, Wesley overwhelming every one of his senses, and he was falling apart, feeling Wesley fall apart too.

Aftershocks danced through him as he lay panting on his side. He was still facing Wesley, and leaned in to brush their lips together, light as a butterfly. "Thank you," he whispered, and it could have been for anything, for saving his life, for understanding what he'd struggled to say, for being everything Sebastian needed, because maybe he didn't have magic and didn't know if it was coming back, but he would be okay, because he could rely on Wesley to help him.

Wesley smiled, eyes a little dazed. "Don't fall asleep just yet. You'll never be warm enough without covers."

Sebastian fumbled for the blankets. "Come here," he said, trying to roll Wesley over onto his other side so he could spoon up behind him.

"*You* come here."

A half-huff, half-laugh escaped Sebastian as he was

the one pushed over onto his other side. "Wait, what are you doing?"

Wesley's arm was curling around his waist, his chest warm against Sebastian's back. "You're a smart man, you'll figure it out."

"But I *like* holding you."

"Yes, and now I understand why. I've commandeered this position, and it's your fault for showing me how nice it is."

Sebastian couldn't stop a quiet laugh. "So I only have myself to blame? What if I like this too?"

"You're the one who taught me that, on occasion, reaping what you sowed might not be a terrible thing." Wesley encircled Sebastian's wrist in his hand, over the tattoo. More softly, he said, "Whatever happens next, you know I'm here, duck."

Sebastian pressed impossibly closer into Wesley. "I know," he said, and closed his eyes.

Epilogue

One week later

"Don't give me that look," Wesley said, to the sloth eying him as it dangled from a tree. "I am an unwilling participant in this particular expedition."

Next to Wesley, Rory scoffed. "Funny, the way I remember it, Sebastian mentioned the zoo and you fell all over yourself to make him happy."

"I'm sure that wasn't how it happened," Wesley lied.

"Really," Rory said flatly. "Because Ace's little niece Victoria somehow got herself a kitten. Rescued from Tarrytown, apparently. But I guess that doesn't have anything to do with you wanting to make Sebastian happy either, does it?"

Wesley cleared his throat. "Where did Sebastian get to anyway?"

"They're about to feed the sea lions," Rory said, in a tone that said he knew Wesley was full of shit. "That's gotta be where Sebastian is. I hope Ace is with him."

They made their way back to the sea lion pool, and sure enough, Sebastian was up ahead, watching the barking sea lions with Arthur next to him. The day was brightly sunny, the air crisp but the sky a brilliant blue above the last of the Bronx Zoo's autumn leaves.

Despite the sun, Sebastian was bundled in a scarf and warm hat, but he looked happy, not cold, as he chatted with Arthur and watched the sea lions dive.

"You still think you gotta go back to England?" Rory said, as he and Wesley paused by a pillar.

"I *want* to take Sebastian to San Juan." Wesley's gaze stayed on Sebastian. "But I can't shake Miss Robbins's point from my mind. What if Langford wasn't acting alone?"

Rory nodded slowly. "You know if you're going chasing after answers about Langford, Ace and I are coming with you, right?"

Wesley raised an eyebrow. "I hear you spend sea voyages on the constant verge of vomiting."

Rory gave a grumpy huff. "Yeah. But I'm still coming. Gwen's supposed to be in London again. She can make sure nothing permanent happened to your aura. See what's going on with Sebastian."

Sebastian's magic still hadn't returned. He couldn't see Zhang, he couldn't weaken Wesley's aura, and the lion remained a black, branded outline. Wesley wasn't stupid; he could see Sebastian missed it and was still struggling to manage a world without it. Sebastian didn't seem to think it was ever coming back, but whenever Wesley mentioned it, he would say, with complete sincerity, that he'd rather have Wesley.

Truly unforgivable, to make Wesley's stone heart feel this soft.

"With any luck, it will all be quick, and we can come back," said Wesley. "Mateo's latest telegram says he's doing well at Oberlin; Sebastian could surprise him for Christmas."

Arthur said something that made Sebastian laugh, and the sight of that laughter put a grudging smile on

Wesley's lips. Perhaps it would be good to have company. Sebastian's trauma ran deep, and it might do him good to be surrounded and supported by people who cared about his well-being. Arthur and the others seemed to have had the same idea, and Wesley could admit they were doing a bang-up job being good friends.

To both of them.

Rory cocked his head, listening to the air. "Zhang says we should come to the Dragon House for dinner."

"I require that there be pork buns," Wesley said to the air, in the general direction Rory was facing.

"You sure you and Jade want company?" Rory said, apparently uncaring that it appeared he was speaking to no one. "You two've been hiding out together since we left Tarrytown."

Wesley remembered Mateo's prophecy about Zhang, all the way back in Yorkshire. *She says yes, and everyone is so happy at their wedding.*

Even a cranky cynic like Wesley would be happy for them.

Sebastian looked over his shoulder, then. "Wes," he called. "They're bringing the fish. Come see!"

Wes. Wesley loved the sound of his name in Sebastian's voice. Loved that Sebastian was comfortable enough with him to use it in front of Arthur and Rory. Sebastian was heading toward him, and Wesley started forward to meet him.

But just before they reached each other, Wesley stumbled. He staggered forward, and would have fallen if Sebastian hadn't been there, grabbing him by his arms.

"Wesley." He was pulling Wesley upright. "Are you all right? Did you trip?"

Had he? Wesley straightened all the way up. He

looked behind him, but there was nothing to see but smooth stones leading back to Rory talking to the air.

He frowned. "You think I tripped? Over what, my own feet?"

"It happens to all of us," Sebastian said earnestly.

He was still holding on to Wesley by the elbows, his hands and wrists turned upward. The top of the lion was visible where Sebastian's coat sleeve had ridden up. The sun lit the tattoo in yellow light as the world around them popped in color, the blue sky above, the green of hardy shrubs, the last of the fiery red and orange leaves on the trees. But the lion itself was only the black, brand-like outline against Sebastian's skin.

Except—

No. No, Wesley was seeing the colors of late autumn in New York. He'd tripped over his own feet. There was no other explanation. Life was endlessly cruel and capricious; there was no reason to believe Sebastian's magic would ever return.

He looked up. Sebastian was smiling at him, guileless and fond. "Come see the sea lions," he said. "It's part of your zoo adventure."

Wesley snorted. "The zoo is *not* an adventure."

"It's new and fun and we're here together," Sebastian said. "Of course it's an adventure; you just have to change how you're looking at it."

Wesley glanced back at the tattoo.

Hope and faith were for the naïve. For the gullible who were tricked by platitudes, for the cowards who couldn't face life's brutal truths. They had no place in the heart of a jaded viscount who knew exactly how callous and cold the world truly was.

But then, he'd been convinced there was no place in

his heart for anything at all, before Sebastian had come into his life and changed everything.

"There's an actual lion house we haven't even seen." Sebastian had a teasing grin. "You still like lions, yes?"

When others had seen nothing but a scoundrel in Wesley, Sebastian's magic believed it could trust him with the lion.

Maybe it was Wesley's turn to believe.

He met Sebastian's eyes. "I love lions," he said, with a small smile of his own, and let Sebastian pull him into another new adventure.

* * * * *

Loved Once a Rogue?
*To find more of Allie's books or join her email list,
visit her website at www.allietherin.com.*

Acknowledgments

All my thanks to everyone whose help and support made this book happen:

To C, my zombie apocalypse partner, and to my family and friends;

To my readers—your enthusiasm and love for these books means so much—and many thanks to Louise for the tips about Yorkshire;

To my author crew—grateful to have y'all to lean on in the wild world of books;

To Mackenzie Walton—the best editor Lord Fine & Sebastian (and me!) could ask for;

To my agent, Laura Zats, and to the Carina Press team who bring our books into the world—Kerri, Stephanie, and the art, marketing, and production teams;

And to T, who brings endless light and magic to my world.

About the Author

Allie Therin is the bicultural author of the internationally acclaimed debut series Magic in Manhattan. She also is, or has been, a bookseller, an attorney, a parks & rec assistant, a boom operator, and a barista for one (embarrassing) day. A longtime fan of romance, mystery and speculative fiction, she now strives to bring that same delight to her readers. Allie grew up in a tiny Pacific Northwest town with more bears than people, although the bears sadly would not practice Spanish with her.

Allie loves to hear from readers! Find all the ways to connect with her at her website, allietherin.com.

A murder has Seattle on edge, and it falls to a pacifist empath—and a notorious empath hunter— to find the killer before it's too late.

Chapter One

The question everyone asks, of course, is what do we know about the empath mutation? We know the correlating empathic abilities threaten our privacy and the sanctity of our minds. We know the empaths cannot be allowed to freely use this empathy, because no amount of so-called pacifism gives them the right to use their abilities to discover emotions we do not consent to share.

But there is a far more important question they ought to be asking: what don't *we know about the empaths?*

—C. Stone,
confidential funding memo to the Empath Initiative

Reece supposed if he'd been a *look on the bright side* kind of empath, he might have had a platitude ready, something pithy about how insomnia's single perk was being awake no matter what time someone called.

But platitudes and perks and so-called *bright sides* were for people who could still lie to themselves, and no one had been able to lie to Reece since March. So when his chirpy ringtone shattered the silence of the diner, he instead jerked in surprise and dropped his cup, which crashed to the Formica table and sent orange juice flooding right off the edge onto his jeans.

He cursed and scrambled out of the booth. Under the hard stare of the lone waitress, he snatched the phone up in gloved hands and fumbled to silence it. Ducking his head so he wouldn't have to meet her suspicious eyes, he squinted at the screen.

Unknown caller.

"Great," he muttered. This was obviously going to be good news, an unknown caller at four a.m. on a Tuesday. He put the phone to his ear. "Who is this?"

"We've never been properly introduced."

The man on the other side of the phone had a deep voice and a sugar-sweet Southern accent, and that was the extent of what Reece could read. Even before March, he'd despised how electronics stripped a voice, replacing a symphony with a cheap music box. Now it grated on him to no end to have to flounder blindly with a stranger. "How did you get this number?"

"Seattle's only got two empaths. I'd wager everyone has your number."

Reece narrowed his eyes. "Not my new one. And that wasn't an answer."

His thigh was already growing cold and sticky. He balanced the phone in the crook of his neck as he grabbed a cheap napkin from the dispenser and scrubbed at his jeans. The napkin shredded against the fabric without soaking up any juice.

There was a noise in the caller's background, a rushing sound, as the man said, "Maybe Detective St. James gave it to me."

Please. Jamey would eat her own badge first. "Maybe you be straight with me or I hang up."

"Aren't you awful prickly for an empath?"

"I don't like phone calls." Were those cars Reece was hearing? A highway, perhaps?

The deep drawl rolled through the phone like a lazy river. "I'm Evan Grayson."

The hairs on the back of Reece's neck rose. He knew that name from somewhere, like the echo of a dream that had vanished in the daylight. "Should I care?"

"You—"

"More importantly: are you driving right now?"

There was a pause.

"I knew it," said Reece. "You shouldn't talk on the phone when you're behind the wheel. It's dangerous for you and everyone else on the road."

"That's not more important than my name."

"Yes it is. Cell phones cause one out of every four car crashes in the US."

"You've got no idea who I am," Grayson said, "and the empath priorities of a Care Bear."

"Just doing my part to keep the streets safer. Somebody should and it's obviously not going to be you." Reece sat back down on the dry side of the booth. He was still being watched by the waitress, but then, she'd had eyes on him since he came in. More specifically, she'd had eyes on his gloves, and it wasn't the stare of someone wanting a phone number from the short, skinny guy covered in juice. He lowered his voice. "So, Evan Grayson, what do you want?"

"Are you sitting down?"

"Dancing, actually. I can't contain my joy that I'm party to your four a.m. reckless endangerment—"

"Tell me you're sitting."

Sittin'. Reece glanced out the droplet-streaked window at the dark street beyond, where a liquor store's neon signs illuminated the flecks of sleet in the falling rain. Even stripped by the phone, the out-of-place accent was a shot of unexpected warmth against the freezing November night, and Reece's defenses were apparently cold traitors because he found himself answering instead of hanging up. "Yes, I'm sitting."

"There's been a murder."

Reece fumbled the phone. He seized it in both hands before it could fall. He clutched it too tightly, clenching his teeth.

Grayson's voice floated up from the speaker, tinny and distant. "Did you drop your phone?"

Reece put it back to his ear. "No," he lied.

"Now you know why you needed to sit. I'm used to empath pacifism. Most of y'all don't even like that word."

Reece took a hard breath. Blew it out. He couldn't make out a single emotion in that drawl and had no idea if he was being mocked. "So why tell me about it?" he said tightly, trying to shove away encroaching thoughts of human cruelty, of pain and suffering beyond his help.

"Because this murder is gonna be the biggest case of Detective St. James' career and she's got nothing."

Reece's stomach dropped. "Nothing?"

"No leads. No theories. No clues. The city's not gonna take her failure well. You might know what an unhappy press is like."

He swallowed hard. He knew exactly how unforgiving the press could be, and the thought that the news might drag Jamey through that same mud—but no, she wasn't a fool who ran her mouth like him, and there was no better person to solve a major crime. "If there's something to find, she'll find it."

"Unless finding it would take an ability she doesn't have. An ability only a handful of folks with delicate ears have. Pretty sure you know where I'm going with this."

"What I *know*," Reece said, free hand balling into a gloved fist, "is that Jamey would call me if she needed an empath."

"For a petty theft? Sure. Grand larceny, even, assuming no one got scratched. But the way I hear it, Detective St. James would take a bullet before she called her precious baby brother to a homicide."

Reece tightened his jaw. "I would help her with anything."

"That's why I called. She's at the Orca's Gate Marina." And Grayson hung up.

Reece stared at his phone in disbelief, then slapped it down on the table with a huff. He didn't know Evan Grayson from the president. He could be a bully wanting to ridicule the empath aversion to violence. He could be another anti-empathy activist who'd dreamed up a new conspiracy. He could be simply *lying*; thanks to the phone, Reece wouldn't know.

He bit at one gloved thumb and worried it between his teeth. He'd noticed Jamey's car was gone at three a.m. when he'd given up on falling back asleep and gotten off her couch for a drive. But he hadn't thought anything of it. Jamey didn't need much sleep and sometimes she was out at night. It didn't mean she was on a case. It didn't mean Grayson was telling the truth. And it certainly didn't mean his sister could use his help.

He found himself dialing her number anyway.

Four rings, then voicemail. He dropped his phone to the table again and buried his face in his hands, his pulse too loud in his ears. Was he really considering going to the scene of a—

He cut off the thought before the word formed, but

he was already on his feet. If there was even a chance
Jamey needed him, he would be there.

As he approached the register at the end of the bar
counter, the waitress came over with dragging steps
and stopped a few feet away. She pointed at his hands.
"You never took off your gloves."

His fingers automatically flexed inside the stiff ma-
terial. "Of course I didn't—"

"I thought you were just cold when you came in. But
you're an empath, aren't you?"

Great, another place to cross off his list of insomnia
haunts. "I'm also a Pisces, but no one ever asks about
that." Under her relentless stare, he reached for his wallet, pointing back to the booth with his other hand. "If
you have a rag, I can—"

She recoiled. "How did you know I was pissed about
having to clean up?"

"There's juice everywhere, anyone would be—"

"Are you reading my mind?"

"Emotions aren't—"

"I thought the gloves keep us safe from empathy!"

Reece bit his lip, then said, "They do."

He knew it would be a lie before he said it. And sure
enough, the sound rang sour in his ears, like hearing
himself sing off-key.

The gloves did block his empathy, that part was true,
but it would take only a second to yank them off and
get bare hands on her bare skin. Only a second for the
touch of his hands to shred every mask and expose her
true emotions to him, clear as words on a page, whether
she wanted to share them or not.

And she was still safe. He'd never read her without
consent. No empath would. It was a lie to say the *gloves*

kept people safe because what kept people safe was the empaths themselves.

But he wanted to drive the fear from her eyes, so he chose the lie she and the rest of the public needed to believe.

No one knows the gloves can't stop you from hearing those lies now—

Reece quickly shoved the thought away. He put half of his meager cash on the counter, enough to cover the juice, tax, tip and extra for the cleanup. "Sorry about the mess." At least it wasn't another lie.

He pulled his hood over his dark hair as he pushed out the doors of the diner, the bell jingling too brightly behind him as he darted through the sleet to his car.

It was closing on five a.m. by the time Reece arrived at the marina north of the city, and his clothes were still damp with rain and juice despite blasting the heat the entire drive. He slowed his car as he approached the turn-in, his pulse speeding up. There was a police perimeter set up at the entrance, and what looked like most of the force in the parking lot beyond, whirling red and blue lights bright against the night's tenacious darkness. Mixed in with the cruisers was an ambulance, a black Explorer—and the unmarked navy blue Charger the Seattle Police Department had given Jamey.

Reece gritted his teeth. He'd wanted Grayson to be wrong.

He pulled up to the barricade and an officer in a puffy coat tapped on the driver's window, which was luckily the one that still worked. The previous owner had not been kind to the car, but that's why it had been in Reece's budget. He managed to roll the window halfway down with only a grunt of effort.

The officer shone his flashlight into the car, making Reece's eyes water. "This is a crime scene. You should be in bed, kid."

Cold rain peppered Reece's face as he held up his consultant ID card, a recent gift from the SPD's public relations front man, Liam Lee.

Your big mouth might make me less work if the press knows you're officially part of the team, Liam had said, when he'd created the card for him.

Your big sister is worth putting up with her wreck of a brother, more like, but Reece would grudgingly admit the card came in useful.

"Oh!" The officer glanced at the card, but he was more interested in the gloves. "You're the detective's brother. I've heard about you. Did she call you in?"

"Why else would I have come?" Reece said, because *no* was the wrong answer.

The officer jerked his head toward the chaos beyond. "Go on in. I'll tell her you're here."

Reece drove down to the lot and parked his Smart car next to Jamey's navy blue Charger. He killed the engine but sat in the car, fingers clenched tight around the steering wheel. The tiny space seemed claustrophobic and overheated as he tried to pretend his rapid breaths weren't loud enough to drown out the rain dotting his roof.

This Grayson guy had been right about where Jamey was. Based on the slew of officers on scene, he was likely also right about why. And as much as Reece wanted to turn around and drive anywhere else, Grayson might also be right about Jamey needing his help.

He stared at the whirling red and blue lights as he tried to slow his breathing. The police would let him help, even on a case like this. *Especially* on a case like this. No matter how much buzz the empathy bans were getting, they weren't in place yet, and most law enforcement were still happy to exploit empathy if it got the results they wanted.

A shock of freezing wet air swirled in as the driver's door of his Smart car was yanked open.

"What are you doing here?"

Jamey had found him, her tall figure bundled in a thick coat and a hat tugged over her dark curls. There were stress lines at the corners of her deep brown eyes, but the sight of her was still steadying enough to slow Reece's heart to something close to normal.

He tried for a smile and managed a grimace. "Possibly having a panic attack?"

She huffed and moved to shield his open door from the worst of the rain. "You don't want to be here."

"I really don't."

"How did you find this place?" She wrinkled her nose. "And why do you smell like oranges?"

Ugh, her nose was too good. "I got a call that you needed my help."

She frowned. "Who?"

"Some guy with this outrageous Southern accent. Said his name was Evan Grayson."

Jamey blanched.

Reece's heartbeat promptly rocketed right back up. "Funny," he said, gaze locked on the fear on her face, "he seemed to think I should know his name too. Who—"

"Out of the car." Reece started to twist out of his seat, but Jamey, as always, was faster. She grabbed him by the arm and extracted him with one easy tug. "Let's go."

"Go where?" he asked, as she steered him through the rain and the parking lot, past a barrier set up around

a Ford Transit with a smashed headlight and toward
a plastic tent stamped *Property of Seattle Police Department.*

"Somewhere I can keep an eye on you."

"Who's Evan Grayson?"

Jamey shook her head. "Not right now," she said.
"This is a homicide scene and you're three seconds from
a panic attack. We're not talking about Grayson too."

"But how could Grayson make it worse?"

"Not *now*. You're already a mess."

"When am I ever anything else?" he muttered bit-
terly.

"Stop," she said. "I know better than anyone that
your compassion's a strength."

She tugged his arm. He sighed and tried to make his
legs move faster.

The tent was at the end of the parking lot, right before the edge of the tarmac and a sharp drop-off to the
ocean beyond. Past the tent was an arched sign that read
Orca's Gate Marina, adorned with a smiling killer
whale that seemed inappropriately cheerful, given the
circumstances. Beneath the sign, a well-lit wooden ramp
led to a collection of pristine yachts and private sail-
boats moored at the docks.

When they reached the tent, Jamey abruptly paused,
one hand on the plastic flap. "Put your hands in your
pockets."

Hide his gloves? He drew back. "Since when do I
embarrass you?"

She gave him a funny look. "Since never?"

He folded his arms over his chest, but that had been
unfair of him. She'd looked out for him his whole life.
Whatever her reason, it would never be shame.

The icy rain dampened his hair as she bent to his eye

level. "I know what you think—that if you show you're willing to hide, it will make people more nervous about empaths," she said. "But just this once. Trust me."

He sighed. "You know I do."

She was studying his face. "You were sleeping when I left. I guess that didn't last much longer."

"I look that bad, huh?"

"Don't be a jerk," she said. "I do notice your insomnia."

"Yeah, well, nightmares will do that to you."

"They'll stop soon." Her promise was twisted into discordance and he cringed. Her shoulders dropped an inch. "Sorry," she said. "I wish I really believed that. You used to sleep like a baby."

He blew out a breath. "You used to be able to lie to me. A lot's changed."

She gestured pointedly around the marina. "I would like to have changed you running mindlessly toward anywhere there are people in pain or you think you can help. This is the last place you should be right now."

There was a strained edge to her voice, a tense set to her shoulders. He tried for a lighter tone, even if only for a moment. "Careful with that concern. People will wonder which one of us is the empath."

She made a face. "No they won't. The touchy-feely shtick is your thing, just like I don't call you for a spot at the gym."

"I don't even know what that means."

"Exactly."

As she pushed the plastic tent flap aside, he jammed his hands deep in the pockets of his hoodie and said, "Grayson's name put fear on your face."

She hesitated. "It was—"

"Don't tell me it was my imagination. I'm an empath. It's never my imagination." He kept his gaze on her. "Nothing scares you. Why does Grayson?"

He watched subtle emotions dance across her face as she tried to decide what to tell him. Finally, she said, "Because I think this is his kind of crime."

The hairs on the back of Reece's neck rose. "You're afraid Grayson might be behind this?"

"No." She ducked into the tent, her words barely reaching his ears. "I'm afraid he might show up."

Don't miss
Liar City *by Allie Therin,*
available wherever books are sold.
www.CarinaPress.com